When Stars Fell Into My Soup

A long tale with many short stories
About those who sparkle differently

A Novel By

Puneet Gupta

Printed in India

IndiePress

ISBN: 978-93-6045-689-4

First Printing, 2025

IndiePress, an imprint of Westland

A division of Nasadiya Technologies Private Ltd.

Koramangala, Bangalore

Karnataka-560029

http://indiepress.in/

Edited by Priya Iyer

Typesetting by MAP Systems

Publishing Consultant: Samyuktha Prasanan

Book Cover Design by Harshad Marathe

Illustrations by Sweta Garg

Reviews from Early Readers

"Puneet Gupta has crafted an intricately exquisite deep-dive into the inner thoughts of Spencer Diaz as he clings to life. Spencer's story – and the stories of those around him – will stick with you long after you close the book."
John DeDakis, USA, Novelist and Writing Coach, Former Senior Copy Editor at CNN

"Puneet Gupta's 'When Stars Fell Into My Soup' is a poignant gem. These real-life stories are an absolute delight for aficionados of evocative language and sensory immersion. Amid humor and heartache, Gupta weaves beauty, assuring each recollection lingers. His prose resembles a meticulously crafted meal—every word a delectable ingredient, every sentence a savory morsel. The emotional depth of the stories will engage your empathy and keep you turning the pages."
Laurie Buchanan, USA, Author of the Sean McPherson novels

"Gupta has a way with words and delivers powerful messages through his writing. The storylines woven through this book are creative, engaging, and touching. This book promises a mix of heartfelt yet realistic storytelling that will leave the reader reflecting well after finishing."
Andrea Couture, USA, Author of 'Embracing What Remains'

"Deeply engrossing, each story is a masterful interpretation of dark realities of life but with a twist of humor and hope!"
Sudha Nair, India, Author of The Wedding Tamasha, Mr & Mrs Nambiar, Knot So Charming and many other books

"Gupta delivers an epic collection of stories, which takes the reader on an incredible cultural journey across every human emotion."
Luke Robert Eckley, USA, Author of Life Boat and God's Country

"'When Stars Fell into my Soup' makes you appreciate the whimsy that comes with knowing people. While reading it, I thought deeply about the stories other people have to tell, the beauty in the mundane and to make the only life we've got count. A book full of starry nights and gripping moments, this book truly lives up to its name- dreamy, chaotic and authentic. For every reader who wonders if their story is book-worthy, this one shows you they all are."
Ananya Mittal, Student and Beta Reader

To Mummy & Papa, for letting me find my path

To Ashoo, for being generous with your love

To Kavita Akka, for listening to my voice

To Anurag, for always spurring me forward

To Harsh, for showing me the power of dreams

To Sweta, for adding new colors to my canvas

To Ananya, for loving the imperfect me

&

And to my detractors, for telling me I wasn't enough!

The Celestial (Dis)Order

This composite novel narrates the legend of **ETHER**, a tale about the ones who are anything but ordinary but afraid to be themselves and be loved. Their voices are often unheard and they stay hidden in plain sight. Just like the lost thirteenth zodiac sign, Ophiuchus, that has disappeared into oblivion in the presence of more potent zodiacs from the families of **WATER**, **FIRE**, **AIR**, and **EARTH**.

Little do we know that the stories of these elements still breathe within the ephemeral tale of **ETHER**. It is a story within stories - Spencer's story.

PART ONE: THE FABLES OF WATER

The Purple Scarf *for the ones who have lost hope*
The Blue Sedan *for the ones who are ashamed of being*
The Red Lipstick *for the ones who suffer in solitude*

PART TWO: THE TALES OF FIRE

The Orange Popsicle *for the ones who yearn for love*
The Turquoise Duck *for the ones who are stuck in darkness*
The Mustard Stains *for the ones who want to belong*

PART THREE: THE SAGAS OF AIR

PART FOUR: THE EPICS OF EARTH

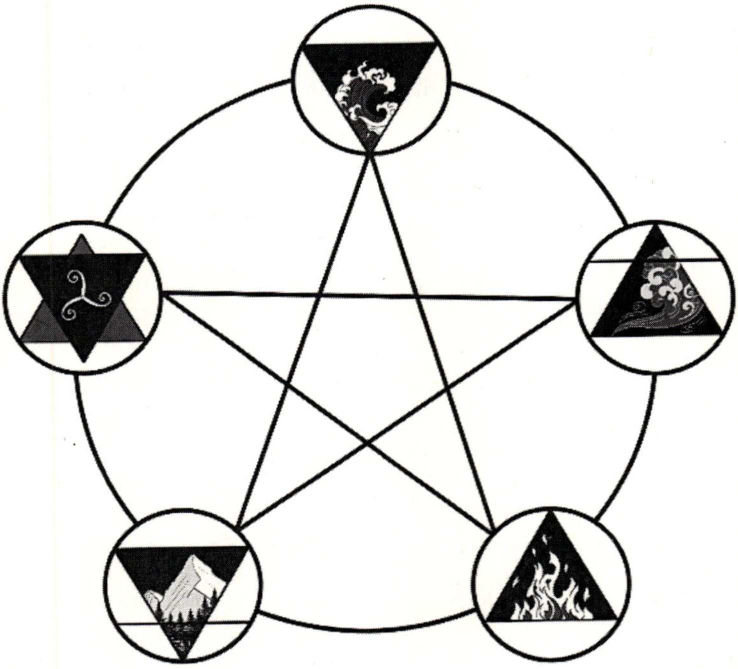

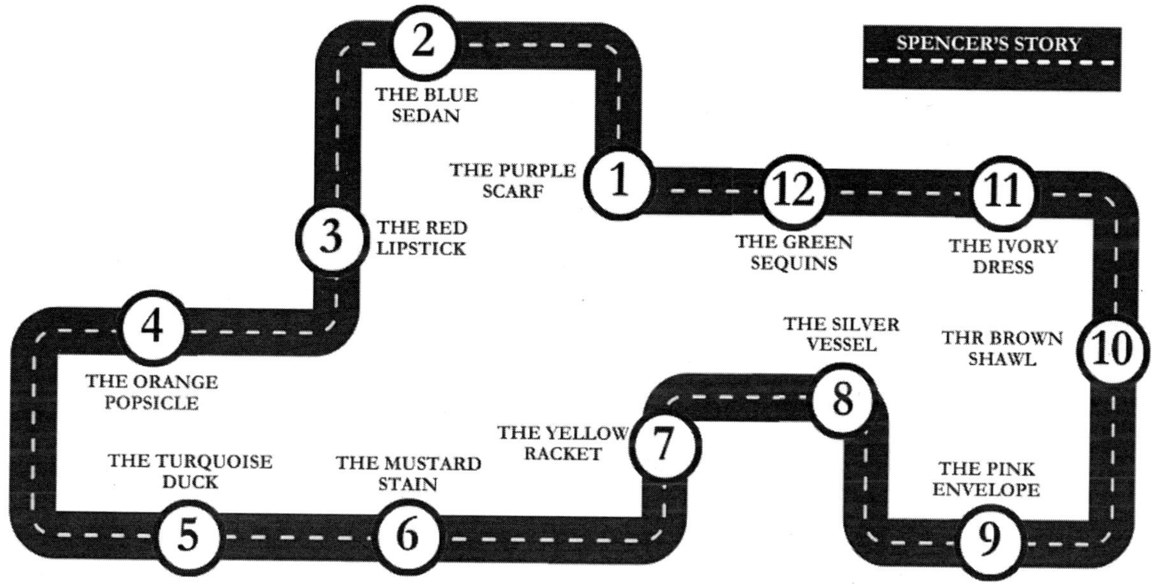
SPENCER'S STORY
1
THE PURPLE SCARF
2
THE BLUE SEDAN
3
THE RED LIPSTICK
4
THE ORANGE POPSICLE
5
THE TURQUOISE DUCK
6
THE MUSTARD STAIN
7
THE YELLOW RACKET
8
THE SILVER VESSEL
9
THE PINK ENVELOPE
10
THR BROWN SHAWL
11
THE IVORY DRESS
12
THE GREEN SEQUINS

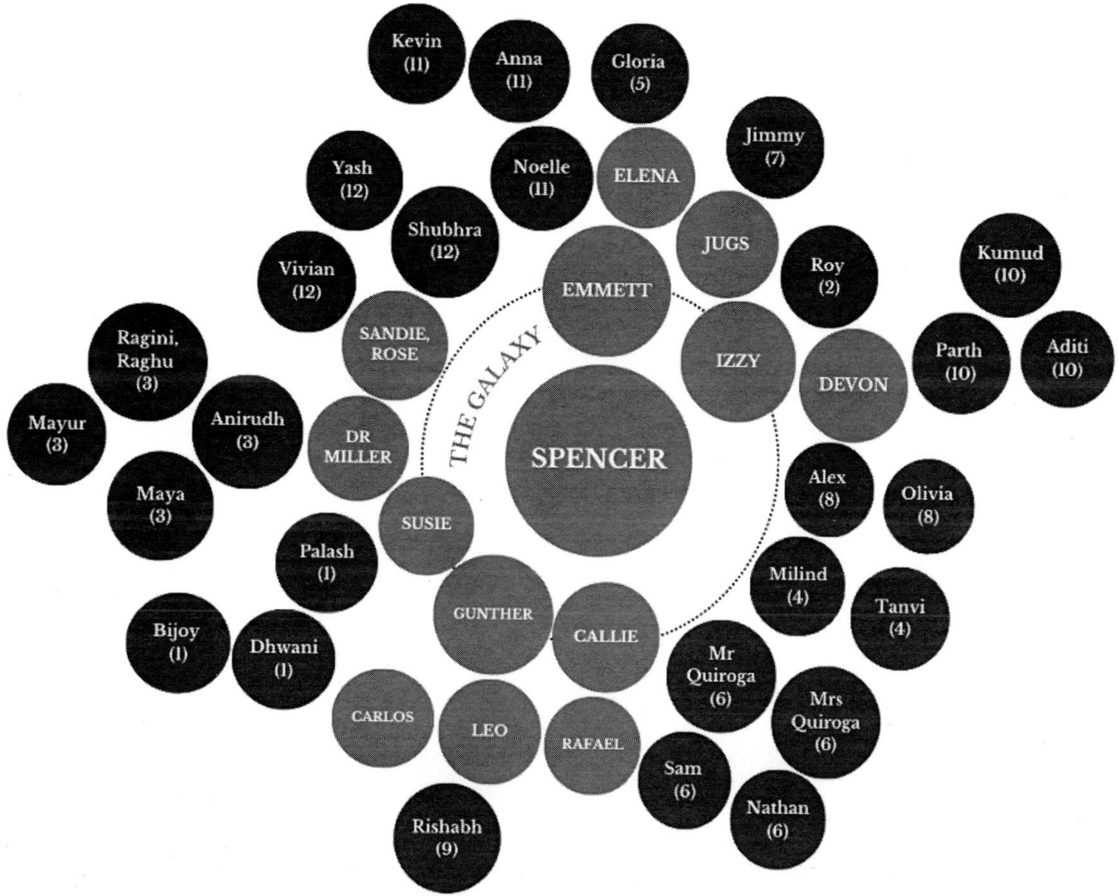
THE GALAXY
SPENCER
EMMETT
IZZY
JUGS
ELENA
DEVON
CALLIE
RAFAEL
GUNTHER
LEO
CARLOS
SUSIE
DR MILLER
SANDIE, ROSE
Kevin (11)
Anna (11)
Gloria (5)
Jimmy (7)
Yash (12)
Noelle (11)
Shubhra (12)
Vivian (12)
Roy (2)
Kumud (10)
Parth (10)
Aditi (10)
Ragini, Raghu (3)
Mayur (3)
Anirudh (3)
Maya (3)
Alex (8)
Olivia (8)
Milind (4)
Tanvi (4)
Palash (1)
Bijoy (1)
Dhwani (1)
Mr Quiroga (6)
Mrs Quiroga (6)
Sam (6)
Nathan (6)
Rishabh (9)

Foreword

A Tribute to the Stars

Dripping, gushing, churning
Unbridled, I am **water**!
Flowing, blowing, whirring
Unbound, I am **air**!
Illuminating, sizzling, crackling
Untamed, I am **fire**!
Thriving, morphing, moving
Unsung, I am **earth**!
Echoing, wandering, searching
Unfound, I am **ether.**

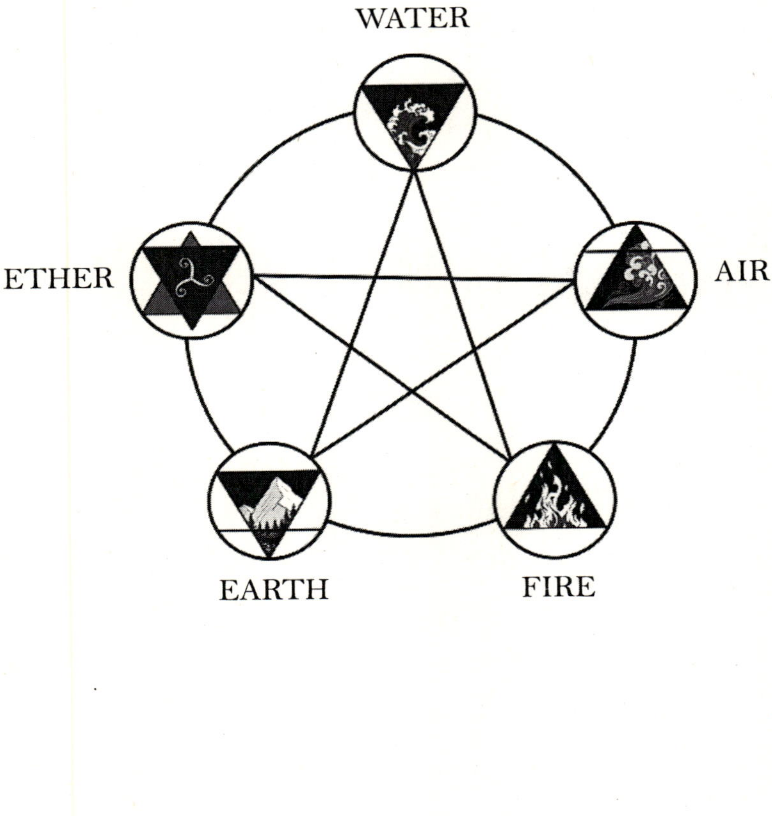
WATER
ETHER
AIR
EARTH
FIRE

Preface

It is an ordinary day. Like the day before. And the one before it. Here and there. Everywhere.

* * *

Yet, when the sun peeks above the horizon on this day, over the tides in the Bay of Bengal, it fills an entire subcontinent with the amber hue of hope. The calls of birds resonate through the air as pots of ginger tea come to a boil.

On the other side of the globe, the sky is dyed crimson, courtesy of the retreating rays of the Texan sun. Finches and doves flutter back to their nests. The aroma from barbecue grills wafts far and beyond with the evening breeze.

* * *

(Del Rio, Texas, US) Spencer puts on his favorite Minion socks and white sneakers. It is time for his evening run – the usual route along the church, the pizzeria, and the pawn shop, and finally right up on Agave Street, ending at the school. He checks the fitness band that Izzy has bought for him. God bless elder sisters! He passes by his father, Emmett Diaz, on his way out. Emmett is smiling as he types something on his phone. Spencer wonders what it might be. He will, hopefully, find out tonight at dinner.

(Kanpur, India) Kumud Mishra wakes up early. She has not slept well, and her mind is busy running through the checklist for tonight's house party. It is her twentieth wedding anniversary. She still cannot fathom why her husband, Manav, proposed to her when he did. She is glad about it, though, and has planned an elaborate menu to floor the guests, especially her sister Aditi.

(Georgetown, Texas, US) Elena checks her reflection in the mirror as she gets ready for the gala at the city hall. She picks the jewelry she will be wearing and lays it on her dresser, smiling. She has not been this excited in a long time. She has to get her ducks in a row. She locks her trunk and stows it away in its usual place. She calls out to the chambermaid to help her get dressed.

(Delhi, India) Raghu's sleep is rudely interrupted by a loud knock on his door at five in the morning. Dada reminds him to take a shower before the taps dry up. Raghu gets up with a mild headache. He sits on his bed, wondering if the day ahead will be tough with Khanna sir's chemistry assignment, which he has yet to finish. He hopes Mayur can help him. Again.

(Del Rio, Texas, US) Izzy and Devon are at the nursery. Devon helps her out in the evenings when he can or if Izzy has an exam, like the one she has tomorrow. It's only been a few months since they met, but Devon cannot find it in himself to stay away from her. He is yet to meet anyone from her family. He is hoping to make that happen during the upcoming weekend.

(Hyderabad, India) Milind tries to concentrate on his breathing. But morning yoga is proving quite impossible amidst the loud noises from the kitchen. He tells his house help, Nandan, to take a break from grinding the soaked urad dal and rice. With quietude restored, he proceeds with *anulom-vilom* and *kapalabhati*[1], hoping for no further interruptions.

---

[1] Breathing asanas in yoga

(Del Rio, Texas, US) Jugs sits back on the couch and lets out a tired sigh. What wouldn't he give to get his students to listen and for the dean to stop breathing down his neck? But he loves being a lecturer at the university. He considers cooking but decides against it. Ordering in is safer for a cook with his skills, or the lack thereof. He is looking forward to speaking with Jimmy later tonight.

(Bengaluru, India) Roy sits on a wicker chair in his balcony, sipping from a mug of cardamom tea. His throat is a little itchy, and his head is clouded, courtesy all the pegs of whiskey from the night before. Venky is to get married in a few months, and he'd dropped by to hand him the invitation. Roy is happy for his friend. But something has been bothering him ever since Venky's visit. A familiar craving takes hold of his thoughts. Again.

(New York, US) Robbie is proving to be an idiot. Again. Even after the divorce, he does not let her be. It's as if he does not want to move on. On the contrary, he keeps looking for reasons to run into her or visit her apartment to pick up some trifle he's left behind. Like a box of what appears to be trash that he extracted from a cabinet in the guest room that morning. Noelle wonders if Aunt Anna would be able to give her some advice. She feels guilty that it has been too long since they last spoke. Soon, she thinks.

(Mumbai, India) Rishabh walks towards the church. The misty drizzle does not bother him. He had volunteered to be there for the breakfast service. So, he needs to get there quickly. He is sure Dhar Sahib would already be up and done with his prayers. Professor Raut may be a different story altogether, and may need help getting dressed. Rishabh checks the time on his watch. At the back of his mind is a question, 'What was Leo's one a.m. plan about?' He hopes that they'll chat again.

(Del Rio, Texas, US) Shubhra gets ready in a dress that Yash loves to see her wear. He bought it for her during his recent trip to Paris. He had wanted her to join him, but she could not get time off from the dance studio. She accessorizes her look with a ruby bracelet and a slender diamond necklace. Yash kisses her on the cheek as she slips her feet into the heels which will most definitely kill her tonight.

(New Delhi, India) Maya does not open her eyes as Anirudh gets ready for office. Anirudh considers waking her up but decides against it. He checks the medicine box, covers her with a blanket, picks up his bag, and shuts the door behind him. Maya throws the blanket off the moment the door clicks shut. She needs to figure out how to win. She cannot lose, not to Anirudh's mother, not now.

(Austin, Texas, US) Sam Quiroga receives the test results. He wasn't expecting much but hadn't seen this coming. Looking at the paper in his shaking hand, he conjures up possibilities of what it means for his future. And his past. He cannot believe that he's been lied to. He wants to run to his best friend, Nathan's, house. But what would he even say? He feels ashamed. There must be another explanation.

(Indore, India) Palash and Dhwani Gaonkar have just finished packing their bags. The bus with the others from Khoj does not leave for another two hours. But they are too excited and cannot wait. They stand in front of the Ganesha statue, hands joined together in reverence, heads bowed in prayer. With a final obeisance, they step out into the cold winter morning with the warmth of hope in their hearts.

(Del Rio, Texas, US) Susie is at the park with Callie. Gunther comes in running, mouthing apologies for being late by half an hour. Apparently, his spectacles broke, and it took a while to find the emergency spare pair. The girls offer him a cookie that he gladly accepts, and they get down to planning the scrapbook for Spencer. It is a present for his 'sweet sixteenth'. Although it's still a few weeks away, they know that printing the pictures, writing the notes, and making it look stunning will take time.

(Shimla, India) Jimmy is on the school bus. The new school is all right. He has made some friends. But he is always looking over his shoulder. It's an old habit. He puts in his earplugs and muffles the sounds of the chattering kids around him. He has to visit his speech therapist after school. He wonders what experiment he'd be subject to today. He leans against the cold glass window and follows the flight of a lonely eagle gliding in the summer sky.

(Unknown Location) Alex looks down at the beautiful lake below. He loves the way the water shimmers in the light of the morning sun, stunned by the golden radiance splayed all around. He is lying next to the glass window on the floor of his cozy, high-altitude home with a book in hand. His fingers turn the yellowing pages he has already read a dozen times. He wonders how his parents and friends are doing.

(Del Rio, Texas, US) Emmet Diaz is getting ready to go out. He is spending longer than usual checking his reflection in the mirror. He swaps his sneakers for another pair he otherwise wears for office meetings. Satisfied, he grabs a Post-it from the dining table and scribbles a message for Spencer and Izzy. He expects to be back before dinner. With a last look at the empty house, he steps out and turns the key.

(Kanpur, India) Parth is at the gym again. He is not sure why. Actually, he does, but wonders if there is another way. His biceps ache under the strain of another curl. He has applied to study in the US but is dreading the odd chance that he gets accepted. It would mean dealing with new people and etiquette. He wishes his cousin, Tavish, could go with him to show him how. But he must go alone. He needs to grow into the person his mother deserves. With a renewed resolve, he lifts the weight again.

(Del Rio, Texas, US) Spencer turns right onto Agave Street. A school bus has stopped right in the middle of the street. He does not give it another thought. He ties the laces on his shoes again, catches his breath, and looks around while leaning against the bakery. He loves the smell of cinnamon and sugar that invariably permeates the air around him. And then, something colors his entire world dark.

* * *

It is an ordinary day.

Just like the day before. And the one before that.

Or maybe not.

Maybe it won't be just another day.

PART ONE

THE FABLES OF WATER

oozing drops of beauty
blessing every single leaf
peasants looking skyward
toiling away with belief
surging in the waves
the currents frothing white
sketching rainbows with drops
splitting that stubborn sunlight
divine in every sensory way
is the sound of falling rain
running through my veins
you keep me grounded, sane
and I hold you ever so close
keeping it a solemn surprise
deep behind the closed lids
of my two dreamy eyes

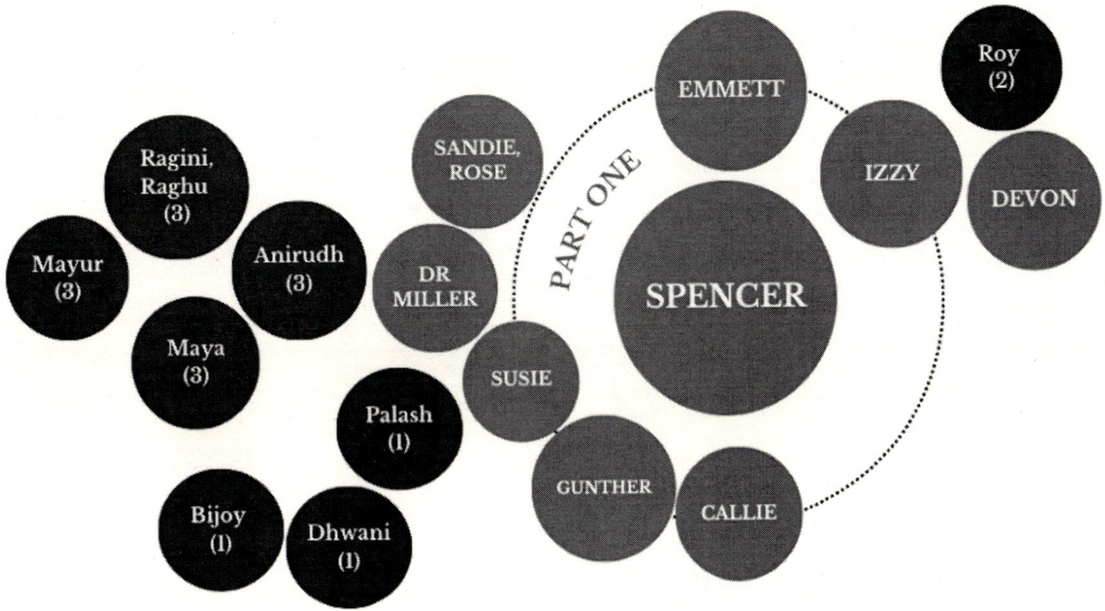
PART ONE
SPENCER
EMMETT
IZZY
Roy (2)
DEVON
SANDIE, ROSE
DR MILLER
SUSIE
GUNTHER
CALLIE
Ragini, Raghu (3)
Mayur (3)
Anirudh (3)
Maya (3)
Palash (1)
Bijoy (1)
Dhwani (1)

SPENCER DIAZ IS AWAKE?

Texas, USA

I think I may be dying. Sometimes, it does not make any sense. This feeling comes and goes, in which I am looking in from the other side of an open window that is open just a crack, such that I can peek in but unlikely to climb through.

Why can't I? I am not even sure I know how to describe it. It must be a dream. This is what dying must feel like.

What else could it be? What is this state of being an invisible voyeur into what ironically seems to be my own life? Let me get back to what I do know.

It is the perky one today, the one who smells like fresh roses. It's hard to make that fragrance out against the deep smells of disinfectants, but I catch whiffs of it whenever she steps closer. I call her Rose. Obviously! I can make out the clickety-clack sounds of her sandals on the synthetic floor. Or at least I suspect it's synthetic. Hospital floors are like that—cold and gloomy.

Click clack. Click clack. Click clack.

She is standing close by. I can feel her presence. I can feel her hand as she brushes strands of stray hair from my forehead. She gently pats my head, just like Izzy always does. She holds my hand in hers … er … my wrist, actually, to measure my pulse. Proof of life. She is spending a long time doing it, though. Should I be worried?

Maybe she likes the sensation of my cold skin against her soft hands. She must be paying a lot for her manicure. Such smooth hands.

I like Rose. I assume she is the day nurse.

I don't know if it is day or night, but there seems to be more of a bustle when she is around, unlike the sullen quiet when the other nurse takes over. The one with a rasping voice like sandpaper grinding against stone. I call her Sandie. I know I have a knack for the obvious.

Surely, there must be some selection criteria for nurses employed in the hospital's Critical Care Unit, like having a minimal level of soothing aura to their personality.

Anyway, I do not hold it against Sandie. Not when she commits to giving me the gentlest sponge bath and a change of baby-soft diapers every single day. *Como la seda.*

It's been a while since I have been here, though I am not sure exactly how long. Counting does not come easy to me right now. I tend to muddle numbers up. It is strange that I find it challenging now, given how many things I am typically used to counting every day.

Brushing four strokes at a time on each side of the jaw.

Two scoops of raisin bran cereal for breakfast.

Checking the front door lock six times before leaving.

One hundred forty steps to the bus stop.

Ten bites to chew every morsel.

Four repetitions to turn on a light and six for a fan.

Twenty-one tiles on our kitchen floor, wishing it was a round number of twenty, or at least an even twenty-two.

Thirteen steps between the ground and first floors of the school and fifteen steps between the first and second. This is something that I have not been able to reconcile with, knowing that standard staircases could have anywhere between thirteen to sixteen steps, and yet, the building constructors chose neither fourteen nor sixteen.

Extraño. People make some odd choices.

I have tried keeping track of time, silently counting seconds, minutes, hours, and beyond. But it does not turn out well because I invariably doze off without warning. No one notices when I do. I tried counting my breaths, assuming that I could extrapolate that based on my pulse. But in vain.

Apparently, I sleep a lot.

If I am to believe Dad, I have been out for twenty-seven days. He tends to exaggerate sometimes, but he sounds sincere when speaking with Dr Miller. I cannot see Dad or the doctor, of course. But I imagine a wide frown on Dad's forehead, deep enough to serve *salsa verde* for a platter of crispy nachos.

He obsesses over his kids the same way I fret about the odd number of vowels in the English alphabet. Why not four or six? He needs to learn how to relax. So do I. I blame it on his genes, although I secretly wish I would grow up to become even half the human being he is.

Abuela says that I have his eyes. That won't do. I need a heart like his. And I would be okay if he hadn't passed on his propensity for loud sneezing down the genetic route. I would rather not give unsuspecting people a heart attack every time I have the flu or an allergy.

Yesterday (or was it the day before or the one before that?) Dr Miller had reminded Dad that he needed to make a decision. And that Dad could take time until he was ready. *Dios mío.* For what?

He said there was no rush, although the chances of my recovery stayed slim. That sounds grim, even to a pathological pessimist like me. I wanted to shout out and tell Dad that he could brood over his decision a bit longer, if nothing else, to diss Dr Miller. But then, Dad doesn't exactly listen to what I have to say these days.

To be or not to be, *esa es la pregunta*. That is indeed the question once again.

This might be a good time to start counting my breaths. Word on the street is that they may be numbered. *Caracoles!* I hope it's not a prime number, or a multiple of thirteen, or both!

I haven't decided yet which way I lean on the whole 'choosing to live' dilemma. While the living world has its charms, I won't exactly mind an early checkout. It would save Dad a lot of trouble. I do not wish him any more horrid nightmares about his son dying, over and over again, in a loop. He'd be able to focus on the good kid he has—Izzy—and breathe easy.

While we are doing a pros and cons assessment, here is something to consider. Who really wants to stick around narrow-minded people who discriminate based on just about anything; or the violent fanatics who mow down innocent people at crowded marketplaces; or the depraved lunatics who peddle drugs to underage teenagers, or the ignorant nincompoops who'd rather inundate the oceans with garbage than exercise restraint; or the unconscionable sociopaths who go around assaulting and raping others?

That's five reasons. I need one more to round it up.

The more I think about it, the scarier it feels, and my resolve to wake up stutters, just like my speech. My attempts at a happy life haven't worked out thus far.

Who is to say they ever will?

I wish Dad would wait long enough for me to make my mind up. Or whatever is left of it after that crashing explosion just before my world blanked out. Just the way my mind is blanking out right now. I cannot stand it when that happens. It must be from whatever Rose has just injected into my drip.

And I fall into a dream. Is this a dream?

I am walking amidst the vast vastness of green everlastingness. Even my vocabulary is a bit of a mess right now. It's not as ... as vast as you would like. But I will try to do better. So, I am walking through this, you know, massive grassland, surrounded by all these foresty things ... trees, I mean. *Por Dios!*

There is an unfamiliar scent floating about, just enough to tease me with its presence, yet not potent enough to be recognized. There is a light shimmer that catches my eye. I stop and approach the base of a ginormous tree—a maple tree.

My hands graze its gnarly bark that seems to be molting, just like my hands did after craft class in junior high what with all that Elmer's glue. I recall Izzy once telling me about how the good folks at the farms extracted pancake syrup from these very trees.

Did she see that on NatGeo? Or was it just a random WhatsApp forward? My sister is quite gullible that way. Wow, that's a big word for me right now!

This shimmery sparkle seems to be reflecting off a piece of glass or a bottle, like the kind they use to package OJ at the supermarket. Orange juice. OJ. Yes. Kill me! Well, don't. Could you wait a minute while I make up my pulpy mind?

The bottle looks old and cracked, though the lid is still intact. It's crusty but intact. Just like me. It's resting against a tiny flag, a faded blue and red one like the one we got at boot camp to mark our trails. It is odd that I should find it here. It doesn't look like the kind of place where someone goes camping. Yet, it is strange how, sometimes, things that are so out of place appear so much at home.

I am trying to take the bottle out of the ground, but it looks like the tree's roots have it trapped. It's like they have learned to grow around it, like an extended family. I try a few more times before it comes loose.

There is a dusty, yellowing paper inside the bottle. I tap the bottle four times and carefully extract that neat roll of exceptionally old-looking paper ... er ... what they call ... a parchment.

Bravo, I've still got it. Suck it, all you suckers who think that my vocabulary is as stunted as the feathers of a kiwi bird.

This paper is covered in moss and grime but surprisingly in one piece. My heart is drumming with excitement. And why not? I have not had an adventure in … forever. Adventure? Really? What's the adventure in a trashy glass bottle with a yucky piece of paper, you think? I agree it's no patch on playing Mortal Kombat, with its multiple levels of adventures for socially awkward teenagers like yours truly.

Mierda, I miss those uber-competitive, sleep-deprived, play-until-your-eyes-fall-off-their-sockets games with Gunther and Callie.

I am unrolling the paper carefully when my eyes catch how my hands look. Hairy. Rough and veined, with a snake tattoo on my right arm and heavy-set biceps to go with them. Nice, but who is this dude wearing my brain on his body?

I stand up and find myself looking down from a greater height than I can recall in my life and times. What? A shiny forest axe and a flask of water dangle by a leather belt on the dude's ample waist. So, is this a brawnier avatar of me in a parallel universe? And if it is, I have a question: Is this avatar still a diehard fan of Johnny Cage?

Maybe all I do in this avatar is walk across the stables and the farm, trying to stay away from … er … trouble? An imminent zombie attack? A hostile alien takeover of Earth?

Mysteriously, I know the name of this avatar of mine with unwavering certainty. Ralph. Of course, he wouldn't have a boring name like Spencer.

The only thing more boring than that name is my life.

I seem to have hit a perennial pause like a stuck record. I've seen a record player, thanks to Mrs Nelson, my friend Callie's mom, who is somewhat of an antique collector. Callie's house looks like a museum. I feel lost every time I visit her place. I feel lost most of the time in other places, too.

I never know what to do except when I am running. Left right, left right, left right. My grades have been slipping since the incident at school. I still haven't decided what colleges to apply to. I worry that Dad does not have enough saved to bail me out. He might have to make peace with just one of his kids graduating.

I try to imagine if he'd rather have a loser for a son or an epitaph for a dead one. It's a tough choice.

Dad has his work cut out for him. I would not know where to go even if he had the dough. I am not good at much. Mathematics is the only subject that I am half decent at. Maybe chemistry. But the rest are a lost cause.

Izzy always knew exactly what she wanted to study and where she wanted to apply. The only clear ambition I have is to own the largest sneaker collection in all of Texas. I doubt that would qualify for a strong college application essay. What a soup!

I ... er ... Ralph unfolds the rolled piece of paper. Sorry, what did I say that was called? I am sure I told you what it was, the thing with the written words and stuff, that thing? Anyway, Ralph's eyes—I mean my eyes—drift to the bottom of the scroll.

Of course, we want to know who our secret pal is.

We are sure that it is from a pal. A note just for us to find. *Misterioso.* A secret just for us to know. Both of us.

It says ... wait, what? That does not make any sense. What's a new nomad? Is that a hippie reference? Or am I mixing it up with some other tribe? But why would someone ... ? And if the age of the bottle and the parchment were anything to go by, this nomad person was not so 'new' after all! *Nuevo nómada?* Puhleease.

Ralph is ... I am ... reading the rest of the note. Whoever wrote it must have been a beatific soul, someone out on a quest of a lifetime. He has written about his thrilling adventures and the joy they bring him. I crave for an adventure. Not this stuck-to-the-depressing-hospital-bed sorta adventure. Something more outdoorsy, maybe?

Is this 'new nomad' person on an extended vacation in the mountains? I wish I could travel to Mount Whitney, Mount Kilimanjaro, or somewhere in the Himalayas. Hike and camp.

Do I have the right sneakers, though?

Would Dad be game for it? I seem to be going adrift. I cannot fully understand what is written. He has written something about setting sail on his vessel shortly.

Vessel? A journey by ship? Interesting.

He speaks of freedom, and there is something about ... *Beep ... Beep* ... his words feel real, as if ... wait, do I know him?

Seems as if ... *Beep ... Beep ... Beep....*

Oops. That doesn't sound right. Only three beeps. *Beep ... Beep ... Beep ... Click Clack. Click Clack.*

Rose is back by my side. She is screaming about something called 'Code Blue'. She lowers my headrest and then the bed. Another person comes running.

Ralph is fading. I can see my vision flicker.

I can hear a heavy clang of metal against the floor, and someone is now on top of me. I sink under the weight of his burly hands on my chest. I can tell it's a man. Both hands. Three beeps. This is hopeless.

Why is this person trying to break my ribs?

Ralph seems to be vaporizing. I don't want him to. Rose asks someone to '... push a milligram of epi'. Two might be better. I feel a numbness start to pulse through my veins. The trees around Ralph are dissolving into a mist. The person on my chest is still pounding at it.

Beep ... Beep ... Beep...

Dr Miller is urgently asking for a crash cart. Was that a Mortal Kombat reference from a level I haven't reached yet? I shouldn't have written Dr Miller off so quickly. The person assaulting my chest is finally off me. Someone shouts, 'Charge to 300. Clear!' At least that's a round number.

I feel a surge of energy throughout my whole being, lifting me like a dandelion floating away into oblivion.

Beep ... Beep ... Beep....

Ralph and the parchment both disappear. The forest is gone. There is darkness. What is happening to me? To Ralph, to us? Is someone there?

Beep ... Beep ... Beep....

(1)

THE PURPLE[2] SCARF

For the ones who have lost hope

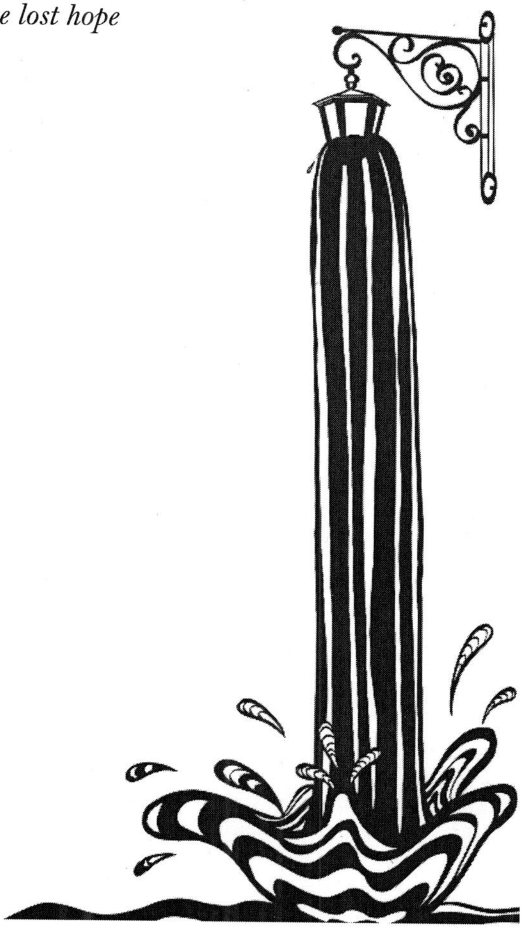

You are the music,

the rain....

And the joy worth

all my pain.

[2] The colors purple, lavender, aquamarine and sea green are often associated with the zodiac sign of Pisces. Those born to this sun sign are believed to embody intuition, magic, dreaminess and spirituality associated with their ruling planet, Neptune.

THE GAONKARS SING A MELODY

Mumbai + Indore, India

My name is Dhwani Gaonkar. I live in Indore. I am a mother.

The applause is deafening. People are up on their feet, clapping, cheering, and hooting. I have been standing rooted to the spot for what seems like an eternity. The four of them—the ones who will decide our fate—are standing too; both the girls are crying, and the gentlemen are bowing down.

I can hear them chanting, 'You are not alone. You are not alone.'

* * *

It's surreal. I am shivering, and my face is wet with warm tears. I must look awful, I think, for I had put on a lot of mascara for this special night. But I don't care right now.

Lights sparkle in my eyes, and I cannot see all the rows of people in front of the podium. I can hear their raucous cheers; sense the emotional sniveling, and faintly make out the whispered words of prayer, though. I look heavenwards, letting my shoulders droop, and my emotions get the better of me.

I sense a gentle touch on my shoulders, and I look up to find Rekha and Colonel Bijoy trying to get me back up on my feet. It is then that I truly remember what we just did.

Rekha, Colonel Bijoy, twenty-three others and I.

All of them have stories just like mine. Some of them are worse. We are bound by the same spirit, spurred on by a profound hope that all is not yet lost. I am sure that the universe has a reason for bringing us together. And I think they feel the same way.

Perhaps we are all desperate enough to believe that there is a spiritual intervention in our pursuit. Maybe it's just denial.

In our most honest moments, there are unyielding, seismic-scale tremors that shake the foundations of our belief. We used to hide these from each other. Not anymore. Sharing them has somehow lent more tenacity to those very foundations.

The unison with which our hearts beat as we chase that dream is something I never reckoned was possible. Looking at them right now, here with me, I am overwhelmed. I know their stories. And they know mine.

Like Dhara and Jeevan at the back of the group, crying. Jeevan is clutching Dhara tight to his chest and she is holding onto him with all her might, lest she loses him too, like their twin boys—Aman and Arun.

It happened seventeen years ago, but her tears are yet to dry. She still goes to the school gate every day, hoping to find them standing there, waiting for her to come and pick them up. She still apologizes for being late to school on that day. She still reasons about what she could have done differently. Dhara and Jeevan are wearing matching gray gloves embroidered with 'A' in crimson red, one for each of their boys. They wear these gloves everywhere, no matter the season.

Rekha opens a bottle of water and offers me a sip. At thirty, she is the youngest among us. She was a chartered accountant for a firm, but that was before…. It has been four years since her daughter was.... She suffered a minor stroke shortly after it happened. It broke her spirit.

She is alone right now. She is alone every day.

Her husband blames her for valuing her job more than what is 'appropriate' for a mother. Her parents supported her in the beginning, through the divorce and relocation. Later, it became convenient for them to let her 'figure' her way forward. Her husband offered alimony, but she denied his charity. Instead, she found us. At Khoj, the collective that we are all a part of.

And it is here that she began her search for her daughter, all over again, with us. Her hair is turning gray from the stress and the dark circles under her eyes belie her claims of getting enough shut-eye. Sleep is yet another thing we have all lost.

Colonel Bijoy, of course, is an exception. He clocks a sack time of eight hours every day. Sometimes more. He is exceptionally regimented about it. He is not really from the armed forces. We address him as 'Colonel' to mock his military-like rules. He is a stickler for perfection, not to mention quite the flirt.

But he has carried on the mission they had once started together. Khoj was their brainchild. Thirty-two years ago, their son went missing from a cricket match they had gone to watch at the stadium. It was his dream to see Kapil Dev live. He was ten. One minute, he was holding his father's hand, and the next, he had been swallowed by a swarming sea of humanity.

They looked all over the stadium, checking each nook and gully over and over, calling out his name until their voices went hoarse and their limbs buckled. The police patrolled the areas near the exit and sent out search parties, but in vain.

Their son was never seen again.

Newspaper articles, pictures and appeals, all died down with time. Folks who had first assured them that their son would return found not-so-subtle ways to avoid them or hung their heads helplessly. Relatives, even friends, started taking steps away, excusing themselves on the honorable pretext of giving the couple privacy.

Moving on, it seems, is vital to finding serenity.

It becomes convenient for others to remain supportive of your loss if you do not mention it. That way, abandonment feels more like solidarity.

But the duo could not move on. They did not want to. Moving on would have meant giving up. The parent in them could not. Instead, they chose to take on the mission of locating their son, no matter what it took. A mission until 'death does them apart' and beyond.

While they pursued their search for their son, they crossed paths with others aching from the same trauma. What started as a personal crusade gradually evolved into a larger cause—to help other parents who were being asked to move on. That is how Colonel Bijoy narrates the origin story of Khoj.

Today, we all stand here on the stage at the famous Filmistan Studio, united by this massive void that each one of us is trying to fill while carrying the burden of guilt and endless worry about what could have happened to our lost children.

Six years ago, I reached the doorsteps of Khoj, located in a small lane near Indore's Sarafa Bazaar, clutching my daughter's purple scarf around my neck and a picture of her in my purse. A friend had told me about Khoj, which sparked a new hope. I was scared to admit it to anyone. Even to my counselor, who'd been helping me fight the losing battle with recurring bouts of depression. By then, I had stopped counting the hopeless hopes I had nurtured because each time I did, and each time they shattered, it left me even more broken than before. Only to trigger episodes where I would lock myself in the bathroom and cry into a towel, lest my husband should find me inconsolable once more.

My husband, Palash Gaonkar, is a simple man and the gentlest soul I have ever encountered. With a doctorate in mass communications, he comes across as a nerd to the uninitiated. Yet, he's the ideal husband, the perfect father, and a terrific guy in every way possible. I like addressing him as 'Doctor Saheb,' something he has surrendered to reluctantly. I've always suspected that he secretly likes being addressed like that. Having been raised in an orphanage in Indore, he did not have a family to call his own before we were married and our daughter Pia came along. He never knew his parents, something you'd expect him to rue. Yet, he never complains about it.

'I've had plenty more than some. It could have been worse,' he says if anyone ever pitied his past.

But despite the brave façade he projected, I knew he was scared of losing what he had with us. He'd confessed as much on a rare evening when he'd allowed himself a third dram of whiskey —on a night Pia was at a friend's place for a sleepover. 'I'll keep you both safe. Always. I will never be alone again. I never want to be without you and Pia. You are my world,' he kept saying, teary-eyed, making me promise over and over again that we would never leave him.

So, when Pia went missing, he just switched off. It was like his soul had left his body. She was just six at the time. She was his pride, his entire world. She was a daddy's girl, as he always claimed. They would talk about animals and gamebirds, watch wildlife documentaries, and make elaborate plans to go camping in the Amazon jungles. Sometimes, with those two, I felt ignored, even sidelined. But mostly, I was jealous that they did not include me in their horseplay.

I'd give anything to be sidelined that way again.

After her disappearance, he withdrew into a shell and never talked about his pain, anxiety, or fear. I was hapless, a teary mess, howling my agony out of my eyes and throat. But his eyes never betrayed him. His face turned to stone, not letting any emotions escape. I witnessed him wither away, piece by piece. The part of him that made him smile was lost.

The man who was my husband turned into a shadow of that cheerful soul he once was. I used to try to get him to open up, but he would walk away. He'd sit alone, stare out of the balcony or blankly look at the newspaper. Whenever our gazes did meet, I saw an unspoken apology and a melancholic helplessness that made my heart splinter.

I did not know better than to let him be. I wish I had.

Year after year, he immersed himself more in his work as a freelance nature photographer and journalist.

Often, he chose assignments that required him to travel, sometimes to places I didn't even know the names of. He still does.

I think it keeps him connected to Pia, to the hope of running into her on one of his trips. A hope against hopelessness!

Pia used to love the stories from his travels. So, now, he writes them in a little red notebook that he keeps under his pillow. It says 'For Pia' on the first page, followed by entries of places he's seen, libraries he's visited, dishes he's sampled, and people he's met, interspersed with a montage of polaroids, flight tickets, food bills, stamps, and news clippings.

I often sneak a read when he is not looking. I will never regret it. It is how I know that he has still not forgiven himself for losing what he held dearest. Not just his daughter but also what made him my husband.

In a few months, he will be on his way to a work trip, a month-long tour across forests in Brazil, Mexico, and the US. Pia would have been jumping up and down with joy if she knew about his tour to the Amazon rainforests—the fruition of their secretly hatched plans, just for the two of them. I was no fun outdoors, they'd say. I wish she could go with him. I wish I could. Instead, I will find comfort in reading the stories he writes for our daughter in his little red notebook, or what I call his 'journal of healing.'

I'm glad he'll get to meet new people. And perhaps find tranquility. Or redemption. Or both.

So, I did not bother him when I learned about Khoj. I snuck out one morning after he'd left for work. I remember how nervous I was that day—nervously excited—in the same way whenever I found a new lead to be pursued in our quest. I stood at the threshold for twenty minutes before I stepped in, wondering what an NGO could do when even the police had failed to locate any traces of Pia during their years of so-called 'investigation,' acting like a clueless bunch of incompetent nincompoops. I told myself that I had nothing to lose and stepped inside.

Meeting Colonel Bijoy and his wife that day filled me with such positive energy that I felt alive again. When Palash returned home that evening, he was astonished to see me dressed up, the house tidy, and a warm dinner waiting for him on the dining table. On most evenings during the last few years, I'd eat early and sleep by the time he came home to a cold, unkind meal in a casserole.

I cannot forget the look on his face, the calm demeanor giving way to a tired smile. He hugged me close, and we stayed that way for long. There was a part of us that was still broken. But it felt like the start of something, an embrace that was a harbinger of a healing we both needed. Perhaps him more than me.

'I'm sorry,' he murmured, his voice like petrichor in the monsoons.

'I know, Doctor Saheb. I am, too. But you've still got me if you still....' I replied.

'I do. I always will. I never....' he grasped for words that never found their way out, even as he held on to me like he was scared to let go.

From that day, I had a purpose. I did not know if and when Pia would be found. Whether it was the breakthrough with Palash, the association with Khoj, or both, I found a solace that had eluded me for years. I would still cry, but I would smile too, sometimes even laugh.

Within a few months, I gave up the aid of antidepressants I had been leaning on for a while. Knowing others like me made it seem a bit easier. There were moments when I'd even forget about Pia, amidst putting together campaigns for other children, filing petitions and following up on leads. At Khoj, we became each other's strength, an extended family of sorts.

It was rejuvenating to talk to someone who'd not tell you to move on, someone who felt the same ache as you did. I did not need to hide my sorrow and bury my tears just to make it easier on the ones around me. I was allowed my grief and my restlessness. I was no longer in my solitary confinement of unbearable proportions.

Besides following up with reclusive cops and visiting slums or red-light areas where someone had spotted something, there wasn't a lot that we could do. There were days when it would get exhausting, even deflating. Because no matter how hard we tried, we never found anyone.

It was then that Rekha came into our lives, almost two years after I joined Khoj. I still remember that day—10 March 2016. I remember it clearly because it was Pia's birthday. Rekha came in with a box of donuts and a beaming smile. Most of us had never seen a donut before that day. I still remember Colonel Bijoy eyeing the mysterious South Indian *vada*-like sweet with suspicion before I told him it was okay to try one. We made a birthday wish for Pia with the donuts. It was the first time I had done that after....

Somehow, I could smile. Somehow, it did not kill me. Somehow, I was okay to take a punt on hope.

A couple of years ago, Colonel Bijoy unfortunately lost his wife to ovarian cancer. We never knew she had been sick. But her demise had Colonel Bijoy doubling his focus on making an even bigger impact via Khoj. 'I have to finish what she and I started together,' he'd say while trying to hide his heartbreak. We knew that feeling all too well.

While preparing for a community support group meeting one evening, Jeevan stopped mid-way while stacking chairs in the meeting hall. He turned around and asked, 'How will they know we have not stopped looking?' He was misty-eyed, feeling powerless, and looking at no one in particular for an answer, yet hoping to find one. Dhara held onto the gloves of her missing twins to her chest, eyes closed, saying another expectant prayer. Jeevan's question cast a dark shadow on all of our minds.

A few days later, Rekha came in with an unmistakable look of triumph. She got us all to gather in the hall. She told us that she had found a way. A way for our children to hear us and hear our voices—to know that we had not given up. Colonel Bijoy was eager to act. So were the rest of us. But a hush dawned over the group when she told us what we needed to do. It was an insane idea. After some sneers and murmurs, the group began to scatter. Rekha tried in vain, but no one was listening.

I, for one, thought that the plan was shockingly brilliant. It was not going to be easy.

I stood rooted to the spot, imagining the picture Rekha had just painted. As members of our tribe were exiting the hall, I caught the beginnings of a faint melody in the air. Barely audible at first, it gradually grew into a full-throated voice. It was Mr Farooq, singing an old Rafi song with his eyes closed. '*Pukarta chala hoon main, gali gali bahaar ki*[3]*....*'

The chatter died, people shushing each other until there was pin drop silence. Though age had taken a toll on what must have once been sensational singing vocals, Mr

[3] I walk through the lanes of spring, calling out...

Farooq's crooning had an unmistakable appeal. Like me, I saw others drawn towards it as well. I saw Ms Desai moving forward to join him, singing along and clapping her hands in rhythmic synchrony. I hadn't seen her utter as many as ten words before that. Soon, Dr Prasad and Mrs Rai joined in, followed by Rekha, Dhara, Colonel Bijoy and even the shy Mrs Nambiar. The effect was mesmerizing. Soon, we all were singing in unison. Even Jeevan, who was certifiably musically challenged, joined in. Mrs Nambiar sniggered when he did, but what the heck?

That evening, amid wet eyes, choking throats, and welling emotions, The Khoj Choir was born.

The following day, we gathered in the hall again. The air was charged with a newfound purpose. The plan was presented, seconded, and approved in less than three minutes. We would participate in a talent show and sing to help our children find us. We had to be the lighthouse to their boats in case they were lost for direction.

Rekha's plan was a bit out there, a bit kooky, but it made sense. Appearing on national TV was a million times more effective than distributing pamphlets on roads and malls.

Maybe someone would remember something.

Maybe someone would say something.

Maybe someone would lead us back to our children.

That night, I did not sleep. And I was sure that I was not the only one.

Three months later, The Khoj Choir was ready to perform at the auditions of a major national TV show.

I still remember the nerves we felt before we went on stage. The tension was palpable. At that moment, all those days of rehearsals came rushing back. Mr Farooq and

Ms Desai had become our mentors. They tried their best to infuse some musicality into croaky throats like mine. The chorus slowly became less cacophonous, and a few lead singers began to emerge.

Ms Rai and I took charge of the costumes. After much debate, we chose white and green, the colors of hope. Colonel Bijoy made arrangements for the bus and filled out the forms. Rekha hired a videographer to shoot our rehearsals and a social media intern to manage our posts. Our Facebook page soon had over eighty thousand 'friends.'

Even Palash took a week off to join us on the trip to Mumbai.

'When do we leave?' he asked, much to my surprise when I told him of the plan. 'How can I help? I want to do something. I need to….' I'd planted a kiss on his lips before he could finish.

From that day, he would come for every rehearsal. There was a longing in his eyes, which moistened every time he heard us rehearse. I hoped it was not from the agony of how off-key and unpalatable we sounded. We visited every temple, gurudwara, church, and mosque on our way to Mumbai, praying that our plan would work and that we'd be blessed with the gifts of meter and tune.

Earlier today, we hugged each other before stepping on the stage, but no one talked. The silence was deafening. The anchor announced our group and the thirty of us slowly trooped up on stage. Colonel Bijoy introduced Khoj and talked a bit about our story and mission. Then we sang.

'Yeh hausla kaise jhuke, yeh aarzoo kaise ruke[4]*….'*

---

[4] How can this courage wane? How can this dream stop?

I know we messed up some of the lyrics and definitely went off-key in a few places. Fortunately, three minutes later, it was over. We stopped and took a bow. This is where I am right now....

* * *

The applause is deafening. People are up on their feet, clapping, cheering, and hooting.

I have been standing rooted to the spot for what feels like an eternity. The four of them—the ones who will decide our fate—are standing too; both the girls are crying, and the gentlemen are bowing down.

I love tears. I cry a lot.

Behind us, pictures of our children with their names and our contact numbers are flashing on gigantic screens that they use as backdrops. The audience is hysterical. They are all still standing, clapping, and hugging each other. Crying. Sniffling. I can hear them chanting.

'You are not alone. You are not alone.'

I am on my knees, sobbing uncontrollably and looking pathetic. I pray that our children have heard us and that they know. I hope that every Indian is memorizing the smiling faces of our children.

In this auditorium full of strangers, I have found my belief again.

I have always had faith. But today, I have found a new path or at least the possibility of it. I tug at the purple scarf around my neck and hold on to it. It has been twelve years, and I can still smell her in the folds of that scarf. I speculate when I will see Pia. I yearn for when she will look into my eyes and hold my hand. I close my eyes and pray.

'Yeh hausla kaise jhuke, yeh aarzoo kaise ruke....'

We are through to the next round.

Doctor Saheb is standing next to me, holding me steady. For the first time in ten years, I witness him cry without reservation, not embarrassed about who is looking. There is a touch of abandonment and relief in his eyes. He does not want to be strong right now. He is still gripping tightly onto my hand as he slides down to the floor. I sit next to him and he buries his head into my shoulder. It has taken a long time for him to get to this point. Right here is our first victory.

Later that night, he would go into Pia's room and cry some more into her favorite blanket. It would be the first time he'd do that since her disappearance. That will be our second victory.

The thing with tears is that they have the habit of sacrificing themselves to let their love affair with the eyes reach its climax.

The lights on the stage dim as we exit. Walking down the steps, I clutch Pia's purple scarf with a smile. I cannot wait.

the promise of a dream

that lost joy aching in that heart

tonight, a different tale begins

Pisces (Feb 19 - Mar 20) | *Neptune* | *Aquamarine*

I may be lost for now, but find me in your smiles.

SPENCER DIAZ SMELLS COCONUTS

Texas, USA

In case you were wondering, I survived 'Code Blue'. Blue is not my favorite color anymore. I will need to do something about my blue sneakers once I wake up. If I decide to wake up, that is. As it turns out, 'Code Blue' is not a dress code for nurses and attendants.

Turns out I have had a few of those in the past few weeks. Turns out that they can be deadly.

But somehow, I have clung on to dear life. I am okay for most parts, but sometimes, my head spins. The way it does right now. More like swaying. It happens when I am thinking hard, something I have been doing a lot lately. One moment, I am deep into a philosophical debate with myself, and in the other, I am floating in mid-air, rocking to the rhythm of a fluid movement.

I feel like a serpent, perched steadily but aware of a light-footed nothingness that comes with having no feet. I think I am dreaming. Dreaming while floating. Only my dreams seemed to be built entirely of rain clouds, for they don't stay once they have poured all over the dry cracks of my dysfunctional brain. Dr Miller must have a more suitable word to describe it, but that's what it is. A ginormous brain fart of epic proportions.

A cool breeze is caressing the right side of my face. Sandie must have left the window open. I don't mind it; it's better than the conditioned air I breathe every day. I can hear labored snoring somewhere to my right. I can tell it is Dad, producing his signature cacophony of snorts and whistles while he catnaps. *Ay ay ay!*

Poor guy, he must be tired from all the waiting. And the tribulation of having to decide on the most dreadful thing a parent can be asked to do ... whether to pull the plug on their child—I'd say 'favorite child'—but then, I don't lie, at least not without reason. Everyone knows that Izzy is his favorite. And I don't envy her for that. She is not just my sister but also my best friend.

Her name is Isabella, but everyone just calls her Izzy. Dad has virtually raised us both alone. Mom was never really in the picture, even before she left us. A business tour or conference was always more important than my birthday or Izzy's prom.

She was, at best, absent from our lives.

I blame her for a lot of things—for Dad's never-ending loneliness; for Izzy needing to grow up before time; for my recalcitrant stutter, and a lot more. There was nothing warm or fuzzy about her like Mrs Nelson, or Mrs Moreno —not the mother we needed her to be. It is fitting that she is not in any of the photographs we have in our house.

No one ever mentions her or reminisces about their times with her, or even acknowledges that she ever existed.

It's a silent pact that we have made as a family. Dad made sure of it. *Ángel de Dios.* He knew that it would hurt too much otherwise.

So, he simply erased her existence from our lives. Life handed Dad a horrendously dirty slate, but he wiped the heck out of it until a clean surface emerged, one on which to rebuild our lives.

Just the thought of Mom hurts. A physical pain. A suffocation that is determined to stifle me until my last breath. Just like this cold hand that is holding my palm where the cannula is inserted, injecting what I am sure is a magic drug to make me rest. Rest more.

Hala! Do they even want me to wake up?

But I still have a few minutes before I lose my wits to the power of sedatives. Should I make a go for it once again?

I try making a sound. I imagine that I am opening my mouth and yelling.

Only, I cannot hear myself. Are my noise-canceling headphones still on my ears? I had them on when I was running that day. I am not deaf, for I can hear the bustle around. It's futile—trying to do this 'yell and tell.'

Dad is still snoozing, though I detect a change in the cadence of his snoring. He lets out a huge yawn and groans. The way mortals do when they have slept for too long, yet getting up from bed does not feel justified. I can hear him drink water the way he does. Glug. Glug. Chug. He lets out a small cough and then drags a chair, the metal screeching against the synthetic floor. I can sense him close by. I can smell his musty cologne. He never let me use it, even if I begged him.

He told me that every man must find his own fragrance. Whatever that meant!

He touches my face—the gentlest of touches—as if he is scared of hurting me. He kisses my forehead and sits next to me. I can tell by the way the bed tilts slightly to the right under his weight.

Dad is speaking. To me? But then, why does his voice seem to be traveling away from me? Oh, there must be someone else with him, visiting me. Who could that be, still visiting me after all these days? Tía Gabriela, maybe? I remember her dropping by a few times. She has always been kind to me after mom left, bringing paella and chili for us and taking us out for picnics with her daughters. Dad is telling this person something, but I am not able to make out exactly what.

Is Dad whispering? Is he trying to hide something? Does this mean that he believes I am listening?

It is heart wrenching how he is trying to hold on to me, still hopeful for a miracle. Supercalifragilisticexpialidocious. That's one of the longest words in English and it exactly describes what I feel right now. Sorry, I know weird crap like that. That's kinda my thing. However, I am amazed that I can recall the word without it getting stuck or all jumbled up inside my head. Hunh.

I wish Dad knew that I keep having these weird, one-sided conversations with him inside my head. *Ay ay ay.* I just realized it must mean that at least I am not brain dead. Not that I know what it feels like. But I am sure it must be an awfully unwelcome way to be.

I have to focus, but I can start piecing some of what is being said. Bits at first and then complete sentences. And just like that, I am back in the business of eavesdropping. *Venga!* Don't judge me. I am just lying there in my deep, slumbering state of zen, doing absolutely nothing to no one. If citizens of the world want to keep their secrets, they should find a more private space.

What is that accent? Arabic? Indian? My head is aching trying to do this geolinguistic positioning thingamajig.

The other person is definitely not Tía Gabriela, Dad's sister. I'd know her mellifluous voice anywhere. It's a man. And it's someone I have met, but not able to remember who or where. He keeps calling Dad 'Em'… like he knows Dad well … as if they have spent years talking to each other. The only two other humans who call Dad by that name are Abuela and Tía Gabriela. He had one more sister, but she went missing when they were all quite young.

Abuela told me once that Tía Elena was the smartest of them all, not just academically but also in resourcefulness. She wanted to become a psychologist and had lofty ambitions and elaborate plans that inspired her siblings. But one day, she disappeared, never to be found again. The police suspected abduction, but no leads ever panned out. No one knows if she is still alive. Abuela told me how devastated Dad was when this happened.

Poor guy! People tend to bail on him quite often.

Presently, the man with the yet-undeciphered accent is emphatically making a point. 'You don't know that Em, not for sure, at least....'

'I don't know how to ... It's so freaking hard. What would you do, Jugs, if it were you instead of me here?' Dad asks.

Jugs? Ew. What kind of a name is that? Why does he sound like that?

'Go home, Em. Take a shower. Get some shuteye. You have been in this room ever since Spencer ... I will stay with him until you get back. I promise I will not leave him alone even for a minute. And I'll call you if anything changes. You know I will. But you've got to take care of yourself, be strong for his sake. This isn't over yet. Em?'

Although spoken by another, they are exactly the words I want to say to Dad. He needs to give it a break ... the hospital chairs, the cafeteria Jell-O, the incessant worrying, and the hopeful waiting for miracles. He needs to believe that I am okay, that I am just taking a short sabbatical, although I don't know if I am accepting a permanent position yet. I love this Jugs person for trying to make Dad see reason. *Gracias a Dios!*

'I can't leave him. Not again. What if, what if I am not there and he.... Or if they, I mean, if....' Dad is incoherent, not able to contain his voice down to a whisper anymore. I can tell that he is crying. I want to hold him in a tight bear hug.

I hear footsteps. Jugs walking over to Dad? I can smell a strange aroma. Is that coconut? 'Come here, Em. Oh, you poor man.' He kisses the air, and I feel Dad's weight shift slightly even as his sobs, sending little tremors through the bed. 'I should have been there. That day ... with everything going on, he has been on edge. I shouldn't have gone to the cabin. I should have stayed home. It was a mistake. Just like when … only if I had….?'

'You know where I stand on that. You should have told him long ago. He would have seen it your way.'

What is going on? Who is this man with the coconut odor?

I feel him walk away, leaving Dad sitting on my bed. I hear him slide the window open. Sandie, the evening nurse with the raspy voice, won't be happy. But then, who is happy? Like really happy? Not Dad. Izzy? Maybe. Not me. Gunther? Callie? Mrs Nelson? Dr Miller?

What do you do when nothing that ever made you happy is enough anymore?

How do you move past the ache that filters away all the colors from your pictures, leaving behind a monochromatic aberration others insist on calling your life?

I just do not see the point in trying. Mrs Garcia, our school's student counselor, will vehemently disagree, I am sure, but then I fathom she is not happy either. Have I lost that part of my brain that stores joyous memories?

There is a possibility that I am making this grotesque story up in my head. Do I have that much brain trauma? Just like I'd made up that weird story about Ralph and the glass bottle with a secret message?

My eyes are heavy. I am hovering in space again, balanced on nothing but the air beneath me. This is how Iron Man must feel: light and invincible. If only I could figure out who Jugs is and what he is lecturing my Dad about.

Who is this man? A priest? Is Dad turning to religion for me? Unbelievable. *Por favor!* And what is Dad going on about?

Oh, I remember now. Dad was away at the cabin that day when I…. But what mistake? My stomach is churning. I want to tell him that I understand, even when I do not know what he is apologizing for. But I do want to know.

I think I can solve this mystery. I mean, not in the real world where I am as still as a stale cucumber in a trash bin. But in this other parallel world where I am in this uber-evolved, sharp, hyperaware state of being, anything is possible.

I am sure I'll crack it wide open if Dad just speaks to me about it. And that is just the thing. I know that he won't. He never does.

A cold is settling in my veins. My eyes are drooping, and my head is beginning to loll. I am zoning out. *Ay ay ay!* It's like a bloody power cut in the penultimate scene of the latest Avengers movie.

All of a sudden, the air underneath my feet is sucked into a damp vacuum, and then it's all dark again.

(2)

THE BLUE[5] SEDAN

For the ones who are ashamed of being

Stepping towards the center stage

Unshackled, free from my cage

Of misery, sorrow, and fear

A brand-new beginning so near

---

[5] One mostly associates the colors blue, sky blue, sea green and white with the zodiac sign of Cancer. And just like the Moon anchors you at night, Cancerians are known to be the emotional anchors for others and connect to the heart of all matters.

ROY MEETS LOVE, POSSIBLY?

Bengaluru, India

The walls are dull gray or cream. Roy cannot tell. They are plastered with some cheap shiny paint on top of roughly laid brick walls. 'Do they try to make these places look ugly on purpose?' Roy wonders. He notices the top right corner of the ceiling. 'Technically, it's top right from where I am sitting,' he thinks as he soaks in the oddly symmetrical room. He finds this detail quite comforting.

Two windows are placed right in the center of two facing walls and two doors, each placed at the end of the remaining two walls. A naked hanging light shines overhead, swamping the room with an odd warmth that he finds unexpectedly soothing. He would have preferred white light over this yellow, balmy one, but he is not complaining. But then he never complains anyway.

Not about the long queue at the ticket counter. 'The cashier is trying her best!'

Not about the hordes of trash piled on the sides of the street. 'How can the municipal corporation keep finding new places to dump the tonnes of garbage we generate?'

Not about the unusual delay in getting his LPG cylinder delivered. 'Poor delivery boy. What can he do if it rains so hard and the roads are inundated?'

Today is no different. 'After all, I am not perfect either! Far from it,' he argues.

When the two officers enter the room, the first thing he notices is how similar they look. Both are about thirty-five, well-built, fully bearded, and wearing gray trousers with white shirts.

'Are they trained to look dull and morose?' he ponders.

Although being fully bearded doesn't mean much. Practically half the species with Y chromosomes in India now has a beard, thanks to inspirational style icons in Bollywood and the Indian cricket team. It is hard to tell one man from another on the street.

'Why do these officers bother with grooming their beards when their telltale potbellies and breathtakingly tight shirts tell another story?' his mind wanders.

He can't help thinking that way. But deciding it's time for him to focus, he casts aside this train of thought, for there are matters far graver than India's herd mentality of metrosexual male styling. He needs to curb his OCD and focus.

'Do not obsess about irrelevant details,' he tells himself. It has taken him two weeks to get here. He is not going to blow this by being himself.

The two officers introduce themselves, almost as a formality. He does not get their names properly and is reluctant to ask again. So, he names them Grumpy and Goofy in his head. They ask him to state his name (Roy), address, and details about next of kin.

He patiently answers their questions about his marital status (single, are they trying to imply something?), his job (Business Analyst), and his age (thirty-one). He wishes for them to ask about the car he drives (a Jeep) or his driver's license number (of course, he does not remember).

Goofy lays a worn-out register and starts to scribble furiously. 'Look away from the folded edges. They don't need to be straightened,' Roy tells himself.

From where he sits, Roy can see the logbook that is the unlucky recipient of Goofy's penmanship. Goofy seems intent on exacting vengeance for some sin of the shoddy old register. He has issues. 'Oh, and I am the one to judge. Right!' Roy chides himself. The ballpoint pen in Goofy's hand tears through the skin of the pages as he writes something into the register.

Grumpy stands next to Goofy and stares intently at the page as if willing to change what or how Goofy is writing. Once done, Goofy looks satisfactorily at Grumpy, seeking an approval that never comes. Grumpy grunts and shifts his attention to Roy. He pulls a chair beside Roy and sits down, looking him squarely in the face.

'The chair does not need to be aligned to the table. Slightly askew is perfectly fine, too,' Roy decides.

Roy shifts in his chair without blinking, half expecting to be hit in the jaw any second. This goes on for a full three minutes. Goofy does not seem to know whether to disturb the boss man or let him play this amateurish game to see who blinks first. Then, without a warning, Grumpy gets up and leaves. Goofy looks at Roy apologetically and saunters off with a silly smile. Roy, once again, is alone in the dull gray, oddly symmetrical room. He sets the chair at a right angle, the right angle for a chair to be in.

'I cannot control everything, but this I can set right!' he argues.

He sits on the uncushioned metal chair for a while. But soon, his hip starts to go numb. He has been sitting there for over an hour now.

'Do they make these chairs hard and cold on purpose?' he speculates. Unsure, he gets up and stretches his legs and moves towards the window on the opposite side of the room.

'This must be the rear wall of the building,' he figures. The view from the window is the side alley of a lodge, dilapidated and green with mold.

'A wall that needs a hard scrub, or better still, rebuilding from scratch,' he reckons. He can feel the stench of dampness creeping up on him.

He returns to the chair and sits down with a shudder.

It is starting to drizzle outside. Roy can hear the pitter-patter on the glass window facing the lodge.

'Shit, the storm warning!' He remembers hearing it on the news that morning. The sight of rain floods his mind with memories of the cursed road trip that started all this. Four buddies. A rented SUV. A long weekend. Destination Ooty. Or Ootacamund, as it's called now.

'Do the officials have no work other than renaming perfectly named places?' he rues. 'It must be a disorder, much like my own disorderly compulsions.'

There are certain things in one's brain that one has no control over, notwithstanding the sincere intent. The stronger the desire to control, the less compliant wayward things tend to become. You wish you could feel less of one undesirable emotion and offset that with more of another one you yearn for.

You consider whether not feeling the latter has anything to do with an overdose of that undesirable one in the first place. You reckon it may be a way for your brain to deal with what it cannot fit into a pattern. You want to do something about it. But you do not know where to begin.

You eventually end up confused.

His thoughts linger on the scenic drive along the Nilgiri ghats on those meandering roads to heaven. He recalls how excited he was about the trip. Venky was getting married, and the trip was his bachelor's party. After all, drunken raves with strippers are a no-go in this part of the world. Shaz and Lucky had tried to talk him out of it—the wedding, not the trip—but Venky couldn't stop blushing. Their mate was utterly smitten, what with texting or calling his fiancée every thirty seconds. So, they had booked a homestay, packed a load of grub—cola bottles, potato chips, chocolate biscuits, beer crates, and water—and hit the road.

Shaz was still using a cane to support him while walking. A nasty fall at the metro station led to a fracture in his right ankle. So, Roy and Lucky were going to take on driving duties. Shaz was the designated DJ. Venky … he was just a fool in love.

'The kind of love I hope to be in someday,' Roy thought.

He had taken the first turn at driving. At Mandya, Lucky had taken over. They were all okay until Mysore when Lucky asked to switch again. The next stretch of their journey was known for lush green landscapes, spotted with dense trees that were a domicile to many tropical birds. With his recently-acquired passion for digital photography, Lucky wanted to take shots of the verdant foliage and birds. Thanks to the innumerable 'perfect spots' for his pictures,

Roy had managed to cover just about thirty kilometers in the next two hours.

It wasn't until their bellies started to grumble with hunger that Lucky relented, and they began looking for a restaurant or roadside *dhaba.*

As they stepped out of the car for a rather late lunch, Shaz groaned. His newly-healed leg was cramping since he had been sitting in the car for long. He had taken his painkillers but was still in discomfort. Venky had suggested that he lie down for some time.

So, they flattened the back seats and used the sleeping bags to create a makeshift bed for Shaz. The three of them played cards and posted pictures on Facebook while they waited for his pain to abate. Lucky also took a quick nap.

'Some people can nap just about anywhere and at any time. I wish I could....' Roy had felt jealous. Pissed at his compulsions, he plugged in his earphones and slowly submerged himself under the waves of familiar comfort courtesy of his trusted iPod playlist.

It was late evening by the time they resumed driving. Shaz was navigating. Lucky was driving. Roy was in the back seat with Venky, who was humming along with the remixed version of *Humma Humma.* Roy liked the original one better and lamented the lack of originality. Lucky had deemed his quip nonsensical, and Venky had ganged up with Lucky against Roy, taunting him for being too old-fashioned. Arguments were made about plagiarism, inspiration, and innovation. Compelling theories were proposed with growing vehemence about the best era for music.

Shaz pleaded for them to quiet down. They did not listen. Shaz did not want to miss the next turn to lead them into the Bandipur National Park. To distract them, he had started naming the animals they might spot while driving through the sprawling acres—elephants, wild dogs, deer, and tigers. When that did not work, he tried exotic birds—cormorants, partridges, whistling thrushes, scimitar babblers, and honey buzzards.

With that, he hit the jackpot.

Lucky was no longer arguing. He zoned in on driving, shifting gears, and accelerating, anticipating the perfect night shots he could capture with his brand-new camera lens. And with Lucky's departure from the din, an unusual silence filled the SUV. Shortly after, they passed the checkpoint, where an officer noted down the number of their SUV.

'Who can even read what he is writing? What with the irregular slant of his letters,' Roy observed.

The road ahead was not well lit. It was impossible to decipher the path. Direction signs were far and few. They saw one saying there was a birdwatching spot nearby to observe vibrant blue and beige roller birds. Lucky desperately wanted to click some shots. But since Shaz was still in pain, they decided to drive to the spot instead of walking. Lucky was behind the wheel again, despite Roy's offer to drive.

It was supposed to be Roy's turn to drive.

Roy should have driven.

Roy knows that.

Roy has not said this to anyone.

They had been driving for a few minutes when Venky uttered a vehement, throatful cry.

'Tigers. Stop. Stop. Stop. Tigers. There ... there were tigers there. Turn back.'

Startled by the sudden sound, Lucky braked in panic, and the SUV swerved, throwing Venky against Roy and

Shaz against the window. Roy's newly acquired manga book slipped out of his hand, the page he was reading melding innocuously into the ones he had yet to peruse. The SUV screeched as Lucky lost control and skidded along the dark road. And then ... the SUV hit something. It was dark and they could not see what it was. They wondered if it was a deer, or a dog, or a fallen branch from a tree. After a few minutes, Shaz rolled down his window and craned his neck out. Nothing.

He turned to Venky for reassurance, only to find him shaking and breathing heavily.

Panic. Embarrassment. Guilt?

Lucky exchanged a muted look with Roy and turned the headlights to a high beam. There was nothing on the road.

Armed with their lone torch, Roy decided to get down and take a final look. The others resisted, but he had to know. Amidst flashes of headlights of the swerving SUV and the distant street lamp, something had caught his eye.

With every shred of prayer in his heart, he hoped it was just his imagination playing tricks. He did not find anything unusual. He called out, 'Anybody there?' a few times, but no response. Soon, the others got out of the car, and with the torchlights of their phones, they looked too. But no one found anything.

As they returned to the SUV, Roy noticed a dent in its front grille and a broken headlight. He notices such things. Always. Even when he would absolutely rather not. There were some scratches, too, and a small patch of blood. No hair or hide, just blood. Roy rushed inside and dragged out the crate of water bottles they had purchased earlier. Venky and Lucky appeared by his side. Without a word, they washed off the blood.

'Blood never washes off. It always leaves a trail behind,' Roy worried.

Meanwhile, Shaz found the broken piece of the grille and shoved it into the trunk. Lucky took off his shirt and wiped the surface they had just washed. Roy's breathing was heavy—the sight of blood had made him queasy. Shaz tried to calm him down. Venky urged them to drive away before someone discovered whatever animal they had hit. He took charge of driving in a situation he knew had quickly turned sour. He moved slowly and carefully.

They made their way out of Bandipur around ten in the night. From there, they drove on in silence until they reached a run-down hotel near Masinagudi. Lucky kept apologizing and looked distraught. Venky and Shaz took turns convincing him that the slippery roads were to be blamed. Soon, they were talking to their girlfriends or fiancées, seeking the comfort of their assurances.

As always, Roy sat alone in silence, counseling himself to slow down his racing mind. 'It was not real. There is a thing as too many crime dramas and sci-fi shows on Netflix,' he scolded himself.

The rest of the night was a blur. They made an unplanned stop to allow themselves time to think about what had happened. Shaz asked if they needed to inform the forest officials. The quartet agreed they did not need to stir the burning pot anymore. Venky emphasized that they stay calm and forget the sordid night, looking at Roy for support. Lucky and Shaz nodded in consent.

Early the following day, they checked out and visited a temple nearby and offered prayers for the well-being of the maimed animal. They prayed for its survival. They prayed for atonement. Roy prayed for more. He had not slept the previous night, even when they had stopped to rest. Flashes from the accident kept dancing in darkness whenever he tried to get a shut-eye. Tossing and turning on the hard mattress of the motel bed, clutching his crumpled manga book, Roy's prayers went on through the damp, starless night.

After breakfast at a local *idli* stall, they started for their resort in Ooty. On the way, Roy observed Lucky as he surreptitiously dumped his blood-stained shirt into a pile of burning trash, making sure that it was burnt to ashes before they drove away. Shaz kept checking the local news but saw nothing about Bandipur.

Somewhere on the way, they visited a local mechanic to get the grille repaired and the headlight replaced. Hopefully, the rental car dealer wouldn't notice. Hopefully, he does not have Roy's problem of 'seeing too much'. They used cash for it, something they learned from Law & Order.

With all traces of the accident wiped off, an awareness of relief washed over their tired bodies and thoughts. The shock of the accident still hung in the air, but it was gradually wearing off as they got farther away from it. At least for some....

At the resort in Ooty, Lucky managed to arrange a medley of raunchy dance numbers to which Venky and he danced all night while the others watched and drank. They even got a young couple on vacation to join in —Izzy and Devon. The girl was an American but spoke with a strange accent. Roy guessed she was Spanish. Or Mexican?

The guy, Devon, had a complicated background. His mother was an American, a professor, and his father an Indian, a banker. They'd come down for his parents' silver jubilee anniversary celebrations at a fort in Jaipur. Amidst all that, they had sneaked away to spend some alone time. 'Alone time is the kind of time I happen to be an expert at,' Roy thought.

Devon shared colorful stories of his time researching black corals in the Gulf of Mexico for the past year. Izzy smiled lovingly through his anecdotes, snuggling her head on his shoulder. There was a calming ease between them. They belonged together like the moon and the stars. They fit. Seeing them made something churn inside Roy.

The same old feeling of being trapped inside a bubble.

Izzy invited the group to Texas if they ever visited the US. The four friends promised to take her up on the offer of an authentic homemade Mexican meal. After a few drinks and dancing to Bollywood songs, the couple excused themselves and walked away into the vast, lush greenery under the moonlight.

'True love can feel so easy. I could do with some of that in my life,' an intense yet familiar yearning took root within Roy.

He was lost in a silent reverie on the beach for the rest of the evening. 'Is this what love is supposed to be like? If I could feel that for someone … anyone.' Roy kept thinking that night.

He had never been in love, never crushed so hard that his heart ached, never had that one person he wanted to share everything with. He ached for romance, but he had never aced that game.

He reiterated the words he had spoken in his mind for years. 'I am an anomaly, an irregularity that cannot be evened out.'

Even his friends told him he was not 'normal'. He almost believed them.

His friends talked about girls they found hot or lusted over movie stars they found sexy. Knowing he was faking it, he would smile, sometimes even partake in their banter. His body did not crave what theirs did. It wasn't that he was attracted to men, either. He had considered it but was sure that wasn't the case. So, he had found companionship in his books and music.

He knew there was something different about him. Over time, he came to a well-researched conclusion, too. Yet, he felt like a missing key to some undiscovered lock or a stray card lost from its deck.

He did not know what to do with this awareness of not fitting in or of not knowing how to feel what he was expected to. None of his books had the answer. He was not even sure what the question was. Days like that day made it worse, trapping him, weighing his heart down as if a flurry of notifications lingered over his head, reminding him about missing a meeting he did not know he had to be at.

That night, back in the room, the boys played poker, half-watched movies, and guzzled two more crates of beer. A compilation of steamy 'love-making' scenes from Hollywood flicks and porn sites was Shaz's 'thoughtful' gift to Venky. He insisted that it was quite befitting for a bachelor party. Roy faked a compliant smile, then presented Venky with a scrapbook with pictures capturing twelve years of their friendship.

They spent the night talking about the photos that brought back vivid memories of flunked exams and failed romances. Venky confessed how the thought of the first night with his wife was freaking him out. Lucky called him a loser. Shaz told them about the naughty perks of being physically compromised. Apparently, he had been getting a lot of attention from girls in his office since the accident. Of course, he had conveniently peppered in the trivial and you-know-that-so-absolutely-never-happened detail of getting injured while trying to save a schoolgirl from falling off an escalator.

'Things people do to find a mate. And also the things they do with them. Things I can never bring myself to do. Things I wish I would at least give a try,' a deep sense of inadequacy welled behind Roy's eyelids. He plugged in his earphones, closed his eyes, and attempted to strangle the unwelcome thoughts.

He recalled a line from one of the mangas by Tsubasa Yamaguchi. 'If it is blue to you, then let it be blue, whether it's an apple or a rabbit.' Those words comforted him. He let himself be blue, at least for the time being.

Roy is startled by the sudden sound of the door to the oddly symmetrical gray room opening. Goofy is back, alone this time, carrying a big mug of coffee and a recorder. He sets up the voice recorder on the table and arranges his papers. Grumpy joins them, strolling in with the arrogance of someone used to having his way around. He sips his coffee, and Goofy settles down on another chair. The sight of the steaming coffee makes Roy feel hungry. 'It's the rain,' he thinks, as he craves hot onion *bhajia* and his iPod, which is presently in the locker outside.

Grumpy turns on the voice recorder and formally announces the commencement of the witness interview. He asks Roy to state his full name, address, and phone number for the records. Again, really? They then ask him to narrate the incidents of the night in question. Roy repeats his story, just the way he had done earlier, but slowly, lest G&G should miss something.

Goofy nudges him to be more specific.

Roy has rehearsed his answers and double-checked the details. He is ready for cross-questioning. 'Bless you, Law & Order. Bless you, American TV. Bless you, Netflix,' he chants in his mind.

He narrates details about the trip to Ooty with friends but leaves out the mention of a bachelor's party. He tells them about their meal in Mandya, about the comic book he was reading in the car, and the photography session by Lucky, but skips the part about the stash of beers in the SUV.

He tells them, truthfully, that they had been running late and that they entered Bandipur when it was getting dark. He knows that lying about that will raise suspicion, given that the entry and departure times of their SUV were logged into the decaying forest registers in slanted, terrible handwriting.

He tells them that the evening was dark and the roads were slippery with rain. He tells them that he had heard the loud and intense screeching of an accident from a distance.

He looks straight into Grumpy's eyes. He says he is sorry for not being more helpful and not knowing more. Grumpy tells him that it is okay, clarifying that the reason Roy's being interviewed is that the SUV was rented out in his name.

Roy clears his throat. He looks at Grumpy and asks if the animal that died in the accident was a protected or endangered species. Grumpy looks puzzled. He looks accusingly at Goofy as if he has forgotten some essential part of his duty. He switches off the voice recorder and looks at Roy, befuddled. And then he hollers out a flurry of abuses. He grabs Roy by the collar and confirms his worst suspicions.

'You think we have nothing pissing better to investigate than some dandy deer being run over by a freaking car?

Do you think we are pinheaded idiots? Is that what you've been going on about? Some stupid deer getting hit? Faaaaack....'

Goofy looks frazzled and apologizes. He seems a bit paralyzed under the pouring ire of Grumpy's gaze. He pleads with Grumpy to let it be, afraid that someone might see them harassing a witness. Grumpy lets Roy go and clears his throat, still bristling with rage.

'There weren't any buggering animals killed that night. The hit-and-run involved a local farmer from the area. He was thrown off the main road and sent flying into the shrubbery. That drunk idiot was riding his bicycle without any tail light. He got thrown far off the road. He had bled to his death by the time the forest ranger spotted him. You understand that, Mr Roy? A man has died. His frigging skull split open. Do you understand, you dope-faced moron?'

Roy's brain is drowning in a deluge of questions. He is shaking, jolted by the revelation of a truth he had already suspected. Amid the raucous screeching of the SUV against the road, he had heard an ominous clang of metal against metal. His vision of crooked wheels flying through the air was not just a figment of his imagination.

'It was his blood. A person, not an animal! We should have looked harder. Heck, we should not have run away.' Roy is hyperventilating with this guilty realization.

Grumpy looks worried, cursing the moment when he had caught Roy by the collar. Goofy gets Roy a glass of water. Grumpy leans in and asks, 'So I assume you did not see anything. Such a waste of time. Do you at least remember what color this car was? Did you happen to see the number plate?'

Roy does not move or blink, yet notices the smudges on the bottom of the glass. His eyes are racing in all directions, trying to catch up with his distressing thoughts. The sounds and images from the night are playing underhanded card games in his brain.

Grumpy is losing patience. He bangs the table especially hard. Roy stares blankly at him.

Goofy asks him if he is alright. Roy requests to be excused for a bio break. As he enters the bathroom stall, tears break free. He presses his hand over his mouth lest someone should overhear him sob. His worst fear has come alive.

They had killed someone that day. Not an animal but a person, a human being. Manslaughter? Their SUV had hit him and cracked his skull. Murder? That wretched man had died on that forsaken muddy road. A forgotten roadkill? Roy wants to call up Venky. But his phone is in the locker outside the station.

He is alone. He has a decision to make.

He curses Lucky for being desperate to click roller birds; Shaz for taking the long nap in the car delaying their drive through the forest, and Venky for maniacally shouting, 'Tiger, Tiger' and triggering the accident.

Goofy knocks on the door, asking him to hurry up. Roy flushes and comes out, smiling apologetically. He is not smiling on the inside. Back in the gray-walled room with asymmetric doors, Roy apologizes to Grumpy as well. He tells him that he is suffering from food poisoning.

'A lie that cannot hurt anyone,' Roy reckons.

He tells them that he is sad for the deceased man's family. Not a lie. Grumpy tells him that the farmer who died did not have any family and was an abusive drunkard with at least two prison spells in his past. Roy feels relieved but does not say so. Not a lie. He despises himself for taking solace in the fact that the life they had taken was less than perfect. Not a lie.

Grumpy reads out the details of a blue sedan Roy had reported seeing speeding in the forest area. He is trying to confirm if Roy had noticed anything unusual about the vehicle. Roy makes up oddly specific details about a muddy rear bumper and a slightly crooked number plate.

'A final lie. The most important one. To lay this matter to rest. For my friends,' he decides.

Roy tells them that he might have been mistaken about the exact color of the car since it was dark. He reiterates that he could not be entirely sure if the sedan indeed was blue, covering his bases and leaving enough ambiguity in his statement. 'Having OCD can have its merits,' he fathoms.

Goofy asks him to sign the declaration. Once done, Roy gets up and offers a handshake. Grumpy looks offended but Goofy grabs his hand and leads him out of the gray-walled room. Roy gathers his phone and bag from the locker outside and exits the police station. He sanitizes his hands twice. Then, once more, for good measure.

Roy hails an auto rickshaw on his way back to the apartment. He puts on his earphones and plays a random song on his iPod at peak volume. The cool breeze bathes his face, and he feels something he cannot place as an emotion he fully understands.

Once back home, he steps into the shower and washes off the dregs from the day, scrubbing his skin red.

Blood. It never washes off. No matter how hard you try.

He cries in the shower, sobbing uncontrollably under the hot, scalding jets of water burning into his bruised skin. Someone deserves the punishment, he knows. They cannot get away with it. They may have evaded an arrest, but there will be a lifetime of penance.

He contemplates not telling anyone about the dead farmer. A decision takes shape in his mind.

'It can be my burden to carry. Others need not know. They may not have even seen the sparks or the wheels.... It has to be me. After all, I am already condemned to a lifetime of being alone and unloved, of self-doubt and dark visions. What's another reason to loathe your life?' he considers.

Pain is a small price for cowardice, a surprisingly acceptable barter to those who choose to trade.

'Pain can be my chosen companion for a life I know I will be spending alone. A life of wanting to be loved but not knowing how to love somebody back in the way they might expect to. A life that's been passing me by, even with me striving to keep a grasp on it with all my might.'

Roy is convincing himself to pay that price.

'Better me than my "normal" friends who still have a shot at happiness,' he further argues. 'There is nothing to gain from telling them anything, not when they have much to look forward to. Unlike me....' he sinks deeper into the miasma of his depressing thoughts.

Just then, his phone buzzes.

He turns the shower off, dries himself, and takes a deep breath. There is a new message from an unknown number—pictures of people he cannot recognize at first. Then, a wave of recognition dawns on him. It's Devon, the guy they met in Ooty. He has sent a selfie of Izzy and himself, their heads leaning against each other's. The picture is a bit grainy as if it was taken under poor illumination. They are at a library or some bookstore, with stacks of dusty-looking books in the background. They seem disheveled and tired, but the fatigue does not reach their eyes, which sparkle with life. 'They make it look so … so….' he cannot find the right words to finish that thought.

The message reads, 'Hi Roy, and hello to our other "dancer" friends. Devon and Izzy here. We thought of saying hello. It was fun hanging out with you guys the other night. Thank you for teaching us all the crazy dance moves. Please send us pictures from Venky's wedding. Izzy says that her offer for homemade chalupas still stands.'

Roy cannot help but smile.

Long after he sends gushing responses, emojis, and compliments on the pictures, he lingers on, checking out how perfectly together they both look. He reminisces about the evening when he'd met them, taken by how naturally at ease they'd seemed, not caring to create the perfect impression. He recalls how silly Devon and Izzy had looked dancing to Bollywood songs and how they both knew it too, yet it did not stop them from mimicking the gyrations of the four strangers they had just met.

They did not care how they appeared to others. They liked who they were. They were perfectly okay to just be!

They were the kind of people who would be okay with the creased pages of a register, the scribbly handwriting of a security guard, moldy green walls or chairs not placed at right angles. They were the kind of people who were okay taking a selfie of their disheveled selves in a dusty library. They were comfortable in their skins and wore them with pride.

Juxtaposed against how he strives for perfection in everything, for the first time, Roy realizes that the compulsions he feels are not about the things around him but about the need to control the narrative or manage the perceptions about him.

For the first time, Roy discovers the root of his need for perfection. Shame.

He sinks into his bed, the weight of this realization awakening something in him. Memories he had carefully concealed threaten to resurface, the susurration of buried ghosts from the past raising their heads once more. Snippets of it fill his mind.

'Dude, live a little. Ask Tanya out. She is clearly into you!'

'Are you gay, bro? Tell me if that is the case. I don't want to share the showers with you and realize you were checking my junk the whole time!'

'I don't understand why you'd not give this, us, a chance! Is there someone else?'

'Have you seen a doctor? The one who.... I mean, in case the plumbing has any issues, man! If you know what I mean.'

'You can have a drink with us, can't you? What secret are you guarding?'

'We know you will not enjoy the party. It's not your kind of place. There will be a lot of close dancing, booze, and girls.'

'What the hell? I was just trying to kiss you! And that's how you react? What an asshat you are! Push off, you jerk.'

'Find someone, or you will die alone one day. Is that what you want?'

Roy had faked smiles, hurried goodbyes and excused absences to navigate these conversations, which had eventually metamorphosed into 'leave him alone', 'he is always like this', 'whatever', and other forms of indifference. With time, he became a part of the background for his group of friends, an arrangement that worked for him as well.

It helped him forget. It let him bury the discomfort of the questions he did not have answers to. Not then.

The ignominy became bearable. The ache dulled. The pressure abated.

The perfect solution had presented itself, and he had committed himself to nurturing it.

It was self-preservation. Or so he thought until Devon and Izzy's picture appeared on his phone. Strangers from another corner of the globe, grinning like a well-fed Cheshire cat, reminding him of the beauty in imperfections.

He cannot help but scan the titles when he notices a vivid pink cover with a funky neon font. The title reads 'Loveless'. It's a book he had come across on Amazon just the previous night while doomscrolling. Coincidence? A sign?

He feels a tug at his heart. A few taps on his phone and an order for the book is placed.

He knows what the book is about. It's about him, in a way. Strange as it feels, Roy is inundated with meditative calm, a belief that he is not alone or abnormal. He wants to try being his imperfect self—even if that means being aromantic or asexual.

With a silent thanks to Devon and Izzy, he utters the words he's never dared to.

'I am an ace. But I matter. I can do this.'

A smile starts to form on his face. Despite the crippling burden of guilt, his shoulders feel lighter, and his jaw unclenches, even if just a little bit.

He feels less blue.

The fog is starting to clear.

A phone call brings him crashing back to the present. Shaz is asking him why he is still at home. He quickly irons his new designer *kurta*, not fussing about removing every last crease in the fabric as he'd typically do. Tonight is a celebration. Tonight is the time to dance with friends.

Tomorrow is another story.

Tomorrow, he has a truth to tell them—about the blue sedan and what transpired with Grumpy and Goofy. He decides he does not need to bear the weight of it alone. Not when he wasn't the only one at fault. Not when there is a chance that his life will amount to something more than nothing. Not when he's just become friends with himself once more.

They will need to find a way through it. Together.

Meanwhile, he will try to figure out a few things.

Perhaps he will attend a Sunday run at the park with that queer group he knows of.

Perhaps he will redefine the semantics of what he has always assumed to be a gargantuan error.

Perhaps he will find a way to ace being an ace.

Perhaps it will all be okay.

Perhaps the blue will fade away.

the stillness of this night
a truth caught in that dark cobweb
behold my gleeful face now

Cancer (Jun 21 - Jul 22) | The Moon | Pearl

I may not know the right path, but allow me to fail.

SPENCER DIAZ MISSES HIS GANG

Texas, USA

Flashes of hot and cold greet me as I slither towards something or away from someone. It is as if my body's thermostat is broken, as if I am being dunked into a volcanic pit by a massive hand of pure ice.

I know why I feel restless. It's the knowledge of my indecision and the lack of intent to get there. Limbo, though boring, is a state that suits me well, at least for the time being. I have enough practice in procrastinating decisions.

Despite researching for months and even a dozen field trips later, I haven't made up my mind on which college to apply to. I don't have the faintest clue about what I'll wear to the annual ball. Heck, I haven't committed to choosing my favorite superhero or tennis player yet. I am so pathetic at it that I couldn't even decide a number to bet on at the roulette table when Tía Gabriela took us to the casino that one time. I knew it was going to be an even number, but which one? Twenty-two, sixteen, thirty-six, and twelve seemed equally good to me.

My social media handle is another thing I have deferred because there are quite literally a million possibilities. It should be something befitting like @a_clueless_guy_waiting_it_out, though it won't be easy getting any followers with that handle. There is a reason why I am not on social media. This particular world is not ready for me yet. Maybe a different one?

It's the weekend. I am sure because Izzy is here with me. She has classes on weekdays, and the nursery keeps her busy as well. It must be tough to juggle it all, even for someone with her multitasking skills. Today is quickly becoming my favorite day of all the days I have been at the hospital. Izzy has brought in a picnic basket. *Genialdad!*

I can hear her fussing about as she sets it all up. I imagine a red and white checkered mat on the floor, a cane basket with a heap of muffins, empanadas, and tamales, and bottles of gazpacho with nectarines and guavas. I can smell them. Izzy would have picked the perfectly ripe ones like she always does for me. Oh, my nose is tingling with joy. Can they see me smile? Dad seems to be in a better mood too. Unlike last night, or was it a few nights ago when he was acting all sappy? *Maravilloso*. I can hear him chuckle at some or the other joke that Izzy cracked.

Izzy is my favorite person in the world. She is an angel. I have never seen such gorgeously blue eyes on any human being on Planet Earth. Her teeth are like pearls, her laughter like the sweet sound of a little wind chime. Abuela once told me that she looks a bit like Mom. I chose not to believe her. I told her so while she was making her signature chalupas for me. She did not protest. I took that as a win.

No one knows her better than me. Like the fact that she tugs at her right earlobe when she is thinking intensely. Or that she scrunches her nose when she is getting emotional and fighting back tears. She usually fails at that. She has social skills, you see. Unlike me, who uses his blank, expressionless face in most worldly situations where he needs to interact with living beings in all forms including humans, dogs, and cats. And ferrets. And hamsters. And birds. And reptiles. You get the picture. Being with Izzy feels like lying in a hammock and being serenaded by a psithurism of leaves. If petrichor were an emotion, it would be the one of having her by your side.

By the way, I think Dad is more than a wee bit tipsy. How they let him inside the hospital in this state is a mystery.

Did he play his grieving Dad card? Can Sandie not smell the whiskey on his breath? I surely can. I was awake when Dad arrived. That was a while before Izzy showed up with her picnic basket. Dad sat by my bed and kissed my head. That happens a lot these days. I need to tell him to ease up a bit on that. I don't want him turning into a soppy sod.

He kept saying sorry, though I am not sure what for. He told me he wanted to confess. He must have seen my still posture as a sign of approval as he went on about how he should have fought harder to save his marriage; for Mom to stay with us, yada yada yada.

He told me that he regretted missing my elementary school play, the one where I played a tomato. *Caracoles!* Why now? It's been ten years. He did not miss much. He tried to show me a picture of my first day at school when I had cried unstoppably, telling me that he wished he'd never sent me there and had home-schooled me instead. Ew. Dad schooling me would be a gross new nightmare in itself. I'd rather stay in this halcyonic coma. *Por favor!* He told me that he loved me. And that he should have told me all this sooner.

I agree. But these many tears are excruciatingly many to count.

He promised that he would make an effort to be a better father. He begged me for another chance to make it right. He promised that he would not let me slip away, that he would fight for me, and that we would travel together all over from Peru to India and New Zealand to Austria.

'Do you know how much that would cost, Dad? Hello, we aren't first cousins to the Prince of Arabia! Could I negotiate a trip to Sneakercon instead?' I mutely holler.

He sang me the lullaby that he used to sing for me as a toddler. And then he slept right there on the chair, his face next to mine. And snored. And completely slobbered my shoulder with his stinky drool. *Ay ay ay!*

Izzy is making a ruckus, and I hear Rose come in and shush my crazy family. They are creating too much of a scene. I can hear Izzy giggle and put something on my face. Sunglasses? She had promised to get me a pair for my birthday. Is it my birthday? Ah. That explains the smell of fresh blueberries. Izzy must have baked my favorite cake with fresh blueberries. I love her so much. Why couldn't all humans be her clones? I would so much like to live in a world full of people like her.

It would be a world where I did not have to deal with ridicule from schoolmates or receive constant inputs from well-meaning teachers to become better than 'just average.'

If I ever live in such a fantastic world, I will stop trying to fix my stutter. In fact, I will stutter my way through everything all the time, just for the heck of it. Did I mention that I stu…stu..s.s.s.s.tutter? It gets worse when I try to count how many times I repeat each letter. It reminds me of compound interest from math class.

In this world, I'll be popular.

I'll have my gang of misfits, a clique of those who don't fit into the molds of normalcy. Like Cuckoo Callie, Glassy Gunther and Rando Rafael from my class. I don't know why nicknames always insist on such alliteration, but somehow, they do. I am Snoozy Spencer. In this new world, misfits would rule. Callie Nelson will not get made fun of for her freckles. Gunther Delgato will not get picked on for his super thick, nerdy glasses. Rafael Blake will not be bullied for having ADHD. And Spencer Diaz's embarrassing existence will not go viral all over campus.

A chill runs down my spine at the memory.

I remember walking down the corridor, a hundred eyes staring me down, suppressing their laughter, averting direct eye contact lest they should catch some infection I was harboring. I did not know it then, but I found out later when Rafael Blake forwarded the message to me. He had been attentive, despite his ADHD, and been a good friend. He knew it would matter to me. And it did. It still does. I was labeled. Branded as a weirdo. It hurt to see my classmates turn on me. *Traidores!* And for what? I can feel the pain even in my comatose state.

My breathing starts to get a bit uneven. I can feel it—a certain tightness around my chest as if someone is sitting on top and wringing the life out of me. And then I hear it.

Beep ... Beep ... Beep....

Here we go again. The unbearable trio of beeping. I can hear the panic in Izzy's voice as she calls out for help. I feel a stethoscope examining my chest as it rises and sinks. Another hand on my wrist. Someone removes the pillow under my head and lays me flat with my hands by my side. I hear Rose asking Dad and Izzy to leave the room. I have an airbag in my mouth and oxygen being pushed into my lungs.

I can hear Dad cry out in anguish.

Izzy tells me that she will never forgive me if I die.

I am sure she is scrunching her nose a lot this very minute. I want to tell her that I want to live and that she should relax. But I cannot get any words through. I count backwards from a hundred to settle myself down.

Hundred. Ninety-nine. Ninety-eight. Ninety-seven.

I feel a warmth emanating from where the cannula needle pinches into a blood vessel on the back of my palm. Ninety-six. Ninety-five. My breathing is still ragged, but I feel a slumber setting in.

Ninety-four. Ninety-three. Ninety-two.

I want to stand up more for myself. Back me up a lot more than I do. That is, if I survive whatever freak show in hell is happening right now in my hospital room.

Ninety-one. Ninety....

And then, I am surrounded by a silvery gray nothingness that looks ethereal. Scary but fascinating at the same time. Like a chimera.

There are no walls in this space. Or floor. No windows or skylights.

My vision is clear despite the conspicuous lack of a source of illumination. I feel a sense of foreboding. An ominous heartbeat in my chest fighting to explode out. I glide through the vast emptiness of the space, straining my eyes to find anything to latch on to.

'Where are you, Izzy? Please stop tugging at your earlobe.'

This emptiness is unsettling. I don't know for how long, but I stray aimlessly, seeking something to anchor on to. I detest this vacuum.

'Dad? Have you passed out? Gosh, I hope you are not bawling again.'

I try a different tactic.

I stop moving. And wait for something to change. For someone to break into or escape from the galactic void of a sinkhole that this place is. Are those ripples I see below me?

Is that water? It's far below me somewhere. It's not flowing, just like a puddle of water in a pothole on the street. I bend down, trying to reach it. And the space around me mysteriously bends and warps until I am in the puddle. Only, it's not water. It's thicker. And stickier. Like....

Wait. Is that? *Qué bárbaro!* No.

I want to check my neck and stomach for cuts and bruises. But I still have no hands. I have no stomach. Or anything else for a body. I scream. But no sound emerges. I retreat. I run. Or slither. Or whatever I am doing. I am losing control. That's never okay.

This is completely mental. I must be dead, and this must be hell. But where the hell in hell were the other hellmates? Or was hell a lonely looney cell with no walls and windows and a sticky puddle of blood? I have often imagined the concept of an afterlife. But this beats anything that I had ever pictured.

I shut my eyes and refuse to open them even when a cold hand tries to pry them open. A bright light is shining in my left eye. Then, the right one. And then left again. I keep my eyes shut lest the effulgent beam should blind me. But my strength is failing me. I let go. I am sure this is the end.

It's a relief, finally accepting this, until I hear Izzy's voice, 'Happy Birthday to you, Spencer, Happy Birthday to you….'.

And just like that, I am sixteen. Spencer Diaz is formally a man. Almost.

And most probably, I am still not dead.

(3)

THE RED[6] LIPSTICK

For the ones who suffer in solitude

Circling around the why
And what of who I am,
Concluding that today
I shed the garb of a sham.

[6] Conventionally, one associates red, maroon, brown and black colors with the zodiac Scorpio. Ruled by the planet Pluto, people with this sun sign are intense and crave deep connections but are selective about letting others in.

ANIRUDH PLAYS HIDE & SEEK

Delhi, India

Raghu is busy finishing his homework, scribbling feverishly in the old notebook with pages that are starting to crumple near the edges. He had hoped that this notebook would last him the entire year. It is a bit hefty to carry in his backpack every day, but it was a fair bargain, just like the shopkeeper with the tobacco-stained teeth told him. He must not let his thoughts wander, Raghu tells himself.

It is becoming tough for him to focus, given the rowdy music blaring from the speakers outside. It is always the same in the *chawl* where he lives. There is either a prayer ceremony or a wedding—some reason for loudspeakers to be blaring. He is struggling with the fourth question on his chemistry assignment but does not give up.

He never gives up. But he does not have much time. It's getting late for his evening appointment, and getting ready is a ritual in itself. He needs just fifteen or twenty more minutes to crack this problem of rogue molecules and wandering atoms. He can feel the answer within his grasp. Only if it....

A man calls out to him from outside, reminding him that he has just five minutes to leave. Raghu does not respond, frantically willing the unwilling electrons into their orbits. He usually loves chemistry, but not when he is racing against time.

The man calls out to him again, repeating verbatim what he'd said earlier, in a rehearsed and detached tone, albeit louder than before. Raghu shouts back, acknowledging that he had heard the man the first time, but puts away his books into the backpack. He marks the page with a makeshift bookmark he tears off from an old newspaper.

The man hollers, his voice filled with impatience, asking if Raghu is ready. Raghu's reply is calm and measured. He addresses the man as *Dada*, an endearment for an elder brother. He assures *Dada* that he will be ready in a minute. *Dada* grunts back in response.

With brisk movements, Raghu steals a glance in the mirror and picks up a comb. He is glad he'd shaved that morning. He usually does not, but that shave will last him several days. Thanks to his genes, he isn't too hairy. There are some boys in school who, he can tell, shaved more often. Their faces have a certain grown-upness, making them appear out of place at school. He can just tell.

No one messed with these boy-men at school, letting them bask in the glory of their 'we-shave-like-real-men' haloes.

Raghu pulls back his hair while frantically combing the ends with mild ferocity. He then puts on an elastic band to prevent his hair from falling onto his face. Mayur, his best friend at school, once asked him why he grew his hair so long. Raghu fibbed that it was a religious thing. But he knew that long hair made things easier for him with *Dada* and his appointments.

He is a bit nervous about the evening. Trying to relax, he breathes in and out through his mouth. Then he picks up his cell phone, looks at the old wall clock, and decides to call Mayur.

Raghu beams with delight on hearing Mayur's voice and sings him the 'Happy Birthday' song before his friend can say anything. Mayur thanks him, and they both laugh at how silly it is to sing that toddler song for a teenager. Raghu tells Mayur to save his mobile number, a new Jio prepaid connection. Raghu prays for a long life for the Ambanis for making data affordable for poor students like him.

Mayur chuckles and asks him what time he'd arrive. Raghu apologizes for not being able to make it. He fabricates a cock-and-bull excuse that Mayur's house is too far from his *chawl* and *Dada* has not permitted him to travel alone by bus.

Better make *Dada* the villain.

He cannot tell Mayur why his appointment for the evening is more important. Raghu decides it is better that way. 'Mayur may not like it now, but no one should piss over a teenager's sixteenth birthday! Yes, it is more acceptable this way. It's not as if Mayur's parents would be too excited to see me at their son's party, dressed in a shabby, hand-me-down jacket,' he rues.

Dada had given him that jacket, courtesy of a benevolent lodger in the apartment complex where *Dada* works as a watchman. Mayur's parents are junior doctors and work long hours at a government hospital.

'They sound like lovely people, but I am sure they would not approve of a delinquent, smelly nobody from the *chawl* darkening their doorstep. Especially not on their son's birthday of all days,' Raghu concludes.

Mayur is still pleading for him to come to the party, even if for a short while. Just then, *Dada* bangs on his door, screaming and asking him to come out at once. Raghu covers the phone with the palm of his hand and assures *Dada* that he will be out in two minutes.

Mayur hears him anyway. He asks Raghu, 'Are you performing tonight?' Raghu is quiet. He apologizes and tells Mayur, '*Dada* had fixed the show a couple of days ago without asking me. I am sorry I lied to you.'

Mayur says, 'I understand. Still, try to make it,' before hanging up.

Raghu can tell that Mayur is hurt, but he tells himself that Mayur will not hold a grudge. Mayur lets him be. He is okay to let him say whatever he feels like and do what he wishes.

It is always easy with Mayur. He never judges him for bringing bread and jam in a faded pink plastic container for lunch or for wearing shoes with soles as worn out as a beggar's rags. Mayur does not hesitate to sit next to him in class. He is not ashamed of Raghu or of being his buddy.

And that is why Raghu loves him.

Raghu knows that other students gossip about him, give him cold stares, and avoid him like the plague, as if he is contagious. But not Mayur.

Once, at school, DoucheyGuyFrom11C (who is this douchey guy from 11C as you may have guessed) dragged Raghu into the boy's toilet and started pushing him around. Raghu never knew what he'd done to deserve it. He howled in pain as DoucheyGuyFrom11C shoved him to the floor and started kicking him to a pulp.

No one tried to stop him.

Luckily, one of them had the gumption to call Mayur, who came running and pulled DoucheyGuyFrom11C off Raghu. Mayur was furious. He pushed DoucheyGuyFrom11C to the wall and punched him in the face. He had never seen Mayur like that. He was not even remotely afraid of DoucheyGuyFrom11C, who was at least a foot taller and a few inches wider.

That day, Raghu silently vowed never to let anyone or anything hurt Mayur. And that had meant hiding a few things, stowing away certain realities. Minor inconveniences! Not going to Mayur's birthday party at his parents' swanky apartment fit right into that strategy.

'It's not like I am lying,' Raghu tries to make himself feel better after the call with Mayur. 'I am choosing not to share a few things for his sake. He will agree if he knows what I know,' he says aloud with resolve.

Deep down, he knows that a lot of this justification is for his own sake.

Raghu sends a message to Mayur on WhatsApp. He says sorry again, and then a few more times. Eighteen times, to be exact. He wishes him 'Happy Birthday' again, accompanied by twelve different emojis. There is no response.

Just then, *Dada* announces the arrival of the taxi, his voice warped with a mouth full of the billowing juices from his fresh *paan*. Raghu keeps looking at his reflection in the mirror, sitting at the edge of his study table as he adds finishing touches to his make-up. He is dressed up in the costume for today's show, another hand-me-down from some rich *sethani* for the needy watchman's family. The silver ornate lining on the costume has turned blotchy black now, but it will have to do. The shoddy show must go on!

Raghu picks up the phone again. Still nothing from Mayur. He puts the phone down and picks it up again. He texts Mayur, asking him to meet up an hour before the class the next day. He tells him he needs Mayur's help to finish the chemistry assignment. As an afterthought, he adds a GIF of a bald guy, something Mayur would understand was a tribute to Khanna Sir, their Chemistry instructor.

He can hear the taxi honking outside. With some final touches to his makeup and clothes, Raghu is ready. This is an act that he has rehearsed and mastered by now. Although pivotal to the show, it's not the role he'd have auditioned for. It will have to do for now.

'Tonight's show will help with the annual school fee that is due in three days. Even after taking off *Dada's* share, I should be able to save at least seven hundred rupees, maybe eight hundred, if the tips are reasonable. It all depends on the audience and how well I perform,' Raghu exhales with an air of determination.

A few days ago, Mayur had caught Raghu staring at the bulletin board reminder that the annual fee was due in three days. He had understood what was bothering his friend. He knew that Raghu was an orphan and struggled with money for school fees, lunch, and even shoes. He offered to help pay Raghu's fee with his pocket money, but Raghu refused. He assured Mayur that he would manage. Mayur insisted. It was then that Raghu had told Mayur that he worked in the evenings and holidays to pay for his rent and other expenses.

When a worried Mayur questioned him about the kind of work, Raghu told him about musical shows that *Dada* arranged with an old troupe he'd been a part of. Mayur looked solemn but did not prod further.

Raghu did not offer any more information. 'Mayur does not need to feel guilty for having a perfect set of parents to take care of him. Any more of the truth would be too much. It might spoil everything we have,' he had reasoned.

Finally ready, Raghu picks up a glittery bag from the table—a prop for his performance—and covers his face with a scarf before leaving the room. Once inside the taxi, he waves goodbye to *Dada* and checks his bag one final time. He stares out the window at the litter-strewn street lit with amber lights from bulbs illegally suspended via makeshift hooks on power lines. There is a song blaring on a loudspeaker … *'Balam pichkari, jo tune mujhe maari*[7] *....'*

He contemplates when he will be able to leave this clamorous street behind forever.

Forever.

He checks his dull reflection on the shiny screen of his phone and tells himself that doing shows like the one that night was just a temporary arrangement until he could save enough to join an acting school. He yearns for the day when he will learn from a proper instructor and do shows at ginormous auditoriums for which people like Mayur's parents will buy tickets and dress up in their best clothes.

'It won't be like that tonight,' he muses but smiles nonetheless at the fantastic life he has conjured up in his dreams. Tonight, he is still the orphan who was taken in by *Dada* and offered a place to live. Tonight, he is meant to be a performer that *Dada's* troupe has trained to act and dance. Tonight, he would do it for the rent and the school fee, and smile through it. But tomorrow could be another story.

---

[7] My love, you splashed me with a jet of colors

Not the 'tomorrow tomorrow' but the metaphorical tomorrow.

A tomorrow where his teachers will be proud of him, a tomorrow where he will return to Baroda, the city of his forgotten childhood. He conjures visions of his family still looking for him. Or what is left of it after his parents died in that fire? A family he had abandoned, packing a few clothes and a photo album, hopping onto the dirty blue train that brought him to Nizamuddin Station, Delhi.

* * *

In the other part of town, Maya is sitting on a comfortable settee, looking absent mindedly into the dressing mirror. She is getting ready, arranging a heavy helping of *sindoor* into the center parting of her hair. Her hair is unbraided and falls casually on her shoulders. Her hands are laden with two rows of zirconium-studded bangles that jingle as she puts in her dangling earrings.

She picks up a *bindi* and puts it on carefully, perfectly centering it between her brows. She sits there looking at herself in the mirror. Beautiful but adrift in her thoughts.

Anirudh walks over and sits on the ottoman nearby, unbuttoning his sleeves, which are too tight over his muscled arms. Some men like to work their muscles. Most of them like to show them off as well. Slowly, he takes off his tie, shoes and socks, one by one. He unbuttons and removes his shirt and belt, which falls to the floor with a clunk.

Maya snaps out of her reverie and turns around. 'Will you have tea?' He grunts his refusal, goes to the closet, and takes out a fresh towel.

'Going for a shower,' Anirudh replies in his heavy voice, walking away.

She is about to say something, but his tall, dark frame is already behind the bathroom door.

She stands outside, listening to the sound of the running shower and her tuneless but dashing husband humming a Punjabi song.

'Did you bring the items I'd asked for?'

There is no response. She steps out into the living room, where a brown tote bag is reclining against the sofa. While she inspects the contents, Anirudh's phone starts to ring. She picks it up more out of a reflex than from a habit of answering her husband's phone.

The home screen has a picture of him working out at the gym. 'Self-obsessed much?' she sniggers.

It is Mr Batra, Anirudh's office manager. Anirudh runs a business selling medical supplies. His company, Medicallis, distributes gauze, bandages, syringes, tapes, central lines, strobes and probes to healthcare institutions all over South Asia, Europe, and North America.

He often travels to these places, attending weekend conferences and networking events. He always asks Maya to join him on these trips, but she never goes. She does not get involved with his business, nor does she understand it. Yet, she begrudges Anirudh for all the time he spends away.

She tells Mr Batra that Anirudh will call him back.

But Mr Batra says, 'That won't be necessary. I just called to inform him that he left his wallet on the desk when he left the office this afternoon. That's all.'

'Afternoon?' Maya wonders.

When Anirudh steps out of the bathroom, Maya tells him about the call.

'Reckon I am going senile? I am glad I was not pulled over by a traffic policeman on the way.' Anirudh chuckles.

Maya does not laugh.

She tells him, 'Your mother called earlier, asking if she should come and help with the evening's function.' Anirudh looks away.

Maya clarifies, 'I told her not to, with her knees acting up.' Anirudh does not react.

There is an uneasy silence between them; the kind that has a history, the kind that speaks a lot even in its wordlessness. Maya leaves the room. Anirudh does not have anything to say that would change something. He drops the towel to the floor and changes into the green kurta his mother gifted him during Diwali. He got a bunch of compliments the last time he wore it.

He is used to flattery. He toils hard at the gym. It's his one addiction.

Maya walks back into the room, wanting to talk. She has something on her mind. He can sense it too.

'Why are you late? Strolling in at 6.30 p.m. when you were supposed to be back by five o'clock.'

He grunts and ignores her. She picks up the towel, his shoes, shirt, and socks, and paces about the room, placing each item in the right place, mumbling about his spoilt, unsanitary ways of living. As she drops his shirt into the laundry basket, she picks up an unfamiliar scent. She raises the shirt to her face, and it confirms her worst suspicions.

The telltale smells of infidelity? It must be!

She has had her doubts, but now she is sure that her husband is having an affair. A secret mistress? A second wife?

Why else does he spend so much time sculpting his body into shape? She wishes she knew who the unscrupulous bitch was.

She comes back to their bedroom. 'They will be here soon. Are you ready?' he asks while examining the pockets of his kurta.

Maya is sitting at the edge of the bed, sullen, taking off her earrings. Before he can say anything, she tells him, 'I am not feeling up to it.'

He is surprised by this last-minute u-turn. It's always some tantrum. 'What's it this time?' he contemplates. They had discussed the matter earlier, and he thought he'd convinced her.

He sits next to her, 'You are overthinking it. Everything will be okay.' He wishes he had said it with more conviction.

'It is a massive decision. You pushed me into this. I need more time to think. You should not have told anyone before we decided. Together,' she argues.

'Telling your mother was not right, and you know it.' Her voice is shrill and laced with bitterness.

These taunts set Anirudh off too. But he controls himself. 'Ma needed to know. And please try to relax.'

Maya is in no mood to back off, 'You should have thought of that before deciding to speak for the both of us!'

Sensing he is on thin ice, he tries a different tactic. He tries to soothe her, 'It is a simple family ritual. There is no need to make a big deal out of it. It is symbolic. It will be over before you know it, Maya.'

She replies, 'It is not the ritual that makes me uncomfortable. It's the fact that a stranger will come to our house and give me what I may not even want.'

He argues, 'It is not my call. Ma insisted this has to be done. She wanted an entire group to come. It was I who convinced her to limit it to just one.'

Maya smiles at him sarcastically, holding her hands up in mock reverence and says, 'And that's just bloody incredible, isn't it, Anirudh?'

He gets irritated and asks, 'So what would you rather have me do?'

Maya does not back off. 'Don't you act like a debilitated victim here. Don't play that card with me!'

Anirudh curses, 'Then stop being such a freaking drama queen.'

Maya kicks the door, 'Why don't you leave me alone? Just leave me and my drama alone. Go away. Forever.'

He tries to reason, 'You need to learn to trust me. Please don't make a....'

His words are drowned by her laughter, 'Trust you? You? But how can I trust you when you lie, sneaking around so that you can snuggle into your girlfriend's panties? Do you take me for a dumb moron? All you care about are your biceps and your whores. How can I be happy with the adulterous piece of scum that you are?'

He stands there, stunned.

She rallies on. 'You do not need to fake it anymore. Your cheating and deception are why we should not have this ridiculous ritual to bless the baby. There shouldn't even be a baby. Not now. The silver lining is that your mother won't need to worry about it being a girl.'

Anirudh's eyes flicker with something that is neither rage nor shock. It is an internal dialogue he is struggling to verbalize. He looks helplessly at Maya, who storms off to the bedroom before he can say anything.

Just then, the doorbell rings. 'Gosh, it must be the....,' he thinks as he opens the door.

A person wearing garish makeup and beaming a broad smile walks in wearing bangles, bindi, red lipstick and a sparkly handbag. She introduces herself as Ragini and congratulates Anirudh on the exquisite house. There is a bright scarf casually draped around her neck. She claps her palms together, thundering like the clang of a hammer on an anvil. He tries to stop her, but she continues to wish him, this time on becoming a father, unabatedly carrying on with her vociferous, flat-palmed clapping. The living room echoes these sounds.

With great effort, Anirudh requests her to stop. 'Sorry, but my wife is not well. We cannot do this today.'

Ragini is still smiling, asking, 'What, sir? Trying to save money, sir? You look like a film star. Big muscles, but acting like this? Why, sir?'

She is determined not to let him get rid of her. She warns him that she will expect nothing but a generous *baksheesh* at the end. And with that, she starts to dance and recite a holy prayer for the parents-to-be, replete with blessings for their unborn baby.

Maya walks in, determined to stop the charade. Before she can utter a word, Ragini holds her head in her hands, closes her eyes, and chants a hymn to ward off evil spirits. For some reason, Maya finds herself unable to pull away. She lets Ragini bless her and the child with eternal bliss and fortune. She does not object when Ragini takes out a speck of *kajal* from her own eyes and puts a *nazar ka teeka* behind Maya's ear to keep evil away, reminding her that a *kinnar's* blessings never go unheard.

Anirudh looks apologetically at Maya as Ragini pulls them both towards the settee, fishes out two marigold garlands from her shiny bag, puts them around their necks and says another prayer with her eyes shut.

Once done, Ragini gets up and extracts her phone from the bag. She tells them that no ritual is complete without a celebratory dance. 'Hope you like the songs I have chosen. Bollywood top 10.'

The hall is soon reverberating with music *'Balam pichkari jo tune mujhe maari, ki seedhi saadi chhori sharabi ho gayi....'*

Ragini dances with incredible expressions, a smile beaming on her face all through. She gyrates, palm claps, and waves her hands in circular movements to keep away evil from the family.

She showers them with blessings and rose petals and appeals, 'Please love the child, no matter if it is a boy or girl.' Beads of sweat form on Ragini's face as she continues to dance. 'Your child is lucky to have such a loving couple as parents.'

Maya suddenly gets up, takes off the garland, and throws it on Anirudh's face.

'Loving couple, yeah, right!'

Anirudh gets up, too, embarrassed and humiliated.

'What are you doing, Maya?'

Ragini does not realize what has happened and assumes that they want to join in the dance as well. She holds Maya's hands and nudges her to dance. Maya shrugs her hand off bitterly, slaps Ragini, and storms out. Anirudh follows.

Ragini is not dancing anymore. The song continues to reverberate through the room. *'Balam pichkari jo tune mujhe maari, ki seedhi saadi chhori sharabi ho gayi....'*

Ragini is dumbfounded. She turns off the music and stands rooted to the spot, tears flowing down her face. She can hear muffled sounds of crying, Anirudh's voice rising and Maya shrieking back. Ragini stuffs her phone back into her sparkly bag.

'What is wrong with her?' she thinks. 'What about my payment?'

Just then, Anirudh comes back outside. They exchange a look. He looks down, his hands joined in front of his face in apology. 'I am sorry.... She is.... I told you she is not.... Sorry.'

Ragini asks. 'Is the baby okay, sir?'

Anirudh shakes his head sideways. 'She does not want to keep the baby.'

He hands Ragini two five-hundred rupee notes, who looks too shocked to say anything. Anirudh figures that he ought to do better, especially after what happened. He takes another four notes, shoves them in her hand and repeats his apology.

Shame and guilt are often the best drivers for unbridled benevolence.

Ragini wraps her bright scarf around her head, getting ready to leave. Anirudh looks sullen, lachrymose.

'Can you make one final prayer for us? For me to have the resilience to fight for her happiness, our marriage? Please say a prayer with all your divinity. Please. For our family?'

He continues, 'Maya is … not well…. She gets tangled in her thoughts. There are days when…. She is caught in this web of suspicions spinning in her head. Her sickness has turned our lives upside down. All days are not so bad, especially if she remembers to take her medicines. But then she…. The doctors are … I mean….'

His unspoken words swirl in the miasmic cesspool of guilt that he is nurturing. 'If I could tell someone … anyone. What can I do? She needs space alone. So, I stay out of the house and spend hours lifting weights and boxing, hoping to sweat the helplessness out and to punish myself for not being strong enough for us both.'

Looking at Ragini with desperation, deep furrows lining his forehead, he says, 'She has always been my person, the only one I have ever loved. But I am so lost…. She wants to … but that is our baby…. Please. Please pray that she will trust me again and agree to let me help…. She needs more than just … I hoped that the baby would make us whole again. But now…. What she wants.... How can I do that to our baby?'

Ragini holds his head in her hands, closes her eyes, and says a silent invocation, a heartfelt one. And with that, she runs down the flight of stairs she had ascended with hope just fifteen minutes ago.

* * *

Ragini enters her room with heavy steps. She takes off her bright scarf. Her *kajal* has become a dark pool of smudges from all the teary sniveling in the taxi. She takes off the gaudy earrings and bangles, the fake eyelashes and the clothes. She scrubs off the red lipstick and the mascara, tearing off the anklets and throwing them on the table.

She sits down in front of the mirror and looks at her reflection. Raghu's face. 'I am done. She is done!'

He repeats this over and over again. He puts on his shabby, smelly jacket and lets his long hair loose as he collapses on the bed.

He is replaying scenes from the evening in his mind. 'How can I carry the burden of that?'

His stomach is grumbling. He picks up the cold sandwich that *Dada* has left on the table. He does not know how to honor the faith that the hapless father-to-be had shown in Ragini. Raghu knows that Ragini is a lie—was a lie—a convenient falsehood that has helped him make a living. But what about the lives of others she touched? He joins his hands and closes his eyes in earnest worship, hoping that the almighty listens.

To a young boy trying to survive.

He opens his eyes to a realization—the fact that while some truths need to be told, some others need to be lived, whether you like it or not. While other people may or may not understand his truth, he needs to accept it nonetheless. The worst thing is to distance yourself from the ones walking with you simply because you are nervous that they might not want to be by your side. It ensures that there is no companionship. It promises a lifetime of solitude. It guarantees that you lose.

His eyes moisten, but he steels himself, chewing at the dry sandwich until all that is left are the hard crumbs on his paper plate. He takes out the six notes from his bag, places *Dada's* one-third share on the table and puts away the rest in his blue geometry box. Just in time. He wonders if he should get back to his chemistry assignment but decides that Khanna sir's homework will have to wait.

Instead, he picks up his phone and calls Mayur. Thankfully, Mayur answers. Raghu asks if it is too late for him to come over to the party.

a dainty but proud branch
that pregnant wad of gnarly old stamps
unload that burden too heavy

Scorpio (Oct 23 - Nov 21) | Pluto | Topaz

I may be alone today, but I will find my pack.

PART TWO

THE TALES OF FIRE

razing to cinders what I touch
soaring high beyond walls
gasping in my vicious clutch
everything crumbles and falls!
but I, too, play another game,
with my raging fury in check
as the most gentle flame
like a dew drop on the neck!
dual as such my nature,
a benign trickle, a roaring flow
seeking reverence for my stature
born to burn and glow
not just outside but within
that which nestles in the soul
the passion, desire, and want
spurring it to the next goal

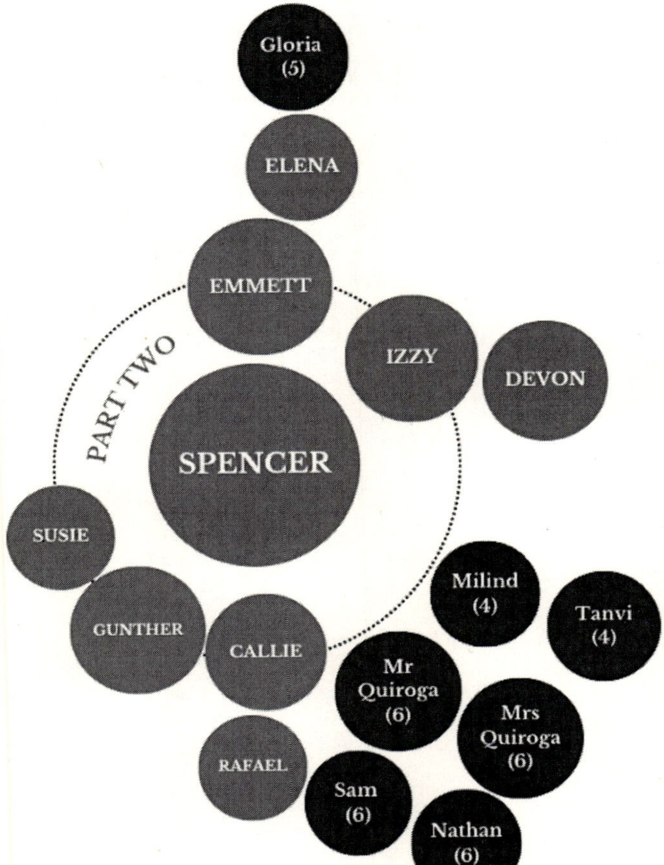
Gloria (5)
ELENA
EMMETT
PART TWO
IZZY
DEVON
SPENCER
SUSIE
GUNTHER
CALLIE
RAFAEL
Milind (4)
Tanvi (4)
Mr Quiroga (6)
Mrs Quiroga (6)
Sam (6)
Nathan (6)

SPENCER DIAZ MAKES A LIST

Texas, USA

The sounds that echo inside my sorry mess of a brain are becoming too many to handle. Whatever fate has in store for me, I seriously hope it is better than hanging here in balance.

A comma. A coma.

And it is all making me feel so desperately lonely. Why can't I wake up? Why won't I let myself come back? What am I so afraid of? Why does everything taste so acrid? Why am I getting recurring nightmares?

I have been conscious for a whole hour. At least it feels like an hour. However, I have no way of telling if it has been that long. Once, I tried counting the seconds and totaling them into minutes. I reached twenty-six minutes before Sandie tugged at my catheter.

Ridículo. And then all meaning of time was lost as she emptied the urine bag and reattached it to my, well, you get the picture. It isn't pretty. Of course, I haven't seen it, but I can feel it. Urgh.

Anyway, I think I should have rights as a sixteen-year-old. And one of them is to reject the idea of urine bags and catheters. If only they could read my mind. Wow. They should totally read my mind. There must be some doohickey that can read brain waves. Aren't they scared I have gone brain dead? I am sure their stupid detectors can catch all this cosmic brain activity I have been experiencing. Science and medicine have supposedly made incredible strides. Or was that all just hokum?

You need to know about my lists. I make a lot of them. Right now, I am preparing a mental list. Not that I can make any other sort of list. A list that I am memorizing. I keep adding items to it and then state it aloud, I mean think it aloud, I mean just think about it. Urgh. This is too tough to explain. Well, you know what I am saying. I mean thinking. Oh, forget it. I am just going to sleep. Or not. I need my morphine. It's become such a habit. You see what I just did there? So, I go over my list in my head.

Go to the cabin with Dad.

Bake cookies with Izzy.

Return Susie Boyle's diary.

You must want to know what that one is about. Well, it's a long story. Don't distract me. It's hard enough to keep track of my thoughts.

Go to the cabin with Dad.

Bake cookies with Izzy.

Return Susie Boyle's diary.

Find out who Jugs is.

Buy tickets to Sneakercon.

Dad will throw a fit about Sneakercon. The tickets won't cost much, but it's in Vegas. I can imagine him raising his voice just a tad as he says, 'You already have a gazillion sneakers, Spencer! How many is it now? Fifteen? Twenty? Is there a thing as one too many sneakers in a teenager's closet? We are running out of space in the garage!'

But I know he won't stay like that for long. He never can. He will give in eventually. He always does. He tells me that he cannot say no to me. I think I exploit that a little bit. And I have twenty-three sneakers, Dad. Only. *Por favor!* But he should be glad that I have not yet asked for an iPhone—say for my recently celebrated sixteenth birthday—but Dad is pretty busy routing all his savings to fight for my life right now. He is such a darling that way. Now, where was I? The list goes....

Go to the cabin with Dad.

Bake cookies with Izzy.

Return Susie Boyle's diary.

Find out who Jugs is.

Buy tickets to Sneakercon.

These will have to do for now. I knew I had some more to add to my list, but I cannot recollect them now. This is tiring. Curse this stupid stuck-to-the-freaking-lifesaving-ventilator state of being a vegetable that Dad is spending a lot of money to keep fresh. Although, I am relieved that Dad told Dr Miller that he did not want to pull the plug on me. Thanks, Dad. God bless you. I knew that you'd not rush into accidentally killing me. Thirty-eight days now and counting. But I am getting distracted. Um, where was I?

Go to the cabin with Dad.

Bake cookies with Izzy.

Return Susie Boyle's diary.

Find out who Jugs is.

Buy tickets to Sneakercon.

Make a thank you card for Dad for not killing me.

I can ask Susie to help me make the card. She is fantastic at such things. The art journals she doodles in and the personal diary she keeps are a riot of colors, images, sketches, paintings, writing and whatnot. She doesn't talk much, but she is always nice to everyone, even the bullies. She is the only white student who speaks to us. Her parents are Irish. But she was born here in America. She is kind. Always kind. She has flowing golden hair that looks like sunshine. I hope she is better now. Why did it all have to get so mucked up?

I don't want to talk about it. Or think about it. I will focus on Dad's cabin. And the cookies. We'll bake peanut butter ones. Izzy loves them. They were a rage when he made them for a bake sale in Leo Moreno's backyard. Everyone loved them. Mrs Moreno told us that those were some of the best cookies she had ever had. I like Mrs Moreno. She is sweet. Her auburn hair, her colorful patterned dresses and the way she smiles all the time. I don't think I have ever heard her raise her voice. Mr Moreno does not talk much, though. But he is cool. He always wears a fedora, even inside the house, which I find a bit strange. Maybe he has a bald patch he is trying to hide.

Grown-ups do that a lot. They hide their faults, even though it draws more attention to what someone might not have even heeded otherwise. Grown-ups are weird about such things.

How can someone's state of being invite others' judgment?

I have always been bumfuzzled by the premise. But Mr Moreno is just the right amount of weird, I guess. He picks us up from school on Tuesdays and always gets us frozen yogurt on the way back. I guess that made up for the shitstorm that hit us later.

We were all lucky, all things considered. The campus police did well to lock us all in the loading dock by the basement no more than two minutes after the first shots were heard. This was not the first school shooting in Texas. And something makes me feel it won't be the last. We were so scared.

I still remember Susie holding onto my hand, clasping her diary in the other. I could see beads of sweat rolling down her face, soaking a few stray strands of her sunshine hair. Her diary has these yellow flowers on the cover. Eight flowers. I counted. She had caught me staring at them once and told me they were called sunflowers, certifiably shocked I hadn't seen one until then. I had agreed without protest. Those flowers could not look more like the sun.

We stayed hidden in the darkness of the loading deck, anxious eyes scanning the cold emptiness of the space around us. Every sound made us jump. I don't remember how long we were there.

But then, Susie suddenly got up and started towards the door. I tried to pull her back to safety. She looked scared, but she kept saying she had to find her sister. Others tried to reason with her, but her decision was made. She left her diary and bag right there by my side and walked out the door and into the scary school corridors beyond. For her sister. Would I do that for Izzy? I would like to believe that I am brave enough to do that. But then, I am not doing so great fighting for myself, am I? *Suficiente.* To think of being capable of more is unbearable.

After being rescued and picked up by our morbidly worried parents, I remember how we cried and collapsed in their arms. Even some jocks on our football team. Weren't they supposed to be tough and rugged? On the way home, I simply crashed in the backseat of Dad's car. I had never seen him more worried.

Until now, maybe? Maybe if I could look at him now, I could tell. Poor guy, he has had to deal with the possibility of my death twice in the last year. Worrying about death so often must be quite taxing.

It was only the following day that I thought of Susie again. I ran down to the living room, calling out to Dad, shouting my lungs out. He ran up to me and held me back as I raced for the door. Izzy was there too. She looked worried for me. Dad looked me in the eye and helped me find my breath. I told him about Susie Boyle. He promised me he'd make some calls and find out. He stepped out to the backyard, his ash-gray pupils heavy with a weariness I had never seen before. I kept pacing the living room while Izzy held my hand. She was scared that I would run away.

Thirty minutes and a few calls later, Dad sat me down in the kitchen. He held me close when he told me that a stray bullet had injured Susie and that she was in the hospital, where they had to perform emergency surgery. Her sister was okay. But Susie was not out of danger. The news did a number on me. It was guilt. I should have stopped her. It was my fault.

I should have insisted she stay there under the loading dock's protection. I should have kept her secure. She was one of the very few people I could call a friend. I should've tried harder. I should have been brave. I should have looked out for her instead of counting the number of rivets on the boiler. I remembered that I had brought her bag back home from school. I needed to return it to her family. And her diary. But I decided to hold on to it for a while.

I needed a bit of sunshine right then.

The school reopened a couple of days later. Dad suggested I take a few days off. But I insisted that I needed to go back. I could not read his expression, but he did not contest my wish. Staying cooped up in my room was, anyway, not working. I assumed he did not know better than to give in. I make a lot of assumptions that simplify the tough questions in life. There were black commandos at the school entrance and one of those full-body scanners that they use at the airports. We had to walk through them, emptying our pockets of loose change, phones and even gum. *Increíble*. Several classes had to be canceled or rescheduled since students could not get in fast enough.

Just before lunch, the principal held an assembly. She told us that there were no fatal injuries or deaths and that the shooter—now identified as Carlos Gomez from junior year—had been apprehended and handed over to the law enforcement authorities.

Carlos? *Absurdo.* No ... that wasn't possible. Not Carlos!

The reason behind the shooting was not clear, although she did say that Carlos had been struggling with severe mental health issues and would get treatment. Bullshit. I was not buying that. Carlos was the most harmless-looking fellow ever to walk the school corridors. The principal urged us to take it easy for a few days and not worry about grades or exams for the time being. However, we were all to be interviewed by investigating officers and our parents had been informed to bring us in. That kinda made 'taking it easy' not so easy anymore. The school was never the same again.

As I walked the corridors, I could not help but stop by Susie's locker. I still had her diary with me in my bag. I decided I'd return it to her when she came back to school. What was I thinking? That the diary would, somehow, be an added incentive for her to fight for her life?

Dad picked me up and I requested that he take me to see her at the hospital. Am I at the very same hospital right now? We ran into Mrs Moreno and Leo, who had also come to check in on Susie. *Gracias a Dios*. Relief swept over me when Mrs Moreno told us that Susie was awake and lucid.

Leo would not look at us. He was scared, his eyes full of tears. Leo is gentle and caring. Seeing him like that was tough. He was aching for Susie and for what Carlos did. His shoulders drooped, like he was weighed down by an encumbrance too heavy to bear. Too afraid to ask for support. I hoped he would see Mrs Garcia and unload. The shooting had messed us all up—some more than others! Anyways....

Damn. I let my thoughts go astray. Again. I need to get back to my list. Where was I? Ah yes....

Go to the cabin with Dad.

Bake cookies with Izzy.

Return Susie Boyle's diary.

Buy tickets to Sneakercon.

No, there was something else before Sneakercon. What was it? It was ... umm ... Oh, screw it. Who am I kidding here? This is hopeless. I am pathetic. I am sure I look like a shaggy, wilted carrot by now.

Where is Sandie when you need her? Some morphine. That's all I ask for. I want to snooze.

I want to forget about the world where lovely humans get hurt. A world where parents are scared to send their kids to school. I want to not worry about Dad. Or what he would do if I were to check out from this dear world sooner than he had ever imagined.

I wish I could return Susie's diary and tell her that I was sorry for her pain and that I wish I were as courageous as her.

I wish I could still see her sunny smile again. That would mean I need to wake up. But I still haven't taken a stance on matters concerning my imminent death.

I sense Sandie back by my side, turning me over like a sack and sticking another needle in my punctured left butt. I will be flipping Sandie off when I wake up. She needs a special course on bedside manners.

(4)

THE ORANGE[8] POPSICLE

For the ones who yearn for love

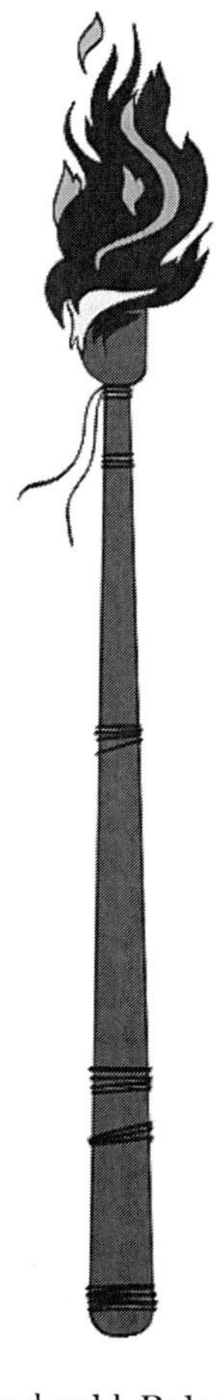

Answer that question once more
Closing with resolve that open door
What if to be whole, to be alright
Means walking alone into the night

[8] The zodiac Leo echoes the colors orange, yellow, red and gold. Ruled by the Sun, people with this sun sign express creatively, shining their light with an individualistic identity that bravely protects what or whom they love.

MILIND TALKS TO THE STARS

Hyderabad, India

Milind has this remarkable knack for acquiring sprains regularly as though regulated by some divine timetable. Every couple of months, he would end up with his neck or back so sore that it would virtually cripple him. That morning, he had been kneeling on the old, dusty wooden cabinet when Nandan, his house help, sneaked up on him and booed so loud that even a bazillion-year-old mummified Egyptian king would have woken up.

So, it wasn't any surprise that Milind leaped two feet into the air and banged his head against the top row of kitchen shelves. The impact sent several bottles of spices flying, only to land all over the floor. 'What the hhhheck?' he cursed Nandan silently. But he did not lose his temper.

Milind never gets angry. It is not in his nature to yell or shout. He makes it a point not to.

'Obvious Rrreasons.' He tells himself that being sensitive is one thing and being hyper is another. It is one of the things that Tanvi—his girlfriend of three years and, more recently, his fiancée—likes the most about him. And if something does manage to push him over the edge, he reprimands himself for losing control and works on his breathing, a trick his counselor had taught him many years ago.

'Breathe in. Breeeathe out. Breathe in. Breathe out.'

Today, he is in control of most things apart from his hunger. It knows no restraint. He eats six or seven times a day, though just a few bites each time. Strangely, he empathizes with Obelix, the menhir-carving, motley Gaulish hunter from the Asterix comics series, whose appetite is legendary. It is a practiced joke for Milind's friends, and Tanvi too, to offer him a snack as soon as he walks into a room. Despite this reputation, his friends find him surprisingly lean, even as he is turning thirty in a few days. Much to the chagrin of his portly pals on their low-carb or keto diets! They attribute it to his freak metabolism or genetics.

'Only if they knew the whole truth, but it would appear reasonable to thank my parents for it at my wwwedding! Better than....'

He had just finished making a sandwich when Nandan startled him. The sandwich now lies on the floor near the dustbin. A cockroach creeps out from under the cabinet and explores its feast, oblivious to the gaze of its assassin. Milind is about to crush it under his slippers when Nandan walks in with a broom and dustpan, smiling sheepishly. Nandan has a soft heart, and Milind does not want to step on it along with the cockroach. Ffforggggive.

'It is not worth it. Breathe iiiin ... Bbbbreathe out.'

Milind retreats to the living room and picks up the cordless phone, leaving Nandan to sort out the pestilence. He has other things on his mind. He's already tried his parents' landline four times since morning, but no one has picked up.

'Where can they be so busy? Some senior citizen wrestling tournament?' He curses them under his breath for not buying a mobile phone despite his repeated requests.

He sends messages to Tanvi to wish her luck, although he knows she won't be checking her phone until evening, being away at the *Odissi* conclave. He tries his parents' landline again and is about to give up when Appa answers. He sounds exhausted, as if he has endured a long voyage. His voice is parched and hoarse, and he is saying words that are listed in the dictionary but defy all logic.

'What are you sssssaying, Appa?' Milind sits down with a thud on his reading chair as the phone call ends. As he does so, a sharp pang of pain hits his neck.

'Why? Why now?'

He cranes his neck gingerly from side to side in an attempt to soothe the nerves. He is hoping that this phone call was just something he had imagined.

'This is not happening! What is wrong wwwwith them?'

He instinctively brushes his right palm against his left arm, which feels sore under the full-sleeved maroon T-shirt he is wearing. He always wears full sleeves. Nandan appears from the kitchen and places a freshly- prepared cheese sandwich on the table, smiles apologetically at Milind, and leaves.

Even as he tries to relax, Milind's eyes are brimming with anxiety while his jaw starts to twitch, as it does whenever he is afraid or tense. He closes his eyes and tells himself to relax. Breathe in. Bbbbbreathe out. But his head won't listen.

His left arm feels scratchy under the fabric, but he ignores it.

He is busy working out the meaning of what he has just heard. His brain is playing out the various explanations and possibilities, forming and unforming scenarios, but unable to make any sense of Appa's words.

'Breeeeeeathe....'

He picks up the sandwich and starts eating, determined to act normal and be normal. But his heart is pounding and his breathing labored.

Thirty seconds later, he passes out and slumps to the floor, the half-eaten sandwich falling with him. His dreams are disturbed and gloomy. He finds himself in the middle of a war field after sunset with dead, mutilated bodies everywhere and a reeking stench of blood. He is buried beneath a mangled pile of corpses, his hands covered in slime and gore. He struggles to escape but in vain.

A fire is raging nearby, burning what looks like shrubs of rhododendrons.

'Is that candy?'

Nearby, in a pile of burnt trash, he can make out the broken rim of a bicycle.

'My bicycle? And coloring books, my tiffin box and crayons. Is that a birthday cake?'

His face is wet. It feels dirty. He tries to wipe it with his callused palms. But it won't dry or clean, no matter how hard he rubs and scrapes. He feels cockroaches crawling over his skin, hissing and chirping all over his body. He brushes them off, but they just keep coming. And then he starts to fall into an abyss, darker than the darkest blackness he has ever seen. And then it starts to rain.

'It is a strange, red rain. Is that blood?'

With a start, he wakes up and finds Nandan leaning over and splashing water on his face, staring blankly into his eyes. He looks down at the cordless phone that is still in his sweaty hand and smashes it on the floor with repulsion, the kind he felt for vermin-like cockroaches. He knows he needs to get a grip on himself, but he cannot keep his body from shaking.

'Breathe in. Breathe ououout. Bbbreathe in. Breathe out.'

He cannot get his pulse to settle down, although he is rubbing his chest with his palm. Nandan looks extremely worried and asks if they should go to the hospital. Milind staggers to his feet and puts on his slippers.

'I nnnnneed to go out. I need to ggggget out of here,' he stutters incomprehensibly to Nandan and leaves his apartment.

Fifteen minutes later, he finds himself standing in the middle of the *sabzi mandi*, the Indian equivalent of a vegetable market. He does know how he has ended up there. But there he is, at the edge of a blue tarpaulin next to an electric pole, ready to be serviced by a waiting *sabziwala.*

'Why am I hhhhere of all places?'

His arm feels like it is on fire. He wills himself into thinking about something else.

He looks around at the cacophony of mankind. He doesn't want to be here. He does not want to pick tomatoes with just the right firmness or onions of the perfect shape. Llllike Appa used to do with unflinching dedication. He doesn't want to be among the swarm of sweaty, loud strangers bustling close by.

He doesn't want the sounds of honking cars, shouting vendors, and blaring radios to swallow his thoughts. Amma hated coming to the *sssabzi mandi.* Yet she would come every time.

'Why?'

He closes his eyes, pressing his eyelids shut tightly, willing his mind to take charge of the situation.

'They are not here. Look at the sky. Find your stars. Breathe in. Breathe ouououout.'

The sounds slowly fade away, and Milind feels like he has suddenly been transported to a vacuum chamber. He opens his eyes, a stream of sweat running down his back. His breathing feels normal. He can move, but everything and everyone else in the world is frozen in time, like they are posing for a picture. What he sees now is the same as what it was a moment ago, which was the same as the moment before that.

'The present is the right time. The future is overrated. And the past is too hyped up. It is the moment now that is lucid. Stay here. No one can take this moment away.'

Slowly, but surely, he starts to relax. His grandfather, Ajja, had taught him this ritual, which took him to this place that would always be his and could be whatever he wanted. Thinking of Ajja makes him chuckle! Ajja was such a goofy oddball. Even at seventy, he would dress up in jeans and have the latest flip-phone.

'He was such a dude.' Milind loved him more than anyone. And then he died and left Milind all alone to deal with all the mess.

His much-fancied moment unfreezes when someone elbows him in the ribs. Ouch. 'Sorry *beta,*' a sweaty lady in a gaudy printed *sari* is saying with a fake smile and a phony look of concern. Before he can say anything, she has turned back to haggle over the price of capsicum.

'Of course, she did. This is what grown-ups do. Fake apologies and lead phony, two-faced lives. They cleave you and simply turn away like nothing is bleeding, like the red carpet can hide the stains of the new pain dripping from your arm. Typical.'

Milind massages his ribs and looks around aimlessly, still rooted to the spot.

'First my neck, and now this. Urgh. This day could not get any worse!'

The *sabziwala* is playing his part cheerfully. *'Madam, thoda aap adjust karo, thoda main karta hoon. Chaliye bees rupay de dijiye. Theek hai?* This settles the deal and the lady trots away, gleaming in the glory of the six-rupee discount she fought so valiantly for. The bloody power of compromises.

'Ssssmall victories. Bbbbig smiles.'

He curses at her solemnly inside his head. She has ruined his moment in the vacuum chamber.

'And for what? A six-rupee discount? How self-centered can people be?'

A storm of rage threatens to build inside him. But before it can gather any momentum, his brain shuts it down. Like a reset button.

'Pppeace, not rage. Think about Tanvi. Good grief! What do I tell her?'

He notices that the *sabziwala* is grinning, looking all smug and victorious.

'What is his problem? Urgh. Didn't the lady just....'

And suddenly, he realizes that the *sabziwala* might have settled for an even lower price if the woman had persisted, that he must have kept a margin for haggling, and that the woman must still have paid over what the capsicum was worth.

'Bigger victories. Bigger sssssmiles.'

'The hidden ppppower of compromises.'

Milind gets even more irked by the sweaty lady in the gaudy *sari*. He despises the woman for being so delighted with what was her failure at a simple negotiation.

'Why do pppeople give up so easily? Do they have no spine or self-respect?'

He is getting exceedingly distressed and infuriated. And for some reason, he is letting himself be.

'What idiots? Some ttthings are worth fighting for. Sorry, Ajja, but she has earned it.'

He thinks about his counselor from boarding school, Sister Cara, who had taught him the breathing trick all those years ago. She'd taught him tricks and techniques to calm down. They were different from Ajja's methods but effective. He recalls sitting in her room with the ruddy old chairs and a stack of withered books in the corner.

Her room always felt cold and he was glad for his full sleeves.

She would ask him questions about his family and parents. She would ask him why he pushed someone in his class or threw another someone's notebook down the gutter. He remembers sitting silently through everything, determined not to let anyone know. Sister Cara never knew.

'She gggave up, just like this sweaty lady haggling over the price of stupid capsicums. Everyone eventually gives up, even on those who are counting on them to have their bbback.'

He makes a sudden u-turn and starts walking back home.

On the way, he gets a call from Amma. He does not pick up. He decides that the call with his mother needs to wait until later. But he does not want to go back yet. He enters a park and sits on a bench. Amma calls again. He answers. And he listens. And he hates everything he hears.

'Why not all those years ago? Why nnnow? Two months before my wedding? Why are some folks sssso selfish?' he asks aloud to no one.

It is getting dark. The itch on his arm is becoming unbearable and impossible to ignore.

Nandan has sent him a zillion WhatsApp messages asking where he is and if he is okay.

'At least someone cccares. But then I overpay Nandan for what he does. Mmmaybe this is the only way to get others to care for me as well. Not Tanvi, of course. She sees something in me that is worth sticking around for. I hope.'

He stares at the broken excuse of a pavement and the overflowing drains. His palms are balmy, and his eyes are itching, fighting back emotion and straining against the dust in the air.

'Why is everything freaking going to the dddogs? This is sssshit. How can someone ssssimply stop caring? What even....'

He passes by a flock of rowdy boys and girls riding their mud-soaked bicycles and is in half a mood to yell at them to shut up.

'Such a ruckus! Shut up, you idiots.'

But he stops himself from getting too mad.

'It's not their fault. Wasn't I jjuust like them?'

The kids are in some sort of high-stakes race. He can make that out from the jeering and cheering kids all around.

It looks like the dumpster at the end of the alley is the finish line. He can feel the concentration on the faces of the racers. And he can discern the careless, free spirit of childhood among the cheering squad.

'When did I stop being like them?'

Perhaps the day when the carpet in their house could not soak up any more of the anguish dropping slowly into its frazzled fibers.

A nostalgic cloud begins to draw upon him. Flashes from his thirteenth birthday, vivid and alive. He had returned to his parents' house from boarding school. It was the day when Appa had bought him his first bicycle. It was a Sunday. He had gone to his best mate Ankit's place and they had taken turns riding it all through the afternoon. When he had come back, he found the living room empty but could hear his parents' voices, raised and angry.

He wished they had chosen another day to conduct their shouting contest.

Perhaps they thought he'd spend more time with his friends.

'It was my fault for being back too early. I shhhould have known better. Why did I have to ruin a perfectly nice day?'

He had quietly walked up to the dining table, listening to his parents over the sound of the TV with practiced ease. They assumed no one was listening, as alalalways. They were wrowrong.

It wasn't about money or love, this one. She wasn't complaining about his limited income, though it was bound to come up sooner or later. She would harass him for being impractically honest. After all, what was so wrong with accepting gifts from clients? And he would taunt her for being an unscrupulous nag. But that day, she was not accusing him of taking her for granted. And he was not coaxing her to leave him for good. That hollering match wasn't about family or neighbors or in-laws.

He had wrecked his brain trying to comprehend what it was about. They both kept mentioning other people, but they were irrelevant, all of them. Neither of them was willing to lose their ground—him shouting, her crying, them cursing and abusing each other. Perhaps they did not care who was listening.

'I was lilililistening. I was always listening. I don't recall who won. I just knew that I had lost. Agggain. Why did Ajja have to die and leave this vapid excuse of a family behind?'

Milind knew what would happen next. So, he sat at the dining table and distracted himself with lunch from the casseroles laid out. He labored through the lukewarm meal, chewing with intent as he blocked out the sounds that threatened to become more violent. If only the food had the same heat to it as their fight. He quietly got up, put his plate in the sink, washed his hands, and escaped to his room. He heard crockery being smashed and doors being slammed.

He laid in his bed, held his pillow over his head, and went to sleep—his very own vacuum chamber amid green farmland where candy grew on shrubs. MiliLand, with a river of cola flowing through it, depositing chocolate silt on the banks and mountains covered with pillowy marshmallow snow. No one shouting or throwing things at anyone. No grown-ups. No stutter in his speech. As good as new!

He wished Ajja knew how he had conjured this place all by himself—for himself and nobody else. Just the way Ajja had taught him. He shut his eyes, pressing his eyelids tight and freezing that perfect moment. He locked and sealed that perfect moment of bliss ... that he could return to whenever life threw a curveball.

When he woke up that evening and walked out of his room, they both beamed at him, looking abnormally normal.

The room was decorated with streamers and the cake set on the table. As he watched them bustle about cheerfully, he tried to fathom how they did that.

'Wow. They are exemplary at hhhiding things.'

They could not hide everything, though.

He could see Amma's pink lipstick expertly hiding a swollen lip where Appa's fist had made contact. The sleeves of Appa's shirt were rolled down and buttoned to cover where his Amma's nails would have cracked his skin.

'Thanks for teaching me the trick, Appa. It came in handy. It still saves me from staring eyes of strangers. Hyhyhypocrites. Savages!'

His parents sang the birthday song in chorus while his buddies smeared his face with icing. They thanked the guests for their presents and handed them some picayune return presents, the expense for which had been a raging topic of discussion for three days leading up to the birthday. They blessed him when he touched their feet.

'I did not need their bbbblessings. It was never the blessings I needed!'

They were smiling. He was smiling. Everyone was smiling.

'Ssssmall victories. Big smiles. Gargantuan lies.'

That was the first time he cut himself with Appa's shaving razor. It was the first of many slashes on his left arm. Not too deep but enough to nudge drops of blood to fall quietly into the carpet. No one would ever find out. The truth stayed hidden under the sleeve of his shirt.

That was the last birthday he celebrated at home.

The next few were spent at the boarding school in Dehradun until he turned seventeen. By then, he had twelve cuts on his left arm and three each on his left and right thighs. He always did that in the night, always in the dark, not trusting himself to stand the sight of the crimson ichor that would ooze out of his veins. He would sneak up to the terrace with his blanket and his 'let's-practice-dying' kit with a cutting blade, cotton wipes and disinfectant.

He felt serene there on the terrace, alone in the company of the stars. He knew Ajja was there somewhere amid them, watching over him. After he was done, he would lie on his back, talking to the stars.

He would wonder if there were other boys out there in the world, looking up at the stars right then and asking why they existed, why they stammered, why they got bullied for something they could not control, or why their life was such a shithole.

'Did they cut themselves, too? Did they also wish to disappear but were too scared to cut deep enough?'

Sometimes, he felt that the stars answered, shimmering in the night, telling him it was going to be okay and that he was not alone. He prayed that the stars would carry his voice across the oceans to other young boys and girls like him and bring them peace.

He desperately wanted to know that he would not be alone forever. That, one day, he'd find someone to celebrate his birthdays with. It was only after he met Tanvi that he believed that the stars had granted him his wish. That was seven more cuts later.

Today, thinking of those times, a million questions start to pop up in his head. He feels it might be time to relook at the once-lacerated skin on his body that tells the story of his past. He needs to face the questions that have been piling up for a long time, eating away at him for years, the resounding hum of which has become impossible to ignore now.

'Was this nnnormal in all families?'

'How could she forforforgive him for being called a thankless bitch? How could he ignore the repeated innuendos of cowardice?'

'Did they love me? Was I a disappointment? A mistake?'

'How could he punch her in her fffface? Why did she throw the ashtray at his hhead?'

'If they hated each other so much, why did they stay tototogether?'

'Was there a ffifinish line to their race?'

'Did they care if I was okay or not?'

'Why did they never shshow up at my bbbadminton tournaments?'

'Why did they send me to boarding school?'

'Did it not matter that their only son struggled with a stammer?'

A rambunctious ringing of bicycle bells brings him back to the present, eighteen years later. The race has just gotten over. The winner—that tiny boy in a red T-shirt—is ecstatic, high fiving his comrades. It is time to celebrate. He shimmies happily for a while, raising his fist in victory while teasing the losers.

The gang of kids slowly moves to an ice cream cart, excitement written all over their faces. Together, they look merry—no anxiety about the world; no signs of that competitive ferocity on display not but ten seconds ago. They looked so at ease, licking away at those orange popsicles.

This is their perfect moment—with their orange popsicles—just like his perfect moment in his candy farm by the cola river.

'Small victories. Bbbbig smiles. Bigger victories. Bigger smiles.'

Milind remembers being such a kid once. He would win sometimes but lose a lot more often. The pain of his loss would sting for a few minutes, knowing he'd not been adequate enough to win. But he knew well how much he liked being a part of that flock.

Walking back home with his bicycle, he would enjoy the cool sweetness of the orange popsicle. And soon, they would all be smiling at how Raman had torn his shorts, giggling at how loud Dheeraj had farted that day or drooled over the homemade cake Ankit's mother had sent for them. And just like that, he would forget the pain of his loss.

He knows that he has lost something today. But it is a miracle that his parents—their family—had lasted this long in the first place. It is a compromise he is willing to make.

'It may actually all be worth it. What am I upset about anyway? Am I even upset? Had I not known this day would come, maybe secretly prayed for it, too?' he thinks.

Slowly, a sense of serenity starts to descend on him. His breathing relaxes and he lets his feet walk him back to the apartment. Everything will be okay. He looks at the sky, still starless.

'Ajja, I will not let Tanvi down. I won't let this ruin my pperfect moment.'

He reaches a bustling junction as the evening traffic honks away with a vengeance; the hoi polloi jostling to get by and street hawkers yelling their lungs out. A few minutes ago, this had disturbed him immensely. But not now. He is steady. He stops at the chemist's and buys a spray for his neck. Then he visits a Chinese food truck and picks up a takeaway of chow mein and *gobi* manchurian for dinner. 'Nandan will do a gleeful dance when he sees this!' he imagines.

Back at his lodgings, after dinner, he sprays the sore muscles at his nape with the muscle relaxant as Nandan massages it gently. It's Nandan's way of saying sorry for startling him earlier or as a token of his gratitude for the Chinese takeout. Shortly after, Tanvi messages that the dance conclave is going superlatively well and that she'll speak with him the next morning.

And a heart emoji.

Followed by a kiss emoji.

And a naughty GIF.

And another good night kiss.

He feels lighter with each message.

'We'll never be llllike them. We could nnnever be like them. Because ... well ... because there is nothing that I need to hide from her and nothing she needs to win against me. Because ours is not a freaking race.'

Later at night, Milind spreads his yoga mat on the terrace and lies down, looking up at the starry night. He thinks about the moon, surrounded by innumerable stars and yet, so okay to be by itself. At peace. Serene. Knowing that the Earth is around to keep it safely orbiting in the gravitational pull of her love—the purest form of love imaginable.

'I miss you, Tanvi. You are my star on Earth. And then there is Ajja, of course. Up above the world so high, like a diamond in the sky.'

He remembers the days in boarding school when it seemed hopeless and bleak. Yet, somehow, magically, he'd found his light. Someone to celebrate his birthdays with. He offers a silent prayer for every child like him. Anyone who needs to be okay with being alone, anyone blaming themselves for the strain of their parents' failures, and anyone who was missing a certain someone in their corner to celebrate their birthday with.

'I've got you. I am here. You are okay. We are okay.'

'I hope you, too, find your stars.'

'Until then, just breathe. Breathe in. Breathe out.'

And just like that, the last remnants of his anxiety dissipate. Slowly and surely, the clouds of the why or why now of his parents' divorce are parting. He feels exhausted with emotion.

Tired. Spent. Just like Amma and Appa?

At that moment, he realizes how utterly and painfully exhausted they must be. After all, his parents had been racing for a remarkably long time. And finally, they decided to stop running. They had reached their finish line.

A finish line.

A line beyond which they could sit down, look away and breathe. A line that, once crossed, would swathe them with the relief of knowing that they could stop now.

They need not slash the skin on their outstretched arm again.

They could finally let it heal.

He rolls up his sleeves, letting the evening breeze soothe the ridges that furrow his arm. Burying the specters from the past can be painful, but acknowledging them sometimes does the trick.

He knows that their timing sucks, but shortly, it won't matter, just like it won't matter who won or who lost the race. Because it will be time for their very own orange popsicles, their very own perfect moments as they walk their separate paths in search of what they both had once willingly yielded to—the possibility of a win.

'Breathe in.'

'Breathe out.'

turn around and face me

deeply entwined with that barren, solitary stump

inhale the fresh morning breath

Leo (Jul 23 - Aug 22) | The Sun | Ruby

I may stumble sometimes, but I will rise again.

SPENCER DIAZ FAILS TO FORGET

Texas, USA

The truth of our past is buried deep inside us, often forgotten by others who were in those moments with us. But sometimes, they remember it and hold on to it for us. And that makes forgetting it tougher. There are many things I want to forget. Really, really forget! *Para Siempre*. I want to forget some things forever. Enough to get a freaking lobotomy done to erase them permanently from the cesspool of my memories.

It would have been nice if this accident had erased it. But alas.

I am standing in the kitchen. Our kitchen at home. And Mom seems to be cooking? She never cooks. I must have died in my sleep when no one was looking at my vitals. She is smiling, wearing an apron with pink flowers. What the hell is happening? It's summer, I can tell, for the windows are open, and I can smell freshly mowed grass. Mom tells me she is going to make me my favorite mac & cheese.

I must surely have checked into hell. I wish I could have said adios to Izzy and Dad. Is this the afterlife? Will I be punished with Mom's cooking for eternity? She's the worst cook ever and I would rather starve than eat her cooking. Or anything else, for that matter.

Dying sucks.

But I can still hear the incessant beeping of monitors and the tug of the catheter on my pecker. Phew. Not dead, then. I must have slipped into my favorite hobby of daydreaming.

What else would explain Mom cooking?

I would have to ask Mrs Garcia. She'd have something to say about it. She usually has something to say about everything. Although she also has something to ask you about everything. In case you are wondering, Mrs Garcia is my counselor. She is not my 'personal' counselor. We are not that rich. I'd go as far as saying that we are just barely short of being penurious.

But let's save that for another chat and get back to Mrs Garcia. She is the counselor we are supposed to see at school if we need any aid—like if someone is bullying us or stealing our lunch money. We need to book an appointment and visit her. It's fairly easy, actually. She also takes walk-ins but only if it's an emergency. As in if you are thinking of jumping off the roof or drinking rat poison kind of emergency. But most of the kids at school avoid her—it's not very cool to admit that you are spiraling out of control just because you can't handle the usual unpleasantries life is dealing you.

She is nice, though, all things considered, especially her positively hideous turtlenecks. Sorry, but the Egyptian mummies are asking for those to be returned. And the ghoulish cat-eye glasses that make her rather pointy face look even more angular. Not to mention the joshua tree at the far end of her room, which she calls her chamber for some reason. I am sure there is some metaphysical or neuropsychological significance to its presence in that otherwise overly colorful 'chamber'. I have unwittingly picked up a few fancy words from her vocabulary. But again, I digress.

As I said, she is nice enough. She tries to help us the best she can or the best that we allow her to. She has little chance of succeeding if we just keep dishing out half-truths and invented lies. All that binge watching of crime thrillers and courtroom dramas does come in handy, no matter what Dad says!

She got a lot of flak for Carlos, whom she'd been counseling for the last several months. His sessions were also on Wednesdays, just before mine. I like Wednesdays. They break a five-day week neatly into two perfectly equal halves. Perhaps Carlos did not want her support or anyone else's for that matter. He used to just sit in the chair, staring at the floor or running his fingers through his curly hair while Mrs Garcia tried this and that. I could see all that through the narrow gaps between the blinds on her windows.

In my defense, I had nothing better to do while I waited for my session. And eavesdropping is kinda fun when you are trying to read lips. It was either that or counting the brochures on the rack outside. I cannot figure out what happened to him or what made him snap like that. With the gun and....

Were there any signs? Did we all miss them?

Carlos never spoke with anyone at school other than Leo. They were close— those two—like Siamese twins. Inseparable. Best mates like Frodo Baggins and Samwise Gamgee from The Lord of the Rings.

Gunther Delgado, Callie Nelson and I would often stay back after school to talk. Or bitch about things. Talking sounds much better. Susie and Leo joined in at times. We would invite Carlos too, but he never came.

I remember Leo asking me once what Mrs Garcia talked to students about. I think he wanted to know what Mrs Garcia talked to Carlos about. It was nice to see that he cared about his best friend. I did not know what to say. Not everything Mrs Garcia discusses with us is sane. I still cannot comprehend why she is obsessed with each one of us talking to her about those bizarre splotches of ink on her notebook. I am certain the school pays her well enough to buy another one. But never mind.

People can be weird and still be nice. And she is nice. *Lo juro por Dios!* Very ... nice.

When I meet with her, we talk about Mom a lot. She asks me strange questions about how Mom smelled. Urgh ... it's just gross to think about it. Lavender. She smelled like lavender. Or what she liked to sing to me. I cannot picture Mom singing, ever ... unfathomable. She asks me if I miss Mom. I tell her it's hard to miss someone who I barely know or remember properly. She asks me if I am angry at Mom for leaving. I repeat my answer.

How can I be angry at someone I have no recollection of being with?

I mean other than that picnic at the beach that we went to on Memorial Day weekend. Or when she took me to the planetarium and told me all about the eighty-two moons of Saturn. I remember that day. And some of my birthdays when she was home and treated us at Applebees, even if it was a school night.

She could be normal, like other moms, if she tried.

I wish that she'd tried harder to be one.

Or that she did not have to try so hard in the first place.

Or that she had not given up on us.

I do not think that Mrs Garcia will get it. So, I keep telling her that I do not miss anything about Mom. Picnics on the beach or birthdays at Applebees aren't worth leading Mrs Garcia on. She would perhaps try to convince me how fabulous Mom was, but I am not interested in buying what she'll be selling. She might even convince me as to why Dad is not entirely justified in his bitterness towards Mom. I don't want to consider Mrs Garcia's plethora of alternatives to reconcile with what I already know for a fact is the truth.

Poor guy, he was left alone to deal with the incorrigible mess their son has turned into. But some thoughts are better kept private, tucked away from the prying gaze of cat-eyed counselors sitting in the shadow of prickly joshua trees inside the school rooms they refer to as chambers.

I do not think Mrs Garcia has anything against Dad personally. But she does not know him like I do. He is lonely. And sullen. I can see it in his eyes. He was lonely and lugubrious even before Mom left us. It's older. It's deeper. He carries the weight of it every day. But despite all that, he's been the best Dad a boy can ask for, particularly one so broken as me. *Gracias a Dios.* Even with two jobs and a bazillion errands to run every day, he always has dinner with us every night.

His day job is as a marketing executive for a sports equipment company, where he makes schmoozy sales calls to pitch their wares. He seems to be outstanding at it. I had met his boss once at a 'bring-your-kid-to-work-day' event. She told me with great ebullience, 'Emmett Diaz is one of the best sales managers on my team.' I remember feeling skittishly proud while Dad intently stared at the floorboards.

In the evenings, Dad works as an accountant for a mom-and-pop store downtown. I have not seen him sit and relax on the couch, kicking back with a beer and watching a game. Although, when you think of it, he is pretty peculiar that way. He doesn't enjoy soccer or baseball. He is more of a jogger. I've seen him put on his lone pair of ragged sneakers and go out for a run as late as one in the night. Maybe I should lend him one of mine. If our sizes match, that is. I reckon he has trouble reaching slumberland, just like his broken son.

One more thing in common with the most awesome guy. Cool.

I must ask Mrs Garcia about it without telling her anything. It might be the breakthrough she's been waiting for.

I remember Dad talking to us in the kitchen on the evening that Mom left us. He'd just served us pizza with soda for dinner. That was the first red flag, for he has a fundamental issue with soda. He told us Mom had left him a letter, which he did not ask us to read. He tried to act normal, in control, like a grown-up. But I could see how much he was holding back. He kept apologizing, unable to look us in the eye. Izzy was scrunching her nose a lot and tugging at her ear. We were all silent for a while. A long while.

I remember walking up to Dad, holding him in a tight embrace and telling him that I loved him. Izzy did the same. And then we were all crying. I knew what Izzy and I were crying for. But I had a suspicion that Dad's tears were for a lot more.

The weight he'd been carrying around since Tía Elena disappeared. The guilt that never left him. The tears that never dried. I hoped that someday he would trust us to share some of it. I prayed that he would not blame himself.

Although, I am not the most steadfast person to stack his hopes onto. I tend to disappoint people. I have a bit of a history of making rash statements, impulsive decisions and being plain stupid. We all remember that time I decided to give myself a haircut to save on pocket money. Or when I caused a minor explosion of sorts in the science lab at school by mixing baking soda and vinegar for my volcano project. And when I thought I could win the 'Inferno Challenge' at Taco Rico by eating the world's top ten hottest peppers and chilies. No matter what anyone says, I maintain that I did not cry like a baby or drink a gallon of milk. *Que disparates?* Anyhow, I have a feeling that Dad does not trust my judgment.

But more anecdotes about my unparalleled awesomeness have to wait. Right now, Dad is talking to someone on the phone, although in a hushed voice, and I need to eavesdrop. Probably some schmuck from work. Or Tía Gabriela checking up again. Or maybe Mrs Garcia has called to see if Dad could look into the murderous wrecking of her notebook with grotesque splotches.

I am funny, aren't I?

But all this thinking about mac & cheese, pizza and soda has made me hungry. My stomach is grumbling. Maybe Rose will hear the sounds and decide to bring me a snack. Or at least a refill on my drip.

(5)

THE TURQUOISE[9] DUCK

For the ones who are stuck in darkness

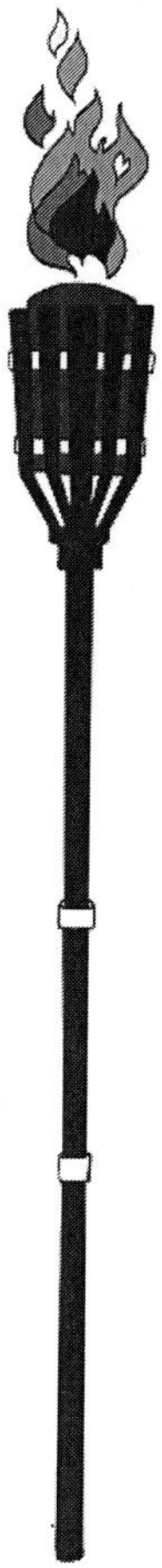

Holding on, clinging to life dear

Gripped by one ominous fear

Eroding, shredding bit by bit

Just a flicker where fires once lit

---

[9] Sagittarius, as a zodiac, radiates colors like turquoise, plum and deep blue. Jupiter, their ruling planet, imbues people belonging to this sun sign with a thirst for the truth, spurring them toward new experiences and higher knowledge.

ELENA, LOST & FOUND

Georgetown, Texas, USA

'I, Gloria Stevens, did not sign up for this. I was better off living with mamá,' she is fuming, her mind busy with too many thoughts.

'It is not in the drawer. I have checked. Even took it off its hinges and patted the far end with my hands. Found that old handkerchief lodged behind the rails of the drawer. But not the damned duck. I have looked through the musty cartons tucked away at the back of the attic. Maybe I should look again, take more time to look carefully, now that the maid is done cleaning. I'm sure to have another manic attack of sneezing looking for the stupid duck.'

Although she is usually okay after a few puffs of her spray, should her allergies surface, there is such a thing as too much of it—steroids and whatnot. So, she decides to finish breakfast before starting to look again. Hunger is making her fidgety. And she doesn't want to break any of Miss Elena's artwork. The boxes in the attic are full of expensive vases and her sculptures. She needs to be alert.

After her second shower for the day, she steps into the kitchen. Barefoot on the cold floor, she looks at the hospital-like whiteness of the space. White tiles, pale countertops, amber lights and jaded walls. The most colorful things there are the ash-gray stovetops.

'This kitchen always gives me the creeps.'

'What on earth drove me to come here? This is what a mid-life crisis must look like. What was I thinking? Trying to rediscover myself at this age, alone in this city? Damn you, Eat Pray Love! Damn you, Julia Roberts for making it look so easy, so desirable! Damn you, Miss Elena. If I ever saw such a dreadfully cold person....' she rants as she whisks two eggs for breakfast.

'I should have done my research on her before coming here. I genuinely felt bad for her, the frail old woman, when we spoke on the phone. I was taken in by my naivete. I am so pathetically gullible!' she continues to mumble as she pours orange juice into a tumbler.

'And now I am stuck here, in this humid, patrician nightmare, eating chalky pancakes and stone-hard muffins in the name of sophisticated opulence. I am sure that I will go completely berserk, scrubbing the ceramic tiles in the dining hall every four weeks and dusting the great rug in the hall every six,' she thinks, a shiver rolling down her spine.

The limpid scrambled eggs beside the slightly charred toast on the white ceramic plate further depress her mood. Colors are important to her. So, she squeezes a big dollop of blood-red ketchup on her plate. Better. Much better. She sits there, staring at her plate. She doesn't feel like eating. She dips her finger into the ketchup and draws a smiley face.

Only it looks more like the sinister Joker from the Batman movies.

She gobbles up her breakfast, washing it down with a glass of cold orange juice from the fridge. She makes a mental note to go to the supermarket, to stock up on vegetables and fish.

'I must try to get her in a good mood before I tell her about my ... theory? While I am at the supermarket, maybe I'll buy a few duck breasts too. Damn. I just cannot get the cursed ducks out of my head!'

She wracks her brain, trying to remember where she had seen it. Unable, she heads to the attic in haste.

'There's a lot of ground to cover or boxes to uncover. I don't understand why Miss Elena must keep so much junk in the attic. Some of the things she calls art look more like heaps of trash. But then, I am not known for artistic flair. I am more of a spontaneous, camping-with-friends-on-a-mountain-top kind of gal,' she ponders, mumbling and muttering the whole time she searches.

'Either way, I think Miss Elena is a hoarder. But she wouldn't acknowledge it if it were written in pig's blood in bold letters all over the large wall in her library. Why does she even have those hideously naked busts of randomly famous Romans lining the great hall?' The only name from that lineup of busts that Gloria remembers is that of Morpheus— thanks to the dude from the Matrix movies.

'Isn't it time for her to move on? She is almost fifty, though she looks older with her pale skin and lifeless eyes. With her husband off to heaven, she need not bother so much with the decor and the drapes. Anyways, not my monkey, not my circus.'

Gloria had brought it up once, making sure not to sound impertinent, but her employer had snubbed her off, saying, 'Henry and I lived it up while he lived. He would not want me to penny pinch now, would he?'

'Paying your overworked staff a bit more is not exactly penny pinching, I should have told her. But I am an honorable woman with perfectly pleasant manners.'

Gloria is not even sure if her employer would understand her worry. 'But now is not the time to think,' she decides, resolving, 'I need to find the damned duck first. It is critical to my chances of ... of ... I know in my bones it's important.'

Miss Elena's chambermaid (of course, she has one of those) tells Gloria that breakfast was served at nine (the usual) in her bedroom, and now, Miss Elena has gone for a walk in the garden. The butler (they have their own Jeeves) is with her, walking a safe distance behind, alert to run to her aid if she trips or faints. She'd objected to this arrangement at first but surprisingly gave in without much of a real fight.

'Mr Henry made sure she was never alone. He was a caring husband, and she knew better than to argue with him. I know she realizes her frailty, although she would never admit it.'

Deciding to explore the attic, her thoughts wander. 'I wonder why her family never came to visit her. Not once? Georgetown may be old-fashioned, but we are just minutes from Austin!'

She recalls asking once, only to be told, 'I have no one other than Henry,' with a tone of finality to the discussion, before adding, 'Henry was the only family I was meant to have.' Something about the way Miss Elena said those words had unsettled Gloria. She knew it was a lie or a morphed truth. She had seen a strange sadness in her employer's cold eyes; her lips curved downward, resolved to curb any emotion from escaping. Gloria knew there was something amiss but did not press further.

'How come there are no pictures of her family in a mansion with at least seven hundred framed photographs hung all over its walls? Why would she lie about that?' Gloria wondered as she ascended the steps to the attic.

Despite all her whining, Gloria admired her employer's gumption.

'To do what she's doing is not easy. I am thirty-six and feel lonely and at sea in this house. I don't know how she does it. Are books and music enough? Or playing old records on her gramophone or reading journals with no pictures and freakishly tiny letters for hours?'

'Is that why the ghost is back?' Gloria conjectures as she reaches the landing outside the attic. She rubs her forefinger on the wooden cabinet near the landing, expecting to find dust. But the maid has done a magnificent job.

She shakes off the shivers and gets to work. It's going to be a long day. She starts with the first box. It is filled with miniature pieces of glassware collected from Turkey and Russia, trinkets that no one would care to look at again. But Miss Elena said that they had 'immense sentimental value' for Mr Henry.

'Was that sarcasm?'

She sifts through the boxes one by one, carefully enveloping them back in their bubble wrap. But there is no sign of the turquoise duck anywhere.

'Surely, I have not conjured it all in my head!'

Her back feels sore after a couple of hours, so she decides to head back downstairs. When she reaches the entrance hall, the butler announces with a smirk, 'The ghost has arrived. He is with Miss Elena now.' They share this inside joke, the butler and Gloria. The ghost is their nickname for the writer hired to author a memoir, a biography to chronicle Mr Henry's adventurous life. He was commissioned by the man himself, a few months before he died.

'I am not sure how I feel about it. Does she want to honor her late husband's dying wish? I bet a clause in his will mandates her to get it done.'

Simply put, Gloria does not like the ghost. For her, he is too polite, too proper, and ever so caring, offering to help with chores that are 'none of his god-damned business.' Gloria feels he should focus on his writing, which she presumes would be insipid at best.

'I'd know a good writer when I see one—temperamental and adrift in their world of words. They are not so ... friendly and chatty,' she had gossiped with the butler. But the real reason why Gloria chose the nickname was because she felt he was dead.

'Not "dead" dead, but his skin is like parchment; his lips white, like a corpse in a morgue,' she'd exclaimed to the butler, drawing from her vast experience of watching CSI Miami. 'Miss Elena is blind not to see it, but she is literally getting her story "ghost-written"!' Gloria had chuckled, almost choking at her own joke.

Presently, Gloria retreats to her room and lies down, bracing for the bustle for lunch. She is restless, her thoughts drifting to the day they found Mr Henry dead. In the glasshouse!

The doctor had been called but it was already too late.

A suicide. The note in Mr Henry's handwriting was unmistakable. Gloria had read it before the police took it away from her trembling hands. Through tears of disbelief, she saw how Miss Elena sat alone on the couch in the hall, staring into the distance, frozen by what she assumed was shock. She sat in silence. She did not cry—not even a single tear.

'Until then, I had never imagined Miss Elena without Mr Henry. They were like that pair of decorative ducks that go together. Two ducks. Two!'

She gets out of bed and removes her old Walkman from a locked drawer. The Walkman was the last gift her father had given her before he left. The tape is already in it. She had found it while cleaning Mr Henry's room, tucked away inside his coat pocket. She'd kept it on a whim, wanting to hear what was on it. She could not make much of it then and was in half a mind to throw it away. But something made her hold on to it and keep it hidden.

She plays the tape. She has heard it a hundred times, the words etched into her memory. Direct and unambiguous. But she cannot comprehend them.

'Is it conceivable? Am I letting my need for adventure get the better of me? But if Sir Arthur Conan Doyle has taught me anything, coincidences should not be ignored. I feel I am on to something.'

A ringing clatter of spoons in the hallway snaps her out of her Sherlocking. This investigation will need to wait for a couple of hours.

At the lunch table, she observes Miss Elena talking animatedly to the ghost. She seems cheerful. A bit of color is starting to return to her wrinkled cheeks. The ghost's plate is almost empty—just two pieces of potato, a few beans and a bit of fried rice. He aimlessly pushes the food on his plate with a spoon, occasionally remembering to take a bite. The ghost is nodding but his thoughts are elsewhere.

'What has gotten into him? He is quite unlike himself today,' she exchanges a look with the butler.

Gloria interrupts their chat on the pretext of offering bread. Miss Elena dismisses both the bread and her rather unceremoniously. Gloria's eyes meet the ghost's, their gazes locking for a fleeting moment. He looks haggard. She cannot help but feel pitiful. Strangely, she does not try to hide the concern written all over her face.

'Something is off. I must find out. But right now, I need to find an opening to speak with Miss Elena.'

As she contemplates her move, the ghost excuses himself to the men's room. Miss Elena turns to her and asks what she'd been looking for in the attic. She is surprised her employer knows. She lies to her like a pro, 'Crockery, we are short a few plates.' Before Miss Elena gets busy with her meal, Gloria takes her chance.

'How are you feeling, Miss Elena? Did they give you back the letter? The one….' Miss Elena nods, pointing to the library with her head. 'Under the globe. I don't know what to do with it. It's not something I can frame and hang on a wall.' Her casual tone bothers Gloria.

'Should I smile? How can she be so….' Gloria is unsure how to finish that thought.

After lunch, when the maid and butler go off for their afternoon nap, Miss Elena retires to her room with the ghost and Gloria retrieves the letter, folded neatly inside a transparent pouch. She reads the letter and her suspicions are confirmed. It's the exact words. Verbatim.

The exact words recorded on the tape in Mr Henry's voice—spoken over and over and over again—as if rehearsing for a perfect audition.

'Why would Mr Henry rehearse his declaration of suicide on tape before he wrote it down in that letter and killed himself?'

'It was redundant. Unnecessary.'

'The only explanation is that Mr Henry wanted to leave behind a tape instead of a letter, perhaps a more personal goodbye to Miss Elena. But he could not keep his composure enough to go through with it.'

Replaying the fateful day in her mind, she recalls something else. There was strange music playing on his phone. It had been less than a minute since they'd heard the gunshot that the butler, the maid and Gloria were out in the gardens. The music had drawn them to the glasshouse.

The maid had let out a chilling cry as she turned the corner, walking right into a pool of blood. Gloria stood transfixed as the butler held onto the maid, who was howling uncontrollably. Miss Elena walked gingerly towards them.

And just before Gloria turned away to help Miss Elena, she noticed it. The turquoise duck.

It was odd that it was there. Bizarre.

'Why would someone leave a crystal duck in the glasshouse, that too only one from the set of two I had cleaned so many times?' But there it was— behind the geraniums, where it had no reason to be. Gloria had picked up Mr Henry's phone and switched off the music, careful about touching it only with her apron. Leaving fingerprints was a sure-shot way to become the prime suspect.

'Thank you, CSI squad,' she had thanked her TV stars for her presence of mind. 'I would rather not want become their prime suspect.'

Back in her room, the tape she has been listening to has the same weird music playing in the background. Each recital of the dying man's declaration was followed by a clicking sound and a few moments of silence, followed by pitiful crying, apologizing, and shouting in exasperation before the recording was abruptly stopped.

'What is that clicking sound? Who is he apologizing to?'

Determined to find these answers, she puts on the earphones again, rewinds the tape, increases the volume, and closes her eyes.

She doesn't realize when she dozes off, but when she gets up, it is nearly dark. She washes her face and heads straight to the glasshouse. The blood has long since been washed off. She approaches the geraniums, now in full bloom. The duck is still there, covered in mud and leaves. It looks more at home now. She kneels where she believes Mr Henry would have been sitting when he shot himself. She knows this because the police told them—a blood splatter pattern and whatnot.

As she kneels, her eyes level with the duck. She focuses on the voice and the strange music from the tape and raises an imaginary gun to her head.

'Looking for something, Gloria?' a grating voice startles her.

She loses balance and trips onto the gravel. It's the ghost. He offers her his hand, but she is too scared to take it. She is flummoxed by his intrusion. Although Miss Elena had waited a few weeks before summoning the ghost to finish the work on Mr Henry's memoir, Gloria never felt at peace in his presence.

'What the hell is he doing here?' she thinks, her body tensing.

Gloria makes an excuse and starts walking away, but he blocks her way. She maneuvers away, but then she hears him call after her, 'She scares me, Gloria.'

She stops in her tracks and turns around. 'Who?' she asks. He stays muted. She knows who he means.

He nods, his eyes flickering with doubt.

'Have you seen her? How can she scare you?' Gloria inquires.

He holds his finger to his lips and shushes her. Before she can react, he pulls her into the glasshouse, eyes scanning the bay windows while beads of sweat flow down his brow. He is paranoid.

'What could Miss Elena have done to frighten you so much?' Gloria's asks.

He lets go of her hand once they are out of sight. He wants to say something but cannot seem to find the words.

'She ... I think ... It's not that she told me ... but that day ... she ... when I ... I mean, it was clear ... in that story…. When Mr Henry.... It's just in my head … but then she ... I felt it ... Although I might have imagined it.'

He is a foot shorter than Gloria, a zombie-faced weakling. Somehow, at this moment, he appears more human to Gloria than ever before. She feels sorry for him. She can see that he is not faking this. Something has rattled him.

'I won't be coming here again, Gloria. Please tell Miss Elena that I have an emergency. Don't tell her that I spoke with you. I will leave town, the state even. I will not come back. Not if she paid me a million bucks. I don't want to lose my mind like she … to think that I let her....'

Gloria tries to comfort him. 'Miss Elena must already be in bed. No one will know what you tell me. I promise your words are safe with me. You can trust me. Please. Tell me everything. From the beginning.'

He looks her in the eye and lets go of the bag he's been clutching tight to his chest. It falls on the gravel with a soft thud. He sits down next to it, steadying himself against a metal column. He is quiet for a few moments. But what he says next stuns Gloria.

'It's all wrong. She is wrong. What she made me do ... Gloria, I am terrified of heights. I'd never do that of my own free will. But that day, she.... She is a witch or a part of the occult. I just looked into her eyes for a minute. And the next thing I knew, I was on the ledge, ready to jump.... She is crazy. A witch. A witch.'

He stops talking suddenly, his eyes fixed on something. He looks petrified, his voice deserting him. Before she can ask him anything, he is up on his feet, grabbing his bag and running out of the glasshouse, blabbering in absolute terror. He keeps looking over his shoulder at the rows of geraniums. She follows him outside, but he is already several steps ahead.

'The evil bird. Those blue eyes. The evil bird,' she hears him mutter over and over to himself before she loses him in the darkness of the moonless night.

She stares after him briefly, then returns to the glasshouse. She gets down to the floor where he'd been sitting and turns her gaze to the rows of geraniums, right into the piercing eyes of the turquoise duck—the evil bird with blue eyes, drenched in the mist that fills the glasshouse.

She is distracted throughout the dinner service. She steals glances at Miss Elena, who seems perfectly normal. Once or twice, she catches her looking, but Gloria smiles back politely. As soon as dinner is over, she retreats to her room and shuts the door. She doesn't know why, but she feels jittery. Her hands are cold. She shuts her eyelids and tries to breathe. But the air in her room seems to have thickened. She thinks of all she knows and writes it down in her diary.

'Mr Henry committed suicide using a gun—a shot to the right of his forehead.'

'Mr Henry killed himself kneeling by the geraniums which he loathed.'

'A turquoise crystal duck is sitting behind the rows of geraniums.'

'The turquoise crystal duck is one of a pair. I cannot find the other one.'

'The ghost was spooked out of his wits. He said he will never come back.'

'The ghost said Miss Elena is a witch.'

'Miss Elena made the ghost stand on the ledge?'

'The ghost called the turquoise duck "an evil bird".'

'One turquoise duck was behind the geraniums when Mr Henry died.'

'Strange music was playing on Mr Henry's phone when he shot himself.'

'The same strange music is heard on the tape with Mr Henry's voice.'

'Mr Henry made the same dying declaration over and over again.'

'Mr Henry kept apologizing in the tape.'

'The exact same words from the tape were in his suicide letter.'

'Did the ghost learn something while writing the memoir?'

'Why is the ghost so afraid of Miss Elena?'

She hesitates before writing the next few questions, afraid to ask them and fearful of the answers.

'Mr Henry did not seem suicidal. Why would he kill himself?'

'Did the ghost discover something he should not have?'

'Miss Elena didn't look shocked when he shot himself. Or even sad. Why?'

'Mr Henry had no reason to kill himself. Did Miss Elena have one?'

She is appalled by her thoughts. 'Miss Elena is a sickly woman who is unsteady and infirm beyond her age. It is not possible that she ... she was not even in the glasshouse when ... she came out of the house long after we all ... long after....'

And another question forms in her head.

'The sound of the gunshot was deafening. Ugly. Unmistakable. She must have heard it. What took her so long to come out?'

'I remember I gave her Mr. Henry's phone afterward. She had switched it off and kept it in her purse just before the police arrived and bagged the evidence—namely, the gun. I remember him checking the safety on the gun before he packed it away. It had clicked harmlessly into place as he....'

And just like that, a flash bulb lights up inside Gloria's head. Bright and clear. She knows without a doubt what the clicking sound in the tape was. Nervously, she adds a few questions to the list.

'Why was Mr Henry practicing shooting himself with the gun's safety on?'

'What was that strange music playing on Mr Henry's phone?'

'Miss Elena switched off the phone. Why? Why then?'

'Why was he kneeling next to the geraniums?'

She is still swimming in the sea of her thoughts before she falls asleep. She wakes up when the maid knocks at her door the next morning. Gloria tells her she is sick. The maid enters her room gingerly, assuring her it is okay, for Miss Elena had left in the morning to meet the lawyers in the city.

Gloria waits for the maid to say more. Predictably, she is more than keen to gossip. She lowers her voice and tells Gloria, 'Oh dear! You did not hear it from me, but the mistress wants to sell the estate and move away. I am already looking for another place to work. Awful, isn't it?'

A few minutes later, Gloria snoops into the room where Miss Elena and the ghost work. She is there on the pretext of tidying up. She digs around, hoping to find answers or the manuscript the ghost is writing. But all she sees are stacks of books on psychology, psychiatry and even some on hypnotism. That does not surprise her. After all, Miss Elena has been studying and researching the human mind for almost thirty years. Mr Henry had told her when she had just arrived.

'Someone who would be perfect at playing mind games.'

There is no sign of the ghost's work anywhere in the cabinets, drawers and shelves. Finally, she checks inside an old travel trunk. She extracts the papers and the books that fill it, looking for clues. Nothing. She rams the lid in frustration. Something rattles. She opens it again and sees a latch on the underside of the lid, which she had not noticed before.

She checks her watch. Miss Elena won't be back for another couple of hours. It's now or never. She slides the latch and extracts a small box filled with trinkets that must have belonged to a schoolgirl. Lockets, charms, a rabbit keychain with a house key, a faded lip gloss, a library card for San Felipe Memorial School, two notebooks, some pens, a photograph of three children—a boy and two girls, an old tape recorder, and three cassette tapes. The photograph has names written behind it: Three Musketeers—Elena, Emmett & Gabriela Diaz: Corn Factory, Del Rio, 1983.

'Is this Miss Elena? She looks so pretty. Are those her siblings? Is that her family?'

The cassette player intrigues her, given her recent discovery of the other tape. Cautious not to make a sound, she closes the door to the room. The first cassette tape she puts into the player is dated over twenty years ago. It screeches when she plays it, and she can barely make out the voice of a young girl. 'Elena from the photograph? Our Miss Elena?'

The voice sounds scared. Gloria can only decipher a few sporadic words, the magnetic tape damaged either from repeated listening or age.

'Sorry Papá, I did not … never trusted Henry … liar … He … forced … inside me, all over me … dragged … old house in Idaho … chained like an animal … until I stopped … to leave … Papá, he threat … kill you all … the worst … lied … all over… wish I would die….'

Gloria's mind is going bonkers. 'What the heck? Did Mr Henry abduct her and.... Is this for real?'

She rewinds the second tape and listens to it with urgency. It's more of the same, albeit the voice sounds feebler but unmistakably Miss Elena.

'... burns and welts ... my skin ... at night. Henry is a monster no one sees for one ... married ... feels wrong.... Henry does not think I will run away ... villa in Georgetown ... came into money ... all over the world ... like his pet ... hell ... come home ... so close.... Sometimes, I hold a knife when he ... kill ... blood everywhere ... cannot do it. I want to ... back to ... free.... I miss Em and Gabbie. I am so close, but.... Papá, are you still there? I hope....'

Gloria cannot process what she is hearing. 'Mr Henry, a monster? Is this why Miss Elena is so.... Did he....?' She feels sorry for her employer and is furious at herself for assuming the worst of Miss Elena. But she still cannot explain the mystery of the duck and the frantic pleas of the ghost.

The last tape is dated two weeks before Mr Henry's death. When she plays it, she is shocked to hear the same music as on Mr Henry's tape. And then she hears the ghost's voice, apologizing, crying uncontrollably, sobbing, his voice quivering. She rewinds a bit, plays again, and hears him say, 'I want to jump from the window.... My life is not worth living. I must die. I am sorry. But I must die. Help me. Please help me. I am so sorry.'

Gloria listens to the tape again—the same music, the same crying, and the same apologizing—over and over. She flips the tape to the other side, rewinds it to the beginning, and plays it again. She can still hear the music, but it's all quiet otherwise.

And then she hears Miss Elena speak. 'Listen to the music. Focus on the beats. And look into the eyes.' The ghost's voice asks, 'Are you sure about this?' Gloria hears the windows being slid open. The ghost goes silent.

Miss Elena keeps saying, 'Follow the bird's eyes. Follow the eyes. The bird will guide you. You know what you must do, don't you? Follow the bird's eyes.'

'Follow the bird's eyes,' he replies in a voice that does not sound like his anymore. Gloria hears a desk being pulled.

She hears footsteps on the wood. She hears the hinge of the window creak under the strain of a heavy load. And then she hears an emphatic knock. She is shocked to listen to her own voice in the tape, dull but clear, 'Miss Elena. Miss Elena, you have a call. Miss Elena?'

The music switches off abruptly.

Gloria hears hurried footsteps on the wood. Her voice on the tape goes on. 'They want to invite you to an event. Shall I transfer the call here?'

She hears the windows being shut, and then Miss Elena whispers, 'That's enough of a dress rehearsal. It is ready. I am ready. You will wake up now.'

Her mind is going a thousand miles now, and her heart is racing. With trepidation she has not known until that moment, she goes to the bay window and slides it open. It is raining outside, and a gloomy white mist is pouring into the room through the open window. Through that mist, Gloria finds the other turquoise duck, sitting on the ledge, staring into her eyes—the evil bird.

sound of a penny drop
in the abyss of this mortal world
listen ... my nightmare still echoes

Sagittarius (Nov 22 - Dec 21) | Jupiter | Turquoise

I may take time to find my way, but that is alright.

SPENCER DIAZ GOES FOR A RUN

Texas, USA

The definition of love is subjective. And so is the concept of a soulmate.

So, the idea of finding that special someone sounds like a witch hunt. Izzy, however, claims that she has found hers. When did she have the time to look for one? She is always busy with college and, of late, her work at the nursery. How did she even meet someone, fall in love, and decide that they are date-n-mate material? Sounds like a big fat lie. I called it when she told me. I mean, not literally, because she hasn't 'told me' told me.

She just spoke to me when she thought I wasn't listening. Welcome to the benefits of a pseudo coma or whatever the hell one describes my state as. His name is Devon, and according to Izzy, he is remarkable enough to possibly be God's most extraordinary gift to mankind after Wi-Fi and mobile phones!

What kind of a name is Devon?

He is her senior at college and is graduating this fall. She told me that they met during a party at the house of a friend (of a friend?). Since when did Izzy start enjoying random parties? She told me that he is a perfect gentleman and had walked her home because she had had one too many drinks. Since when did Izzy start getting drunk? Is she going through something?

I need to get her to meet Mrs Garcia.

Izzy is too trusting. She might not realize that she is making a mistake with this Devon dude. He might turn out to be a total fraud. What does he do for a living? I bet he runs a yoga retreat to scam unsuspecting septuagenarians of their life savings. Maybe he drugs and robs them.

In my head, he is such a rascal. And just like that, I conclude that I do not like Devon. Why is Izzy being so gullible about it? I seriously pray that they haven't yet had....

I wonder if Izzy is lying to me just to shock me into waking up. I know a thing or two about lies. The thing about lies is that they are sort of addictive. One small one leads to another not-so-small one. And then that leads to a few more oversized ones. Until the lie becomes you and nothing else remains but the hiding and cheating. Even with the people you love. The lies take over everything, even the air you inhale. The guilt of it chokes the last bits of you that remain like a potent dose of poison you concocted for your own personal hell.

I am digressing again. All that is neither here nor there.

Sorry, where were we? Oh yes, Devon. Liar. Cheat. Scum.

I don't want Izzy to rush into anything. She needs to be sure of this dude or else she will end up like Dad—resenting the very person she thinks is the love of her life. What is love anyway? A myth propagated by people who make romcoms? I bet that love is what Dad had felt all those years back when he proposed to Mom.

Come to think of it, I am a bit fuzzy on the details of how that proposal went down. What did Dad do to woo Mom off her ambitious feet? She isn't the kind of person you can win over with just a warm smile and a kind heart. I know that because I know that she betrayed him. And I lied to cover it up. *Qué vergüenza.*

I need to get some me-time with Dad. He needs to know about Devon's dark secrets and checkered history of hideous crimes. Izzy needs to zip it until then and not make this a bigger deal than it is. She needs to realize that it is just a phase. What does she think will happen? Does she believe that she will have a happy ever after with this guy? She is certainly delusional. The odds of that happening are worse than a panda giving birth to a piglet. Even the evens of that are not looking great.

Dad and I will disintegrate if she leaves us for Devon. We won't just wake up one fine day and start sharing our inner thoughts. Doesn't she know that Dad is like an envelope and I am like a postage stamp about to go out of circulation? And the only thing that is holding us together is her. She is the freaking glue. Super Glue. I am sure I can come up with a better analogy than that.

But you get the point, don't you? So, enough of your whining to an objectionably gangly teenager in a coma.

My unbridled anger and clenched fists are suddenly brought into perspective by the soothing yet firm voice of Dr Miller. I remember meeting him the day I visited Susie at the hospital with Dad. The day we ran into Mr and Mrs Moreno. And Leo. Wait! So, Susie was at the same hospital then? *Extraño.* That's not bizarre. Or is it?

I wonder what Leo is up to these days. He seemed so out of sorts after Carlos. It must have been tough to lose your best mate like that. I can only presume where they took Carlos. Some juvenile detainment facility or rehab center? I shudder to think how it must be for him there.

Hope it's at least better than the jaw-droppingly happening life I have got going at my bachelor pad in the hospital.

Wow, I am going bananas. *No bueno.* Keep it together, Spencer. Dignity, man! Get a grip!

Back to Dr Miller. He is explaining something to Izzy, Dad, and the random-polite-stranger-who-smells-of-coconuts, 'Jugs.' Who is he? Why is he here so much? Coconut? Focus, Spencer. Focus on the voice of the good doctor.

'... will tell you exactly as I see it. The promising news is that Spencer has turned a corner. There is no remaining trauma to the spine or limbs— everything seems to have healed there. We see no signs of any infection—the antibiotics seem to be working. His brain function is steady, but we'll need to monitor it. He is still not out of the woods. Right now, our main concern is his lungs. The surgery was not enough and the damage caused by the shrapnel was too extensive. *Asombroso*. His only hope is a transplant. Sadly, you and Izzy are not a match, nor are any friends and family we've tested thus far.'

'How about....' Dad interjects.

'Oh yes, Señora Gabriela, Spencer's aunt, offered to be tested, but she does not qualify on the count of her medical history. We don't know when we.... And the longer we keep him on the ventilator.... *Increíble!* But let's not lose hope. Spencer is young and otherwise healthy and that improves his chances. I just want you to know all the facts. I can see you at noon tomorrow to discuss this further.'

I can hear Dad muttering something. Keep breathing, Dad. I can hear Dr Miller walk away. Izzy comes and sits by me. I think she wants me to answer. I just don't know how.

The race is on. The clock is ticking. Hell, I like races. Always have. And why shouldn't I? It's one of those things that I am genuinely splendid at. I have won a medal at every school race I have ever been in. I run every day. Before school. After school. Weekends. Just like Dad.

Strangely, we have never gone on a run together. One would imagine that it could be the thing that brings us together. Yet, we try to make it a point that we always run alone.

Just like this race, the one I seem to be running against time. What was it that Dr Miller said about shrapnel? Was it a bomb that exploded? What the hell happened to me? I need to remember. I need to figure this out now, not tomorrow, not the day after. Close your eyes and think, Snoozy! Think. *Por favor.* Remember.

I try to recollect. I am running past the bakery downtown. I have a sip of water from my flask. I see Mr Moreno driving past in the opposite direction. I wave to him and he smiles back. I run on, past the library and the dry cleaners.

Left right, left right, left right, left right.

I have my ear pods plugged in, and I am zoned out, listening to my running playlist. I pass by the church, the pizzeria and the pawn shop. I turn right onto Agave Street. I like running up the incline on the street—a challenge that I never turn away from. So onward and upward I run.

Left right, left right, left right, left right.

There is a school bus stopped in the middle of the street. It's odd to see it there at that time of the day. Maybe it's broken down? I check the time on my watch. It's almost half past five in the evening.

I hear some noises in the distance over the music in my ears but cannot see anything. It's getting dark anyway. I am out of breath and need a break. As always, I halt near the bakery.

I lean forward on the lamp post, my back towards the street. And then there is a sinister explosion.

My world goes blank.

(6)

THE MUSTARD[10] STAINS

For the ones who want to belong

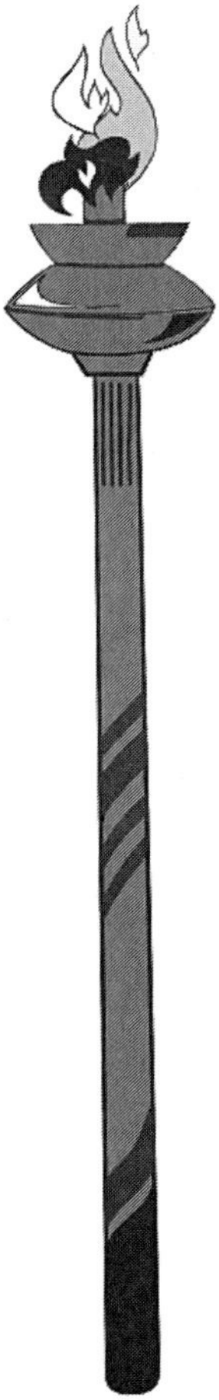

Bristling leaves, the dawn of the day
Chirping birds flying to the bay
Brought a smile, distant but alive
A will, a new promise to thrive

[10] Mustard, rust, saffron and yellow are the vibe of the zodiac Aries. The ruling planet of Mars fill those with this zodiac with a deep passion and bias for action, an eagerness to act and the spirit to take challenges head on.

SAM AND NATHAN GO CAMPING

Austin, Texas, USA

I go by Nathan—it's short for Nathaniel—your average, nerdy, school-avoiding teenager who hates getting up in the morning.

Mrs Quiroga is calling. It's still a bit early in the morning. I have that awful bitterness coating the insides of my mouth. As a policy, I do not speak with anyone without first brushing my teeth in the morning. I decide not to pick up. I am sure she'll assume that I am still asleep or taking a shower. She'll understand. I make a mental note to call her back.

Samuel Warren Quiroga, or Sam as everyone calls him, has been my best friend since the fourth grade. What made us so, I would never know.

I do know a little. A bit of it was fate. The rest of it was perhaps my math teacher, Mr Hinkleson.

* * *

When Mom and I first moved into town, our life was a big pile of muck. Like literally. There were cakes of mud all over my jeans, shoes, and even my worn-out 'I Love Vermont' hat. Heck, there was filth all over the doors, tires, and most of our boxes in the U-Haul trailer straddling my mom's pathetic Prius.

Given how the car had heaved and cranked all its way from Montpelier down to Austin, I was glad to have made it without Mom having to jump-start that green monstrosity of a vehicle on a stranded highway. As if sensing that its life was ebbing to a final halt, the wheel cap on the rear tire fell off as soon as we idled up the driveway of our new abode. For some reason, that car has always been quite loathsome to me, even when it was not covered with goop in twenty shades of nasty.

I bet that's why Dad was so accommodating about who got the car as part of the divorce settlement. I reckoned he'd be content in a world free of the dilapidated green *merde* that was now my legacy. As if there wasn't enough other awkwardness to make a boy stand out in a crowd.

Speaking of crowds, Mom enrolled me in Mason-Rice Elementary. She dropped me at the school gates on my first day.

Naturally, she would have thought it impossible for me to walk the two hundred meters from our new house to my new school alone. Sometimes, I do not get Mom at all. At other times, I do not even try. She is complicated. I guess Dad figured it out the convoluted way. Anyways, Mom won custody. Yippee yay!

I waited for her to leave before I began my ascent along the twelve steps at the school entrance. My heart was pounding in my chest. It felt like the eyes of the entire school were on me. They weren't. No one as much as looked at me.

I was glad that my gift of invisibility still worked. Cool. Otherwise, it would have been difficult to hide my super cute acne that resolved to tear through my fair skin and explore the world outside with a vengeance. Or my scrawny build and a head full of blonde perms that stay tucked under this oversized hoodie! Let them discover my many gifts one at a time, slowly, very slowly. But being so gifted had an undesired side effect. Well, a few!

Frankly, I must have looked messier than an upside-down bowl of instant noodles. I must not boast of my numerous natural talents so trivially.

I made it a point to smile widely at anyone who looked my way. I worried that my silence would be misconstrued as arrogance or contempt. Yet, somehow, no one ever smiled back. I wondered how to break the ice and let them partake in a bit of the awesomeness in me!

Most kids at school stayed away from me. Some inferiority complex, I assumed. I imagined it was tough for them to be in the company of someone so precocious! So, I had my lunch alone in the cafeteria. As days passed, this became a pattern. And I always sat on the last bench of the corner-most row in every class. Slowly, the new school became an imitation of my old school. I and me alone.

When I cycled back from school, the kids playing on the street would make way for me to pass, stealing glances at me as I glided away on my cycle. There were numerous times when I opened my mouth to say hello, but all I was able to manage was a gurgle or a hiss.

What can I say? I had style!

I liked Austin enough, though, better than Montpelier, which was dark and frozen for most of the year. I hated the cold. It's a sinister season that must have been created by the devil himself. Not happening! I decree that the damned season be banned.

I was on one of my evening rides through the block when a boy ran straight into me. I could not blame him, for the boy's eyes were glued to the chaser behind him. A white terrier barking its lungs out. I let out a throaty groan as we both hit the pavement becoming a mechanical sandwich of sorts in the process. I was the bottom loaf, the bicycle forming the layer of crunchy goodness in the middle, capped by a panting black-haired boy on top. Luckily, no one got hurt.

The terrier looked satisfied with the results and made a retreat. The boy—Sam—apologized; got up, and helped me back up. He took off his bandana (folks in Austin wear some weird mishmash) and tried to clean himself up, and then me. Sadly, his bandana was dirtier than a machine-shop rag, and all it did was add grease to the grime on our faces. We looked like two runaway delinquents who'd been illegally squatting in an abandoned warehouse for months.

I smiled my popular smile at him. Sam let out a guttural laugh, pointing to my face, holding his stomach like it would fall off. I always knew my smile could bring joy to the beholder, but this was something far beyond.

Sam stepped close to me, still laughing, checking his own reflection in the bicycle mirror. The howls of laughter that followed were even louder. He put his hand on my shoulder, and for the first time in many years, I broke character. I started laughing.

Sam walked back home with me that day. As we walked and talked, Sam told me that he also went to Mason-Rice and that we should hang out at school. He was a year ahead of me. But he did not seem to care. At one point, Sam touched the acne on my nose and asked me if it hurt. I told him it did not. When we reached our house, Sam did not find the green Prius ugly or odd. I felt he was the most perfect person I'd ever met.

Sam mentioned playing catch with his dad on weekends and asked if I wanted to join them. I beamed another smile at Sam and confessed that I'd most likely suck at it.

'Hand-eye-feet-brain coordination is not my forte. So yeah … we'll see?' I told him.

Sam chuckled and told me that I was funny.

'Yeah, bro. I've got swag or what? About time that someone saw that!' I replied.

More guffawing laughter followed. I breathed easy for the first time since we had landed in Austin. It felt like an intruder was trying to burgle into my impervious vault, and I was handing him the keys and a torchlight. Some accidents are surprisingly acceptable ... they lead to the most pleasing of outcomes.

More power to the beauty of accidents.

At almost five feet, Sam was a good four inches taller than me, and the tallest in his class. He wasn't lanky like me either, his shoulders were wide and neck thick. Kids would tease him about being too big for his age, but he always brushed it off.

He introduced me to the school baseball team and the coach. He told me about the best ice cream shop and the 'sick burger place' that I had-to-had-to-had-to-go-to. God, I love these have-to-have-to-go-to places of all types of places in the world.

We connected over our mutual dislike for math, especially the horrendous way Mr Hinkleson taught the subject—with boring anecdotes about theorems and bizarre trivia about axioms. I would laugh my ass off every time Sam impersonated poor Mr Hinkleson, his impression of our teacher's snorting down pat to the last note. Our friendship grew wings.

'My new friend. My only friend. My best friend,' I would chant every time we parted ways. Yet, I never said that aloud to Sam. You see, I did not want to jinx it.

This was fourth grade. Sam and I stuck together all through the school year. Sam skyrocketed to be six feet four inches, while I peaked at around five and eight, but somehow, I never felt the need to find cover around him. Strangely, though, he would make an inordinate amount of effort to appear shorter when others were around. I got the distinct impression that he would rather not be the tallest Quiroga in his family, looming a good one foot taller than his relatively diminutive parents.

We would cycle in the evenings and sample flavored yogurts at the Dairy Queen on weekends. I showed Sam my collection of miniature ninja turtles, and he regaled me with stories of hikes he'd gone on with his parents. We discussed our plans for what we'd do when we grew up— everything from a dashing astronaut to a suave banker.

I was never alone at lunch again.

Sam introduced me to his other buddies—there were a lot—an abnormal number of people to call one's friends. Whatever his shortcomings, being popular was not one of them. Sam was just.... I still cannot find a better way to put it. Sam was just Sam.

This carried itself into high school, and we were practically inseparable after that. On weekends, we would go on short hikes with our parents, who, for some reason, always chose to camp at the base. By junior year, Sam had even cured me of my inexplicable desire to shear the perm off my head and my obsession to fix my walk.

My gait's a bit wonky if you pay close attention. 'I am trying a new walk,' I had told Sam, who had looked at me like I'd recited a pagan verse. He flicked me on my head, saying, 'You're fine, Nathan. At least you are not a boy in the body of an ogre.' It was an odd thing to say, but I ignored it. Sam was never at peace with his size.

That had been enough. I no longer needed the gift of invisibility. A part of me had become ready to share my natural awesomeness with the world around me, although I did consider if the world was prepared for it.

Sam's father, Mr Quiroga, runs a local business—a diner—near the downtown library with his wife. After his graduation, Sam joined the diner too. He was supposed to take over the family business when he grew up. Sam was a one-man army—bartender, cleaner, sous-chef, all rolled in one. Simply put, the Quirogas made the most scrumptious tuna sandwich in the whole of Texas!

Every time I ate the sandwich, their unique homemade mustard sauce would ooze out from the sides and stain the table napkin. Mrs Quiroga would complain that the turmeric-hued mustard stains were too tough to get out and urge Sam to discover an easier-to-wash substitute. Sam would laugh it off. According to him, seeing the stains on the napkins was the perfect way to know that diners were getting the right amount of sauce.

'Stains are the best part,' he told me. 'It is what makes it all worth it,' he said. I was mesmerized by how Sam found these interesting ways of looking at something as banal as mustard stains. But then, Sam was being Sam, I figured.

When I graduated the next year, I took up a job at the local newspaper, where I still work. My pay grade was well below that of the editor and slightly above that of a delivery boy. In other words, it was just the perfect launchpad for a rising star in the world of journalism. My uber-scrawny looks were now accentuated by wide-rimmed glasses and rolled-up shirt sleeves. When not chasing local stories, I would drop in at the diner and lend Sam a hand with polishing the wine glasses, filling up squeeze bottles with mustard sauce, setting the tables, and laying out the yet-to-be-stained napkins.

On weekends, we would often go to the Big Bend National Park, our favorite hangout. There was a meadow clearing just off the top of the hill where we would camp at night. We would make a small fire, gorge on smores and gaze at the stars. Sam always said it helped clear his head. I was never sure what in his perfect head might need clearing.

But he loved it there. And so, I loved it too.

Sometimes, Sam would not speak for what felt like an eternity as we lay there in our tent, trying to trace Ursa Major, Hercules, or Orion in the night sky with our fingers. I assumed it was fatigue. Sam did not like me asking about it, so I let it be. Even when I insisted, Sam would shrug it off with a smile.

This was then.

* * *

Mrs Quiroga had called earlier today. I had not answered. I was still in bed then, making a mental note to call her back. But it completely slipped my mind. So, I am royally embarrassed when I see her waving through my office window, looking solemn.

I meet her outside on the pavement. I can see she is extremely worried. I take an early lunch break, and we walk down toward the diner. I can see the redness in her eyes and the nervous twitching of her hands. I offer her my most pleasant smile. Once we are at the diner, I ask her if she is okay. And she breaks down into a mournful flood of tears, like a house of cards collapsing. It takes all of my natural talents for effortless socializing not to run away.

What I hear next lands me a blow so hard that I feel like my ribs have cracked.

'Sam is hurt. He … has been in the hospital for the last three days. It was scary … he was hanging on by a thread….' Mrs Quiroga says. 'I needed to speak with you, Nathan.'

No, this can't be true. Sam, Sam, Sam, Sam, Sam!

At that moment, I realize why the diner had been closed the last few times I'd walked past. When I sent a message to Sam asking about it the day before, he just replied, 'Deep cleaning,' with an emoji that looked much like white table napkins. Without the mustard stains, of course! I figured I'd leave the Quirogas to it.

I should have made more effort, paid a visit, or….

I have a thousand questions in my mind, most of them starting with 'why?' I do not realize I am shaking, fighting back the wetness pooling in my eyes.

* * *

On one of our camping trips, Sam had made me take a solemn oath never to cry. This was when I opened up to him about my fears of loneliness and how I tried to put up a brave, happy face for others while I wept in solitude. I had not realized it but I had cried throughout most of my little confession.

Sam had drawn me into a bear hug, cackled vehemently and then told me that I had to get rid of him before I could even think of enjoying any alone time.

As always, Sam has just been Sam.

We were brothers, even though from two very different mothers. I knew I would never be alone again. I believed that Sam meant what he said. I had agreed to his deal. And I had held my side of the bargain.

Until now.

* * *

'I am not going to betray him now. Not ever.' I brace myself and take a deep breath. 'For Sam. For my brother,' I find myself chanting, a quiet prayer in every breath.

Mrs Quiroga tells me now, in a squeaky voice that sounds hoarse from crying, 'You are his best friend, Nathan. And you need to know.... You see, a few months ago ... Sam ... well ... he took one of those genealogy tests. You know, the ones that can trace your family history. He did not ask us for permission, of course. If he had ... not that we would have ... but this is.... There were things he did not know, things that we could have explained to him before.... When he saw the results, it was quite a shock to him.'

I am perplexed. It must show on my face, for she continues, 'If we had known, we would have.... But it was too much for him. It would be for anyone if their ancestry maps to a partially Nordic gene pool despite both parents being from multi-generation all-Texan families.' I try to speak. Instead, I blabber something incomprehensible, as if I have a toad stuck in my throat.

Mrs Quiroga carries on, 'Sam knows about our families, of course. He's met them during Christmas, Easter,

Thanksgiving and such. My own parents stay at a very nice retirement home in Rocksprings where my brother Jonah owns a thrift store. Jonah is Sam's favorite uncle, always bringing him weird trinkets from the store.'

I can sense that she is leading me to something but is hesitant. I decide not to rush her.

I let her carry on with her account. 'My husband's parents have long passed, but the rest of his family are based in El Paso. They run a chain of hardware stores, you see. My husband is not particularly cozy with his siblings but makes it a point to stay in touch, being the eldest. His sister married a local tradesman, Stephen Blake, in Del Rio and has a son, Rafael. He is a fine young chap, so observant. It's too bad about his ADHD, but I hear he is getting better. You hung out with Rafael last spring with Sam, didn't you, Nathan? You're all the same age. Almost … nearly.'

I ask, 'But how…. Is Sam okay, Mrs Quiroga? Please tell me. Is he....' my heart thrumming.

Sam, Sam, Sam, Sam, Sam!

Her hands quiver, and she tries to steady them by intertwining her fingers. She struggles to steady her gaze as she says, 'Sam confronted us last week. He wanted answers. Whose birth video had we shown him? Who was the child we had lovingly played with in those grainy clips? Did we have another child he did not know of? Why had we lied to him? Was his entire life a lie built on deception? We tried to explain, but the problem is that he was right.'

My jaw drops. What? What is Mrs Quiroga saying? Is this what a brain melt feels like?

Mrs Quiroga tells me the rest of the story, although it is not a story. The truth. Sam's truth. The same truth, which when the Quirogas finally told Sam, had broken him.

It nearly broke me too.

I implore again, 'Where is Sam? Please tell me, Mrs Quiroga?'

Sam, Sam, Sam, Sam, Sam!

Mrs Quiroga's eyes are filled with shame and something more. Fear. Shame. Guilt?

I know whatever it is, it is killing her, but she is willing herself to go through it for Sam's sake. Some parents just love their children that much.

Her voice shakes and her hands tremble as she says, 'I am his mother, Nathan. I mean, I am Sam's biological mother. But his biological father ... well ... he is not in the picture. He died a few years ago in jail. He was....'

There is a long pause. I can see her trying to calm her breath.

Eventually, she speaks, her eyes averted. 'It was a long time ago. We had just started the dinner service at the diner. Things were starting to look up for us. We had a European tourist come in just after ten, clearly drunk. He was from Denmark or Norway or some such place. It was late, almost closing time. When we told him so, he was not ready to listen. Well, he caused quite a ruckus. Sam's father tried, but the man simply refused to leave. He threatened some other customers who tried to talk sense into him. He was a hefty fella, towering well above us all. You know how these Scandinavian folks are. No one wanted trouble, and they all left, one by one, until it was just us.'

Mrs Quiroga pauses. I can tell that this is not easy for her, but she soldiers on, driven by a steely grit in her eyes. 'When Sam's father tried to usher him out, the ruffian started to yell. Voices were raised. A scuffle broke out. He punched Sam's father and then knocked him out flat with the butt of a gun he had tucked into his belt. A gun in our restaurant. Can you imagine? It was mortifying. You hear cases of drunken shooting ever so often, but nothing can prepare you for when it happens to you.... I hoped that one of the customers who'd left hurriedly would call the cops.'

She closes her eyes, clearly tormented by reimagining the horrible day. 'There was broken glass and blood where Sam's father had fallen. I ran to his aid. He was bleeding so much from his brow and nose. I feared the worst. He was not moving. But the man grabbed my wrist and pulled me back by my hair. He slapped me, tearing my lip. I could taste the metal in my blood and my head spun. I tried to call for help, but no voice came out. My throat was burning as if someone had fed me embers. Sam's father was still not moving. I prayed he was not dead. I tried to get up but the man shoved me on the floor, pinning me down with his weight. I could smell the filth of his sweat and the alcohol. I could not move. I froze. And then, he ... he....'

Mrs Quiroga's body trembles and she collapses into tears once more. Her eyes are bloodshot and her voice is broken. 'He held the barrel of his gun to my forehead, choking me until I went quiet, while he....'

Sam's biological father was a violent psychopath, a rapist.

I cannot breathe. I do not know what to say or do.

'Why is the world so full of horrific people? Why do people hurt others? Why are there driving tests but nothing for gun licenses?'

My hand finds Mrs Quiroga's as she rests her head on my shoulder. Her tears fall silently on my neck.

Sometimes, no words are needed.

Sometimes, silence is the perfect conversation.

Sam, Sam, Sam, Sam, Sam!

After a while, Mrs Quiroga speaks again. The fear in her eyes is clear as daylight. 'There is more? Sam?' I ask, fearing the worst.

'Since that day, when we told him, Sam locked himself away from us, from everyone. He would not go out of his room or even his bed. He would not even touch the plates of food I left outside his bedroom door. Finally, three days ago, I used a spare key to unlock his room. Only to find him unconscious, barely breathing, covered in blood, a paper cutter near the sleeping bag he was in … he … he tried to…. Why? My Sam … my baby … my baby….'

The world stops. My pulse halts, and a panic grips me. I cannot believe what I heard.

Sam, Sam, Sam, Sam, Sam!

Mrs Quiroga wipes her nose with a handkerchief tucked in the belt of her dress and says, 'He is alive, but … Nathan … it might be a while before he … well … I just wanted you to know. I need to get back home. Sam is getting discharged from the hospital. So … what I am trying to ask is … will you help us, Nathan? You know … maybe … maybe if you tried, he might be able to forgive us. We were just … it was … we were just trying to protect him.' With that, she gets up and disappears into the kitchen, leaving me alone amidst the stacked chairs.

Minutes later, I find myself in an alley, kicking the trash bins with a vengeance.

'Why did you not share this with me, Sam? Why not tell your best friend?' I recoil from the shooting pain in my foot, but my wrath is boiling. 'Why did you have to be so selfish, Sam? Why?'

I groan so vociferously and curse so profanely that a few people gather outside the alley. I bark at them and tell them to mind their own business. 'Why could we not go to the Big Bend and gaze at the stars to clear our heads? Talk it over? Or smash something with a baseball bat?'

Eventually, I limp back to the office and slump in my chair, still shivering. I cannot think. I cannot breathe. 'Did he not know that he was loved? So … so loved? How could he not know? My brother….'

I take the rest of the day off and lock myself in my room back at home. I do not let myself cry. I won't break my promise to Sam even if he does not care enough to stay alive.

Mom calls out for dinner, but I do not reply. When she knocks on the door, I pretend to be asleep, my mind barreling with questions.

'I am glad you are okay, Sam, but what the hell? How could you?' I do not call Sam or text him. Not yet. Sleep eventually takes over.

The next morning, I am standing outside the driveway of the Quiroga townhouse. The newspaper is still outside on the lawn. I wait, unable to work out what to say to Sam. I cannot imagine what Mr and Mrs Quiroga must be going through. I am determined not to leave Sam alone, though suddenly worried that Sam might not want me there.

I cannot leave him alone. He is like oxygen to me. 'Let him push me away if he wants to.'

I cannot do anything to change the truth of the time gone, but I know that I will not abandon Sam. Yet, no matter how hard I try, I cannot think of the right way to be with Sam just then.

'Sam will have to suck it up and accommodate whatever imperfect version of me I present to him. Like he always does. I just need to show up.' I conclude my inner ramblings with a finality.

Sam has been my boulder for ages and I realize I can at least be a little rock for him. Or maybe a large pebble.

When I reach Sam's room, I can see him lying curled up in his bed, his face turned away from the door. His feet dangle from the bed, for it no longer fits him. Mr Quiroga had proposed to trade his bed for a longer one, but Sam had grunted his refusal. Shock courses through my body as a realization dawns. This must be why Sam took the damned test. He wanted to know.

'I should have sensed something amiss. How could I be so oblivious to Sam's angst about his body? And I used to think I had it tough.'

Standing at his door, I know he is not asleep. He is not making that funny breathing sound he usually makes when he sleeps. And he never sleeps on his stomach. I walk in and look around the room. It seems the same as always—pictures of famous monuments and forests from across the world plastered on the walls—all the places Sam wants to travel to, the sights he wants to see. Then there is the big jar with the gazillion spoons from our yogurt tastings at Dairy Queen. I never understood why Sam collected those. But I am not one to judge. After all, I am a proud owner of a canister full of odd-shaped twigs and gravel.

After what seems like hours, Sam peeks at me from under the sheets. I do not see him, but I can feel his eyes on me. It is a good thing, I surmise. But that is as far as it goes for now.

It's late in the evening when Mrs Quiroga arranges a soft mattress for me on the floor. I refused to sleep in the guest room when she offered earlier. 'I will not leave Sam's side.'

It is two more days before Sam agrees to go out on a drive with me. At least he is out of his room. I drive him to Dairy Queen in the evening. Sam seems skittish and nervous, looking over his shoulder while we taste some twenty-three flavors of frozen yogurt. After the ninth or tenth one, we cannot taste anything anymore. But we keep going, Sam starting to smile at the stupidity of our dogged pursuit. We even try the purple and green ones we had once sworn never to.

Seeing my tongue turn a wicked shade of grey draws out a loud chuckle from Sam. Whether he is laughing at me or with me, I do not care.

I am glad to see glimpses of my friend again in the boy who is here with me. I leave a ten-dollar tip in the jar and profusely thank the confused-looking guy at the counter while Sam washes the dribbles of yogurt off his face. Back in the car, he gives me a gentle smile before putting on his seatbelt.

A few days later, I run into Mr Quiroga at the supermarket, who looks haggard but stands upright, as always. He says hello and pats me on the shoulder. He knows about the drive Sam and I took. 'Thank you, Nathan, for being there for Sam. He is blessed to have you by his side,' he says.

It is then that I see the black soot and blood on his clothes.

'What has happened now?' I am alarmed.

Mr Quiroga notices my consternation and follows my gaze scanning the butcher shop his clothes look like. He quickly throws on the jacket he has in his hand and draws me aside to explain. 'I've just returned from Del Rio, having had to travel to deal with a truculent supplier for the diner. I did not want to leave Sam, but my wife.... Well, she convinced me to go. Plus, I thought I could meet my sister and her family. I haven't met them for a long time.'

I nod as he continues, 'But as luck would have it, there was an accident not far from the restaurant where I had to meet the supplier. A blast in an illegal meth lab, I later found out. Would you believe that?'

I scan him again for any injury. Their family does not need any more of those right now.

Mr Quiroga goes on, 'I rushed over there, only to find debris, billowing smoke, fire, blood, people screaming, panic and worse.' Most people would run away from a blast, not toward it, but the Quiroga family is logically peculiar that way.

I ask, 'But the blood on your shirt? Are you sure you are okay?'

Mr Quiroga leans a bit on the shopping cart. 'The blood on my shirt is from a young boy, not much older than you and Sam. I found him by the roadside, bloody and unconscious but breathing. Just like when Sam....'

Mr Quiroga is quiet for a moment, and I know that he needs a minute to wall up his emotions. 'I lifted his limp body in my arms, hauled him into my truck, and rushed him to the ER at a nearby hospital. I must have broken a dozen traffic rules. But....'

Mr Quiroga is a good cookie, the best kind that there is. He is a good person. More significantly, he is a great father. Sam's father. The only father Sam would ever need.

'The world could do with more people like you, Mr Quiroga. You inspire me,' I tell my friend's loving father.

Mr Quiroga's eyes get misty, but he smiles. His reply melts my insides. 'Someone was looking out for Sam when he … so … it's only fair that we pay it forward. I will pray to the saints that the boy lives. His name is Spencer. Spencer Diaz. His parents must be sick with worry.'

Mr Quiroga pats my shoulder again, smiles and walks away, pushing his rickety shopping cart. I am left gazing at how much Sam takes after his father in his generosity of spirit.

It is another two weeks before Sam and I go back to work. Sam does not want to go, but I make him, for my sake, as I have no more sick days left. My mind is distracted the whole day. I keep sending him messages about this and that. After work, I meet him at the diner, offering to help with his chores for the dinner shift. Sam sits at the back, hiding behind a stack of chairs, polishing cutlery and folding napkins with a forlorn look in his eyes. He looks preoccupied. He has an aura of melancholy that has not left him in days. His smiles are labored. I sit with him, filling mustard sauce into the squeeze bottles.

'I am here, brother.'

Sam, Sam, Sam, Sam, Sam!

We work in silence. I see him stealing glances at his parents. Mr Quiroga is ferrying crates of produce from the loading deck. Beads of sweat fall down his nose, his wet shirt clinging to his lean frame. Mrs Quiroga is busy with the *mise en place* for the evening, with bandages on her fingers that have calluses from the daily scrubbing and cleaning of the stoves in the diner's kitchen.

Sam normally helps out with these chores, but today, he....

Mrs Quiroga is julienning carrots when she looks up and catches Sam's eye. She manages a faint smile that tells me more of her pain than anything she'd said at the cafe the other day. This time, Sam does not look away. I register a defenseless apology in Mrs Quiroga's gaze—the guilt of a parent who does not know how to heal their son.

I know Sam can feel it too. Tears are flowing down his eyes. But he does not make any effort to hide them.

I place my hand on his trembling ones and he does not flinch.

'I've got you, brother!'

Sam looks at me with pleading eyes, shivering and broken. I am not sure what he needs right now from me, but I do not look away. I do not try to hide my emotions. I am crying, but I don't care.

Then, suddenly, Sam pulls his hand away, gets up and rushes past the stack of chairs into the kitchen, where he pulls Mrs Quiroga into a tight embrace. Mrs Quiroga collapses to the floor, upsetting bowls of beans and meat onto the floor. Sam holds on to her tight as she lets out a piercing wail that is so full of anguish that the diner seems to drown in it. Sam is crying and apologizing. Mr Quiroga rushes in, alarmed by the sounds, dropping the jars of pickles he is carrying as he trips over the slices of tomatoes on the floor.

The kitchen is a mess.

But I have never seen anything so beautiful in all my life.

The Quiroga family stays huddled on the floor, with Mr Quiroga kissing Sam on his head more times than I can count, and Mrs Quiroga caressing Sam's wrists with her bandaged hands.

I look away, trying to be less of an intruder at that moment. I pick up the bottle of mustard sauce lying sideways on the table and cap it. And I pick up the napkins that Sam has been folding to wipe the puddle of sauce on the table. Maybe I should have fetched a washcloth from the supply closet instead. But I don't bother.

Someone once told me that the stains are the best part.

hidden amid the fallen leaves
clinging to the long longing for belonging
bathed in the morning dew

Aries (Mar 21 - Apr 19) | Mars | Diamond

I may be lost for now, but do not give up on me.

PART THREE

THE SAGAS OF AIR

walking past the hills
climbing up the mountains
nursing the heat, the chills
tearing away the vicious rains
across the prairies and deserts
serenading flora with my whirl
soothing farmers and herds
the whisk, the swoosh, the twirl
sounds of your whispery breath
ragged, labored, and slow
I bring you back from death
divine, magical is my flow
a new zeal soaring in the veins
I rise, yet again, with hope
taking charge of the reins
riding towards the next slope

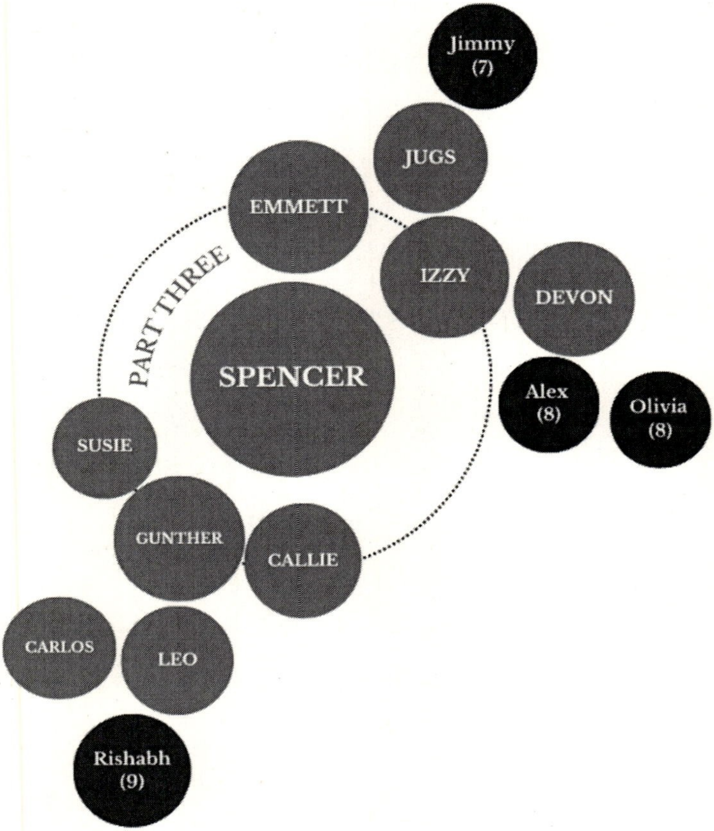
PART THREE
SPENCER
EMMETT
JUGS
Jimmy
(7)
IZZY
DEVON
Alex
(8)
Olivia
(8)
SUSIE
GUNTHER
CALLIE
CARLOS
LEO
Rishabh
(9)

SPENCER DIAZ TALKS TO THE STARS

Texas, USA

The world, before it exploded on me, is certainly not adequate, but ... perhaps ... just perhaps ... not too lacking either.

I see the stars. I see the moon.

I am lying on my back, sprawled over my sleeping bag that I have unrolled on the terrace. It's not our terrace. We don't have one. I am at Gunther's place for a sleepover. Callie was here too with Susie until Mrs Nelson, Callie's mom, came to pick them up.

We had a nice dinner—extra-cheese pizza and soda—with a lot of being-by-ourselves-without-anyone-hovering-over-us. What more can a bunch of gawky teenagers ask for? I am sure our parents have some idea about how utterly unadventurous we are. Quiet kids, they say. But the adults underestimate us, claiming to have called our bluff. What do they know about the nefarious plans that our Mortal Kombat-addicted minds can hatch?

Callie Nelson wants to neutralize 'excessive' physical beauty by brewing a 'normalizing potion'. She wants to take physical aesthetics out of school bullying.

Susie plans to become the President of the US and make gun use punishable by life imprisonment. Susie Boyle, POTUS.

Gunther wants to make fruit loops mandatory for lunch. Trust Gunther Delgado to come up with revolutionary, history-altering ideas. And that might as well be. He wants to study computers and become a game developer or a coder someday. I'm not sure if that is him or his father talking, but Gunther usually seems excited about the prospect, especially about all the money he'll make. He will undoubtedly add a unique perspective to the field, if I may say so.

I would like to know if being an athlete pays well. I wish it would be enough to pay my bills. I would hate to be poor.

After Callie and Susie left, Gunther offered to show me his terrace, which was to be accessed by the stairwell outside his window. I had never taken a stairwell, certainly not from the eighth floor of a high-rise building. To my surprise, I said yes.

What? Who's this dude with the need for cheap thrills?

Gunther went ahead of me, carrying his sleeping bag. He had told me to bring mine too. If he could do it with his oh-so-thick glasses, I could do it too! With that deeply thought-out argument, I ascended four flights of stairs to arrive at the marvel that is his terrace.

I stood there, stunned, for a long time, looking, turning my head this way and that. I had never seen so much at once—the sky, the buildings, the bridges in the distance, the night lights, the billboards, the stadium, the roads, the highways, the shops, the street lamps—the whole cheesy enchilada.

Surrealista. This would become my favorite spot.

Gunther Delgado is a perfectly satisfactory comrade. Within ten minutes, he was out like a log. The dude snores, making whistling sounds like a small trumpet being blown entirely out of tune. I should have recorded it. But I left my phone downstairs. His glasses were askew on his face. I gently took them off. I wondered how it was for him.

He is not stupid, as some kids at school claim, just weirdly eccentric in his sense of humor. And even more gangly than me. But then, who am I to comment on social graces and panache? I am the guy who dozed off and tripped on his shoelaces in the middle of the school play while playing the role of a tomato. 'Snoozy Spencer'. Get it? Glassy Gunther is undoubtedly better. Or maybe not? I don't understand the dynamics of slurs.

Interestingly, it does not seem to affect Gunther. He smiles his way through. And not a fake smile to convince others, but a smile that radiates from within. 'They just don't get me. But it's cool. One day, they will, and then it will all be fine,' he says when we ask him why it does not bother him. He is resilient that way. I am a bit jealous of him, for I can never stay out of my head about all this.

Gunther says, 'A bully gets to be one when we let him think that we are ashamed of being us.' *Eso es cierto!* For a guy who believes that a pop-up toaster is the most splendid invention by humankind, those are some seriously heavy words!

That night, I snuggled into the sleeping bag, staring at the sky. I could not get over the stars. All those stars. They seemed to be so within my reach. Their incontrovertible infiniteness made me relax. I no longer felt the burden of counting them, trying to even out their collective presence. It was not for me to worry about.

I raised my hand and waved it slowly, trying to make waves in the night sky, getting the stars to twinkle as my fingers touched them. *Asombroso*. All the loneliness that I had bottled inside me started to leak from the sides of my eyes.

I did not wipe the wetness away. I did not hide my face. I felt okay being seen for the first time in a long time. I decided to talk to the stars. I confessed to being so afraid of everything, though I cannot remember when it started.

Although I do know, I know exactly.

It was not long after I saw Mom with Jeffery, her business associate. I was six. But even then, I somehow knew that what they were doing behind Dad's back in his own house was wrong. I did not tell anyone about it. Not the day I found out. Not the day he was crying in my arms when Mom left us. Or any day after that when I saw him suffer in solitude.

They call it lying by omission. I was an accomplice in their dirty game. The stars twinkled. I took that as a sign to go on.

The stars understood. So, I went on, baring my heart about school and the kids who call me names. 'Dude, I need a freaking snooze button just to talk to you!' they would say. Just because it took me a long time to finish my words and even longer for my sentences. The harder I tried, the more challenging it became for me to talk. The more I focused on saying things properly, the less my words cooperated.

I asked the stars why kids like me were born. Or why we lived? Death would be easier than living a panicky life, surrendering instead of justifying to everyone why you mattered even though you couldn't even say a joke without faltering? When you are the freaking joke.

But then, no one else can be expected to take you seriously when your mother is torpedoing and wrecking her way through everything you've held dear in life.

Scum. Lies. Screw you, Jeffery. And to hell with you, Mom.

Mrs Garcia tells me that I put too much pressure on myself. And that speed of communication is not the key. I did not tell her, and she does not get that speed is everything. Everything.

Speed is why I run. Running gives me a thrill. A feeling of control. It makes my fears dissipate and my lies blur. At least for a while, until they catch up eventually.

Now, I talk to the stars whenever I feel overwhelmed, for they are my new friends. They don't say much, but they shimmer in comprehension and flicker in commiseration when I tell them things I don't tell anyone else. I promise them that I wouldn't let anything else change. I confess to them that counting helps me live my life as a regimented recipe of twos and fours, eights and twelves, and how it has become a part of me that I can no longer part with.

I can see them twinkle as I speak of the new sneakers that Dad got me for my last birthday. My most cherished possessions. I wore them to the track and field meet at school. And I won the silver medal. It hangs proudly on my wall, next to the few others I have won over the years—two golds, another silver, and one bronze—four in all. I want to be an athlete when I grow up. Athletes do not need to talk much to anyone. It's not like being a clerk at a bank, a checkout counter at Walmart, or a teacher—all of which require too much verbalizing.

And Mom saw to it that I was ruined for words. Forever.

So, I train hard. I run every day, giving my legs and my lungs a sound workout. It's for the future. My future.

Izzy knows how much I want to be an athlete. Dad too. He is nice that way, he cares. He just does not have a way of letting go. He needs to learn how to chill. I am not going to break so easily, Dad. I have my issues, but Dad needs to find another project rather than try to fix me.

He needs someone else to fuss over and love. He lets Izzy be for some reason. And that does not work out well for me. We argue. He never raises his voice. Ever. I throw fits and yell. And he lets me. I sense that he is afraid of something as well.

Guilt? Shame? I cannot figure out what it is.

The last time I was on the subject of him being a horrible parent, I might have said some harsh things. I am an awful person with a compromised judgment, remember? Sometimes, I feel I do not deserve him. Or rather, he deserves to have a better son. Or at least not have me as his son. He deserves a son who dares to speak the truth and allows his father to carry on with his life after a decade of it being on pause—a son who is more worthy of his love.

The stars are blurring now and the night sky is dissolving. A sooty darkness is taking over, drowning the beauty. Where are my sneakers right now? I cannot find them. I need to run. Fast. I am rooted to the spot. I am back on Agave Street, but the world looks sideways.

I am lying on the street.

People are running helter skelter. I try to look up, but my head is pounding. It hurts to breathe. *Ay ay ay.* The school bus has toppled over, its windows are shattered. Were there any kids inside? I hope they are not hurt. I see smoke and dust billowing from a ginormous hole in the wall nearby. *Que demonios.*

I cannot see the sky. My ears are ringing. My head hurts. My eyes are watery. My legs won't move. I cannot breathe.

One two three four.... One two three four.

And then I see a bright light. Are those flames?

Dad, help me, please!

Why is it raining fire from the sky? Why is everything swimming in front of my eyes?

Dad! I call out again. Dad! Izzy!

But I cannot hear my voice. Something is not right.

Que esta pasando? Is this Death?

I hear the sirens blaring. The first responders? Please save the poor kids on the school bus. I can wait. I am dispensable. I have already had a second chance at life. It is okay if my time is over. Dad and Izzy might be better off without me. I wish....

I love you, Dad, Izzy. You are my favorite stars.

Stars that fell into the soup that my life is.

I am sorry, but I do not know if I have another fight left in me.

I am tired. I am afraid. I don't know if I can ever be what you deserve.

I know that this is not what you ordered. Maybe this is one way to return your faulty shipment.

I just wish I could say goodbye … and sorry. *Lo siento.*

(7)

THE YELLOW[11] RACKET

For the ones who must hide their voice

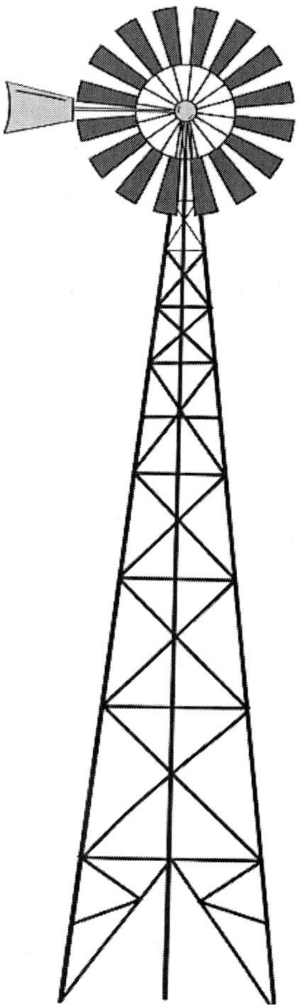

I am but you, only backward

floating on a cloud,

In this miasma of words,

Finding my voice proud

[11] The zodiac Gemini finds its connection with the colors yellow and green. Blessed by their ruling planet Mercury, those under the influence of this sign are inquisitive, curious and especially adept at adapting to changing environments and circumstances.

JUGS WRITES JIMMY A LETTER

Shimla, India

The day begins with the sound of clattering steel utensils in the kitchen. The milkman has arrived. It's half past six in the morning, for God's sake! I hold a pillow over my head. It muffles some of the morning commotion of my hyperactive joint family—sounds of flushing toilets, whistling pressure cookers and ringing doorbells. I try to stay in bed just a while longer. There is a booming knock on my door.

'Wake up, Jimmy.' Knock. Knock. Knock.

Oh, shut up! I hurl my pillow at the door.

They mean well, my family, but they don't know how to stay quiet. My solace is the bathroom attached to my meager room. It's my salvation. I go inside and it always dulls all the sounds out. Sometimes, I wish there was a big bathtub there in which I could zone out at night, away from the crazy cantankerous clamor outside. Instead, I have a folding chair that I sneak into the bathroom. I put it behind the shower curtain to sit or draw in my sketchbook. In silence.

My family likes to 'talk'. Or what they pass off as talking! Interestingly, the talking typically involves the same back and forth every day—like a worn-out rag doll being tossed about. One would imagine that Mummy would stop asking Papa how his day has been, for he no longer responds with, 'Very hectic. Lots of work. What's for dinner?' Or that *Bauji*, my grandfather would run out of complaints about this fruit or that vegetable becoming costlier than his right kidney. You'd hope that my sisters, twins, would stop giggling about every single thing that I draw in my book.

My family is stuck in a loop. From Monday to Friday, it's a race against time. Saturday is burdened with the onus of relaxation. And Sunday is too close to Monday to plan an adventure.

So, we go nowhere and do nothing. Well, most of us don't.

I am not a revolutionary kind of fellow. I know I cannot change the world. Hell, I don't think I can even change my family. But I do have rebellious thoughts. Not enough to start a movement or anything but drastic enough for someone who's been taught to be 'safe' and to 'stay out of harm's way'.

So, while I am certain I will not grow and become a start-up entrepreneur, my world has truckloads of imagination. That is something even my family cannot take away from me.

My world, Fantasmica, has color. It's a kingdom ruled by the fair and beloved King Jasper. There are no words in Fantasmica, but there is music. There is no money, but everyone is rapturous. The community there does not fight or argue. Folks do not complain about vegetable prices or giggle at someone's sketches. My world is simple, and it's captivating. And it plays out all these brilliant stories every day, stories that another human would find tough to fathom.

My world is, therefore, a secret. I haven't told anyone about it. I don't want to make my world over crowded, you see. I am quite selective about who I let in.

At the breakfast table, the usual chitchat plays out. I am zoned out, but not enough to filter it all out. I wish I had those noise-canceling headphones. Papa is going on about the rush on metro trains. Mummy is hyper about some wedding next month—her cousin sister's daughter's—and insists that all of us go. *Bauji* has been farting on about a bout of constipation.

Did you notice the clever wordplay there? Guess not. No one does. The world doesn't get my wit. Whatever!

Bauji declares that he will have only fruits until his bowels clear. The twins are arguing about the dress they want to wear at the wedding, both pitching their ideas to Mummy, who is putting jam on bread slices, while she brings up the uber urgent topic of the amount of gift money to be set aside for the newly-wed couple.

Papa tells her one thousand should be enough. *Bauji* tells him it should be one thousand one hundred and eleven. The old man's got ideas! Mummy feels strongly that it should be fifteen hundred because that's what we gifted another cousin's daughter when she got married the year before.

What's with the cash gifts anyway? Did anyone bother to ask the bride what she wanted as a present? Anyone?

The discussion veers around the value of money; the government's obnoxious tax policies; the maid's salary and hatred for the new mayor of Shimla before they settle on *Bauji's* suggestion. Meanwhile, I have my toast with butter dunked in a cold glass of plain, unflavored milk that I poured for myself. Never mind a young, starving teenager when you'd rather have a banal discussion about gifts!

At thirteen, I have not yet become a priority for my parents. I hope one day I will.

With that thought, I pick up my bag and head out to the bus stand. The school bus is already there by the time I reach. I find my usual spot in the back row empty, with others avoiding it like an affliction. It suits me well—the lone seat at the back of the bus facing the side window next to the spare tire. It helps me avoid any eye contact with the driver or the other children on the bus.

I take out my sketchbook. I carry that with me everywhere now. I don't want to find the twins ever laying their hands on it again. They are my sisters, but I do hate them!

From my spot on the bus, I can observe all the shenanigans at play and overhear surreptitious whispers about the contraband. That's me, duh! Strangely, they do not feel the need to lower their voices when talking near me. And about me. They forget that my hearing is just normal. But I guess they have nothing to fear as I am, for certain, never going to utter a word about it to anyone.

Because I don't say anything to anyone, ever. Not a word. Never.

Thrice a week, I go to see a speech therapist in the evenings. I think it's a big waste of time. I just go and sit in his room and lie down on what he calls a couch. It's more of a decrepit beach chair padded with pillows. I listen to him ramble. He must think he is helping me in some way. At least he sincerely tries to.

I feel sorry for him, especially when he comes up with new experiments or games to break my silence. When I am overwhelmed with pity, I make some sound, letting him think that I am trying. I can see the joy it brings him when I do that. He scribbles perkily in his notebook throughout our sessions. He must have been one of those studious front benchers in school.

It has been two-and-a-half years and he has not managed to get me to speak my name again. What keeps him going, I cannot fathom. I might have given up by now. But then, he gets paid quite handsomely for it, if I were to go by Papa's 'talks'.

He never asks me how I am doing or how my day has been. Yet, he does not hesitate to remind me how I am wasting his hard-earned moolah. I want to tell him that he can save money. Why pay someone else to talk to me when he could.... Never mind!

On my way back from therapy, I always stop by this old *mithai* shop near Mall Road. I often walk this way, letting myself drown in the din that envelopes the air. I don't know what it is, but that old Superman poster on the wall calls out to me. So now, I just walk in, point to my sweet craving for the day and hand out a ten-rupee note. The *halwaai* hands me the delight in a paper cup or plate.

Just like me, he never speaks. I like him.

There is this tacit arrangement that we both are cool with. He is the only person I smile at. He never smiles back, going about very business-like weaving spirals on oil, magically turning them into *jalebis.* These sweet spirals are pretty magical, just like the delicacies one gets to eat in Fantasmica. Today, I have chosen *rasmalai,* served in a diminutive but cute earthen *kulhad* with a bamboo-wood spoon.

I need to sit down to eat or else I will spill the sweet milky syrup all over myself. There is no room on the wooden bench. A man in his forties scooches over and makes room for me, pointing to the now vacant space next to him.

He smiles as if coddling a child, tapping the bench with his palm, saying, 'Come over here, it's okay.'

Over and over again.

I freeze as I look at the man's crooked *paan*-stained teeth and checkered shirt. My senses are now fraught with panic as he repeats, 'Come over here, it's okay;' 'Come;' 'Come here,' 'Come on.'

I take a few steps back and bump into the *halwaai*, dropping my *rasmalai* over the pavement. The *halwaai* gives me a disapproving look, but before he can say anything, I make a run for it.

I do not turn or stop until I reach home, running out of breath while a paranoid mist threatens to escape my heavy eyelids.

When I enter the house, I am still breathing hard. I stop when I find Jagjit Chacha, or Jugs as I call him, sitting in the living room, sipping *adrak chai*. He is my father's cousin and he used to stay with us for a bit when I was younger. He looks up at me while he sips his tea.

My face turns pale and I cannot control my tears anymore. I cannot help letting it out. I cannot stop thinking about the man at the *halwaai* shop, the dried *paan* stains on both sides of his mouth. Is that where the Joker found his inspiration?

Mummy is alarmed to see me. She wraps me into her arms and orders the twins to fetch some water. She keeps fussing, asking if I am alright and whether anyone has said anything to me. My eyes are locked with Jugs. He lets out a slow breath, eyes still latched on me, nudging me to relax. I do not register Mummy's words as I gulp down two glasses of cold water without stopping for breath.

I find an excuse to go to my room and lock the door from the inside. I lay down in bed, draw up my blanket and close my eyes. Next to me is my neon yellow badminton racket.

I always have it by my bed. It gives me strength.

It is a strange color for a badminton racket. Or so I thought when Jugs gifted it to me for my fourth birthday. But it did not matter. The bright yellow made it stand out from the black and blue frames that everyone else had. It was exceptional. Playing badminton made me feel like I was flying in the air. I loved it. I would regularly get my racket re-wired, and no one, not even the twins, was allowed to touch it. In Fantasmica, badminton players command the highest level of respect.

I do not play anymore. I miss it.

The last time I played was approximately three years ago. It was the same summer when....

I cling onto the frame with all my might, sobbing uncontrollably until I drift into Fantasmica, the land without evil. Vroko, the djinn, comes to life as I drift deeper into sleep, carrying me on his magic silver carpet over deep blue waters, my yellow racket by my side. My long robes are billowing in the breeze as I gaze upon the verdant greens and the deep blues of Fantasmica.

My red parakeet, Mr Prattles, flies up and settles on my shoulder. He gives me updates from across the kingdom, cooing in his unique musical language that can be heard only in Fantasmica. He tells me about the discovery of unicolor rainbows and purple, flying peacocks. He shares tales from the music carnival and narrates the new play that people from my kingdom have written about me, a paean of sorts called, 'The Legend of Jimmy, The....'

'Wait, whose voice is that? Mr Prattles?'

'Jimmy. Jimmyyy, Jimmmmyyyyyy.'

The urgency with which my name is being called out is growing steadily. On no, that's Mummy.

Her voice echoes deep concern for my well-being. I get up, unlatch the door and then lie down again. She walks gingerly into my room and sits next to me; caresses my hair and plants a gentle kiss on my head. I recoil at her touch. She withdraws, quietly gets up and leaves. She probably thinks it's another tantrum from her troubled son who has made a habit of imagining problems when there are none and who would rather cry in the loneliness of his room than talk to his family.

I have not spoken to her or anyone for almost three years now.

She has made peace with it. Typical! Just like she made peace with Papa's drinking and with *Bauji's* taunts. Just like she made peace with what I had told her. I don't know if she ever believed any of it. But I know she has long forgotten about it. Or, at least, she pretends to have forgotten about it, just like everyone else.

I will never forget.

It's less than a minute since she's left that there is another knock on my door. Again. I do not lift my head to check. I know it's Jugs. I can tell from the telltale odor of coconut oil from his hair. Coconut is the national fruit of Fantasmica. I am glad he is here. But I shut my eyes and pretend to be dozing.

He draws up a chair next to me and sits there, not making a sound. I feel the dab of his handkerchief on my face as he wipes my tears while I focus on orchestrating the sounds of sleep-breathing. He runs his slender fingers through my hair, a habit that has not changed. His hand lingers a while longer. He pats and kisses the top of my head gently as he gets up to leave.

I reach out and hold his leg at the knee.

He smiles as if he knew all along that I was just pretending. He looks at me but does not ask me anything. He will give me time until I am ready to tell him. I calm down. He has that effect on me.

After dinner, Jugs offers to buy me ice cream. The twins are not invited. For a change, my parents think it's better to do it this way. Good riddance. If there is anyone in the world who can prioritize me over the sinister sisters, it's Jugs!

We walk in silence to a nearby ice cream parlor. They have just modernized it and turned it into somewhat of a sit-in cafe. Some changes can be nice! We are their only customers at the moment. In my trademark style, I point to a picture of a choco bar. Jugs orders a *kulfi* for himself.

I cannot stop shivering. He puts his hand on the base of my neck. I do not flinch. I know I am safe with him. But I keep looking over my shoulder, half-expecting the man from the *halwaai* shop with his *paan*-stained teeth and checkered shirt, afraid of hearing his words.

Those words.

As we bite into our frozen delights, I remember the day when I had first told Papa.

* * *

Papa had come home late. I could tell he was drunk. Mummy had warned me not to say anything, but I was genuinely scared to go back to school. I had told Mummy earlier that month. But she had shushed me, telling me not to tell anyone else.

She was uncomfortable knowing.

She did not accept or did not want to accept.

So, she was okay sending me back every day for more torment. I had hoped Papa would understand. He did not. No sooner had I told him that he slapped me. He called me a scoundrel. He threw his shoe at me and kept telling me that I had a sick mind.

I was ten, for God's sake! Why would I make that kind of filth up?

I kept saying that I was not lying.

He kept hitting me and Mummy just stood there, looking and feeling powerless.

I told my parents that I hated them. I called them cowards and impostors and told them that I loathed my life. I promised them I would slit my wrists.

And then I could not speak anymore.

Had Jugs not returned from office just then, I don't know what I'd have done that night. He took Papa away and put him to bed. He sat Mummy down and gave her a glass of water with Disprin. And he took me to my room, wiped my face, and held me in his arms until I fell asleep. When I woke up the next morning, he was still holding my hand, my head against his chest.

Over the next few days, I stayed in my room. Jugs stayed with me. We watched cartoon films and read comics. No one else was invited. I could see Mummy and Papa talk in muted voices, but Jugs did not let them speak with me. Every time they tried, I hid behind him and closed my eyes, refusing to say anything in response. I could tell he wanted to talk to me, to understand.

So, I wrote him a letter, telling him my truth—when it started, who was involved, and how scared it all made me feel. He did not say anything when I handed it to him.

As he read it, I was scared, afraid that he might get upset with me as well. But as he read on, two things happened. He started to shiver and his eyes melted into tears.

Something inside him snapped.

He raced across the room and embraced me tightly, telling me I had nothing to fear, assuring me that he would keep me safe and unhurt. And I trusted that he would.

Since that day, Jugs has been there to rescue me every time I have needed him. He is the inspiration behind Jasper, the true and only king of all the realms within Fantasmica—from the valleys of the north to the great plateaus of the south; from the islands in the west to the canyons in the east. He is the fair one, the kind one, the one who blesses everyone with his divinity. Jasper is loved by everyone and Vroko has sworn to protect him for eternity. Mr Prattles loves Jasper, too, almost as much as he loves Jimmy.

* * *

What happened earlier today at the *halwaai* shop had, perhaps, just been a panic attack. And nothing bad actually happened. I had not let that man hurt me.

I feel Jugs' firm hand on my shoulder. I realize I have been trembling. He is trying to help me calm down. I see him tearing up, the same way he did that night three years ago.

I know he cares for me, but there is something else.

I recall all those times when I'd seen him hang his head and look away from me as if trying to hide emotions that were too much to handle. There is something about me that triggers this in him.

* * *

Jugs left for the US around two-and-a-half years ago. The six months before his departure were, to say the least, eventful.

The day after that fateful night when Jugs rescued me from my father's rage, he lodged an FIR with the police station without asking for my parents' permission. He also visited the principal's office to make an official complaint and ensured that the school expelled one of its own, refusing to accept anything but retribution.

He did what my parents did not do or even approve of him doing. My happy-to-turn-a-blind-eye scared-of-god-knows-what parents, who told him that he was a cousin and that he needed to maintain his boundaries. They blamed him for bringing disgrace to the family name. They told him to pack his things and leave. I hated them for it.

Hail Jasper, the mighty king!

I loved him for rooting for me while he fought the case in court, renting a room next door to ensure he was nearby. He had understood my words when my parents had not.

He had felt my pain. And more than anything else, he had cared to do something to make me feel inviolable again. I would never be pushed into dark corners. No one would force me to pull my pants down. I wouldn't let anyone's breath or hands sully my body. Never again!

The following month, Jugs enrolled me in a different school. I was happy to make a fresh start. But I was not ready to trust anyone. The deadening volume of silence had permanently muffled my voice. I had already stopped talking to everyone. Mummy did not know how hushed to be around me and Papa averted his gaze every time I crossed his path. The twins were too young to understand anything, but they also learned that they needed to leave me alone.

For them, I was an oddity in their lives with no explanation or justification. And it suited me just fine.

The night before Jugs was leaving for the US, I tried to force myself to sleep. I conjured Vroko and ordered him to burn a forest down to ashes. Mr Prattles calmed me down and reminded me that fires in Fantasmica did not burn anything for real. Then I ordered Vroko to waylay Jugs' plane or plead with King Jasper to brainwash Jugs into staying. Vroko's eyes reflected my sadness.

I could not sleep that night.

At midnight, I quietly went to his room. The door was open, as always. His packed suitcases were lined below the window. I sat on the floor next to his feet, determined to meet him once before he left.

But I woke up the next morning right there on the floor, a thin blanket covering my lanky frame. Jugs had left. I had wanted to say goodbye, but I knew he did not want me to go through that pain. Underneath the blanket, I found a handwritten note tucked under my yellow badminton racket:

'Jimmy. I am sorry to leave you like this without a proper goodbye; I did not want to wake you up.

I am going away today, but I am not leaving you. I wish I could take away your pain. But that is not how it works. I will come back someday soon. I promise. But until then, please be my brave little warrior. Sometimes, others may make you feel that you need to be strong. They may expect you to put on a face that says you are okay. It is OK not to be OK, at least for a while, as long as you keep trying to feel like yourself again. Take your time, but promise me that you will not give up.

Know that the demons from the past may still linger around for some time. So, what you must do is learn how to fight them. Remember what I told you, what we practiced? They cannot hurt you now—you are not alone. Try to focus on your books and go out to play with your friends. Eat jalebis and paint in your book. Fight not to let what happened take all that away.

Write to me any time. I will send my address to your Papa soon. You know you call me anytime you wish to hear my voice. I promise not to sing. I know you think I am pretty out of tune. Whenever you choose to speak is your decision. I will wait to listen whenever you are ready, my little warrior.

You know how special you are to me.

Love, Jasper.'

* * *

A rattle of chairs nearby brings me back to the present. The ice cream cafe. My Chocobar ice cream has half melted by now. Jugs is slowly eating his *kulfi*, waiting for me to ... to do something. Anything. He is just there.

After he left, I had never written to him. Not once. I did not know what to write or how to go about it. How could I tell Papa to post my letter when he resented Jugs for messing with their lives? For my parents, Jugs had been the enemy that tore their family apart. They had only been too elated to see him leave.

I secretly wish that Jugs was my father. I wish I could go with him forever, leaving my broken namesake of a family behind. He is here, again, sitting next to me when I need him. He never forces me to say anything, to be anyone, or to do anything for him. He quietly lets me be.

Most of all, he can feel my pain. Even now, he is so affected by it, as if he has lived that horror himself, as if he was there watching an unimpaired view with his own eyes, in the dingy sports room at school ... as if....

And then I know.

I get up and go over to his side of the table. I stand in front of him and look him in the eye. He is perplexed. He picks up a tissue and cleans a bit of chocolate from my face, smiling gently. I look at him with inquiring eyes, probing to find confirmation of what I know must have happened to him.

He asks me if I need anything, holding up the bottle of water. I don't speak. He gets up and clears the table. We pay and leave.

I am still staring at him. But I don't talk.

We go to the park, where we sit down at our favorite wooden bench by the fountain, looking at the street dogs playing without a care in the world. He holds me close, instinctively guarding me against the evening breeze. I hold on to him tightly.

He looks at me again and tells me that he is sorry for leaving like that. He knows that I know what he is talking about. I do not react. He tells me that he is around for a few weeks and promises to spend time with me every weekend.

I hold on tighter, a nervous smile on my face.

He talks about his life in the US and how he missed being in India. He tells me about his cooking disasters in the kitchen and his struggle with escalators. He speaks of his boss, the university dean, who seems like a first-rate jerk by the way he treats others. He tells me about his friend Emmett and how I'd love to hang out with Emmett's son, who is just a couple of years younger than I am.

I know Jugs is just trying to cheer me up. Then, he asks me again if I am okay, or if I need him to do anything.

And he is stunned to hear my first words after three years.

'You can tell me, Jasper. You can tell me about your monster. Don't let him win. Don't surrender. You fought for me. Now, let me fight for you. I can be your little warrior.'

deep inside the dark forest

hidden away under the warm blue moon

a silent prayer finally breathes

Gemini (May 21 - Jun 20) | Mercury | Citrine

I may have been hurt, but I am not weak.

SPENCER DIAZ CRAVES MORPHINE

Texas, USA

I am feeling less dizzy than usual. My head does not hover inside itself so much now. The monitors seem to be beeping less boisterously. I heard Izzy talking to Dad, telling him how some color has returned to my face. Is that the sound of hope?

Dad told her that he believed that I would bounce back now that my brain was getting stronger. They do not mention what is bothering them. I am still placed twelfth on the transplant list if Sandie's gossip is to be believed. If I do not find a donor soon, there will not be much of a bounce back happening. They should quickly find a bucket for me to kick ... just in case.

See what I did there? I still got it!

Izzy was here last night with Devon. She offered to give Dad a break, and he relented grudgingly. For crying out loud, come on. *Vamos!* Dad does not seem to mind Devon, who, to my surprise, does not sound like a drug dealer. No serial killer vibes, either. I bet sociopaths and murderers do not talk with modesty and respect. But what do I know? Anyways, he is a marine biologist and is leading a high-profile research project on the preservation of corals. Houston, we have a problem! But he sounds way too geeky to be a scamster. I might need to let this one go for now.

But just when I was about to change my opinion of him, he said the most unthinkable thing. 'Have you checked if your mom is a match? I mean, that might just work. She is his birth mother, after all.'

Izzy should have shut him up. *Qué absurdo!* Instead, she asked, 'Do you think she would? Dad will lose his marbles if I….'

That idiot Devon went on, 'You need to at least try, Izzy. This might be Spencer's only shot.'

Dude, this is not some fishing expedition of yours? We are talking about a woman who left her entire family for … for what? Jeffery? Her career? Not wanting to be my mother? I do not want a lung from that treacherous woman who played us all.

Mom is not welcome back in my life. Or Dad's. Or Izzy's.

Devon needed to shut up. Instead, he convinced Izzy. *Cáspita!* Devon is back on my blacklist of dudes who are not allowed to date my sister. I would think a marine biologist would have more tact than that. Unacceptable. Izzy should break up with him right now. It's a matter of principle.

People need to think about other people—people whose lives are affected by their words and actions; people who depend on them for being there in their lives; people who may or may not be able to survive without them, no matter how pathetic their presence has been; people who know them for the liars they are but still crave their pathetic presence in their family.

Mom is people. I am people. Dad and Izzy are people.

People cannot saunter off whenever they want without heeding other people. People tend to go berserk when other people go AWOL.

My head hurts. I want to sleep. Just seal my eyes and drift off. I wish Rose would hit me with some morphine right now.

I can hear her whispering. Is that the sweet smell of hospital gossip? Is that Sandie? Rose and Sandie just have enough time to exchange hellos and enquire about me at every shift change. Sometimes, Sandie tells Rose about her dickhead of a husband and Rose complains about her neighbor's nagging. They seem to be in a chatty mood today. I bet they are pitying the morbid, short life of their absolute favorite patient, Spencer Diaz.

But there is something naughty about their chatter today, sans all the downcast pall of gloom that the hospital is. Are they fighting over who gets to give the charming hunk lying on the bed a hot sponge bath and a change of diaper? Gosh, I am such a player.

I soon figure that the subject of their giddy attention is not me, but a certain visitor in the lobby, who is waiting for an appointment with Dr Miller, Dr Alvarez and some of the other senior doctors. I wish I could see the dude. Rose is guffawing about how perfectly he fits the definition of tall, dark and handsome. Sandie oohs and aahs about his biceps that barely fit in his tight blue shirt.

I need some tips from this guy. Who is this mystery visitor casting such a spell on my nurses? I cannot get any girl at school to go mad about me like that. There are plenty who get mad at me, but never about me. *¡Así es la vida!* It's quite strange that I haven't had a single drive-me-crazy romance in my three years of post-pubescent life. I was hoping that the hormones would do their trick, but I guess it takes a lot for someone to see me that way.

In all fairness, when I turned fourteen, I did sorta ask Violet out for a mocha latte. But she just sneered and left me standing like a noob in the corridor. What was I thinking? She would rather stick chewing gum in her hair than go out with a snooze button.

I haven't been able to bring myself to that level of extraordinary courage ever since.

My current strategy is to let love find me.

I am not desperate for it or jealous of those who have found it. Although it would be nice to have a girlfriend, to belong to a special girl for whom you are a special guy (and not an especially needy guy). Callie promised that she'd help me, but I am not sure how. She has the social dexterity of an amputated octopus. I need to up my ante if I do not want to die a virgin. Let me put that on my bucket list if I survive this.

Presently, Rose and Sandie keep coochie-cooing about this supposed eye candy of a man before I hear Dr Miller speak from a distance.

'Welcome to Verde Vista Memorial Hospital, Mr Anirudh. Sorry to keep you waiting, and more so after your long flight from Delhi. I had a long surgery. This is Dr Alvarez, who heads Trauma, and Dr Kauffman from the ER. We reviewed the proposal from your firm ... er ... Medicallis? The mobility aids and rehab equipment look promising. Some of our trauma patients could use them, especially the ones recovering from brain injury. We have a few active cases in our Critical Care Unit, even as we speak. To think that we can accelerate the recovery for these patients who haven't walked for months ... it's priceless. We would love to discuss a few more things, especially the lab results and clinical trials. Why don't we go to a conference room to discuss this further? This way, please.'

I hear Sandie and Rose giggle like college girls as their handsome hunk walks away with the doctors.

By the way, I just realized that Sandie's real name is Sandie. What are the odds? Okay, I might have heard someone call her that before I gave her that name. That does seem more probable. But I just also found out that Rose is not Rose at all. Her real name is Simona.

That's a nice name. Rose is better. I guess she just has to get used to being called Rose.

All this distraction alleviated things a bit. But it's not enough. I hope Izzy is not trying to be a hero. She does not need to beg that woman. Not for me. Our lives are complicated enough as it is. I don't want to … I mean.… She does not understand how.…

Mom did not just cheat on Dad. She did not just desert us. She started this whole chain of horridness that our lives have become. Certainly mine.

The beginning of my stutter.

My insatiable need to count.

The bullying.

A life of fear and loneliness.

The anger at being abandoned.

And turned it all into a murky soup of pitiful existence. The sessions with Mrs Garcia don't seem to have helped. *Ay ay ay.*

However, I am very clear that I do not want anything from Mom now. *¡Nada que hacer!* Nope. Never.

She does not get to feel righteous about saving my life. She does not get to be my mother after all this. I will not let her ruin us again. She will not take anything more away from me. Not again.

This needs to stop. *Por favor.* I am relying on Dad to shut Izzy down. Izzy needs to deal with it as does Devon.

I must have slept off, seething with these emotions, for when I wake up, I can sense Dad by my side. It is Dr Miller's voice that wakes me up. He is not alone.

I hear him saying, 'Mr Anirudh. This is Spencer, the patient I was telling you about earlier, from the blast downtown—the Patient Alpha for this trial.'

Did he say Patient Alpha? I have never been an alpha anything!

Dr Miller is a rockstar. He continues, 'We've been doing regular physiotherapy and induced activations, but there has been significant muscle atrophy in the last few weeks. I hope the equipment we've commissioned from you can help. His father here, Señor Diaz, just gave consent.'

A deep bass voice, which I gather belongs to the too-sexy-for-his-own-good Mr Anirudh from India, says, 'Hope you are well, Señor Diaz. Did I say that right?' Damn, he is a charmer. Isn't he? Sandie and Rose did not stand a chance. Good on you, Mr Anirudh.

Dad responds, 'It is perfect. Thank you. Days like today, people like you are the reason I can keep going, while my son....'

Mr Anirudh steps closer to Dad, perceptibly close to my bed, and says, 'Thanks to Dr Miller. I just hope that this trial can help your son. I am glad to meet you, to know he has someone fighting for him while he can't.' I feel his voice get heavy, and then he goes quiet, his words veiling something behind them.

Dad also seems to notice it, for he asks, 'Do you have any children of your own, Señor?'

Mr Anirudh clears his throat before responding, 'Well, almost.'

'So, a little one on the way? Son or daughter?' Dad can barely hide his excitement for a stranger he met ten seconds ago. That's such a classic Dad thing to do.

Mr Anirudh does not speak, but I can sense him trembling when he leans against the rails of my bed as if sand has given way under his bare feet on a barren beach. I have become such a ninja at the subtle discerning of human movements!

Dad asks him, 'Is everything alright, son?'

Mr Anirudh seems caught off guard by this sudden warmth from Dad. He clears his throat and replies in a voice that lacks the certainty it held before, 'I lost the baby ... and my wife soon after ... It was a few months back. It was ... she was not well.... It was an accident, of course. She did not mean to.... It was tough for her to.... We tried to.... Well, it happened. So ... yeah.'

There is a stunned silence in the room. Time seems to stop. The tremors from his hands stir the sedentary stillness of my existence. Dad manages to speak, '*Oh Dios, ten Piedad!* I am so sorry, my dear.'

After a few moments, Mr Anirudh lets go of the rails, finds his voice again, oozing a serenity I know must be fake, and says, 'I may not be a father, but I can imagine the torment you must feel. I will pray that Spencer is up and running marathons once again. We need brave young men like him to build a better world. I wish he wakes up soon.' He squeezes my shoulder gently and turns away as he says goodbye to Dad.

I say a secret prayer for him in return. I hope he gets to be a father someday. I have more than an inkling that he'll be a good one, just like mine.

I hear their footsteps retreat into the hospital corridor.

My room is quiet once more.

My head is not thumping now and my breath is steady. I do not feel any pain. There is no darkness lurking around the corners of my eyes.

I think of the stars in the sky above Gunther's terrace.

I thank my friends from the Milky Way and beyond for sending a dollop of hope my way.

(8)

THE SILVER[12] VESSEL

For the ones who are forever alone

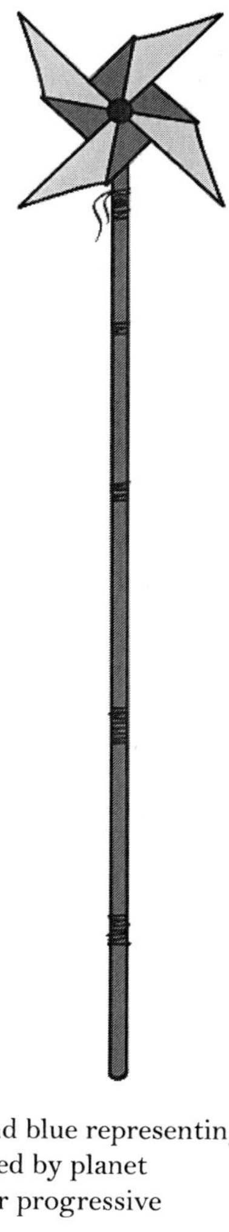

Waking up after being awake

Decisions, choices I must make

Now, at this moment, today

Like a mound of wet clay

[12] One often finds the colors silver, aquamarine, violet and blue representing the zodiac of Aquarius. Those with this sun sign are ruled by planet Uranus and known to challenge the status quo with their progressive thoughts.

ALEX IS HOME ALONE

Unknown Location

The name's Alex. Alex Stanton. That sounded a lot more macho inside my head.

I've just touched down for the night. I call it 'touching down' because it sounds fancy. I have fancy names for several things now. My new personal vocabulary. My own new language. I can call things whatever the heck I want to call them. Like nectarines. I call them gornels now.

Why? Just because. Why not?

After all, the main purpose of language is to communicate your thoughts to someone else. But since we are officially not doing that anymore, I may as well damn the old plenary rules laid down by Mr Johnson or Mr Murray or whoever it is that fathered the English language.

The point is that language no longer needs rules; that there is no 'someone else' I need to communicate with and that there hasn't been a need for it for a while.

I have always been an introvert all my life, but that was a choice, I believe, I made. Some may not agree, but I do not feel like using my words when they are not needed or with people who are not in the least bit alluring to talk to.

But this? This is something I did not choose.

I feel like a refugee fleeing the scene of a raging war, forced to seek asylum in another place he must now call his home, mandated to learn an alien language in which he must now express his thoughts. Those who make the rules do not realize what it truly means to be a refugee in your own life.

Perhaps it's not their fault. It must be tough making all those rules for the rest of us—the ordinary people.

Tonight, my vessel has landed in the middle of this lush meadow. And before you ask, a meadow is still called a meadow. I won't change perfectly nice words just to play god with language. I am still figuring out the right way to address my vessel. I call it my cell some days, or my container or pod, or a barge, depending on numerous things that go into that decision. But for now, let us call it a vessel. Besides, what we call it is not important anymore. No one's delivering my favorite *Quattro Formaggio* pizza here anytime soon. Or ever.

The meadow is a vast, verdant expanse of wild growth, edged by a canopy of maple trees, their branches swaying in the evening breeze that runs through my hair. My hair has grown to my waist, not having been cut for over a year. Having just descended from the sky, the air does not feel cold. I take off my parka jacket and scarf, neatly fold them and place them in the drawer at the far end of the vessel.

I look out of the window and see distant specks of other vessels lining the expanse of the meadow. It's getting dark and my eyes cannot make out how many there are. It's been a while since I've been to one of these parks or, as I prefer to call them, waystations. I must stay here for a few days, longer than my previous halts. There are multiple chores to be completed, things I have been putting off for way too long. Like recharging my supply of seeds and manure by foraging the woods at night when no one is looking. I must also desilt the rainwater tank and clean out the solar panels. Plus, the mast needs some repairs. I could wash some of my linen and clothes in the freshwater stream I spotted nearby. Heavens permitting, I might even cut my hair.

It may be a bit of a walk to get to the stream. Other than that frothing delight, I have not spotted even a stray goat in the area nearby.

But right now, I am a bit tired. Maneuvering a vessel with a mast requires skill and I am afraid that even the last three years of free sailing have not helped me master it yet. As a matter of principle and morbid fear, therefore, I avoid landing the vessel as much as I can. Of course, that is only until the batteries and the other supplies last.

I lay down on my bunk, which I call *de chiajeder* (but I will spare you more of my new vocabulary training right now). It used to be fluffy and comfortable when I started my journey, which was two days after the training was over. But it has become flaccid now, with compressed craters where I often rest or sit.

At the academy, there was much to learn and considerable skills to acquire. Some were easier—cooking, cleaning and scrubbing, for instance—because I had been assisting my father with his food truck for years. I had the whole house help thing down pat.

It's useful nonsense like tying sailor knots or catching fish from a stream that I sucked at during training. I knew because of the looks of recurring disillusionment written in Helvetica Bold on my coach's face. Dressed in a surgical suit with an astronaut-like bubble head of glass, inhaling pristine quality oxygen through the ridiculous pump strapped to his back, he looked straight out of a sci-fi movie.

Except that this movie is now my life. All of our lives.

The program at the academy was over in three months. In the end, they did vaccine therapy, followed by what they called holistic rehabilitation. More like an utter waste of time and borderline torture. Plus, a whole battery of medical tests. I had so many needles poked into my arm that I feared I might start leaking. They did not hand out a certificate or a report card when we 'graduated'. Just an entry into the system stating the curriculum had been completed.

I felt nothing when I was told that I had passed. Just a knot at the pit of my stomach, waiting to be assigned a pod. I used to call it a pod, then. I should not have bothered because all the pods look the same. A twenty by sixteen quenelle-shaped oblong elliptical structure made of a super-lightweight metal painted silver.

Why are some mortals so aesthetically depraved? Silver?

I stepped into mine tentatively, carefully considering my steps. I was surprised that the walls looked rather flat despite the outer shape of the pod.

Containers or pods are either waterborne—fitted with their rudders and propellers—or landborne, with old-world tires and engines, or in rare cases, airborne—with a motor and a mast. Since I get motion sickness on boats and roads were bound to be clogged with migrants everywhere, my choice was obvious. A handsome bribe to the selection supervisor sealed the deal for me. I was surprised to see how effortlessly I slid a wad of cash into his welcoming hands.

Did I always have a flexible definition of morality?

Such a social interaction would have been impossible for me just a few months ago. But then everything changed. I changed. I had to.

I was permitted to bring some of my possessions along when the program at the academy began. The crewman told me they were packed in two cartons labeled 'Alex Stanton, 17, Region XIV', kept at the back of the pod. I brought some clothes, two pairs of shoes, some old pictures, a few books, my paints & brushes, two rolls of canvas, a pillow and three bedsheets. And loads of toilet paper and cleaning supplies.

Though many have implied it, I must clarify that I don't identify with the word germaphobe. I just value hygiene as a mandatory life skill on account of my asthma. And there is nothing wrong with educating your classmates about the value of cleanliness.

The crewman offered customizations to my vessel for a stipulated fee. What would he do with the money? Did he hope for a return to the 'jolly good old times'?

I had plenty after emptying all my accounts. I got him to install two solar panels, a simple rainwater harvesting system and wall racks for a vertical garden. I am weirdly big on sustainable energy sources, plastic-free oceans, green alternatives and so on. Some argue that this drives away potential friends. I agree. I know the world's worst conversation starters. It is good that I never got invited to parties.

My most prized takeaway was an old typewriter and some dusty sheaves of paper. There may be some hope for me after all.

I still had a lot of cash left.

So, the crewman made one final modification. A section of the vessel's floor was fitted with a giant fiberglass window, a portal to see the world from above, like the drone videos on Discovery channel. I tried looking down when we first took off, but it did not go too well. I almost peed my cargo pants. But I deny any fear of heights. Anyone would be nervous about it.

Slowly, I learned to enjoy the view, cherishing the unique vantage point, away from the inflictions that plagued the world below. The air up there made me breathe easy and my fear was gone. So was my asthma. I'd stocked up on asthma pumps and epidural pens, but I have not needed to use any of them for months.

The few hundred meters that separate me from the ground give me the equanimity that I've always craved.

As I lay down in the grass now, my thoughts wander to the old times. I mean the recent old times, not ancient old times. The Administration had offered the adult citizens of the New World two options, in a very democratic spirit of decisions made 'by' the people, 'for' the people and whatever the third one is.

Every adult had to pick one, failing which the Care Council in the Administration would decide for them. There was a slight catch. Citizens above sixty years of age—the Wise Elders as the Administration called them—had only one choice.

Which meant no choice!

So did children below fourteen. They were tied to the decision of their parents. The Care Council, however, had very considerately provided an option for parents to hand over the raising of their children, along with all future parental rights, to the Administration. A secure future for a petty fee and a single signature. If parents chose to bring their children with them, they would need to arrange for the resources needed by their progeny, and no one had any savings left.

For qualifying adults, the first option was to move to one of the bubble colonies set up by the Administration. Each colony comprised not more than a few thousand individuals curated by a supercomputer with no-one-gives-a-damn-intelligence called Tyche, after the Greek goddess of fortune.

Who comes up with such pretentious names for machines?

Bubble colonies had closed borders, allowing no movement in or out, run by a self-sufficient motley aggregation of humans across different professions.

Wise Elders stayed in a special home inside the bubble colony. All the men in these colonies were mandated to undergo a tiny, simple procedure called vasectomy. Snip snip! Couples wanting to be parents would need to be cleared by the Administration for an IVF, which was 'apparently' the best way for controlled growth of the colony.

Inter-colony visa rules were just as straightforward as airlifting the Redeemer Statue from Buenos Aires to your backyard. The Care Council would arrange for yearly vaccines against new strains of deadly viruses and other contagions that have wiped out half the world's population in the last ten years. If you still contracted the infection, you'd be quarantined out at the Island of Dawn.

More like the Island of Your Last Sunset!

In short, the first option sucked.

So, I chose the second one.

It essentially involved signing off a waiver from being cared for by the Administration. A clean chit to them saying, 'We couldn't care less.' In return, they would take you through a generous three-month crash course to train you at the 'tools' you may need for survival such as food, energy, illness and safety, while strictly staying within a personal bubble —the pod or the vessel.

Paying for these personal jail cells was the cherry on the cake. Those choosing this option were called the New Nomads, who would be exempt from all citizenship rules and would not need permits or visas to travel by land, air, or water. However, they would not be permitted to stay in any one location for more than ten days and would necessarily stay at least ten feet away from another New Nomad. An electronic chip would buzz an electric shock right to your bones if you ever forgot.

You could take walks out in the open, just not while holding anyone's hand. You could sleep under an open sky, just not cuddle next to someone unless you are really into experiencing blood-curdling shock waves.

Tonight, I look up to the starry night from the lone window in the vessel. And I am filled with a strange longing for what I left behind. My parents. I had not told them about my decision. I did not know how. I looked at the empty road for a long time after their bus took them to the colony.

'They'll be fine. I'll be fine. Eventually,' I remember thinking.

Nothing ever remains bad forever. Unless it's drizzled honey on French fries. There is no redemption there. I remember when I waved *au revoir* to my only two mates, Caleb and Mino, both miraculously destined for the same bubble colony. Saying goodbye to them made my heart wrench.

I maintain that I did not cry like a little girl on the way back, despite what the cabbie may claim.

Person by person, my childhood neighborhood withered away, leaving behind dry skeletons of the past. Until what was left of it all was a few nutcases like me who had chosen the life of a New Nomad.

Mino had begged me to reconsider. I overheard him speak with Caleb as they fretted, 'Alex won't survive alone. Not with his asthma. What if he has another panic attack? What if he gets sick? I wish he would....'

I loved them for it. But I could not bring myself to budge, for I had already lost so much to fear and logical reasoning. After twenty-nine lockdowns, eighteen vaccines and three hospital visits, I was done. I just could not sign up for a lifetime of trepidation. I would rather die of a disease than let life be taken away ounce by ounce.

I wanted to tell them all this, but words have never been my friends. It's not that introverts do not feel. They just don't know what feelings are okay to share.

Since then, I have crossed paths with other New Nomads, and my belief has grown stronger. Sometimes, when we touch down and our vessels have windows facing each other, we get a peek inside each other's lives. We have chats about our journeys and share stories of the loved ones we've left behind.

Strangely, I feel lonelier after these conversations than actual days of being by myself.

Surprisingly, over time, I have become okay at striking conversations, with necessity being the mother of inventions and all.

But I mostly talk to myself or to the pictures I have, like the ones of my parents. Unlike before, I now tell them everything—I do not hold back anything. I even talk to my classmates, particularly to Caleb and Mino. I like these conversations. There is no interjection, no judgment, no one teasing you for saying the wrong thing.

There is no need to filter anything anymore.

I am like a new mutated strain of the old Alex.

I know I am different now. I mimic the cry of a wolf in the distance. I marvel at hearing the buzzmouths, my new name for crickets. I shush myself when I hear the rustle of the leaves. I feel the smell of the freshly- cut grass. And I write down the thoughts in my head. And I read them back to myself later. It's all fine. I wish it had always been this fine. I wish I had gone with Caleb and Mino to their bubble colony. Maybe.

My musing circles back to the present, and I see hundreds of fireflies floating at the edge of the canopy, like the lights in a discotheque. Gosh, I wish I had gone clubbing when I still had the chance. The sight makes me want to dance. And sing, of course, because my phone has long since died, and there is no laptop or boombox. So here I am, in my undies, gyrating to 'Being Alive' with shameless glee and merriment that I never thought I had inside me.

Mutant Alex knows some moves. Groovy!

As the night turns to day, I am still awake. I have an undersized loom and I have been weaving this fabric using an Incan pattern. My stomach grumbles and I must cook something. Just then, I hear someone call out from a neighboring pod. I wave back and I am suddenly embarrassed at my nakedness. I quickly duck, fetch a pair of bottoms and pull them on.

She is giggling when I stand back up. The sound of her laughter is like that of a gushing spring, full of life. We are about thirty feet apart and I was not even aware our voices could carry that far. Surprisingly, they do. She tells me that I sing well. Holy cluck!

Did she hear me murder those pop songs last night? Then she tells me I dance better, suppressing laughter that eventually escapes her.

Someone, kill me now!

Her name is Olivia. She is the prettiest girl who's ever spoken to me. Caleb would tease me endlessly if he knew. She looks Greek or Turkish, but I cannot be sure. She tells me that she has baked olive bread. I tell her about the carrots I'd glazed yesterday. I show her my latest loom magic. She holds up a piece of knitting she has been toiling at.

She beckons me closer to the window, holding what looks like a lasso. I wonder if she is Spanish as she swings it wildly and throws it toward me. I catch it with my natural flair, which involves not toppling over the window ledge and almost breaking my neck. Mino would be so proud of my athleticism.

We soon have a rope bridge across our windows, with a small pulley and a little basket to ferry stuff. She ships over half a loaf of olive bread, which I devour in seventy-nine seconds.

That's me taking it slow. I am not a complete hobo!

I roll the piece of fabric from my loom for her. It would make a dapper-looking scarf, I tell her. She smiles.

This new me is such a heartthrob. A babe magnet?

I smile back. Talking with her is easy, yet the strain of projecting my voice has tired me. This is the first time I have spoken to anyone for that long in nearly twenty months. I realize I do not need a script or an agenda to speak. Words just keep flowing. I share without inhibition and inquire without apprehension. All those conversations with myself are certainly paying off.

I do not feel inadequate. It just feels ... right.

Lying in my bed, I have a stupid grin on my face. Trust me, I know. I have seen myself in the mirror when I get like this. I cannot stop thinking about her. I wish I could touch her lustrous skin and run my fingers through her curly, brown hair. I wish we could be together. The yearning is so intense that I want to shuck the tracking chip from under my skin and bury it in mud.

I need to chill.

Take it easy. Don't ruin it, Alex. You have time to figure it out.

Ten days and who knows? Maybe we will fly away into the skies together and take off on a new journey side by side.

Sleep evades me that night. So, I try to keep myself distracted with my task list. The first couple of days, I get up on the roof and drain my rain-harvesting system, clearing out the water ducts and sanitizing the receptacle. I have never been one before, but I am now an aquaholic. That is a legit thing. I am it. I fill up two bottles for her.

What am I doing? This is so unlike Alex from Region XIV.

She waves at me from her window, looking all pretty in her yellow frock, sitting outside on a folding chair, reading a book. We have things in common already—olive bread, water, books, dancing and perennial loneliness. The next few days pass by too quickly.

Day three. I stroll across the vessel and gather saplings. I plant them gently into my vertical garden, my favorite spot in the vessel. I now have basil, thyme, mint, sage, some tomatoes and okra. Plus, a whole lot of wild unknown ones that I have picked up—chrysler, ducati, harley and merc on the top rows (flowering varieties picked from the Scandinavian belt) and iris, orion and homer below those (creepers plucked from the Mediterranean wilds). We don't have CAPITAL LETTERS in my language. They are overrated. I have a spare pot with basil and I ferry it over to Olivia.

She seems positively charmed. Gosh, I am becoming a pro at this!

Day four. I do zilch. Like absolutely no work. I just lay in my bed, share matcha tea and arrowroot biscuits with Olivia across the patch of grass— carefully measured to be more than ten feet apart—and catch a long siesta with abandon.

The stillness of time that I feel at that moment is unparalleled. Like someone has forgotten to unpause a video. Wow, getting a bit philosophical here.

Olivia has done her laundry at the stream. I admire her in the flowing white dress as she hangs the clothes to dry on a makeshift clothesline.

Day five. Washing the vessel's surface is helped by the heavy downpour today. It looks spick and span with all my scrubbing. I intentionally do this part topless. Mino wouldn't believe it if he saw how my lanky self has turned into a muscled Adonis.

Olivia is nowhere to be seen. I wonder what is up with her. I wish she had seen my chiseled abdomen. I wish she had averted her eyes, and then looked again.

Days six and seven. I secure the solar panels and clear out the swatches of dirt that line them. Eco-conservation is no child's play. Tired after a day's hard work, I stay inside in the evening and read a book that I have already read a million times.

I finally see Olivia through the window.

I don't tell her I missed her.

Day eight. I go fishing. Those striped basses are slimy tricksters. Olivia and I decide to go together. We catch a few fish, which she promises to cook with a paprika sambal. Is she Asian? I am pretty excited, although I don't know what sambal is, or even paprika, for that matter! Next, we try hunting, if you define hunting as throwing a sharp rock at a boar and missing it by seven feet.

We both agree that we are better off picking mushrooms, shallots and spuds from an open farm set up by the Care Council on the far side of the meadow. At least some of them have a heart.

Day nine. I am painting the east wall of the vessel. The walls have been randomly assigned a direction; don't ask me how. This wall faces Olivia's vessel. I have painted over the bland surfaces of my silver quenelle, each facade adorned with lively, vibrant visuals of flowers, mountains, or cities I have flown over, even balloons and kites and birds and snakes.

There are no humans in my paintings. Humans make spaces more complicated than they need to, and sometimes, they do not have any space for you. I am better off without them.

Olivia is fine, though. She showers praise on my skill with the brush. I can do it for her vessel, too, if she asks me to.

She does not. I know why.

I need to clear out from the meadow by tomorrow. I am working on where to go from here, my next destination. We keep getting updates from the Administration on routes and permits and new bubble colonies we need to circumvent. Glad to keep my distance. Anyway, none of it bothers me.

I am at peace with being excluded; with being told to stay out of other people's lives; with being abandoned to fend for myself. For the first time in my life, I feel that it is better this way. Like a part of me was waiting for another part of me to find it, and just did.

I am going to wing it. See where the winds carry me. I do not want to plan. I take out my wad of scrolls and spread a scrap of it on my writing desk, my second favorite spot. This has become a tradition.

On my last day at any place, I write down a message to other New Nomads who'll visit there someday. I write about the joy of seeing the forever surprising sights of the world. I write about the thrill of not knowing my future. I write about the hope of finding new companions like Olivia. I write about the transience of friendships. I write about the permanence of the soul. And I write about the freedom of steering my life wherever the heck I want to. I roll the parchment and put it inside a small glass bottle that I'd found in a litter bin.

You'd be surprised how many useful things the bubble colonies throw away.

I step out into the cool night and place it next to a sapling I'd earlier planted at the base of a giant maple tree. I tag the spot with a bright red and blue plastic flag crafted from more litter.

I unhook the delivery basket and release the rope back to Olivia. With a last look at the meadow, I wave her farewell. She never did propose that we fly together into the skies. But it is better this way.

Wistfully, I adjust the sail westward and set off. I do not know what my next adventure is going to look like, but I know that it will be nothing like anything I have seen yet. My tomorrow will never be a pale reflection of any of my yesterdays.

I will fly free until ... until, of course, I run out of coonils, also known as tomatoes. Until now.

on the cliff's ragged edge

smile, little child, at the cherry blossoms

sail alone into the night

Aquarius (Jan 20 - Feb 18) | *Uranus* | *Amethyst*

I may laugh with you, but I don't cry when alone.

SPENCER DIAZ GETS SUNFLOWERS

Texas, USA

It is a special day.

Susie has come to visit me. It's the first time she is visiting. She has come with Gunther and Callie, though they have both been to visit me a few times over the last few weeks with their parents. Gunther tells me that he has decided to grow his hair long. Way to go, Gunther Delgado. Stand out more. Distract the bullies away from your glasses and your freckles. He needs serious styling tips.

I cannot help but smile. My internal non-lip-moving kinda smiling at my fellow misfits.

I am stoked to have my tribe here with me. Sometimes, you find a person who you don't expect to become your person.

But they fight hard to become that. They make you feel like one of their tribespeople. They do not show off. They show up. When you feel cornered, they find a way to sneak into your corner. When you fall, they sit down with you in the dirt. When you bleed, they show you their healed bruises. When you falter against an enemy, they become your shield.

After Mom left, it took me forever to find my way again and make even a single friend. I never fathomed finding even one person to call my own. Now I have three.

I must tell them that when I wake up.

Callie tells me that she has some inconsequential gossip to share. She should know that every school gossip has a consequence.

She begins with something about Rando Rafael. I mean Rafael Blake. Remember him from my class, the one with ADHD? Anyway, it looks like he has a girlfriend now. Wow, this is amazing. Bravo. Some girl named Prisha, one year junior to us. I think I have seen her in art class. She's Indian. She seems super nice. Callie tells me that they have lunch together next to the popular kids' table inside the cafeteria. OMG! I am genuinely stoked for Rafael. He is cool, except for not wanting to bathe every day. He told me after class once. I wonder what Prisha would make of it.

I wish I could ask Callie about this, but she moves on to other news. She tells me about Emanuel, the old man who serves us lunch at school. He is retiring. About time. He looks at least ninety. I like him. He always smiles while he serves us vegetables or cake.

I wonder why people do not smile more. It beats frowning hands down.

Callie goes on with her animated gossip. Gunther chimes in here and there, sounding a bit too chirpy even for him. What's going on? Callie and Gunther talk about some of the kids who got caught in the shooting at school. Most are okay and back to class. They are telling me this to give me hope. *Ay ay ay.* This must be one of Dad's brilliant ideas or Mrs Garcia's.

I wish I could give them a big smile. My lovely gang of oddballs.

Every so often, you find an outsider coming to your rescue when you don't even know you need to be rescued. Like my friends.

Like the good Samaritan who brought me to the hospital. I must find out who he is and thank him properly. I owe my life to him. Had he not been there, I might not have....

Did he check my sneakers? Were they damaged? I hope not. Dad will kill me if I ask him to buy me another pair. Or maybe not, given I kinda died on him a few times already and that he genuinely feels upset about it.

What's that sweet smell? Sunflowers. *En serio!* Susie has brought me sunflowers. She has kept them by the window, where she tells me the sunlight is the best.

She sounds hopeful and upbeat. Nearly dying can have that effect on some. I know how that feels. Somewhat. But I do not wish for any new enrolments to our exquisite came-close-to-dying-but-survived club. Optimism is a drug ill-afforded at the cost of lethal trepidation.

I wonder if others at school are okay. I wonder if they miss me. I wonder if my teachers will check up on me. I wonder if they are allowed to visit me. I wonder about random crap a lot.

Susie is telling Callie and Gunther that she has joined a watch group for eco-conservation. Trust Susie to make life a tad more interesting than it already is. She believes that it is her calling.

My calling is to survive high school and try to find a rich sponsor for my one-of-a-kind sneaker collection.

Susie is going on about her recent trip to the Amazon rainforest and how she met other students, scientists, naturalists, doctors, photographers, ornithologists and whatnot. Hold on. What's an ornithologist? She is bubbling with excitement as she says, 'It's not just the plants and animals. People are healing themselves by finding peace in the wilderness. Like me, after what happened at school.'

Gunther is a non-believer. 'How can one find inner peace when you are not even sure where to poop without being bitten by a viper?' he asks with his usual measured grace. I cannot keep myself from laughing. Gunther should get an award for social etiquette. *Increíble.* The dude is pure genius, in his own unrivaled league.

Susie replies calmly, 'Let me tell you a story, Gunther. On this trip, I met an Indian journalist, a man named Dr Palash Gaonkar. He was shadowing us, journaling the whole caboodle for some report. One night, I was just strolling about when I saw him sitting alone under a tree, writing in a little red notebook by the torchlight, smiling as he wrote. I watched him for some time, curious, amazed at how serene he looked. Like he was sitting on his favorite couch in his living room. I asked him what he was writing.'

Everyone is silent as she goes on.

'He told me that I reminded him of his daughter, who is turning sixteen in March. Wow, I thought, the same age as us. So, I asked him what his daughter was like and where she went to school. And then he told me the most heartbreaking thing. His daughter had been missing for ten years, and he did not know where she was or who she was with. They were at a park one day, playing hide and seek as usual, and suddenly, he couldn't find her. She disappeared. He looked everywhere....'

Callie gasps. Susie tuts and continues, 'Dr Palash has been looking for her ever since. And while he does that, he chronicles his life's stories for her in that little red notebook. A notebook she'd gifted him not long before she went missing. He'd promised his daughter he'd go to the Amazon forests with her when she turned sixteen, and this trip was his way of keeping that promise. He said, 'I know what it is like growing up, not knowing your parents, kept away from what you yearn the most. But my Pia will know of me and our family whenever she finds her way back home, even if we are not around.'

Susie is quiet before she says, 'You know what, Gunther? Dr Palash's eyes were gloomy, but he still smiled as he told me all this.

He told me I was almost the same age as his daughter and wished me a great life. And before he left, he patted my shoulder and prayed that I stayed out of harm's way.'

Susie stops here, processing the last remnants of a thought she has not perhaps articulated to herself yet, although she might have had an inkling for a while.

Then she proceeds. 'What Dr Palash said that night got me to acknowledge and ponder the conflicts in my head. I was in a strange place after the shooting. Nothing made sense. Everything felt futile. Words lost their meaning. I was so pissed with Mom and Dad. I blamed them for asking too many questions, worrying, calling and texting too much, and meddling with my life. I needed space, some time away from them. I did not know how to be around them.'

I hear Susie get up and move away from us.

After a few silent moments, I hear her again. 'Knowing I could have died, I was scared. It hurt to be perennially afraid of every sound and movement around me. And for some reason, I took that frustration out on my parents. I lashed out. Dr Palash's story helped me see something. I realized that day that I was being ... selfish.'

Callie asks her, 'But don't we all find reasons to detest our parents just a tiny bit? I mean, isn't it one of the things we teenagers are supposed to do? I sometimes get mad at Mom just for asking me to leave the door of my room open. Or for putting too much syrup on my pancakes.' I can hear Gunther humming his approval.

Susie responds. 'Maybe. However, we cannot imagine what a parent feels for their child, especially when their lives are at stake. When I met Dr Palash, it was the first time I could see it objectively. I saw his unfaltering submission to the love for his child. I could appreciate my parents' side of the story and acknowledge that side even existed for the first time. He showed me the other side of the coin I was flipping. It woke me up to the possibility of giving my parents a chance.'

'They let us make mistakes. Why can't we let them too?' Susie continued.

'Why do we expect them to be perfect? Why can't they be a bit broken as well?'

'Mom was surprised to get a call from me the next day, my first in two weeks, but the first of many after that day. I gave Dad a long hug when I saw him at the airport.

I will never forget that night in the forest. Or Dr Palash and his little red notebook. I wish Pia finds her way home someday!'

I can tell that Susie is crying. There is silence in the room. Even Gunther has nothing wise to say.

My head is exploding. I hate Susie Boyle right now. Why is she planting such ideas in my head? I had decided long ago that I would never forgive Mom. Just her thought upsets me. I do not want to accept anything or forgive anyone. I cannot forget. *Ay ay ay*. I don't have any more chances to hand out, not after all the crap that Izzy and I have had to go through. She is the anathema of who the rest of us have become as a family.

I cannot breathe. Get out of here, Susie. You and your sunflowery optimism can take a walk. *Ridículo*. I do not need this nonsense.

As if on cue, my friends get up and leave. But before they do, they take turns giving me a delicate hug or a kiss on my forehead. Damn, I love them so much.

And that's the funny thing about love. It's like acne, erupting in the strangest spots where it's certainly not welcome.

(9)

THE PINK[13] ENVELOPE

For the ones who are guilty of surviving

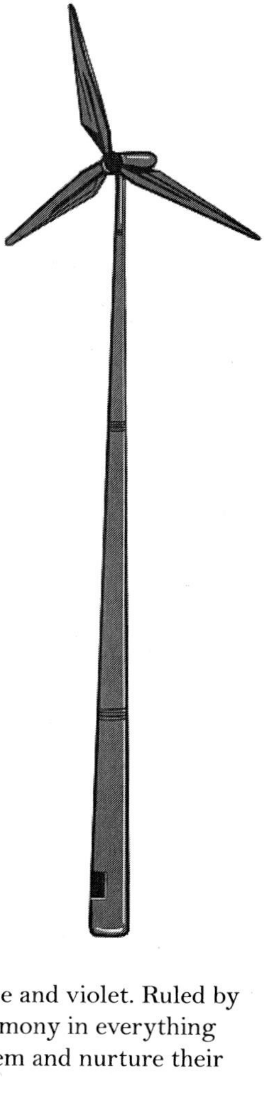

Fighting the noises within

Combating the battles outside

A plain, somber reflection

To find the demons inside....

[13] The colors of the zodiac Libra are pink, night blue and violet. Ruled by the planet Venus, people with this sun sign seek harmony in everything they do, stay open to any surprises life throws at them and nurture their relationships.

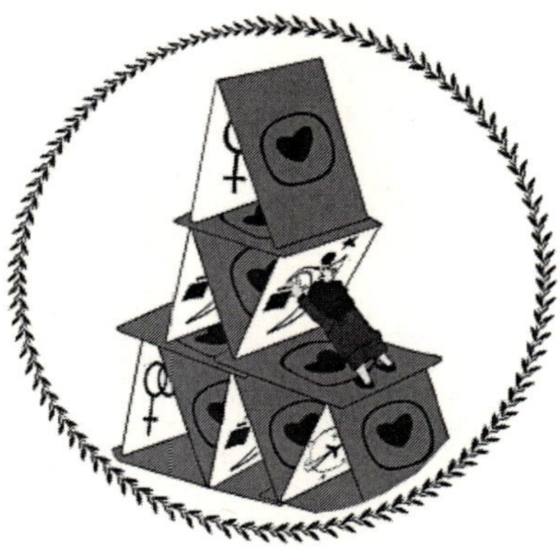

LEO MAKES A PLAN

Del Rio, Texas, USA + Mumbai, India

10.13 p.m.: *It's the fear of the unknown that is tormenting you, Leo. But this is simple, and you know you can do it. You can. This isn't that big a predicament. What happens later isn't the prerogative of your present. You have weighed your options and this seems to be the most viable one.*

Rishabh had christened Babla the 'Iron Man' a few years back for no good reason other than the fact that Babla ironed his clothes. Babla's shop is just outside the apartment building—he is always there, even on national holidays or festivals. Last evening, he'd asked Babla if his family —wife and two daughters—mind his workaholic habits. Babla had replied with a toothy smile that they did not have a choice. Providing books and clothes for his daughters was more important than resting.

Something about the simplicity of Babla's response had unsettled Rishabh. Although he had not registered it the previous night, early next morning, he did. And it left him feeling lonely. He has been pacing up and down ever since, lying in bed and sitting up, trying to shake it off. But it won't leave him alone just yet.

10.19 p.m.: *What others discover about you or what they opine about your choices— does it matter so much? Are you worried about your weaknesses getting exposed? Is this plan sound? Don't know how you've landed yourself in this mammoth spot of bother. And now, what other choices do you truly have? Leo, you have to stop fretting about this. This may not matter to them as much as you think. You get it, don't you?*

Rishabh decides to watch TV for the sake of drowning out the sound of his thoughts. He abuses the plus and minus buttons on the remote for about twenty minutes, gives up and then downs a not-so-chilled Budweiser.

He is desperate to talk to someone. He needs to do anything but be alone with his demons.

He tries calling his sister in the US, but it goes to her voice mail, as usual. Anyway, what would she say? 'Rishabh, Rishabh, Rishabh. You need to take charge; you can't simply waste your life away like this.'

He does not need this sermon. Not right now.

10.24 p.m.: *Don't think again. Just go ahead. What are you scared of? That your family wouldn't know how to deal with the outcome? But that shock would surely be better than a scandal right now.*

Are you worried that your friends would disapprove of your chosen path? But what right do they have to judge you if they haven't felt the anguish of your struggle? Did any of them help you find your bearings?

This is the only way to go about it, to get closure.

Don't you believe in your motto—experiment with life? You need to do this, Leo.

There are power cuts all over the city. And the air is sticky. Damp. Urgh. He reminisces about the previous day. It was a fantastically fine day. He had chosen to spend it with Professor Raut and Dhar Sahib. He listened to the *ghazals* that Dhar Sahib had penned in a hard-bound diary (a present from the church on his seventy-sixth birthday). After that, the three of them had lunch under the noisy white Khaitan fan in the mess. During lunch, Professor Raut narrated a hilarious incident about his wife's baking talents and how she had once charred a pound of carrot cake all by herself and strong-armed him into savoring it on a live feed.

They had laughed so obstreperously that the matron had to shush them more than once.

That day was supposed to be a fabulous day, too. Gosh....

10.44 p.m.: *Actually, it's not surprising that you are faltering. This has been your life's story—second-guessing your instincts, leaving the important decisions to others and jumping into things with not so much as a shred of confidence.*

I have seen you stand in front of the mirror, unable to select the damned shirt you want to wear to a weekend barbeque.

I have been a part of your deliberations about breakfast—eggs or sandwiches.

I have felt the anxious gazes of people in the queue while you go through the gelato menu six times before deciding to have a scoop of vanilla.

I wasn't surprised when you let your father bulldoze you into taking up soccer, even though you hate everything about it. I was there when you packed your guitar and drums into cardboard boxes and stowed them in the attic. And that was certainly not the first of 'our' countless defeats.

Back in the unlit, gloomy interior of his room, still trying to forget his uneasiness, Rishabh wonders what to do. Somewhere in the distance, he can hear the sound of old KL Saigal songs. '*Ek bangala bane nyaara, ek bangala bane nyaara....*[14]'. He sings along for a while but discovers that he no longer remembers the lyrics. He curses his memory for being so scrappy.

He grabs a pack of potato wafers and munches, listening intently to the crunching sound. He switches on his laptop, which, as usual, is low on charge.

'Why are gadgets so needy?'

He predicts the battery will last another hour, perhaps even more. He will charge it later.

10.53 p.m.: *Think about sports legends like LeBron James, Rafa Nadal, or even Tiger Woods. Their serenity is their strength. They don't overthink. They make a choice, and they stick to it. It's the triumph of those choices that makes them legendary.*

Perhaps not Woods, given his ludicrous sexcapades. But who are you to judge?

You have no control over your life. Where you find yourself right now is shocking. It is a relief that you have finally taken a stand.

Equally important now is to see it through.

---

[14] I long for a lovely beautiful home, I yearn for a beautiful home.

Rishabh checks his email and pays a few pending bills that could wait. It takes him exactly seven minutes to finish that. He checks WhatsApp and sees Kishen, Raj, Soumya, Kumar and Shravan online. He does not particularly want to talk to anyone right now. Not them.

So, what next? Cook? Tidy the room? Urgh. He concludes he is too lazy to get up. Eventually, he opens up an incognito tab on the browser and logs into his chat account, the one he uses for meeting strangers.

11.00 p.m.: *The plan you have is perfect. And you have known so for the past few months.*

You knew it while delaying it to get done with your sister's engagement.

You knew it when you went to visit Spencer at the hospital after his accident.

You know ... You have known it all along, yet you stay uncommitted.

Have you forgotten the ache of parting ways with your love, the shining light of hope in this otherwise unbearable stench of social media everywhere?

The night you broke up is etched in my memory, just like the impression one leaves behind when one steps onto a wet patch of newly-laid sidewalk.

There never was a chance for the both of you, was there?

Once logged in, Rishabh sees the usual melee of strangers. Some known frequent fliers as well. Jonas82 and KellyK123 are active and wave. He does not respond. Both of them are utterly useless, with the emotional depth of a disposable teaspoon. They would judge or tell him that he is being irrational. KellyK123 might even try to bait him into some dirty talk, something he knows he has enjoyed in the past. But now, he is not in the mood.

It's not about beating his cravings today. This is something else.

11.06 p.m.: *Don't brood about bygones, Leo Moreno. Relax. It is only a matter of a couple of hours. You will do well. Going by the stars, the hour is the most auspicious, appropriate for life-altering changes. That's funny. I mean the use of the words life and altering.*

The one a.m. plan is your gateway to freedom. Breathe….

He has been idly browsing, not even sure what he is looking for. Jonas82 sent him three messages but has given up. Jonas had been born Jasmine and transitioned last year. He is twenty-eight. He is big on the LGBTQIA rights, something Rishabh is intrigued about. He has let Jonas82 educate him on the lives and tribulations of others like him. He cannot relate completely, but Jonas82 does not judge him for that.

Rishabh went to one of the pride rallies in Mumbai the month before. But he freaked out and left midway, something he feels guilty about and has not yet confessed to Jonas82. He is not in the right frame of mind today.

11.18 p.m.: *Take your mind off it. You have thought about this way too much. Heard of a thing called spontaneity?*

Take a break, Leo.

Talk to someone. Why don't you go online and chat with someone? Someone. Anyone!

Yes, you do that, you scared little coward. Just get this freaking thing called 'second thoughts' out of our system. Tell someone what happened.

Put it out into the universe and let it deal with it.

Rishabh is about to give up when he gets an instant message. He considers not responding, and going out for a walk instead. But he knows well enough that he needs a distraction from himself. Game on, sure_shot_007!

Leo_lives4fun: Hey!

sure_shot_007: Hello

Leo_lives4fun: how r u?

sure_shot_007: I am good. How about you?

Leo_lives4fun: okie. I'm Leo, frm Texas. Del Rio.

sure_shot_007: Rishabh here from Mumbai. India.

Leo_lives4fun: Kewl. sup man?

sure_shot_007: Nothing much. Just feeling a bit down. Want to talk? I mean chat :-)

He wonders if he appears too needy to Leo from Del Rio and if that is even his real name. Should he have used a fake name too? What was he thinking? Figuring he does not have a diddly squat to lose, Rishabh decides to stay the course.

11.26 p.m.: *Voila! You just found the right person. He, too, wants to talk. It is all working out. Another ninety minutes and everything will be ready. An end to their endless questions. A way to get over all the drama.*

One alternative that will give a new meaning to your life, on your terms.

Leo_lives4fun: Gr8. u dont find ppl who just wanna talk.

sure_shot_007: Wonderful. I am glad we can :-)

Leo_lives4fun: so why u feeling low? u stay alone?

sure_shot_007: Do you really want to know?

Leo_lives4fun: can't hurt!

sure_shot_007: You seem like a nice guy, Leo. I don't want to be a drag. This may take a while.

Leo_lives4fun: no 1s w8ing for me nywhr.

sure_shot_007: Hmm.... So, as you guessed, I do stay alone. I have been alone for a while.

Leo_lives4fun: wow. can't imagine. Sounds effed up!

sure_shot_007: I am used to it, but there are days like today when it kills me.

Leo_lives4fun: donno wat 2 say.

sure_shot_007: My parents are long gone and my sister does not often take my calls. She, too, is in the US, by the way. California. My friends are keener to get high than to listen to me rant. So, I turn to strangers to let some of it out.... Funny, isn't it?

11.35 p.m.: *Is that all? If you tell him about your shitshow, he'd know what real misery is. He is brave, and I'll give him that. He is willing to share what is making him feel so horrible.*

Maybe you can do this for him—help him, hear him out. It might make it easier for us, too. To be free of bondage, to forget about gory shootings, to go out listening to Jimi Hendrix.

sure_shot_007: Are you there, Leo?

Leo_lives4fun: ya ... mm listening. promise i won't judge.

Rishabh feels his chest loosen up a bit, his breath becoming less ragged. The lamps on the street have now lit up and clouds are gathering. 'Rains, finally,' he murmurs into the damp air that has been filling his lungs.

sure_shot_007: I am a banker by profession and have lived in Mumbai practically all my life. I fell in love when I was just twenty. She was in my class. I believed that she was my soulmate.

Leo_lives4fun: nice. tell me more of ur story.

sure_shot_007: It's not much of a story. A Mumbai boy (that's me) meets a Tamilian girl (that's her). He asks her out. She accepts. They date. They get married. He is 23 and she is 22.

Leo_lives4fun: Dats gr8. Not many luv stories end well.

sure_shot_007: It wasn't easy. Love marriages can get quite messed up in India. It was for us, what with us being from two different communities. Took 18 months to convince my parents. Her parents didn't approve, ever. There was a lot of drama & fighting, but we got married. And we were so ready to be happy.

11.48 p.m.: *A nice spicy story to take your mind off the one a.m. plan. I give this dude some serious cred. He must have had a lot of faith in his love. He fought. He did not give up. Unlike….*

Leo_lives4fun: i know it's tough 2 make othrs undrstnd wat u feel. why r grown-ups such ass*&^es?

sure_shot_007: We somehow got past it.

Leo_lives4fun: i'm glad.

sure_shot_007: We were young, though. She kept studying for her MBA. But I took up a bank job. I'd help her after office. We celebrated so freaking hard when she received her business school admission letter. Cakes, wine, pizza—the works.

Leo_lives4fun: neat!

Rishabh's gaze shifts to the picture frame by his bedside, of him and Nithya standing by the waterfall, holding hands. At five feet four inches, her head barely reaches over his shoulder. She isn't extraordinarily beautiful. But that had never mattered to him. He is unsure why he still has that picture there.

He knows how much he loved her at the time. But why now? Why still?

11.58 p.m.: *Remember Christmas? There was music and drinks. The decorations and streamers were all over the corridors. Someone even smuggled in beer and vodka. Almost.*

Everyone was there. Except.... Everyone was acting so normal.

No one would talk about what went down before the summer break. I still can hear the screams. I still cannot sleep at night.

I still cannot forgive myself.

sure_shot_007: Leo?

Leo_lives4fun: oh. yeah.

sure_shot_007: Well ... our honeymoon didn't last long.

Leo_lives4fun: oh, wat hpnd?

sure_shot_007: Divorce. 6 years back.

Leo_lives4fun: wtf?

sure_shot_007: Wondering why two love birds should ditch their swan song? Well, our story has a few twists.

Leo_lives4fun: yea?

sure_shot_007: After she graduated, she got a job and quickly made her way up the ladder. Soon, she was earning more than me.

Leo_lives4fun: ego hassles?

sure_shot_007: I didn't mind it. Really. I think my ego is quite like that of a docile pig.

Leo_lives4fun: u r funny. so?

sure_shot_007: I don't know, but slowly, I became a sideshow for her. She was no longer keen to have our usual ice cream or to go for long walks by the beach. She seemed to want to be by herself.

Leo_lives4fun: u talk 2 her?

sure_shot_007: I wanted to fix things. Go for therapy or something. But she simply wouldn't agree.

Rishabh drinks half a bottle of water, feeling parched, as if he has been talking, not typing. Honesty is an outstanding policy but surely a tiring one.

12.04 a.m.: *That's messy. Why is he telling me so much? All that? Loving someone is such a burden. Especially when the person you love turns out to be a coward, unwilling to fight for you. I hate love. Just one more hour to go.*

Leo_lives4fun: u der?

sure_shot_007: Uh. Yes. This is hard for me.

Leo_lives4fun: i bet my skinny ass it is!

sure_shot_007: Anyways ... we were in the middle of all this when my phone rang late one night. It was my sister. My parents had been in a major accident. They were both seriously injured and in the intensive care unit.

Leo_lives4fun: hell no!

sure_shot_007: I rushed to the airport and took a red eye to Ahmedabad. I was too late. They were gone. And guess what? She stayed back in Mumbai. Apparently, she couldn't take a day off from work.

Leo_lives4fun: u effing serious?

sure_shot_007: I came back after a few days, an orphan. I was disturbed, unmoored.

Leo_lives4fun: Hmm....

sure_shot_007: As I thought more about my parents, the idea of being a father myself crossed my mind. I thought that a baby might bring Nithya back to me. Even if it didn't, I'd have someone to go back home to.

Leo_lives4fun: okaaay....

sure_shot_007: I know you think I was being selfish.

Leo_lives4fun: no, i m nt 1 to judge....

sure_shot_007: She was. Told me to my face that I was jealous of her success and wanted to sabotage her career.

12.16 a.m.: *Girls are such bitches. Life is so overrated. I am so over love.*

Leo_lives4fun: and?

sure_shot_007: And we argued for days. She'd come home late, sometimes not at all. It went on for months. Then, one day, she told me we could try for a baby. As long as she was not expected to stay home and be a full-time mother.

Leo_lives4fun: really?

sure_shot_007: I was on cloud nine when we got pregnant. I wanted to feel my baby's fingers curl around mine. I wanted to feel the soft toes and the dreamy eyes.

Leo_lives4fun: luvly.

Rishabh's hands are shaking and words don't come so easily. Each stroke of the key seems heavier than the previous one. A familiar mist clouds his vision, a wetness underneath his eyelids gathering weight.

Leo_lives4fun: U thr? So the baby....

sure_shot_007: Died ... At the end of the second month. Miscarriage. I was not even in the city at the time. By the time I got back, it was all over.

Leo_lives4fun: wtf?

sure_shot_007: I lost the one happiness ... the one that I truly wanted to feel. She went to her parents' house. Told me she did not want to talk about it.

12.28 a.m.: *Un-effing-believable. How did he survive this? This is cruel. What would I do? Leave someone alone like this in pain? Oh, but you do know. Don't you?*

Rishabh's eyes are wet and his emotions pour out uninhibitedly.

He lets out a rough cry of anguish and hits the table with his fist, looking up at the first showers breaking through the cloudy afternoon Mumbai sky. He will throw up. The moist smell of the soil is nauseating him.

Leo_lives4fun: u ok man? u der?

sure_shot_007: Yes … I am. Thanks Leo, but don't worry. I have relived that day every day for the last six years.

Leo_lives4fun: so dat's why divorce?

sure_shot_007: Not really.

Leo_lives4fun: ?

sure_shot_007: One day, as I was filing my taxes, sifting through bills, papers and forms, I found a pink envelope - the kind you use for birthday cards. It was tucked away in her drawer. And inside it were a few old photographs, a couple of visiting cards and a crumpled receipt.

Leo_lives4fun: receipt for wat?

sure_shot_007: For an abortion.

12.35 a.m.: *This can't be real. But why would he make it up? Isn't this too much for a person to handle?*

Being lonely is one thing, but dealing with betrayal is another.

You know how much that feeling can sting! After what Carlos did. After what you saw him do to all those.... How could you ever love him?

The battery on his laptop is nearing the end of its life. Rishabh wants to finish his story. He prays for electricity to come back on. He hears his phone ring. It is Shravan. He turns the phone upside down and slides it under a pillow.

sure_shot_007: Have I scared you off?

Leo_lives4fun: sry. m here. bit shocked. how did u....?

sure_shot_007: I moved out. I cut her out of my life. I could not eat. Or sleep. Started drinking, pot. And then I was fired.

Leo_lives4fun: f$ck!

Leo_lives4fun: how did u even? i wud hv died....

sure_shot_007: I tried. I was ready to jump in front of a train. But as I was walking to the train station, I heard the ringing of bells.

Leo_lives4fun: bells?

sure_shot_007: yes.... a divine ringing sounds from an old, worn-down church next to the train station. And like a remote-controlled robot, my feet walked me inside.

Leo_lives4fun: hmm....

sure_shot_007: They were serving breakfast at an old age home run within the church. The priest asked if I wanted to eat. I told him I wanted to help serve the food instead. I distributed the plates, buttered the toasts and handed out glasses of hot milk. I tied the napkins around the chins of fragile men and ailing women, carried plates of food to the medical ward, and helped some of them eat. I cleaned tables and utensils. I lived.

12.42 a.m.: *I did not see that coming!*

A smile creeps up on Rishabh's face as he remembers how he'd met Professor Raut for the first time that day. He was wearing a faded, threadbare tweed jacket, a gift from his wife, long gone. It was amongst the few things he'd been allowed to bring with him. He had a photo frame with his wedding picture, which he had proudly propped on the lunch table as he ate the yellow lentil soup with wheat bread, hands struggling to stay steady.

His son was an accountant but didn't have a house spacious enough to accommodate his father now that his own son was in high school and needed a separate room for his studies.

'Sacrifices children ask of their parents.' He would never know the feeling.

Leo_lives4fun: so?

sure_shot_007: That afternoon, I heard stories of the inmates—of abandonment by families and failed promises, of unwelcome senility and illness, of forfeited love, and of startling betrayals.

Leo_lives4fun: not da best plc to be?

12.47 a.m.: *Is that where he was seeking closure? Such things do put one's thoughts into perspective, but....*

Professor Raut had pointed Rishabh to Dhar Sahib, who was sitting under the neem tree in the yard murmuring silent prayers. Dhar Sahib had moved to the church dormitory of his own volition. His granddaughter had needed open heart surgery and this was his way of unburdening his family. On the second of every month, he would go to the pension office to collect his dues and deposit almost all of it into his granddaughter's account. He prayed under the tree every day. His vision was failing him. But it never stopped him from writing verses of blessings for her.

'Compromises people willingly make for their children.' He would never know that feeling either.

Leo_lives4fun: u freaked out?

sure_shot_007: The opposite. It was just what I needed. For the first time in six months, I cried openly, without trying to hold back my tears. I cried for myself, and I cried for them.

sure_shot_007: How did they go on? How could life be so unfair? I was mind blown by how they'd willed themselves to live with a smile on their faces, making crutches out of happy moments from a life that had passed them by on their way there.

Leo_lives4fun: i donno....

12.53 a.m.: *This is effing crazy. And here you thought that you had it tough?*

All you have to do is to get your head out of your ass and be brave for two minutes.

sure_shot_007: I found life again that day!

Leo_lives4fun: i wish i cud say sumthin ... why did u say u were lonely ryt now?

The battery indicator is blinking vehemently. Not now, Rishabh thought. He feels a knot in his stomach, hoping to get through this. He prays that the battery lasts for just a couple of more minutes.

sure_shot_007: Because I lost my baby on this day—seven years ago. I still have the only sonogram. To some, it may just be a picture of white and black spots, but it is so much more ... signs of the beginning of a new life.

12.56 a.m.: *You still believe your situation is hopeless? Is this the hardest life will ever be? Is this all you can take?*

Really, how much of a coward are you?

You still have a shot at dealing with your demons, but you just want to escape it.

sure_shot_007: Are you there, Leo? Hello?

Leo_lives4fun: yea. aint da best person to talk abt hope n life.

sure_shot_007: You don't have to say anything. I had this all piled up in my heart. Just telling you about it lightened my mood. Thank you.

Leo_lives4fun: np ... u be ok?

sure_shot_007: Yes. I will.

Leo_lives4fun: u gotta try n 4get.

sure_shot_007: I am trying...

Leo_lives4fun: gud

sure_shot_007: You know there is this woman who helps out at the old age home. A widow. She has a four-year-old son. I have been thinking about her.

A lot. Do you think I should....? Or am I too broken for her?

Leo_lives4fun: no1 othr than u wud know.

sure_shot_007: I guess....

Leo_lives4fun: if it feels ryt....

sure_shot_007: Thanks for being there today.

Leo_lives4fun: i shld be da 1 thking u. dis was ... u hv no idea. abt my 1 am plan.

sure_shot_007: Your one a.m. plan? Tell me abou

Before Rishabh can finish the sentence, the laptop heaves three final high-pitched beeps and shuts down. He stares at it for a few furious seconds, still trying to deduce what Leo's one a.m. plan might be.

12.58 a.m.: *Tell him. You owe it to him. Tell him about your infallible one a.m. plan.*

Leo_lives4fun: u der? wat hpnd?

Leo_lives4fun: ....Rishabh? hello? u der?

Deciding there is nothing he can do just then without electricity, Rishabh gets up, stretches his back, throws the empty bag of chips into the trash and puts the water bottle back in the refrigerator. As he latches the balcony door, his glance lingers on the empty nook near the building's entrance where Babla would ceremoniously return after the rain. He smiles, picks up the photo frame and throws it into the trash.

Leo_lives4fun: guess u had enuf of me. nyway, hv a gud life dude.

Leo_lives4fun: but wait. i didnt tell u my story. it's not as effed up as urs. but I wanna tell u. i want u 2 know.

Leo_lives4fun: i found luv too. didn't think i cud luv som1 so much, but i did. we both did. but it was not meant 2 be. i was scared. i told him i was the da wrong person. every1 says it is taboo. yes, we hv some of those people in effing Texas too.

Leo_lives4fun: n i did not fight for him. For Carlos. i gave up on him, on us. i broke his heart. was easier dat way. i was a coward. i let him go. i pushed him away.

Leo_lives4fun: and then he ... my Carlos went to the school with his father's gun and he ... he ... there was so much blood. he pulled the trigger but it was i who made him feel da way he did. betrayed.

Leo_lives4fun: it is unbearable - dis pain, dis guilt. So many kids got hurt coz of what Carlos did. of what i made him do. i hv tried to 4get it, but it keeps haunting me. so, I created an exit plan. my 1:00 a.m. plan.

Leo_lives4fun: i hv the sleepin tabl8s ready. Abt 40 of em. been stealing em from my parents. they are out of town for 2 days for an effing wedding. i was gonna make it go away.

Leo_lives4fun: only now i don't want 2 make it go away. i wanna figure dis out. 2 find signs of the beginning of my new life in spots of black & white dat I see everywhr ryt now. Just lyk u did.

Leo_lives4fun: i wanna find life again. I wanna support my pals who r still hurting. i will meet susie. and check in on snoozy spencer. he is still in da hospital. i pray he gets betr soon.

Leo_lives4fun: i hope u c these msges. until then...

1:00 a.m.: *You are so stupid, Leo Moreno. So ... so ... effing stupid.*

light mist on the window

carrying the savage breath of death around

washed onto distant white sands

Libra (Sep 23 - Oct 22) | Venus | Opal

I may be scared, but I will not let go.

PART FOUR

THE EPICS OF EARTH

to walk a private path
to build a kindred kennel
to grow a carefree crop
to dig a twisted tunnel
i am the tilled soil
i am the holy place
i am the fertile ground
i am the sacred base
the home to every man
to elephant, to fawn
i was, i am, i always will
from each dusk until dawn
from me is all life born
the carrot, turnip, and tuber
i am the first, the final
i am the ultimate, the uber

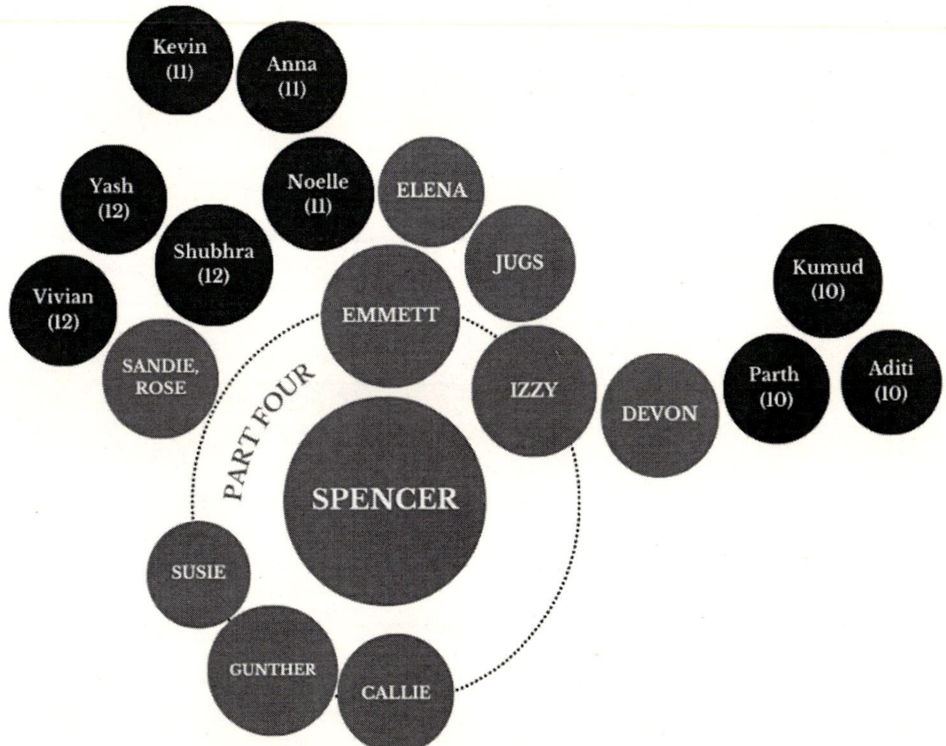

PART FOUR
SPENCER
EMMETT
IZZY
CALLIE
GUNTHER
SUSIE
SANDIE, ROSE
ELENA
JUGS
DEVON
Kevin (11)
Anna (11)
Noelle (11)
Yash (12)
Shubhra (12)
Vivian (12)
Kumud (10)
Parth (10)
Aditi (10)

SPENCER DIAZ VISITS A YARD SALE

Texas, USA

I wake up to the sounds of animated bustling. I can hear Dad, Dr Miller and Izzy all at once. Even Rose. Simona, I mean. What is going on?

The point is that something important is afoot. Am I dying? No, they sound excited and merry. What for? It could only mean one thing.

I infer soon, via my exceptionally keen eavesdropping, that a patient in the Critical Care Unit has succumbed to his injuries. His wife and he had been seriously injured in a road accident. And while she survived, he had been declared brain-dead a few days ago. His younger brother has just signed off on the taking-him-off-the-ventilator-and-letting-him-die form. *Ay ay ay.* The would-soon-be-dead man is an organ donor. Miller says that the lab is running tests to see if he may be a match for me. But he warns Dad and Izzy to keep their hopes in check, lest they should come crashing down later.

With my luck, that is a likely possibility. They should not be celebrating until it's all locked in.

I can discern a tense excitement in my room the whole day. Izzy keeps on coming and tidying my hair and kissing my hand repeatedly. Dad is pacing the room up and down, up and down. Even Rose is cooing her warmth all over me. *Porfi*. Dr Miller will update us in a few hours. Izzy, Dad and Rose need to chill. But they just won't stop. And neither can I.

So, I close the eyes of my soul and channel my inner Ralph. I need to be unperturbed. In case you haven't figured it out, he is accused of wrecking a lot of stuff. Wreck-It-Ralph. Over the years, I have felt a connection with him. Some days, even more than Johnny Cage. Ralph is misunderstood by most and ends up messing things up even when he does not mean to. He is tired of being the villain, but he wants to change. No wonder I dreamt of being him.

In so many ways, I am him. Other than the huge biceps. Mine are like soggy marshmallows. But I need to be strong right now. For Dad and Izzy. And a smidgeon for Rose too.

We should not hope for the best. They must prepare for the worst.

My heart is beating a thousand beats and my stomach is hosting a butterfly soiree. I am not known for showcasing grit in the face of challenges. Hiding and escaping is more my style. The monitors start beeping. A few minutes pass. And my mind starts to drift away. Rose has a way of hooking me up with drugs when I start to lose my wits. I am glad for it right now. Waiting does get a wee bit easier on drugs. Another successful escape.

Sadly, you don't always have such drugs handy. Not when your father shows up alone for your parent-teacher meetings or when you soil your pants during a school shooting or when your mother of seven years disappears on you.

The truth is that there aren't enough drugs to dull out the stinging pain in your heart.

And the irony is that you do not want that ache to fully go away, for it is who you believe you are ever going to be. You have nightmares about what else you might forfeit if you chose to move on. You feel astray without that piercing agony. You crave the loathsome thing that keeps you bound to what you've mislaid. So, you hold on to it with the same ferocity that your consternation grips you with.

You are scared to let it go. You fear that possibility, and that fear is the grandest motivator of them all, a friend who makes sure we do not go awry, a manipulative compass that keeps directing you to what you believe is your destiny.

I am jolted back into the present by the ding of a bell. I can tell that it has been a few hours. Dad is sitting by me, his head propped against my bed, I assume, with his eyes shut. Izzy must have gone to the cafeteria to get dinner. They must be out of their minds eating food from the hospital cafeteria for so many weeks.

How long has it been now? Months?

I have no reference for time anymore. I hear someone enter and they clear their throat. I feel Dad move and get up. It is Dr Miller who speaks next.

'Mr. Diaz. We successfully retrieved the lungs from the donor in the Critical Care Unit. But he was a chain smoker and that's why the tests took so long.'

I can sense Dad's impatience. *Por favor!* He wants Dr Miller to get to the end of his story.

'And while Spencer is a match, I am sorry but the lung has been commissioned for another patient brought into the ER a few hours ago. She is an expecting mother with a life-threatening injury. She was bumped up the transplant list by UNOS. I am so sorry, Mr Diaz.

We all thought it would be Spencer's turn. But let us not give up. Spencer is still fighting. I am sure we will find another donor soon.'

No bueno. After Dr Miller leaves, Dad collapses and buries his head into my chest. He breaks down and keeps saying my name over and over again in a chant, like a mantra.

Izzy is not back yet. I wonder what is keeping her. She needs to take care of Dad. I am kinda numb here. Hello? Izzy? Rose? Where is everyone when you need them?

Wait, who's that? I feel someone enter the room, but I cannot tell who it is. I can smell a perfume that I recognize but not quite place. Lavender? It can't be.

And then I hear her voice. 'Emmett. Why didn't you tell me? I would have come.' Dad is taken aback as much as I am shocked.

'What are you doing here?' he asks her, something that I cannot. 'Did Izzy tell you?' he demands to know.

She comes and runs her fingers through my hair. I am thrashing my head violently in protest. She rests her hand on my heart and says, 'You should have called. I am still his mother.'

Dad is not going to be wooed so easily. 'Oh really? Where have you been for the last nine years, then? Do you still deserve to be called a mother? Mothers do not run away like cowards. *Por favor!* No, you are not their mother. Not anymore. Plus, I hear you have a new husband. How is Jeffery? What does he have to say about all this? Or have you abandoned him, too? Listen to me carefully. If you want to play house, make new kids with your new husband, alright? Leave me and my children alone. Just leave. Now. There is nothing you have to say that will change my mind. *Es definitivo.* Get out and never come back again.'

Dad is standing over me, guarding me from her. I can feel how hard he is holding onto my hand. He has steered Mom away as if shielding me from her shadow.

After that morning in the kitchen, after he told us, he'd gone into the garage and sat there alone. He did not come out for hours.

We left him alone, mostly because we did not know what to say or do. We did not speak again that day. I did not see his face that evening.

That was the last time I ate alone. Dad has never skipped having dinner with us since that night.

The next day, I went to school. When I came back, I saw a huge pile of Mom's things on the curb, with a massive sign that said 'Yard Sale. Everything Must Go.' A donation box labeled 'Donate for Charity' sat atop a small table. He would not keep a single penny from that yard sale.

That day, I'd witnessed how a broken man pulled himself together and took his first steps to move on for the sake of his children. For us. My hero. Like Johnny Cage. After twelve years of being married to someone who always put herself first—before him, before her kids, before her family.

He won't let her hurt us ever again.

I went to my room and gathered my presents from Mom—the vinyl records and Applebee coupons, the laser gun and the board games—into a box and dumped my memories into the yard sale. I did not need all that. I had Dad. *Gracia de Dios.* And that was enough.

I saw Dad sitting there in the yard, clutching the keychain he has had ever since I can remember. A faded rabbit with a carrot. Abuela told me that Dad and his sisters had bought matching keychains shortly before Tía Elena was taken. Dad had not let his sister go and still prayed every day for her return. He was still waiting for her, lost to him for over thirty years. The rabbit keychain was his way of holding on to that memory of Tía Elena.

But Dad would not wait for Mom. He knew it was over with Mom. Forever. *Para siempre.*

Dad has been there for Izzy and me since that day, more than ever before. He held me in his arms when he picked me up from school after the shooting. He made sure Izzy had help from Tía Gabriela when she got her chums. He paid for the lease Izzy put down for her nursery. He buys me sneakers and video games when he cannot afford them. He pampers Izzy with muffins every Friday. He fusses over us much the same way that Izzy does over the hibiscus and plumbago flowers at her potting bench. Her nursery is what paradise must be like.

Dad can get quite protective about stuff when it comes to us. A tad too much sometimes. We get regular shots for allergies and flu; he picks us up if it's getting late at night, and he has a tracker on our phones that he thinks we do not know about. But we understand and we let him.

So, Dad is not going to back off now. He will not stop protecting us. Protecting me. His family. His taunts echo in the closed hospital room. He will not let her damage his kids again.

I can feel his words ricochet and boom around. 'Just leave us alone. Please go. Go. We don't need anything from you....'

Mom simply asks him, 'Not even one of my lungs?' Dad does not speak anymore. *Mierda!*

(10)

THE BROWN[15] SHAWL

For the ones who hate beauty

My thoughts, my lock, my key,

Born to love, share, be free,

My I, my you, my we,

Being the best me I can be!

[15] One often associates brown, khaki and black with the zodiac of Capricorn. Inspired by their ruling planet Saturn, they work with discipline, structure and maturity toward their goals, propelled by their tenacity and practicality.

PARTH MEETS HIS AUNT AGAIN

Kanpur, India

'I am going out. Lock the main door when you leave,' Kumud Pathak calls out to her maid as she hurries out to the waiting car. 'And ask the *dhobi's* daughter to leave the ironed clothes in the hall. Do not let her inside.' She leaves before the maid can even reply. As the door clicks and locks in place, the maid speculates on what has prompted Kumud to depart in such a hurry and so late in the evening.

With that, she starts scrubbing the vessels with renewed vigor. The big *kadhai* is proving tough to clean after being used for heavy frying in the afternoon—*pakoras, pooris* and spring rolls. 'The cook was a skilled one,' she thinks, for he had just taken five hours to prepare a sumptuous spread—from *matar paneer* and *pindi chholey* to fried rice and pasta. The thought of all that food makes her burp. She is sure that she will receive a *sari* or some other expensive gift. After all, it is Kumud and her husband Manav's twentieth wedding anniversary.

Outside, in the car, Kumud's face is flushed with anxiety and she looks quite shaken. Beads of sweat line her brow despite the cold winter air. She never steps out of the house without priming herself. Yet, presently, she is in the crumpled cotton *sari* she had changed into after the guests left. And she is still wearing her flowery bathroom slippers. But there wasn't any time to fuss about all that. There is no time.

'What if it's too late?' she mutters under her breath. Her thoughts are elsewhere.

After a few minutes, the car stops at a signal. Two young girls approach the car—the taller one carries a wad of wiping towels and the younger one holds bright neon scrubbing pads. An odd place to sell cleaning supplies, Kumud thinks. The girls knock at the car window but Kumud does not entertain prolonged eye contact. Just enough to notice that both the girls have remarkably gray eyes, as if life has drained all color out of them. They must be sisters, Kumud concludes in her mind.

The signal turns green and the traffic starts to move. The girls back away, looking deflated, dragging their feet back to the stone partition in the middle of the road. They look tired and dirty, grime plastered on their faces and caked into their clothes. The taller one, not more than twelve years old, is holding the younger one close to her, pressing a hand firmly and protectively on her shoulder. The younger one looks up at her and smiles.

Kumud feels a chill and curses the weather under her breath. The evening is a bit nippy and she wishes she had her brown pashmina shawl draped around her. She tries calling Manav again, but he does not pick up.

'Damn it! Why does he have to go for drinks tonight of all nights?' she laments in frustration, unable to understand why he would choose to spend their anniversary night away from her.

But she knows his celebration is never complete without getting sloshed with his buddies. It is his one indulgence, reserved for such special days, and she has learned to make peace with it since a long time ago. At least he is caring and respectful, she has convinced herself. Seeing him pass out on the couch and dealing with his massive hangover the day after is not too bad.

After all, things could be much worse.

But today, she needs him. This is all too much for her to deal with by herself. Normally, she would have called Aditi, but today, that isn't an option. Aditi and her son Parth were at the party, too, just a couple of hours ago. At seventeen, he is already peeking over Aditi's shoulder. But they had to leave a bit early to attend a school event on the other side of town.

Kumud did not insist they stay. It was better to leave at a safe hour.

The evening had gotten unexpectedly cold and Kumud had lent Aditi her brown shawl. It was a choice between that or the blue one, and Aditi insisted that the blue one simply did not go with the *sari* she was wearing.

Kumud never gave that brown shawl to anyone. It was her mother's gift and Kumud was very possessive of it. Aditi knew how much the brown shawl meant to Kumud, but that did not stop her from asking for it. Kumud tried to laugh it off. Typical Aditi behavior. But, somewhere inside, she was not pleased.

It is the way things are between the two sisters.

The car screeches to a halt and the driver apologizes to Kumud—a cow and a calf are crossing the street, and they do not seem to be in a rush to get to the other side. She notices a spot on the car window where a pigeon has dropped its blessings. She is disgusted by it. She wishes she had a cloth or a wipe to scrub it off.

She blinks her eyes and forces a smile, willing the wetness back to where it's been lingering. She is determined not to crumble under the burden of her emotions. She will not let her dread get the better of her.

'I can do this,' she tells herself over and over and over again. 'I will not let the situation take control.'

Her thoughts go back to the party.

'Parth has started to look like his father,' Kumud had observed, but she kept that thought to herself.

Aditi was beaming with pride about his various talents, from drumming to quizzing. Aditi feels he is somewhat of a genius but worries that he is too shy for his own good and whether he would ever fit in.

'He hardly ever talks to anyone except Tavish,' Aditi had rued. Kumud had known it to be accurate, but she just kept nodding as her sister poured her concerns for her only child.

Kumud's thoughts wander to Parth. 'He needs to loosen up, mingle more, and be….' she finds herself unable to finish that thought. She knows what she wants to say, but her mind cannot coherently connect the dots. Her thoughts are a puddle of nonsense at the moment.

The phone call in the evening has freaked her out.

Parth is two years younger than her son, Tavish, who is in his second year in business school. Tavish wants to become an international economist or strategist at WTO, which Kumud neither fully understands nor appreciates.

'Isn't it better to have more realistic dreams?' she asked him on more than one occasion.

But she knows better than to meddle with his decisions. Particularly not when Manav seems to think it's the best idea in the world, second only to putting pineapple on a pizza. The very thought of the fruity topping sends a shiver down Kumud's spine.

Parth comes over to spend time with Tavish over weekends and they both stay cooped up in the modest room on the terrace. Kumud can overhear their deep conversations about music, video games and ideas to change the education system. Tavish's hope tends to ensconce Parth in its calmness. Aditi feels it is fortunate that the cousins have bonded that way, as real brothers would. But while Tavish is burly and rugged, Parth is lanky and awkward. Tavish is confident and outgoing, while Parth is a recluse.

Parth needs to make more friends.

'Doesn't he ever want to share anything with anyone else? One needs a special permit to sneak inside that egg-shaped head of his!' She wonders what makes it work between the two cousins.

Parth will start his term at a university in San Antonio, Texas, in six months. He is enrolling in an undergrad program aimed at the conservation of soil, wildlife and such. She is puzzled by her nephew's odd curriculum choice but knows better than to quiz him.

'It's not my job. I should not add to any pressure he might already feel. But has he thought this through? How will he survive alone in that foreign land? He is too fragile for this own good,' Kumud opines.

Oddly enough, Aditi has made peace with Parth's eccentric choice despite her apparent consternation about him leaving alone for an alien nation. But knowing that their second cousin Jayesh stays in Texas with his American wife, not too far from San Antonio, has given her some relief. Jayesh has a son, Devon, who is also a science geek and, hopefully, not too old or too American or too snooty to bond with Parth.

'Takes a nerd to know a nerd,' Aditi had giggled apologetically.

The other day, Kumud had overheard Tavish teasing Parth. 'I bet on my left toe that you will not make it two weeks without me in the wild wild west. I reckon I need to come with you. I am certain I can get into the Ivy League. Princeton or Carnegie Mellon, if you will. Given that I am the more gifted one, you should not take my pedigree too personally.'

Kumud could not believe her son could be so mean and harsh. Parth had gone miserably quiet. But before she could intervene, she heard them laughing their guts out. 'Gotcha,' said Tavish. Brothers.

She thought to herself, 'Some shared joke? A sibling connection? Separate but inseparable. Different, but in sync. Racing, but not against each other.'

Her thoughts return to the two sisters at the traffic signal—the ones selling the wiping towels and scrubbing pads—and she is transported back to her own childhood, hers and Aditi's.

* * *

Being the elder of the two, Kumud always had to be responsible and sensible. And Aditi, well, she was the pretty one—the apple of everyone's eye.

'Not like me, always being told off for being too dark or too fat or both. Like a black raven born in a family of colorful parakeets,' she bitterly reminisces.

She loathed it. After all, it was not her fault that she took after their father in her looks.

'How did he land someone as good-looking as our mother for his wife?' she often tried to reason. She had convinced herself that her mother's eyesight must have been weak when she said yes to the marriage proposal. There was no other explanation.

Kumud resented the compliments that Aditi received for her dimples or her butter-soft skin. She despised it, consumed by rage and hatred for Aditi. Sometimes, she wished Aditi were never born. And she hated her parents for treating Aditi like a precious dove.

She found inventive ways to hurt Aditi. Once, she buried Aditi's toys in the garden and burnt her favorite drawing. On another occasion, she let Aditi get too close to a kitchen stove, rushing in to save her just in time from getting her hand burned. Much as she wanted to hurt her younger sister, she didn't want her parents to blame her for the mishap.

The black raven longed to spread its wings for a dance.

Slowly, she learned to accept Aditi as a thorn in her side that would never go away. She immersed herself in her studies, resolving to give herself the best chance at a fabulous career. The only hope her sister had was her appearance and that was bound to stop mattering someday. So, while Aditi went out for movies with friends and spent hours prancing in front of the mirror, Kumud toiled through enormous volumes of coursework and books.

And then, just like that, a few years later, she cleared the monstrously tough UPSC civil services examination.

She could not believe it. And from the expressions of her family members, neither could they. Her father patted her back and promptly posted an update on his Facebook page. All of a sudden, he did not seem to be ashamed of sharing a picture of his ugly daughter on his timeline. Dressed in a cotton *sari*, her mother took her to the temple to ward off the evil eye and even put a small black *teeka* behind the ear of her shy, fat, too-dark-skinned-for-her-own-good daughter.

Aditi did not figure in the Facebook post or the *pooja.*

For once, Kumud knew that she mattered to her parents.

The black raven felt vindicated.

When they returned home from the temple, Aditi sprang a surprise celebration party with their dearest friends. She even baked a cake for Kumud, drawing her into a massive embrace. Kumud could see unbridled joy in her little sister's demeanor, a pride radiating from her being. For her? When Kumud blew out the candle, Aditi wished her all the best in the world and hugged her again.

Something inside Kumud had churned at that moment.

'How can she be so glad for me? Has she not sensed my hatred? How could she not know? Is she faking it? Why?' These thoughts circled Kumud's brain.

But she knew then that Aditi's pride in her elder sister was genuine. Heartfelt. She wonders if the girls at the signal feel the same way about each other.

Kumud knew.

And from that day, the frosty exterior of the insecure elder sister started to thaw. She realized that whatever was wrong with the world around her was not a burden that Aditi needed to bear. She would let Aditi drag her to the terrace and tell her tales about school and examinations, confessing how Kumud inspired her to do better at her studies.

Aditi confided about having a massive crush on a boy in her class, blushing a deep shade of pink that radiated against her pearly white skin. Kumud was awed by the ease with which Aditi went about as if life was so simple! And she realized that she could learn a thing or two from her little sister.

Kumud left to stay at a government campus when her training started, leaving Aditi with her parents. By then, the brick wall that Kumud had built to keep her sister away had all but evaporated. But even as she waved goodbye to Aditi, she still felt envious of her sister's perfect skin and hair, expensive style and fantastic personality.

She still thought herself inadequate, sure that her parents would forget their ugly black raven and be absorbed with their beautiful princess all over again.

She was skeptical of how long her father's timeline and her mother's prayers would continue to feature their elder daughter.

And she clung desperately onto the brown pashmina shawl her mother had given her, a rare gesture to show that she would be missed. As if a mere shawl compensated for everything!

The black raven was beginning to stir again from its slumber.

Years passed, and when the time came, Kumud married Manav, an IAS officer, a few years her senior. He was better than anyone she'd ever dreamt to have in her life—tall, fit, perfectly good-natured and a gentleman. She never figured out why he ever approached her parents to ask for her hand in marriage.

After the wedding, he told her, 'I like how you think, work, and inspire others.'

She was taken aback by the incredibility of the thought. How could she ever inspire anyone? But it would be more unbelievable if he'd said, 'I married you because you are beautiful.' The fact that he did not say that bothered her for days. Months. Years!

She half expected Manav's infatuation with her unsteady mind to eventually be overtaken by a desire for someone else's flawless body. That never happened. But it was not until she had given birth to Tavish that she felt secure. Manav was an impressive man with honor.

Around that time, Aditi started seeing a guy from her college. She still talked to Kumud over weekends, but there was too much on her hands, and Aditi started to take a backseat. Though they did not spend much time together, Kumud still wondered about Aditi's choices and life decisions.

'I just intend to get married to a decent guy and enjoy my life, *didi*,' Aditi had told her once. That was the whole breadth of ambition for a girl who could want anything, have anything. Words like identity, career, independence and security did not mean much to her. It agitated Kumud, but strangely, she did not try to convince Aditi otherwise.

Part of her felt relieved that Aditi would always fall short of her achievements. Finally, Aditi would feel the same void Kumud had been saddled with for years—the onus of being the underdog.

Kumud buried this thought deep inside the crevices of her conscience. With everything going on in her life, she backed off step by step from Aditi's life, maintaining a distance.

She convinced herself, 'I do not want to hurt her. It is for her good.'

During Aditi's wedding with her college sweetheart, she realized that nothing had changed. Seeing her giggling mother and her doting father, she knew that their world, as always, still revolved around Aditi. The beautiful one. The perfect one. She squirmed with jealousy when she saw Aditi dressed as the perfect bride in her pink *lehenga* and dazzling eyelashes. No one even batted an eyelid when Kumud got a nasty migraine and excused herself from several wedding ceremonies.

No one cared. Not her parents, not her sister. No one.

The black raven was mad.

After the wedding, Kumud never checked in on Aditi. And Aditi did not seem keen to talk either. She never called Kumud or her mother. Everyone assumed that the romantic newly-weds were busy setting up their lives.

Then, about two years later, Aditi called her.

Kumud could tell that she had been crying. Tavish was already going to a playschool by then. Aditi was pregnant and her baby was due in three months. She sounded scared and told Kumud she was in a cab and had left her husband. She did not say why. Kumud did not ask.

* * *

Kumud asks the driver to speed up as she falls back into her trance. She recalls how she had not spared even a heartbeat before insisting that Aditi stay with her while she sorted things out.

* * *

Over the next few days, Aditi narrated horrific details of how her husband—her cool college boyfriend—had turned out to be an insecure and possessive monster. He accused her of trying to seduce other men, imagining she was having an affair with everyone from his friends to the building's guard.

He would check her phone calls, messages and emails. His taunts slowly morphed into a kick on the shin or an elbow to her back until she ran out of excuses for her split lips and blackened eyes.

He forced Aditi into what he called 'making love', even when she was hurting or having her chums. He bit at her body and rode her in a drunk frenzy of wild dominance. She was no more than a slave to a man who told her that he loved her at least ten times a day but treated her worse than a doormat.

Love, if left unchecked, can turn lethal.

Aditi despised him. She loathed herself for thinking him worthy of her love. She detested her fair skin and perfect teeth. She despised her silky hair and her full breasts. She hated everything that made him feel the love he claimed he had in his vile heart for her. She wished she was more like her sister—dark and ugly.

Aditi's divorce came through easier than they had expected. Their father had pulled some strings and gotten her scoundrel husband to cooperate. Aditi stayed with Kumud through the rest of her pregnancy, who made her feel protected and cherished.

Kumud was also healing.

A few months after Parth was born, she arranged an unpretentious apartment for Aditi, not far from her own house. She would stop by every day to help out so that Aditi could catch up on her sleep. Not long after, Aditi started working at a job that Kumud helped arrange.

The black raven had finally decided to rest.

Kumud could see how much Aditi had changed over the last few years. Her eyes were still beautiful, but a muted melancholy radiated from them. Her skin was fair, but her scars haunted her.

More than anything, she had forgotten to smile. When they met on weekends, Kumud could see the longing in Aditi's gaze for the promise of a perfect life that had passed her by.

If it had not been for Parth, Aditi would have let herself disappear.

***

The sound of an ambulance siren brings Kumud back to the present. They have reached. Her hands are trembling and her throat feels parched. She swallows her fear and exhales deeply to compose herself. Then, without hesitating, she steps out of the car and walks into the cold entrance to the emergency ward. A nurse guides her to the waiting area.

She is restless and anxious to find out what has happened. She spots Parth standing nervously at the distant end of the hall. She waves to him, but he is focused on his mother, whose legs she can now see from a distance.

Unable to wait any more, Kumud rushes inside and races to the bed, running into a rusty medicine trolley. The edge of the trolley scrapes her hand, but she does not bother to check. Parth notices and approaches her nervously before breaking down in her embrace. She strokes his back and calms him down. He keeps apologizing, telling her, 'I should have been stronger. I should have protected *Ma*.'

Guilt hangs heavy on his shoulders, drenched in sweat and blood. A doctor is standing by Aditi's bed and Kumud cannot see her sister's face yet. There are bandages on her hands—both hands—fingers, palms, everything. The air is rent with the smell of antiseptics. Kumud is scared.

Before she can take a step forward, a police constable sitting nearby gets up and approaches her. He looks sympathetically at her and pats Parth on the back with pity. He tells Kumud how Aditi was attacked by a ruffian on the street where she lives. He had become obsessed with Aditi and stalked her for several weeks, only to be disillusioned by her absolute indifference to him. A stalker Aditi did not know about.

Parth confirms seeing the guy lurking but not thinking much of it then. He apologizes again, 'I am such an idiot. I should have paid attention. I am worse than useless.'

Kumud assures him that idiocy comes in different forms, and he is not it.

Parth tells Kumud, '*Mausi*, that lout was waiting outside our house when we returned from the school function, along with two of his gangbangers, blocking the main entrance. They shoved me to the ground and held me there. The guy told her that he loved her. *Ma* told him to make himself scarce.'

He is shaking as he relives those moments but continues, 'He started yelling, putting on a charade of how hurt he was by her rejection. *Ma* asked him to mind his manners. He grabbed her hand and twisted it behind her. I tried, but I could not move. They were too strong. *Ma* pushed the guy away from her and slapped him on his face. She threatened to call the police. She called out to the neighbors. She fought them.... But before she could run to safety, he pulled her back and threw an open vial of acid at her.'

Kumud gasps, unable to steel herself enough. 'I wish I were strong and muscular like Tavish *bhaiya*,' Parth hangs his head, ashamed of himself.

Kumud cannot believe what she's heard, a deep worry racing through her body. She wants to protect Parth, but her body is trembling with shock. Her heart is pounding from all the effort to stay strong. She wishes Manav would call her back soon. She is scared to turn around and look at Aditi.

'Her face! Her eyes? No! Oh God, no'. The most horrific images run through her mind as she stays transfixed to the spot.

Finally, the doctor moves away and turns toward Kumud. Parth motions her toward his mother. As he leaves, the doctor pats her patronizingly on the shoulder, scaring her even more.

What is he preparing me for? She closes her eyes and braces herself.

And then she turns to look at Aditi. Surprisingly, she sees Aditi's smiling face—as always—fair, unblemished and perfect. But the vial of acid? The bandages on her hands? Aditi's eyes look a bit puffy, but she seems all right. Kumud is confused and turns back towards the policeman. He tells her they have arrested the accused, smiles pitifully, hands her a plastic bag and leaves.

Kumud stares down at the bag with her brown pashmina shawl, which looks very burnt.

Parth explains the rest, a soft mist lurking behind his eyelids. 'I was trying to fight off the guys holding me down when I heard a gut-wrenching cry from *Ma.* They suddenly made a run for it and I sprinted towards her. I saw the vial on the floor, and *Ma* was still standing there, screaming in pain. At her feet was a fuming brown shawl.

We realized later that when attacked, her reflex had been to shield herself with the only thing she had in her hands, your brown shawl, *Mausi.* And so, while the acid burnt the skin on her hands, the shawl protected her from what could have been so much worse.

You were not there, but you saved her, *Mausi.* You saved her,' Parth exclaims, voice heavy with gratitude.

Kumud rushes to embrace her little sister and showers a dozen kisses on her forehead. She doesn't care about smearing her *kajal* all over Aditi's face. She doesn't care about the staring eyes. She wants to take care of her sister. She strokes Aditi's forehead, then takes out a comb from her handbag and starts tidying her hair before eventually knotting it into two side plaits, just like she used to when they were just kids. She then takes a *kajal* pencil and circles a small black mark behind Aditi's ear and under her right foot.

Stay away, evil eye!

Manav calls back and she tells him everything.

She sits by Aditi's bed when the nurses check her vitals and the doctors come over to discuss the treatment to heal the burns. Parth reluctantly leaves to go home and rest. She knows that he blames himself. She knows he will need time. She knows he will be okay eventually, with help from Tavish and her.

Without another look at it, she throws the plastic bag with her burnt brown shawl into a waste bin nearby.

Alone in the sickly ward of the hospital, she knows, for the first time in her life, that the black raven is dead.

a balm for my soul
take away that last dance in me
i have hung my boots

Capricorn (Dec 22 - Jan 19) | *Saturn* | *Garnet*

I may have felt envy, but it came from love.

SPENCER DIAZ DIALS DOWN STUPID

Texas, USA

Over the next two hours, the Diaz family washes more dirty linen than perhaps the daily load from the hospital beds. I mean the linen of the metaphorical kind.

Mrs Garcia could never dream of what went down. Communication is key, she always says. By that logic, blaming the other person is the universal password. A lot of that is happening in my room.

Secrets. Lies. Deceptions. Half-truths. Confessions. All that gossipy goodness comes tumbling out.

All for 'poor Spencer's sake'.

I must give them credit for hashing it out right where the entire staff can hear them. *Excelente!* I am keeping a serious face.

Dead serious. Izzy keeps telling my parents to calm down, back off, or not yell, reminding them they could do this at home. Or anywhere else. But it doesn't look like they can hear her, for they go on.

Sandie has come in once or twice to shush them and they did mellow down for a while. Even Sandie is not taking chances with the only potential donor I might have left. I think Sandie is sweet for that. I get her vibe now. She's got my back.

Mom, as expected, is not doing a great job justifying her vanishing act. She apologizes to Izzy, explaining how she was losing her mind living in the same house as Dad. Dad grunts in response and challenges her to confess the whole truth. He hollers at her, accusing her of being weak and selfish. Mom keeps reiterating that she has always loved me and Izzy and that it was excruciating for her to leave.

She says that she could not be with a man who could not support her ambition, a man who was too old-fashioned to help her pursue her dream. *Perfecto.* She conveniently does not mention sneaking around and having an affair with a much younger man. Gosh, I hate Jeffery.

Dad calls her a selfish bitch.

Mom returns the favor by calling him a shitfaced hypocrite.

She finally goes quiet when Dad says, 'It did not take you long to find your new husband. Did it? Maybe you just got lucky. Unless you were....'

Did Dad know about the affair? I never told him. But the way he says it.... Did he? But how?

Izzy asks Mom something I want to. 'I am sure it was worth it, Mom, abandoning us. I bet it was. So, who's the real hypocrite here? Do not dare proclaim your love for us when all you can do is care about yourself,' she lashes out accusingly.

Mom tells her that she thinks of us every day.

'Yet, Spencer and I have no letters or memories of a phone call from you. Why?' Izzy yells.

Mom tells her that it was for our own sake that she stayed away, for she believed that it would be easier for us to hate her than cling to the hope that she'd return. Dad tells her to stop bullshitting. Plus one on that, Dad. Everyone is reticent for a while. And the silence seems to melt away years of anguish with tears. And phlegm. *Mierda.*

I feel Mom's hands over mine. She is caressing them gently, humming something I cannot make out. I remember she used to hum to herself while working.

She says, 'I love you, Spence. You have turned out to be a lot sturdier than I ever imagined. You are strong. Hang in there, son.'

She always calls me Spence. Is the last letter in my name too much of a burden for her?

Dad tells her, 'He is fit because of all the running he does, just like me.' He is trying to show off. It does not suit him. But it sounds adorable.

Mom says, 'You have raised them well, Emmett. Thank you.'

¡Basta! He does not need her endorsement. Or her thanks.

She calls out to Izzy, who ignores her but comes and lays next to me on the bed. She does that sometimes—lays next to me, holding me tight. I guess those are the days she feels lonely. She does not want one more person from her family to disappear. And I have come very close. Twice.

Izzy tells Mom, 'The only reason I called you is because of Spencer, his life. You are his last shot. Perhaps, his only chance. So, do not bungle this up, Mom.'

'Just this once, please do not frack it all up,' Dad grunts.

Mom's voice trembles as she says, 'I have much to make up for. And I will do my best not to frack it up, Emmett. I've already scheduled an appointment for tomorrow for my labs and cultures. I promise. I will not blow it, not this. *Prometo!* I am here now. I am here.'

With that, Mom leaves. I can tell because I cannot smell lavender anymore.

Dad comes and sits where Mom was sitting until a few moments ago. He holds my hands and apologizes, 'I am sorry for messing up your life and ruining Izzy's.'

He keeps my hands in his, perhaps feeling the blood pumping in my veins, afraid to let go.

Izzy is crying. She tells Dad, 'I love you, Dad. But, if you feel very guilty, you can atone for your misdoings with a giant box of exotic muffins. Beyond that, you have nothing to apologize for.'

I feel sorry for him. I wish he had found someone after Mom left, that he had taken a chance on his happiness again instead of plunging himself into the pool of neediness that Izzy and I have been in for the last nine years, wading against its relentless currents just to keep us afloat.

I say a silent prayer for him.

Some wounds do not stop hurting. And you realize that they hurt because you do not let them heal, because you keep touching them, because you do not let yourself forget about them. They do not heal until the day you feel bitter about having been given that hurt to bear.

It is stupid, yet we all do it. We humans are stupid sometimes. But I do not want to stay hurt.

So, for the first time in many weeks, I pray that I do not die on Dad and Izzy, at least not this way. Not right now.

For their sake, I want to live. I want to survive this.

I want to wake up even if it means that I stop touching my wounds, even if I need to forget how I got them in the first place, even if I have to stop being bitter about the gluggy, tasteless soup life has served me.

I am many things, but I am not stupid.

Love is worth sticking around for and one thing that I am feeling right now is the feeling of being loved. By Dad and Izzy, and Abuela and Tía Gabriela, and Rose and Sandie, and Susie and Gunther and

Callie, and Dr Miller and Emanuel, and Mr Moreno and Mrs Garcia, even Mom.

It might not matter that I do not have that special someone yet, a girlfriend, a soulmate. It might be inconsequential which college I attend or what courses I enrol in.

I still have a chance of figuring all that out—if only I unpunctuate this little coma that I am stuck in.

(11)

THE IVORY[16] DRESS

For the ones who must stay hidden

Invisible in my own skin
Even without any magic cloak
Tearing away at the peel
Wet in my tears, I soak

[16] The Virgo zodiac's vibe is peach, olive, beige and mauve. Ruled by the planet Mercury, those with this sun sign are level-headed and methodical in their actions but are direct and constructive in their communication.

NOELLE FINDS A MEMORY BOX

Manhattan, New York, USA

Noelle is sitting at the bay window in her cosy Manhattan apartment.

Lined by hues of warm blues around the study, she is snuggled into the coziness of her favorite comforter with a colorful array of unicorns, ponies and rainbows splashed all over. It is one of her most prized possessions for reasons she cannot fully comprehend. To be honest, she can. It's symbolic. It's a memory of her Papá.

She'd hidden it away behind her clothes in the walk-in closet when Robbie came to pick up his belongings. He did not see what he did not need to take. He'd always made fun of how it belonged to a teenager, not a 'grown-up' like Noelle.

'As if Robbie would know anything about growing up Mexican. He is a through-and-through city-bred, ungrateful, privileged white guy,' she reasons. 'What would Papá think of my choices as a "grown-up?"'

Alejandro Hernandez, Noelle's Papá, was a second-generation Mexican immigrant who lived all his grown-up life in Rocksprings, just off the Mexico-US border. His father was a renowned dressmaker and tailor in the neighboring cities. People would come from as far as Brackettville, Camp Wood and even San Antonio to get their dresses and suits stitched. His hands had magic, they would say, that could transform the most ordinary fabrics into outstanding attires.

Alejandro had taken the family trade forward as a skilled stitcher, diversifying into a small business selling sewing machines on the side. Noelle wishes she had inherited some of her grandfather's skills but the best she can do as a seamstress is to tighten loose buttons on her office tops.

The reminder does not flatter her.

Presently, Noelle is staring at an antique-looking box on her lap—a memory box—that once belonged to her Aunt Anna, Papá's cousin. Noelle knows that Papá loved her. Noelle contemplates why, for she had never seen her aunt growing up. Aunt Anna never visited. However, she would send Christmas cards and presents for Alejandro and Noelle.

There was never a return address on the cards.

Papá would tell Noelle that Aunt Anna was precious and that Noelle must vow to be in her aunt's life even after he was gone. She'd get pissed at him for saying that, but even as a teenager, she knew that it mattered to him a great deal. So, she had promised.

Noelle had first seen the antique box in the storage container. She is yet to look inside the box. But she is bursting with curiosity. What am I hoping to find? A map to a treasure? Yet, something in her aunt's letter had set her mind racing from the get-go.

'You'll find the real me there.'

* * *

It all started one Thursday morning. Noelle was getting ready for work, which translates to wearing her work coat while still dressed in her yellow pajamas and finishing her customary cereal bowl with cold milk, sitting at the table by the window, observing throngs of people rushing about on the streets below. She works from home most days, given that she mainly carries out virtual meetings with vendors across North America. Such were the perks of being the Head of Procurements.

Just when she was to meet with Señor Emmett Diaz from Del Rio to negotiate a contract, she received a call from an unknown number. She ignored it and got onto the meeting. Amidst Señor Diaz's well-researched and high-spirited presentation, she received two more calls from the same number.

She did not pick up but wondered if it could be something important. She excused herself from the meeting, citing an emergency and promised to reschedule. She would later deny it, but she could no longer bear to listen to the twenty-two reasons why the vendor from Del Rio was the best bet for Noelle's firm. She'd already decided to grant the order to a vendor in Compton, New York, and the call with Señor Diaz was just a formality. The vendor in Compton was a safe bet, tried and tested.

She contemplated why the call with Señor Diaz was even needed. But she knew it was standard process, and it was not her place to question the *status quo.* She just needed to follow it. She had not reached where she had by ruffling feathers.

She called the number and an efficient-sounding secretary from a law firm called McLeary and Barnes answered. She nervously held on while her call was forwarded to Mr Banks, a junior partner at the firm that Aunt Anna had hired.

Over the next fifteen minutes, Noelle learned two shocking truths.

One, Aunt Anna was dead. She'd died peacefully in her sleep of natural causes.

Two, Noelle was the sole benefactor of Aunt Anna's will.

'Why leave everything to me?' she tried to grasp.

Noelle was to visit the law firm's office in the East Village that afternoon, and Mr Banks would walk her through the details of her aunt's will and possessions. Immediately after the call, she called Aunt Anna's number and got her voicemail. She Googled McLeary and Barnes, which was indeed a genuine law firm. Convinced that the call had not been a hoax, Noelle took her first day off from work in more than two years.

Robbie would not believe it. Not after....

By the time she was done meeting Mr Banks, she had inherited twenty-two thousand five hundred and thirty-seven dollars; the contents of Aunt Anna's rented apartment and a letter from her in a sealed envelope. Noelle opened the letter on her way to the apartment, whose keys Mr Banks had handed her in a miniature brown pouch. And she read the last words from a dead woman to her niece, her writing showing an unsteadiness of hand but the resolve of a purpose.

* * *

My Darling Noelle,

Your Papá has raised you well. He was, may God rest his soul, the only one from the family who's stood by my side. Always.

Just like you do now. Visiting me, bringing me yogurt and sweaters from the fancy malls, checking up on my crochet, worrying about my health.

You have always been curious about my years before. But I never told you much. Just this and that. But I want you to know now. About who I was before I was the Aunt Anna you now know me as. Woefully, I am old and frail and cannot write it all down for you.

So, I am leaving you a key instead. It is taped to the underside of my nightstand. Find it and visit Orange Storage in Queens. Container 503. You'll find the real me there.

I hope you'll remember me well. I'll be watching over you!

Yours,

Aunt Anna

P.S.: You should give yourself a break. Divorcing Robbie was the smartest thing you did. He is an idiot. We do not need to suffer idiots in our life.

Noelle's head was spinning. 'Storage container? Queens? A key under the nightstand? What?'

* * *

She stood outside Aunt Anna's apartment for a couple of minutes before she went in. Thirty seconds later, she had the key in her hands. Dangling from the keychain was a tag that read, 'Orange Storage. Queens. 503.'

'What's happening?' she had wondered.

Noelle took more days off as she sifted through the apartment and donated her aunt's clothes and furniture to charity. The only things she kept for herself were old pictures, a collection of stamps, some books, and a stained-glass lamp.

Most importantly, she decided to keep the grand piano.

'It will be my way to remember the music in you, Aunt Anna.'

As much as she wanted to visit the storage container, she kept deferring it until she had no reason left to do so anymore. And so, four days after reading the fateful letter, Noelle found herself standing outside container 503. When she opened the shutter, she was surprised to find it empty.

'Was this a joke? Surely not.'

But then something at the back caught her eye—the memory box.

It's the very same one she has in her lap right now.

***

'About who I was before I was the Aunt Anna you now know me as.'

Noelle opens the memory box and is relieved to find that it just has some old letters and pictures.

'No severed toes or broken teeth! Thank goodness that Aunt Anna was not a yesteryear serial killer.' Noelle sighs.

She looks through the pictures but cannot recognize most faces. One of the pictures has the words Albert and Alejandro. Alejandro.

'Papá? Wow, I would not have recognized you here.'

'Is this Uncle Albert? Of course, I have never seen him before. He died young; I remember. He does remind me of Aunt Anna though, something about his eyes.'

There is a picture of Aunt Anna's parents with Albert standing under a willow tree in their backyard. He has the same golden hair as Aunt Anna. She finds an old newspaper cutting in the box—an obituary for a young boy named Albert.

'It must have been so hard to lose your brother like that.'

Despite herself, Noelle's eyes became hazy, lamenting the loss of an uncle she'd never met. Aunt Anna must have missed him so much. No wonder she kept her pain stowed away in this box.

'Oh, Aunt Anna! Why did you never say anything about him?'

Noelle calls it a night and puts the letters away. She will read them the following day. For the first time in several months, she does not think of Robbie when she falls asleep.

It is not until the following evening, when she picks up the memory box again, that Noelle realizes that the letters are not addressed to anyone she knows.

'There are no postage stamps. Were these letters never posted?'

The envelopes are intact and the writer's name is nowhere to be seen. Just a date. So, she arranges them neatly on the bed, sorting them chronologically. Then, she pours a glass of red wine, snuggles into her comforter by the bay window and starts reading.

* * *

March 06, 1967

Let me tell you how I unraveled. Yes, it happened again. Peter was standing by the the wall, talking to my other classmates. I knew it was him before I even saw his face. So clear was his visage in my senses that I could picture him vividly, even with my eyes shut. He is not tall. Some may call him short. I am somewhat ashamed of this thought, but it soothes me to know that he isn't perfect.

I melt when I look at him. His build, his style and his casual appeal make me go weak in the knees. What will I give to just look into his eyes all day long? I know I appear unhinged—why would he be interested in me? Me. The most off-balance and boring person I know! I am a smitten kitten. Kill me now....

* * *

Noelle is smiling. She knows what a high school crush feels like.

'Very romantic, Aunt Anna. Did not know that about you!' She picks up the next letter and reads on.

* * *

May 20, 1967

Last night, I was with Kevin. He is a couple of years ahead of me in school, but I hang out with him sometimes at the park. We chatted for a short while. How was the day? Did he like his new blue bicycle? I told him about the daffodils that Mom had recently planted. He smiled.

He asked me if I liked anyone in school. I did not tell him about ... well, you know! He reached out and held my hand in his. He has very grown-up hands, hair and everything.

Then he reached over and kissed me. On the mouth. My mouth. It was wet. It was my first kiss. Technically, it was his kiss. But you know how it is, right? I got up and ran away. Oh, I am such a.... I should just jump off a bridge and die. We don't have any bridges nearby.

* * *

Typical. Such a guy thing to do! Noelle is picturing a younger Aunt Anna, with her golden hair tied in a pigtail, running away from this idiot, Kevin.

We do not need to suffer idiots in our life.

Wonders of adolescence. 'Did she tell Uncle Albert about it? Or *Papá*? Did she ever speak with Kevin again?' Noelle speculates.

* * *

June 29, 1967

Wow. Just got back. Had gone out. It was raining, so I carried my favorite umbrella with the dahlia print. Technically, it's mom's umbrella. Anyways, that is not important. Or at least to me.

So, I had been to a dance debut for a friend's friend. It was brilliant—the elegant movements, the graceful hand gestures, the extension of limbs.

Although I got a bit forlorn watching it, thinking about why I never acted on my dreams. Swing dance has been my love. Boy, oh boy, do I like to jazz it up in front of my wall mirror or what! I think I am darn good too, with my expressions and stances, even flexibility. Wish I could learn ballet. But Dad would never agree. He'd never understand why it is so important to me.

* * *

I always knew that you loved music, with the grand piano and your records. But dance?

'Oh, Aunt Anna, why did you not tell me?' Noelle asks no one in particular, feeling more curious with every letter.

* * *

July 18, 1967

Last night, I was reading a book when the phone in the living room rang. Mom and Dad were out, as usual, socializing. I never go with them. They ask, but I feign some excuse. Like my stomach is hurting or I have a test at school. When I answered the phone, it was Kevin, talking as though he were drunk. I told him that I did not wish to speak with him. But he started pleading, telling me that he could not stop thinking about me. He told me that he liked me. A lot. That he wanted to kiss me again if I liked.

He kept talking, my ears aching at the sound of his words. I told him that I was not who he thought I was. He kept on talking in his husky voice, seducing me, telling me how he desired to do things to me and my body and make me feel things I had never felt before. Despite being disgusted by him, I could not hang up. Instead, something inside me started to stir. Heat started to rise between my legs. He asked me if I liked it. I stayed clammed up, scared.

Eventually, I hung up and went back to my room. My eyes could not focus on my book. I kept imagining Kevin's mouth on mine, his hands on my neck and our bodies grinding against each other in the stillness of the night. I was ashamed. But I could not keep my mind away from these thoughts. I could not take it anymore and my fingers finished what Kevin had ignited inside me.... I cannot stand Kevin. Oh, I sooooo don't like Kevin.

* * *

Noelle finds it strange that she is reading such personal stories about her deceased aunt. She thinks it's disrespectful.

'Why did Aunt Anna want me to read these? What did she want me to know? Did Kevin make her do something she did not want to?' Noelle sighs and checks the time on her watch.

It's fifteen past ten already, and she needs to get back to work the following day. She promises herself that she will read just one more letter and then go to bed. She will not keep that promise.

* * *

Aug 27, 1967

I have fallen hard for Peter. Really bad. Like I can't peel my eyes away from him at school. Or at the grocery store where I ran into him by a freak chance. Divine intervention? Conspiracy of the stars?

He said hi and moved on, holding a small bottle of orange juice. I stood there, gawking like an idiot, long after he had left. Dad found me in the aisle and asked me if I was okay. I picked up two bottles of the same orange juice that Peter loves (I am sure I will love it the same way he does) and followed Dad to the check-out counter. Why did love have to be so hard?

* * *

'Oh, this one was too short, Aunt Anna. I cannot just leave things like this. Just one more letter. Or maybe a few more. The meeting in the morning is not so important. I will reschedule,' Noelle decides.

* * *

Sep 12, 1967

I am torn. I am not sure whether I should tell Peter. It's getting close to the date of the school play. I need to see more and more of him every day and I cannot keep it in anymore. Last night, after rehearsals, we all crashed at his place. And I lay not six feet away from him, tucked away in my sleeping bag, but his proximity aroused me. I felt a tingle in my spine and goosebumps all over my skin. I tried thinking about the play, but the oh-so-dirty thoughts kept creeping back. I got up and watched him nap.

How could he look so handsome even while resting?

I am sure he does not feel the same way as I do. So why can't I just.... Goodness gracious. I am an idiot. I think this will kill me someday.

* * *

Oct 05, 1967

The play went well. Splendid actually. After the show, we all went out for root beer. I had been smiling at Peter the whole evening. I walked up to him and smiled, and then we walked out onto the open terrace, talking about the standing ovation we'd received earlier that evening. I hopped perkily on the parapet to sit but promptly lost my balance. He held my hand to steady me. And then, our gazes met. I looked into his eyes and could not look away.

He asked me if I was okay. And I told him how I felt about him. Us.

The words just poured out. He yanked his hand away, all too suddenly, and backed away from me. Not a word. And I could see something else in his eyes as he took steps away.

I should have just leaned back on the parapet and let gravity have me.

My heart aches non-stop. I have cried so much that my tear ducts are on strike. It is very hard to write about it. I don't want to. I'd rather burn myself with a blow torch. Or kill me some other way.

My love story is over. It was short and so not sweet.

* * *

'Oh no ... no, Peter, you didn't!' Noelle is furious with Peter for breaking Aunt Anna's heart.

'What's wrong with the dude? Have you seen her?' she quips.

Noelle realizes that she has not seen Aunt Anna in any of the photographs yet. She rummages through the memory box, but nothing. No pictures of Peter or Aunt Anna. Or Kevin. But surely, Aunt Anna must have been a beauty if how she looked in her old age was anything to go by?

* * *

Nov 29, 1967

Mom went shopping this weekend with friends. And she's bought loads of dresses, shoes and make up. She is always smiling after she goes shopping, radiant and caring. I asked her to show me all she'd purchased. She was surprised but did not ask any questions.

Then she got a phone call and left, her laces and gowns laid out on the bed. I ran my hand through the folds of the fabric, eyes closed, trying to memorize its touch against my skin. I could hear Mom talk from the hall downstairs. I looked around and picked up a flowery ivory dress she had hung by the side of the bed. It looked radiant like the surface of a pearl or the inside of a snail's shell. I brought it down and stood with it in front of the mirror, loving the soft silkiness of it on my face and my hands. I strutted about holding it, pirouetting in front of the mirror and slipping my feet into the new red heels that lay in a box on the carpet.

At that moment, I wanted to wear that dress more than anything I'd ever wanted. My daydream was broken by my dad's voice calling out to Albert from the hall below. Albert was needed in the garage. I quickly hung the dress back in its place, stepped out of the heels, and ran to find Albert. I passed my mom by on the stairs. She was completely unaware of my sneaky excursion with her new ivory dress.

* * *

Noelle remembers how she used to sneak into her own mother's wardrobe from time to time, stealing her make up and shoes for outings and checking out dresses from her closet for parties. On that count, then, Aunt Anna had been a 'normal' kid.

'What did she wish for me to find out from these letters? Was this the real her she wanted me to know?'

* * *

Dec 07, 1967

I am so confused these days. It's getting easy and it's becoming hard at the same time. Sometimes, I surprise myself with the things I want to say. I am surprised that I have those thoughts. I am ashamed and angry about them. I want to explode. I want to yell. Sometimes I want to cry all day. Albert has had it too easy. Mom and Dad love him to bits, overlooking any wrong their dear darling might do. But what about poor Anna? This cannot be. I need to fix this. Just not sure what, how, or when. Well ... that's the way things are.

* * *

'Hold on. What is that all about? Did ... were her parents.... Certainly, there was no discrimination, not like that. But?' Noelle's head is spinning.

She has a lot of questions running through her head. She recalls how Aunt Anna had never once mentioned her parents during their chats. Or any grief she had with Uncle Albert. Maybe because they were dead? Or maybe because it was too hard to remember.

* * *

Jan 17, 1968

A lot of things are tough for me right now.

Kevin keeps calling me to go away with him on a fishing trip. Dad seemed excited about the idea, telling me that it'd be great for us to get a bit of sun. Really? Did he not know how teenage boys just enjoyed hooking up all the time? But then maybe Dad was relying on Albert. He wouldn't know what poor Anna was thinking inside her undersized head with the golden hair. Anyway, I had worked a way out of that horrible fishing idea. I am quite a genius that way!

By the way, Peter has found himself a girlfriend. They hold hands everywhere. All the time. It's disgusting. Specifically, after he shrugged off my hand at the party like I was the yellow plague.

Everyone thinks I am strange. Weird. Sometimes, I feel I should talk to my parents. But they would not understand. For them, Albert is their whole life. They'll never listen to what I am saying. I could speak with my buddies, but then I don't have buddies. It's just the theater crew that I hang out with sometimes. Amongst them, there is Bianca, who seems to like me. Not sure why. She listens when I talk. Maybe I should tell her. But am I even ready to talk? What would I say? That I am going to ... that I want to ... that they need to ... that we.... Darn. This is just so freaking messed up.

* * *

Noelle has poured the second bottle of wine by now.

She is wide awake and her mind is playing a thousand scenarios. She no longer cares about the meeting the next morning or her job for that matter. All she is fixated with right now is the story of Uncle Albert and Aunt Anna.

'What went so wrong? I wish Aunt Anna had given me an executive summary of what to expect.' She picks up the next letter and reads on.

* * *

Feb 04, 1968

Mom was very upset today. Her favorite maroon lipstick has gone missing. She does not know that I stole it yesterday, just like her bottle of gloss last month. She is snapping at everybody. Dad has tried placating her, but she is not willing to listen.

I hope I do not turn out to be a hormonal mess like her. But then it might be very different in my case.

* * *

Noelle is anxious. She does not like suspense and this build-up is killing her. She rips the next letter out of the envelope, tearing it a bit from the edge. She curses at herself for her impatience and reads on.

* * *

Mar 16, 1968

Kevin came by last night. He told me that he just wished to talk. We met outside in the garden, by the big swing. I love that swing. Dad does not like me spending time on it and always finds some reason to call me away. I sneak out whenever they are out on their dinners. They go to a considerable number of dinners.

Kevin asked me what was bothering me. He seemed to genuinely care. I hesitated. But he promised that he'd not judge. There was something in his eyes that made me believe. Other than my parents and Albert, he was the closest to being a constant in my life.

So, I told him. He was not sure what I meant. So, I said it again. He looked nonplussed. Then he smiled gently and held my hand. I let him. He did not say anything. I stayed quiet. We sat on the swing, side by side, for a while. And then he told me he was sorry for kissing me without permission. And for the drunken calling. He asked me if he could still be my friend. He promised to keep my secret a secret. I hugged him. A long hug. I was not sure if it was for him or me.

Telling the truth felt good. I felt good.

I do not hate Kevin. He is not an idiot. Well, not entirely, at least.

* * *

'What did you tell him, Aunt Anna? Why are your letters so damn cryptic?' Noelle is exasperated.

She goes to the toilet, having consumed too much wine. She washes her face and her eyes catch a glint of the diamond ring on her hand. She tugs at it, takes it off and throws it in the medicine cabinet.

'Why would I keep that stupid ring on until now? What was I thinking? Robbie is an idiot.'

She grabs a large tub of ice cream from the fridge. She knows that this is going to be a long night. She doesn't care. All she wants is to get to the bottom of this mystery.

* * *

Mar 22, 1968

So, I thought I'd try it again. The whole truth-telling thing, I mean. I figured if more people knew and were okay with it, I could tell Mom and Dad, too. And they would not blame me for whatever happened to Albert.

My next audience was Bianca. We were out by the playground on a bench, for lunch. And I told her. She got up from the bench, all angry and riled up. I tried to explain. She looked at me accusingly, pushing me away, asking me why I was spewing nonsense. I did not know what I was expecting, but it was not what I had anticipated. She kept saying that I needed to get my head checked. I tried to explain, nudging her to sit back next to me. But she shoved me and left.

Why would she do that? It should not matter to her what I said about Albert or what I felt. She just needed to be my friend.

Why would she choose not to understand?

* * *

Noelle does not want new characters in this story. She does not wish to deal with Bianca. She sounds like a total brat.

'How could you be so insensitive, Bianca?'

Noelle gets a message on her phone, a confirmation from the bank that Aunt Anna's legacy has been credited to Noelle's bank account.

* * *

Mar 24, 1968

I have been calling Bianca for the last two days, but she does not pick up. I went by her house, but she was not there. Or maybe she was and did not want to meet me. Surely, I had not suddenly grown horns. And what I told her was not contagious. So ... why wouldn't she just ... urgh?

* * *

'Stop wasting your time on this moron, Aunt Anna!' Noelle shouts out and throws a pillow at the wall in irritation.

She knows that a big surprise is coming. Like an evil ghoul lurking in the darkness of a blind alley. Stuff of horror films. She resents horror films. And she resents surprises even more.

* * *

Apr 16, 1968

It has been three weeks since the Bianca fiasco. I told Kevin about it and he told me to ignore her. He told me that it was her problem to figure out and not my burden to bear. I have started to notice that Kevin is not such an idiot after all.

He warned me that not everyone would get my story. He seemed quite certain about it. I agree.

But either way, I have to find a way to tell Mom and Dad. I've decided to rip the bandage off on Sunday. Two days to go.

I need luck. And courage. Both. On the double!

* * *

The ice cream tub is half empty by now. Noelle is pacing up and down her bedroom. She is putting together theories in her mind and preparing for the various end-case scenarios as she does for vendor meetings. It is not working. She has no process to follow.

'What was happening on Sunday?' She is nervous and a bit scared to read the next letter.

* * *

Apr 18, 1968

I could not wait until Sunday, I mean tomorrow. So, I tried to talk to them in the morning. But I froze. No words would come out of my mouth. Dad was looking at me quizzically. I blurted out that I had questions about a school project. That took away most of the pre-lunch time. After lunch, our neighbors dropped in for high tea or an excuse to gossip. It was late evening by the time they left. Mom was busy making dinner and Dad was re-reading his newspaper for the third time.

I didn't know what to do. I swear … it was so hard.

I wanted to give it a try. But I will do it tomorrow for sure. Right now, I am afraid to leave my room.

* * *

Noelle picks up the next letter. It looks long, spanning multiple pages. Her heart is racing.

'Is this where I finally find out?'

She remembers her Papá telling her about Aunt Anna all those years ago, and how she was the only one left from her side of the family, and that she was alone. He had reminded her of her promise, urging her to visit his cousin.

Noelle had grudgingly gone to pay her respects, knowing that she'd find a reason not to ever do it again. But that never happened. Something about Aunt Anna had connected with Noelle. Aunt Anna made her feel good about herself. She never preached. She just listened and chose to play the perfect vinyl record to lift the mood if you needed it. She did not dwell on the past.

Only the previous month, she had asked Noelle to teach her all about Instagram. Aunt Anna was indefatigable.

She was how life would desire itself to be lived.

* * *

Apr 19, 1968

I was out in the hall, listening to a radio concert. At about five past two, Mom came bustling out of the kitchen and asked me to switch to MPR Radio. Dad put aside his book. I realized it was time for 'One Truth & No Lies,' their favorite show. I asked them if I could stay back and listen. They seemed okay with it. Dad even patted me on the back.

The show started when we tuned in and the host introduced the guest of the evening, Dr Matthew Hart. He was thirty-five years of age and the recipient of the Rupert Berrett Humanitarian Award for 1968. It had been awarded to him for his work in integrating various diversity groups across New Hampshire. I did not understand what that meant. My curiosity was aroused and I raised the volume.

Over the next few minutes, the host narrated the background of his guest—an activist, a prolific singer and a proud trans man. What did that mean? Dad turned to me and asked me to go to my room. His tone told me that I was not to ask why. I got up and left.

Or so they thought. I sat on the landing of the stairs, outside their field of view but within reach of the radio's sound. I pressed my ears to the floor and listened. Unseen.

Matthew was telling his story. He was born into a small family with limited means and an even more constrained worldview. But he was born to his family as Melinda. A girl? A girl who had known that she was different and lived in fear of being found out. She was bullied for her ungainly walk and unsophisticated manners. She did not know if she was normal or a freak. Her desperate attempts to make friends and relationships failed one after another because she did not fit the pattern. Episodes of depression and loneliness followed. She receded into a cocoon.

I could hear my parents murmur something to each other. The host urged Matthew to go on. Matthew's voice was cracking, but he went on. He talked about battling the urge to kill himself and finding the courage to step back from the ledge of his parent's apartment.

He was silent for some time before saying, 'But I killed Melinda that day forever. I decided to live how God had intended me to be. As a man.' I was stunned. I could not believe that Matthew was telling his story, THIS STORY, on public radio.

He reminisced about having to leave his parents, who'd thrown him out of their righteous, moral lives. He talked openly about his days of homelessness, about singing healing him from the inside, about his surgeries, about finding new friends and about his support group for outcasts like himself. Signing off, Matthew addressed his parents, telling them that he loved them and hoped that they could love him back one day.

I heard the radio go silent. My parents were quiet. I waited for a few moments and tiptoed downstairs. Mom was wiping away her eyes on the sleeve of her dress. Dad drew her into a gentle cuddle, somber and restrained. I realized that my face, too, was covered with tears and snot. It was like a dam had been breached.

My parents were surprised to find me standing there, gasping and crying uncontrollably. Dad got up and held me in an embrace. I held on tight to him as he patted my back and told me, 'You know you can tell us anything. We are here for you. You understand? We are here. And that's a promise, Albert.'

* * *

Albert? But ... Uncle Albert? Aunt Anna!

And at that moment, Noelle realizes why there are no pictures of Aunt Anna with her parents. She is frozen, stunned by the truth. She cannot fathom what would have happened next.

* * *

Apr 20, 1968

I have been in my room since last night. Since I told them about Anna. I am scared. Something is happening. I don't know what. I don't like it.

* * *

Apr 22, 1968

The maid knocked on my door. I was needed downstairs. I was too afraid to ask her anything. An hour later, I was sitting in the back seat of a car with a bag and a suitcase with tags that read, 'Albert Martinez Jr.' I was being sent off to a residential school where a seat was booked in the same name.

Kevin had come to say goodbye. He leaned in and whispered in my ear, 'I like Anna way more than Albert. He was such an ass!'

I could not help but smile. Some idiots are truly adorable.

That was the only goodbye I got that day.

* * *

'I wish I could take away your pain, Aunt Anna. I wish the world were a more understanding place. I wish there were fewer idiots in this world.'

Noelle weeps and prays in silence.

* * *

May 12, 1968

I keep an old picture under my pillow. It's one of my parents, my dad's hand on Albert's shoulder, all of them smiling under the shade of the willow tree.

I wish they'd taken the chance to click a picture with their daughter, Anna, too.

* * *

The empty ice cream tub lies on the floor. Noelle hollers, engulfed by a wave of helplessness. She hates this sensation.

She cannot stand that she'll never be able to tell Aunt Anna how brave she was.

'And I was worried about Robbie? Even though I knew he was a first-rate idiot? Screw him.'

* * *

Jan 12, 1969

I've run away from the school. I have some money I'd saved from my weekly allowance.

I will go and see Alejandro. He will help me. He told me he will, when I spoke to him over the telephone last week.

I am wearing the flowery, ivory dress that I'd stolen from Mom's almirah the day I was leaving.

* * *

Noelle realizes now why her Papá had pushed her to make that promise all those years ago. I miss you, Papá.

* * *

Sept 04, 1970

I telephoned Kevin yesterday.

That idiot kept crying. He was shocked that I was still alive.

Apparently, Albert drowned in a very tragic accident last month.

Apparently, they couldn't locate his slender form in the treacherous currents.

Apparently, his parents cried inconsolably at his funeral.

Apparently, there was an obituary in the local newspaper.

I asked the idiot to send me a copy of it.

He promised not to tell anyone where I was.

Rest in peace, Albert!

* * *

Noelle wakes up at nine the next morning.

She cancels all her appointments for the week. She books a round-trip ticket to New Hampshire. She is on her way to the airport. And in her handbag is a silver urn with her aunt's ashes. She makes a call to her Assistant Manager and informs him of her decision regarding the contract and that Señor Diaz be notified.

Later in the day, she finds Kevin, who runs the bakery in town, much to his surprise.

She tells him about Anna's passing, and he breaks down, remembering an old friend he'd missed, as Noelle holds his hand. He tells her that he came out to his folks a couple of years after Albert's death. He wishes he knew about Anna and could have been a part of her life. Now, he stays alone in a studio by the riverside, choosing to be single, which is not always easy.

There are many teary pauses as he talks about Anna's childhood and his history with Albert. Peter is now in the local government and lobbies actively for gay rights. Kevin doubts if Peter is genuine. Noelle agrees. Bianca had moved upstate with her folks, got married to a serial womanizer and now lives in a trailer park with her daughter.

Karma can be such a vindictive bitch sometimes.

She is feeling strangely vengeful of the bloodhounds who bark the living joy out of small beagles, be it boisterous bullies or big corporations.

She will bat for the ones who are forced to have their voices muffled out.

Noelle and Kevin visit Anna's childhood abode.

They spread the ashes from the urn around the swing in the backyard, under the willow tree. They bury the old memory box under that very spot where Anna first spoke her truth to Kevin.

She is home.

step on the lonely ladder

strings of fire playing on his flute

the divine melody beckons anon

Virgo (Aug 23 - Sep 22) | Mercury | Sapphire

I may be wrong for you, but I am still right.

SPENCER DIAZ GETS A CONFESSION

Texas, USA

This could be the beginning of my end, as some of you may have predicted. But Mom's lab reports came back and I have found myself a donor. Dad has not stopped laughing and yelping all at the same time since Dr Miller shared the 'exceptional news'.

Dad has thanked Mom a gazillion times.

He seems a bit inchoate with his words right now, choking every time he tries to string a proper sentence. Mom has not said much. They are taking her away now to run some more tests.

The surgery is tomorrow morning.

I can hear Dad's phone going off. He silences it, but someone desperately wants his attention. He cannot leave, as Rose … er

Simona is taking me for pre-surgery checks and he'll need to sign another truckload of forms.

He excuses himself and answers the call. 'Hello. I apologize, but I was at the … un hunh. Oh okay. Yes, I understand. Un hun … un hun …. Yes, of course. Sure. Thank you. Thank you….'

As soon as he gets off the call, he calls out to Jugs and Izzy. This Jugs person seems to mysteriously appear whenever the Diaz family is in need. I have grown to like him. Even his coconut scent and his funny sing-song way of speaking.

Dad squeals in joy as he announces that he's been promoted to Regional Sales Head.

He has just sealed a huge sales contract, one that he'd been angling for months with one Ms Noelle Hernandez. She represents a nationwide chain of fitness centers all across the US. Izzy squeals in joy. Dad tells them that the new position will have fewer hours and will add another digit to his salary. *Lo que está sucediendo?* I can hear Izzy jump around. I am sure her eyes are wet with happy tears and she is flailing her arms around as she does when she is rapturous.

'It's the best day we have had in a long time. I wish Spencer could hear this. You deserve it, Dad. You are my hero. Our hero.'

While Izzy is congratulating him, I am making plans on how to splurge all that extra cash. New additions to my sneaker collection? I should be rebranded as Sneaker Spencer.

After the frenzy settles down, Dad goes out to run some hospital errands, leaving me with Izzy, Jugs and Devon. Izzy introduces Devon to Jugs and they are soon chatting away as if they've known about each other for a while.

Strange. How can some humans do that? Not me. I never know what to say. Anyways, who wants to talk to a wiry teenager trying to stutter his way through a conversation? So, I don't say anything.

That's my normal. It's better this way. It's not trepidation. It's pragmatism. *No me crees?* I am pragmatic, if not anything else.

Although it's a happy day so far with a confirmed donor, promotions, upcoming sneaker shopping and whatnot, I know that I am missing something. My comatose radar could not be so off. Dr Miller, of course. I hear him come in. Hope there are no last-minute surprises this time! He tells Dad that they will start prepping Mom and me both at approximately the same time. He talks Dad through the various steps in the surgery and confirms if he understands it. Eventually, he updates Dad about the risks involved, it being a major surgery and all that.

The chances of a failed transplant or unforeseen complications due to prolonged intubation are potential concerns he makes Dad aware of. *Ay dios mío*. He mentions death, but I am trying not to think about it. I don't do well with doom and gloom. He is preparing Dad for the worst-case scenario and advises him to say his *adios*, just in case.

Is he for real? Does he want me to have a panic attack?

It's like he doesn't know me at all. This is the standard protocol, says Dr Miller. He tells Dad that they'll take me away after thirty minutes.

It's Izzy who succumbs to the melodrama first. She threatens to kill me if I do not come out alive from surgery. Er … I think she did not read the memo on that one properly. Devon stays with her as she tells me that I am the best brother anyone could ask for.

I wish she had told me sooner. I could have planned to stick around for longer.

She has brought a lucky charm that she ties on my right hand. I can hear the faint murmur of prayers from her. Then she gets up, gives me a gentle kiss on my forehead and leaves. I know she does not want me to hear her go off the deep end.

Dad is finding it tough to keep it together. When did he become such a wreck? I think I have seen a lifetime of tears from him. It's not a good look for a Regional Sales Head with a six-digit salary. But his voice is calm when he speaks. And the final piece of the puzzle fits in, just like that.

'Spencer. I love you, *mijo*. And I know you know that. But more than love, I am filled with pride for having you as my son. *Mi hijo*. Life has thrown a lot at you, but you still stand tall.

I know it is not easy for you. But you never look away, no matter how many demons chase you. I know you get scared sometimes, but I know that nobody can keep you down for long. You are brave. You are kind. *Gracias a Dios.* And you are funny as heck.

Thank you for giving me so many reasons to laugh. Although I must confess that I don't get some of your jokes.'

He lets out a chuckle. It is a few seconds before he resumes.

'You say that Izzy is my favorite child, but let me tell you that it's always been you. Since the day I first held you in my arms. To think that I am your father, it's just the best damn feeling in the world. I know you have had your share of troubles, but seeing you in this hospital bed has been my worst nightmare.

I have tried to be a good Dad to the extent of my ability, I promise. I have tried hard. I hope you see that, son. But sometimes, I got tired and felt alone and gloomy. It was hard for me too, you know.

I am sorry if I was not there when you needed me, but I tried. I always tried....'

There is a long pause as Dad pulls himself together.

'I struggled with things after your Mom left. I did not wish to afflict you and Izzy with it. You had already been dealt a shitty fate. But I started going to meetings and support groups for single parents to deal with ... you know ... parenting troubles.

It helped. It kept me sane, especially after the school shooting and everything. I was so scared, Spencer. Oh, the horror! The foreboding won't leave me alone. I could not catch a restful wink for days. I would sit outside your bedroom for hours, catching a few fleeting moments of sleep here and there. I never wanted to let you or Izzy out of my sight.

But with each day, it was becoming an impossible predicament to stay agile and available for you both. It was getting incredibly hard. Being there, with the group, allowed me a safe space to let go.'

Oh boy. I never realized how much Dad has been holding back behind that placid facade. He is a lot stronger than he looks.

Note to self. Think twice before deciding to become a parent. It's not just diapers and recitals. You also need to deal with sidebars like the possibility of your child getting killed by disturbed gun-wielding delinquents or accidental fire-pelting blasts in a secret meth lab.

Dad is quiet for a while before he continues. I know there is more to this story than what he is telling me. He knows he may not have another opportunity to finish the story.

'There is something else too, Spencer, that I want to tell you, *mijo*. I should have told you sooner, but I want to tell you now.... We will talk about it when you get better, but I will not be able to forgive myself if I ... if you ... I mean.

I met someone during one of these meetings. His name is Jugs. Well, it's Jagjit, really, but everyone calls him Jugs. He is from a quaint hillside town called Shimla in India. Some of his family still live there. He does not have any children of his own, but he has a nephew, Jimmy. Looks like Jimmy is dealing with some serious trauma, too. That's why Jugs comes to the meetings. We met last year and we.... He's been a major reason why I have been able to function normally, especially after the shooting. If you can call it that. And I ... I want you to ... I want you to meet him, to know him, because he is ... we are ... I mean, he's my ... my partner. Not a business partner. But my....

Do you know what I mean?

We are together.

It was just friendship at first. We'd go on treks, fishing and stuff to unwind and talk. He sucks at fishing, though he makes a mean fish curry. But somewhere along the road, we ... we fell in love.

I have never felt this way for anyone. Not your Mom, no one. I struggled to accept it; I kept pushing him away, but he never gave up. He did not pressure me and allowed me time to come to terms with what it meant. He waited while I was ... well, mostly denying what I knew had always been a part of me. Until....'

I cannot believe what he is saying. I need a minute. Maybe five. *Increíble*. This is insane. While I try to process this, Dad plows on with his monologue.

'Spencer, it was you who gave me the courage. Seeing you walk back into school, refusing to give up on life even after being dealt the worst cards, that was something incredible. You are so brave, my son. You are stronger than you realize.

You have a way of finding humor and happiness in the smallest nooks of life that others tend to overlook. I wish I was more like you. Anyhow, I finally let Jugs into my life. Our lives. He makes me feel intoxicated with joy and he keeps me sane. And the Diaz family could do with some sanity, don't you think?'

Dad pauses as Jugs walks toward me. I can hear his carefully measured footsteps and smell his coconut odor. *¿Estoy soñando?* Is this the person my Dad has fallen for? Did Dad just say he loved him?

Dad continues, 'Jugs is here now. He comes every single day to visit you and me. He brings fresh flowers, my change of clothes and books. He helps Izzy with her nursery and mows our lawn. He even built a custom rack for your shoes, placed it inside the nook by your window and stacked all your sneakers by color and style, just like you would have wanted it. You should see it, *mijo*. It looks splendid!

I introduced him to Izzy a few weeks back. At the hospital canteen, would you believe that? I am sorry to have kept this from you. I was going to tell you that weekend at the cabin, but we never got to that.

Spencer, after a very long time in my life, I feel complete. I don't know what I would do without Jugs. He is my person.

A person who is mine for life. To whom I can fully belong without hiding any part of me.

I have hope. And I hope you will be delighted for your old man, son!'

Dad is silent for a long time. Jugs is nearby, perhaps standing next to Dad. Perhaps he has his hand around Dad's shoulders. Perhaps Dad is leaning against him, letting his guard down. Perhaps Jugs is running his fingers through Dad's disheveled hair. Dad's hair can get messy. Perhaps Dad is kissing the back of his palm.

But surely, Dad is at home with him.

If they could see me on the inside, they'd see that I am smiling. My eyes are brimming with giddy love.

I have never felt closer to Dad than I feel right now. That he would stifle his own life just to make sure Izzy and I have a smile on our faces, it is everything. And more. Because 'everything' does not come close to defining what he has given us. Dreams. Hope. Trust.

I love you, Dad.

I wish you had told me sooner. I wish I was not so selfish to not see your loneliness and anguish. I wish you a lifetime of sick delights with Jugs. Although, I need to find a way past his coconutiness. But I am glad that one more entry on my list is complete.

Find out who Jugs is.

(12)

THE GREEN[17] SEQUINS

For the ones who forget their smile

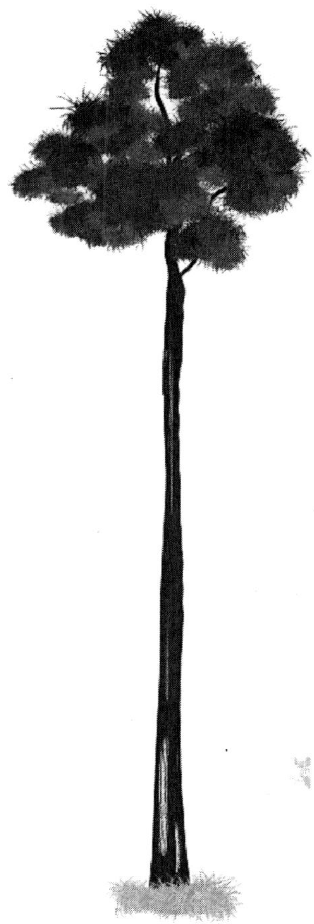

In the crevices of my being
Shy, timid, yet hope floats
Like a buckram, I stand
Stiff, impertinent, my ego bloats

[17] Emerald, along with green and brown are the colors of the zodiac Taurus. Venus is the ruling planet and imbues people with this sun sign with traits of indulgence and self-care, and they try not to waste any time waiting to pursue their dreams.

SHUBHRA GETS READY TO DANCE

Del Rio, Texas, USA

'It will be alright. Everything will be just fine. Do not presume the worst.'

Her sleep is disturbed by a sudden clank so loud that the hair on her neck prickles. Still not out of her slumber, she looks around and notices a nurse bending over to gather probes and syringes into the tray, stretching the stitches of her uniform and accentuating every single bulge of her body.

'How did she ever manage to get into that skirt?' Shubhra Parekh wonders as she blinks herself awake.

A name tag on the nurse's dress says 'Deborah' in bold, blue letters, followed by 'Head Nurse' in slightly trimmer font on the next line. At least my eyes seem to be working all right!

She lets her thoughts stay on Deborah for a few moments, admiring her neat hair and the wispy blue cap like the one they wear at fast food kiosks while serving.

'Do they all buy supplies from the same store?'

She tries to imagine what Deborah might be if not a nurse and cannot quite make up her mind. Maybe an accountant at an unpretentious law firm, judging by the efficiency with which the head nurse seems to work.

'Of course, I must not judge. Maybe she wants to go into sports or culinary science!'

'Mrs Parekh, Mrs Parekh.' Someone is calling her name.

'Mrs Parekh, how are you feeling?' asks Vivian, the other nurse who's been attending to her along with Deborah, adjusting the drip and checking the tubes.

Vivian is smiling, as she always does, her frizzy perm bouncing around. 'She is sweet, that woman. I am trying to fathom how long she's been working here. Is this what she'd always wanted to be?' Shubra wonders.

'I just saw Mr Parekh and he looks fine. Don't you worry!' Vivian informs as she stocks the medicine drawer with supplies.

Shubhra is jolted out of her wandering thoughts.

'I wish she'd stop with all these ominous-looking capsules and syringes,' she shudders.

'You both gave us quite a scare; you did! It was a close call.' Vivian chuckles encouragingly.

Shubhra feels a familiar surge of anguish drowning her again, dragging her back into the darkness that had surrounded her for hours after the crash. She vividly remembers the stench of burnt flesh, the helplessness of her hoarse screams and the panic of being forgotten.

'We did not die. We survived.'

How she had managed to stay alive pinned under the heavy mass of debris, she does not understand. But trying to pull herself out had been futile. She had called out to Yash again and again, but he did not respond. She had wondered if he was dead. His face was turned the other way, and she could not make out if he was still breathing. Panic had set in, and she'd started yelling for help.

'Help! Help … somebody help me! Anyone there? Fire. Fire! Please help. Somebody, listen…. I am here. Help....' the scene replays in her mind.

Anyone would be terrified in that situation. No one prepares to deal with such catastrophes.

'That too alone. Alone?'

She recalls how her throat started to hurt from the screaming, how she'd rest for a while and then start again. Over and over again until her lips started to crack with dryness; it felt like her mouth was ablaze from the inside. She'd seen crows, or was it vultures, circling high up in the dark sky. She'd been sure that death was imminent. But then, without a preamble, the fire had simply died.

It was getting late, the sky already inky at the fringes, the redness of the evening bleeding away into sooty darkness. And so, she kept screaming and hollering until she lapsed into unconsciousness.

Once, when she came to, she'd seen the headlights of their mangled car flickering like a burning flame being doused out by a gust of cruel wind. With that, the last hope of being rescued had disappeared.

'How did it even happen?'

They'd been standing there by the side of the road with Yash smoking his supposed 'last cigarette' of the day.

They'd stopped on their way to an office party—he wanted to smoke under that crusty overbridge.

'Once an addict, always an addict!'

* * *

She'd always loathed Yash for this. But she'd never quite imagined the phrase 'smoking kills' to play out the way it almost did.

On other occasions, whenever he smoked, she'd excuse herself and get away from him on some pretext. He had figured that out but still argued with her about it. She had never said anything explicitly.

'I never said anything. Never. I should have!' she laments.

She recalls how Yash had come home one day and announced that he'd give up smoking, though slowly and gradually. Even then, Shubhra had known that nothing was going to change. He was not serious about it, or her! He'd still smoke at least a pack, perhaps more every week.

'Was that his chosen path to rehabilitation?' she rages quietly.

Soon enough, he'd thrown his hands up, declaring that he had tried but surrendered. Typical. He had other such bouts of exploring nicotine patches and electronic cigarettes, but he'd always come up short. Shubhra knew that he was a slave to the habit and could not be bothered by the inconvenience of being free.

'Why did I not elucidate that to him?' she considers.

Interestingly, every time he started a new remedy, he'd declare that he had earned a night of lovemaking as if her vagina was accepting coupons for totally missing the damned moral of the freaking story. She'd surrender with a smile, knowing he'd not take no for an answer. At least one of them deserved to experience ecstasy!

Every time he heaved his way in and out through sex, she'd feel more and more detached. It was like a chasm that kept widening, keeping them apart even when he was on top of her. She was no longer attracted to him. It was an antithesis to the intense allure she'd felt when they had gotten married. However, that idea of romance had passed quickly for her.

With time, she was convinced she had been mistaken about him all along.

For someone who'd prided herself on being an excellent judge of character, Yash had called her bluff. After the euphoria of their wedding, the adrenaline rush of coming to a new country, and the excitement of setting up their new apartment in Austin had ebbed, she discovered the real man behind the charming persona that was now her husband.

* * *

Vivian has been quietly dressing her wounds. Shubhra knows that her cuts are deep and her body is broken. She cannot help but contrast it with the smooth, dark skin on Vivian's face, admiring the softness of the nurse's hands as she tends to Shubhra's battered body. She knows that doctors had taken extreme measures to save her legs, requiring over nine hours of surgery.

'Thank you, Dr Alvarez. I'll never be able to repay that debt. You saved my future. My legs, my only hope to sail free....' she thinks.

Since Shubhra's pain is a bit more manageable, Vivian is fussing over her appearance, braiding her hair and applying vivid pink nail paint.

'I love this color. Yash will say I look like a slut,' she conjectures, repulsed by the imagined sound of his voice.

Vivian smiles and points to the forehead with a forefinger and smiles. It takes her some time to understand that Vivian is asking her about a *bindi.* She nods and helps Vivian find the pack of *bindis* from her purse. Vivian carefully places one on Shubhra's forehead, admiring her work. Shubhra offers one to Vivian, who preens around like a teenager once she puts it on. Shubhra hands her the whole pack.

'I can always buy more from the Indian store in Austin. Plus, I may not need these if....' Shubhra contemplates.

Vivian beams at her, pocketing the pack of *bindis.* She asks Shubhra if she remembers how the accident happened. Shubhra tells her, 'We had been driving to a party that Yash's office had arranged. I did not want to go, but Yash insisted I come. So ... there I was....'

She does not voice her next thought, 'God forbid if his life looks anything else than "picture perfect."'

Vivian, sensing Shubhra's turmoil, tuts at her considerately, lowers Shubhra's headrest and leaves the room.

* * *

Lying in her bed, Shubhra agonizes over the past year, the perfect bouquet of her subjugation. She recalls their weekend sojourns to fancy Italian restaurants, although Yash knew she preferred Chinese.

'Why pasta and tiramisu every time?'

She remembers the fancy dresses he'd want her to wear, though she felt more at ease in her old jeans. Satin and velvet ... urgh. Her thoughts go back to when Yash purchased an ornate Victorian couch for their apartment, though she preferred the cool bohemian lounger at the store.

'How can anyone like emerald green sequins on sofa cushions?' she recoils at the memory.

She had watched while Yash made the purchase. And she had smiled. She had pretended that she liked it all—the pasta, the tiramisu, the satin dresses, the green sequins, even the frantic grind of Yash's 'love-making'.

'Why did I not say anything? Why did I carry on even when I knew it was pointless?' she berates her own cowardice.

Shubhra and Yash had moved to Texas barely a week after their wedding. She had immensely liked the idea of a foreign country, an alien city—a new start to their new life, without the trappings of Yash's rather boisterous and nosy joint family. She had learned to drive and loved exploring places in and around Austin.

'I was a lot more resilient then,' she reminisces.

At that time, even the gaudy Victorian sofa with emerald green sequins had not upset her for too long. It seemed like an odd choice, nothing more. She was happy living the designer life Yash had planned for them.

'It was fun at first. It was nice being dolled up and posing pretty.'

But slowly, over time, her serenade started to fade. Yash's commitment as the 'man of the house' was unwavering, and his accounting of expenses was relentless. Evenings were reserved for him to unwind and watch cricket or crime shows. Weekends were designed to catch up with his mates, go grocery shopping and have a fancy meal.

Amid all this, Shubhra became confined to being the designated plus one for Yash.

'How had I missed so much for so long?' Shubhra wonders.

Yash was not a monster, for he never laid a finger on her or abused her in any way. He was not a narcissist, for he would buy her flowers and jewelry. He just wasn't the man she'd thought she was marrying.

'It was like living with a stranger. A stranger in my home, my life and my bed. A stranger with a rather rigid curriculum.'

She'd walked into a dance studio out of curiosity during one of her solo trips downtown. That evening, she cooked Yash's favorite dishes and dolled up in a tight skirt he liked. He was pretty pleased, smiling from ear to ear all evening. Later, in the bedroom, she'd broached the idea of becoming a dance instructor at the studio, a place she had instantly fallen in love with. Yash had thankfully been too busy unclasping her dress to object, growling like a tiger on the prowl.

'Why did he make those weird animal sounds in bed?' She shudders at the memory.

She'd taken his grunting as consent, and euphoria swept her deeper into his arms. For the first time in months, she willingly made love to him.

'What can I say? His complete indifference to my decision was such a turn-on,' she recalls.

Dance had been her entire life before marriage, something Yash knew about but never took any interest in. He never even asked what forms of dance she practiced.

'That should have been a hint.'

It was the happiest she'd felt in months. Her appointment at the studio was temporary, but the studio's director seemed excited to introduce *Kathak* as part of their curriculum.

Life was getting interesting. She could not stop grinning even as Yash moaned his way in and out of her.

* * *

'I'll leave you to rest now, Mrs Parekh,' Deborah smiles down at her, diligently updates her charts, inspects the IV needle in her left hand and leaves her to rest, drawing the curtains shut.

'Did Deborah hear anything? She couldn't have. I was just thinking.'

The medicines are making her drowsy, and she drifts into slumber. The pain in her broken ribs and bones in her legs fading into nothingness.

* * *

Deborah walks out to the staff lounge. It's been a long day. She is tired. Her skirt chafes against the skin on her thighs. She wants to take a hot shower.

Vivian is already there, sipping her black coffee while flipping the tired, crumpled pages of the last edition of Vogue. There is a disposable plate with blueberry cake on the table.

Simona from the day shift is there as well, resting her feet on the couch. Deborah pours herself and Simona a coffee from the last dregs at the bottom of the carafe at the base of the oft-broken coffee machine.

Then, the three nurses get on with talking about their patients. They always talk about their patients.

Simona tells them that there has not been much change in Spencer's condition. His vitals look stable, but Dr Miller does not like his odds. She tells them the blueberry cake is for Spencer's birthday. His sister has a whole picnic thing going on in his room.

Deborah cannot help but smile. 'He is a sweet boy, that one. I hope he wakes up soon. Do you feel that he still senses things, people around?'

Simona smiles and says, 'I notice his pulse relax when I give him a sponge bath. And he hates it when I stick him with the shots on his butt.' They have a good laugh at this and Vivian joins in.

They say a prayer for Spencer and move on to discussing Shubhra and Yash.

'Will they pull through?' Simona asks. 'Something's not right between them. I have a feeling. Do you sense that too, Deborah?' Vivian asks the head nurse, her hand turning the pack of bindis over and over in her pocket.

'The pain in Mrs Parekh's eyes is not just from her broken ribs or bones. You know what I mean?' She desperately wants Shubhra to get better. She has not yet made up her mind about Mr Parekh. She feels guilty about it, being a nurse and whatnot.

Deborah considers the situation before she speaks. 'I don't know everything. But here is what I do know. Most of it is what I overheard when the police took her—I mean Mrs Parekh's—statement. A bunch of old bikers had found them, having driven off the highway themselves. They'd called 911. It had taken more than an hour-and-half for the police and the firefighters to rescue the couple. They brought them here to Verde Vista Memorial Hospital; after all, we were the nearest to the accident site. It took Mrs Parekh a full day to regain consciousness. It's been more than a week for Mr Parekh, and yet....'

Simona asks, 'But how did they land up in that wreck?'

Deborah carries on. 'Looks like he had taken the back road to avoid traffic. And then he stopped near the overbridge for a smoke. What's it with men and their vices? Anyhow, she, too, got out to stretch her legs. Then suddenly, there was a resounding bang, and a heavy plank of wood landed squarely on the hood of their Mercedes, smashing glass and steel alike. And before they even had the time react, a freaking truck fell from the overbridge, hitting the road with a crash. The impact threw her off the road onto a grass landing, pinning her under debris. She could not move, poor thing. Her husband was unconscious, lying a few feet away from her but unresponsive. That's all Mrs Parekh told the policemen before she got nauseous and Dr Alvarez pulled the plug on their inquiries.'

Deborah pauses, melancholically sipping her tepid coffee. Vivian sighs in resignation. Simona gets up, unable to contain her billowing rage. She wants to lash out. She is spent from being a witness to so much suffering, exhausted from worrying about her patients and finding herself helpless.

'Someone needs to sue the trucking company. Someone needs to be held accountable. We see too many cases like this when some deranged mofo goes around, fracking the innocent ones. One moment, they are sitting in a class, playing in the park, or smoking on the road. And another, they are fighting for their life!

Just like those kids at the school shooting.

Just like Mrs and Mr Parekh.

Just like Spencer.

What did Spencer do wrong? He was simply running on the street. Was that a crime? Was he at fault? No, he made no mistake. Not him.

Yet, he has not woken up for over a month. He is just sixteen, for crying out loud!

Yet, he is likely to succumb to a lung that was so perforated with shrapnel that it unsettled even Dr Miller.

Just because some shitfaced cokehead thought it would be fun to cook meth in his basement?

Who takes the blame for the ones who died in that blast? People cannot just go about recklessly torpedoing other people's lives like this. They just can't.'

She buries her head in her hands and collapses on the couch, tears pouring out and her voice giving way.

Deborah and Vivian do not have answers. None of them have answers, and they won't get any because there are no answers.

The three nurses sip their coffee in silence.

* * *

Deborah returns to check on Shubhra that afternoon and finds her awake. She offers Shubhra a sponge bath. Shubhra nods and surrenders as Deborah takes charge of her battered body, scrubbing her off with a warm, sterilized thingamabob soaked in steaming hot water with a trace of disinfectant.

She ponders whether she will ever be beautiful again and whether she will be able to dance again. She suspects the worst and the possibility makes her shudder. Deborah apologizes, assuring her that she will try to be more careful.

'Poor Deborah, she doesn't know what ails me—only if she knew my real ache.'

As Deborah gently but steadily swabs her clean, Shubhra turns into another dark alley of her brain. She is daring herself to walk in deeper, to where she has not had the guts to go before.

* * *

'The affair. My husband's clandestine trysts with a certain someone who I do not know. Had I even wanted to know?' Shubhra ponders.

She'd overheard him talking to that someone when he thought she was asleep. He had left the balcony door ajar by mistake, where he was making his trademark mating animal sounds, professing his love for the person on the other end of the phone.

'How had he managed to lure another woman into liking him?'

'Did she know him as I did? Why would she want him?'

She had wanted to feel upset. In fact, she had not felt anything. No jealousy or fury. Just an absolute lot of nothing.

That night, not long after the call, Yash had snuggled up to her in bed, ready to make his conquest. He did not say anything, just growled his way in and out of her body. She'd not made a sound or resisted or reacted to his presence within her. He might as well have been a horny cowboy riding a corpse. All she had wanted at that moment was for him to be done with it.

Her marriage was a kite with a broken spine that would never fly again.

Earlier, she'd wanted to fix things between them. But there was nothing left to fix after that night. They had turned another corner for the worse. The next morning, she tossed away her wedding *lehenga* in the trash. It had to go. She did not need a reminder of what could have been and what was not.

* * *

Recollecting that day, an overwhelming urge to cry overtakes Shubhra. She wants to shed all the pitiful vulnerability she has been bottling. All her emotions are brimming over, threatening to slip away as she lies bare on the cold hospital bed.

'What will Deborah think?' She wills herself not to cry and stays strong while Deborah dries up her body with a soft towel and dresses her up in the hospital gown.

Once done, Deborah draws the curtains open, letting the crisp sunlight pour in and leaves her room.

'This is better.' She decides to look outside and breathe. She can see the tops of cedar elm trees that line the road, their leaves changing to a lovely yellow. Her hospital room is on the third floor. Room 303, her door says.

'I wish I could see more of the sky. But this will do.'

A blustery wind is blowing, with the branches of the proud elms outside swaying wildly. 'A rainstorm?'

The hanging nest of an oriole bird on one of the trees catches her attention. She marvels at its odd design and reflects on how much painstaking effort the bird would have put into building it. One straw at a time. 'Only to be swept aside and torn up in the storm?'

Shubhra's thoughts are interrupted by a soothing, deep voice asking her how she is doing. It is Dr Alvarez on his daily rounds. After reassuring her of her excellent recovery, he clears his throat. His smile fades away a bit as he sits beside her bed. He places a gentle hand on her arm and lowers his voice as he updates her on Yash's condition.

'Things are not looking as good for Mr Parekh. His vitals are slightly better, but not enough. We might need to put him on a ventilator, which can do the breathing for him. We'll need your consent to take any such life-saving measures for your husband. Do you understand that, Mrs Parekh?' Dr Alvarez hands her a form.

'We will do everything to make him comfortable, Mrs Parekh. Please pray for his recovery.'

She looks out of the window at the oriole bird's nest. 'Please survive this storm. Please,' she pleads.

For a moment, Shubhra considers not signing the form. But then, she takes the pen from Dr Alvarez and signs.

'I do not want control, not like this.' And then, she turns her head away and closes her eyes. Vivian comes and pats her gently on the head.

Yash suffers a major stroke the following evening. The doctors need to try an emergency surgery. Vivian keeps Shubhra updated while the surgery is going on.

'Does Vivian have tears in her eyes?'

Shubhra avoids eye contact as Vivian squeezes an injection into her IV line. Soon, she is drowsy. But her dreams keep her busy.

* * *

She finds herself in her posh living room with the Victorian couch and the gaudy cushions with the green sequins.

She is throwing all her velvet dresses and jewelry everywhere, tearing the petals off the chrysanthemums Yash had bought for her on her birthday. A plate of half-eaten tiramisu and a glass of red wine are on the table. A cricket match is playing on television.

Yash is making loud animal sounds on the phone. And she is dancing barefoot on the white carpet with her *ghungroos*, doing the *Kathak chakkars* one after another—pirouetting round and round and round until she collapses in front of Yash, spilling his glass of red wine on the gaudy cushions with the green sequins. And she is laughing.

* * *

The next morning, Deborah tells her that they'll start her physiotherapy and wheels her away in a stretcher to the ground floor. Deborah keeps her company while the therapist asks her to flex or point her feet one way and then the other. He assures her she will start walking within the next few weeks.

'I need to be stronger.'

On her way back from therapy, she asks Deborah to take her to see Yash. Deborah hesitates but relents.

Through the glass walls of the ICU, Shubhra sees the broken, sedated and heavily plastered body of her husband.

'What is this that I am feeling?' she lets out a gasp and a cry as she looks at the number of machines and tubes all around him. She thinks to herself, 'It breaks my heart to see you like this. I wish....'

Tears breach her restraint and start to flow, giving no warning whatsoever. She looks away from Yash, willing herself to stop crying and finds herself looking through the window of the adjoining room, where a middle-aged man is weeping noiselessly at the bedside of a young boy. It says 'Spencer, 16 years' on the nameplate. The man must be the boy's father.

He apologizes, holding his ears and cracking a smile before breaking down again. There's confetti on the floor and helium balloons tied to the bed. One of the balloons reads 'Happy 16th Birthday!' The man holds up the boy's hands and buries his face inside, sobbing reticently into the night.

Shubhra tells Deborah she is done.

Back in her room, Shubhra is wide awake. She recalls the time when she was buried under the debris of the truck, calling out for help. 'Please save me. Fire. Fire. I am here....'

'Help "me". Not help "us"? Why had I not.... Is this truly me? How could I not….?'

When she had gained consciousness, she'd not asked how her husband was. The nurses and doctors had attributed it to the shock. But she'd known all along. She had prayed for Yash to be okay, not to die. She did not want him to suffer.

'But why had my insides not twisted with worry?' she wonders. She is terrified of facing the truth. 'Truth is so overrated. So is love.'

After seeing Yash at the Life Support Unit earlier that day, she knows what she had suspected for the last few days.

'Why do I not want to hold his hands, like Spencer's father? He is still my husband.' Shubhra is tormented by her indifference.

An hour later, she makes a call to her friend Charvi, one of her only two confidantes in Austin. Soon after, she rings the patient's bell.

Deborah has left by now. That's why Shubhra makes her unusual request to the other nurse on call for the night, Sandie, who tells her that she'd consult Dr Alvarez and make arrangements.

Her third call that night is to Amod. He is Yash's younger, single brother who lives in San Jose. She tells him about the accident, slowly revealing details, not letting any panic seep into her voice. She asks him to inform their parents in India and tells him that important decisions will need to be made soon.

'Life and death decisions that I should no longer take,' she thinks.

Yash's condition does not change much the next day. Or the day after. He has still not woken up. On the way back from physiotherapy, Deborah asks her if she wants to visit Yash. She declines. Deborah knows about her request to Sandie.

'I know she wants to know. I don't think I can explain. At least Charvi has not asked too many questions. I hope it stays that way,' she contemplates.

When Yash's brother and their jetlagged parents arrive the next day, they are taken over to the Life Support Unit straightaway. They enquire about Shubhra but are told to wait for the visiting hours. Yash's mother collapses upon seeing her son through the window, even as Vivian tries to help her. His father breaks down, too, unable to bear the sight of his son's battered body, embracing his other son. Amod stands transfixed by the perversity of the situation but surprisingly keeps it together.

Shubhra observes them from a distance. 'Stay strong for them, Amod.' She sends a silent prayer their way.

'Thank you. I mean it. You know what to do with the envelope I've given you. Please tell Vivian that she'll look gorgeous wearing a bindi,' Shubhra tells Deborah and waves her a cheery goodbye. Deborah kisses her forehead as the waiting medics hand her the paperwork. They wheel Shubhra towards a waiting ambulance, ready to transfer her to a different hospital, her belongings already packed in a bag.

'I hope Deborah remembers giving the letter, the ring, and the keys to Yash's parents. I hope they don't come looking for me. I hope....' she worries.

Slowly, though, Shubhra feels a soothing serenity descending over her.

The ambulance is ready. So is Shubhra.

The sirens on the ambulance come alive.

'Bless you Charvi, for making the arrangements so quickly. I owe you one! Here I come, San Antonio. I'm bringing my next dance to you.'

out by the spring alone
walk tall against the proud winter wind
call my name out aloud

Taurus (Apr 20 - May 20) | Venus | Emerald

I may not be your person, but I am surely mine.

PART FIVE

THE LEGEND OF ETHER

The story of Spencer Diaz…
the one that runs through them all

what no eye can see
what no ear can hear
beyond the reach of touch
above the skies clear
what permeates every crevice
what fills every open pore
until it becomes a way of being
down to the pits of my core
what is often left unsaid
what is rarely ever told
inside my heart, my soul
amid the crease of every fold
what wistfully binds it all
what is my foe, my friend
in the essence of every being
from the start until the end

SPENCER DIAZ MAKES A CHOICE

Texas, USA

I feel bright lights shining overhead. It must be time.

I hear the chatter in the operating room that I was wheeled into earlier. Dr Alvarez is scrubbing in with Dr Miller and Vivian is the assisting nurse. I wish Rose and Sandie were here, too. I am sure they are rooting for me outside somewhere.

Dr Miller is talking to me now.

'Spencer, I hope you can hear me. You've been a remarkably gutsy young man, fighting against such odds. Your dad tells me you love to run. I want to give you that, a way to run again. And I need you to fight alongside me on this. I want you to be strong and come out of this, kicking some trauma ass. Your mom is giving one of her lungs to you. She loves you. Your sister Izzy is waiting outside with a blueberry cake. So, let us do this together, Spencer.'

With that, he goes quiet, presumably focusing before starting with the snips and cuts. I want to tell him that I will fight. I want to tell him an umpteen number of things.

I want to run again and I want another pair of sneakers.

I want to go to stupid corporate events and be embarrassed by Dad's boss.

I want to thank Tía Gabriela for the hundreds of nights babysitting me. I want to devour a potful of her delicious paella.

I want to go to the bake sale at Mr and Mrs Moreno's house.

I want to stutter my way through English class.

I want to visit Abuela and listen to her stories over and over again.

I want to have my lunch with Callie and Susie outside at the playground.

I want us to become friends with Leo and help him get over whatever is crippling him.

I want to start hitting the gym and build biceps like Sandie and Rose's crush from India.

I want us to go on expeditions and play a bazillion more rounds of Mortal Kombat.

I want to visit the Amazon rainforests with Susie and thank Dr Palash for his story. And help him find his daughter.

I want to lie down on Gunther's terrace and gaze at the stars in the night sky. I want to talk to the stars.

I feel a few pricks of needles, hopefully, some form of anesthesia.

I want to thank the good samaritan who brought me to the hospital.

I want to tell Mr Anirudh that there is still hope for this world and for the children of the time to come.

I want to find Tía Elena and reunite her back with our family, her family.

I want to hear everything about forest wildlife from Susie.

I want to see Izzy and Devon go out on dates, many dates and get married.

I want to fall in love—crazy, canoodling, cuddly love—with someone I can write my fairy tale with.

I want to see the pictures of Devon's expeditions in the deep blue and green waters from across all the oceans of the world.

I want to meet the young mother who bypassed me on the transplant list and tell her that it is okay, and to hold her kid in my arms and bless his soul for saving his mother's life.

I want to meet Jugs and tell him that he needs to take care of Dad and love him until eternity, and that I will hunt him down if he ever bails on Dad. I want to see their beatific beginnings, the joyful middles, and keep wishing that they never end.

I want to find a special someone who will be my sweetheart and my true love. Did I count that one already?

I want to stop making lists. I want this to be my last one.

But most of all, I want the Diaz family to leave its fears behind.

Fear is a terrific motivator, but it also is the biggest enemy of finding new things that bring you happiness. It binds us, keeps us from flying, and from discovering what could be a happier tomorrow. Fear traps us, paralyzes us and holds us hostage on the island that is our comfort zone. It is a sly foe that beguiles us into a rhythm of safety, luring us away from all that leads us to find the next adventure in life.

I hear faint music in the background. Is that Bach? Way to go, Dr Miller.

Today, I want to be like Johnny Cage and win this 'mortal combat'.

See what I did there?

I want to be strong in body and soul.

I am Johnny Cage.

I am Ralph.

I am a New Nomad.

I am Spencer Diaz and I am not afraid anymore.

P.S.

In case you are wondering, my surgery goes as well as it could have.

I wake up two days later.

Patient Alpha starts with trials for the new rehab equipment.

The hospital discharges him after another week.

Sandie tries to hide her tears but breaks down like a pint-sized princess the moment I thank her for the sensual sponge baths.

Simona decides to go by Rose as her preferred ‘work’ name.

Dr Miller wants me to undergo physiotherapy for three months.

There is a big welcome for me at home when we get back. Izzy’s surprise. Abuela and Tía Gabriela are there. Mr Moreno has donned his fedora and Mrs Moreno is wearing her dress with colorful flowers. Even some of my teachers have come. And my gang of misfits is cheering the loudest. They have brought Leo along. They all take turns hugging me. Even Leo.

Mom goes back to San Francisco. She calls us every week.

Jugs moves in with us a month later. I think I now like coconuts.

Izzy's nursery is flourishing. She has a new spring in her step.

Dad buys me tickets for Sneakercon. This Regional Sales Head gimmick is working well for me.

Devon is taking Izzy to India to meet his family. It's his parents' silver jubilee and they are celebrating at some fancy fort in the royal city of Jaipur. Izzy wants to sneak away for a romantic vacation in the hills. I do not know why love makes you do stupid things.

I am back at school next term and it is my final one. I was allowed to skip a grade.

I made a new friend. His name is Parth. He is Devon's second cousin. He is really smart and is helping Gunther and me build a telescope. He is just like us in more ways than one. I want to talk to the stars up close.

There have been no more shootings or explosions.

I still go for two sessions with Mrs Garcia every week. I don't lie to her anymore.

Jugs and I go fishing on weekends if Dad is working. He sucks at it. I am teaching him. He has a long way to go.

Gunther and Callie tell me that Susie has a crush on Parth. They are trying to play Cupid.

Izzy enrolled for her Masters. Finally, she is studying Business Administration.

I do not count the scoops of raisin bran flakes at breakfast or the steps between the first and second floors at school. I only count my blessings.

I still have rehab and therapy on alternate days. Patient Alpha has done well. The hospital is expanding the trial.

Susie is teaching me how to journal. I doodle or write some nights in my diary. It has a lock and everything. I cannot draw or paint to save my life.

I lay down on Gunther's terrace every so often and talk to the stars. I know some of them had fallen into my soup and made it worthwhile.

Dad smiles more around Jugs.

Izzy smiles more around Devon.

I smile more around everyone.

I still hope to fall in love.

Everybody seems to be living happily right now. I am not too hung up on the 'ever after'. Ever afters are highly overrated.

And here ends the Legend of Ether, the lost zodiac of a timeless being, the sun sign that is a part of nothing but is inherent to everything all the time, the one that effortlessly brings together the zodiacs across bounds of time and space.

HOW THE 'STARS' SHINE

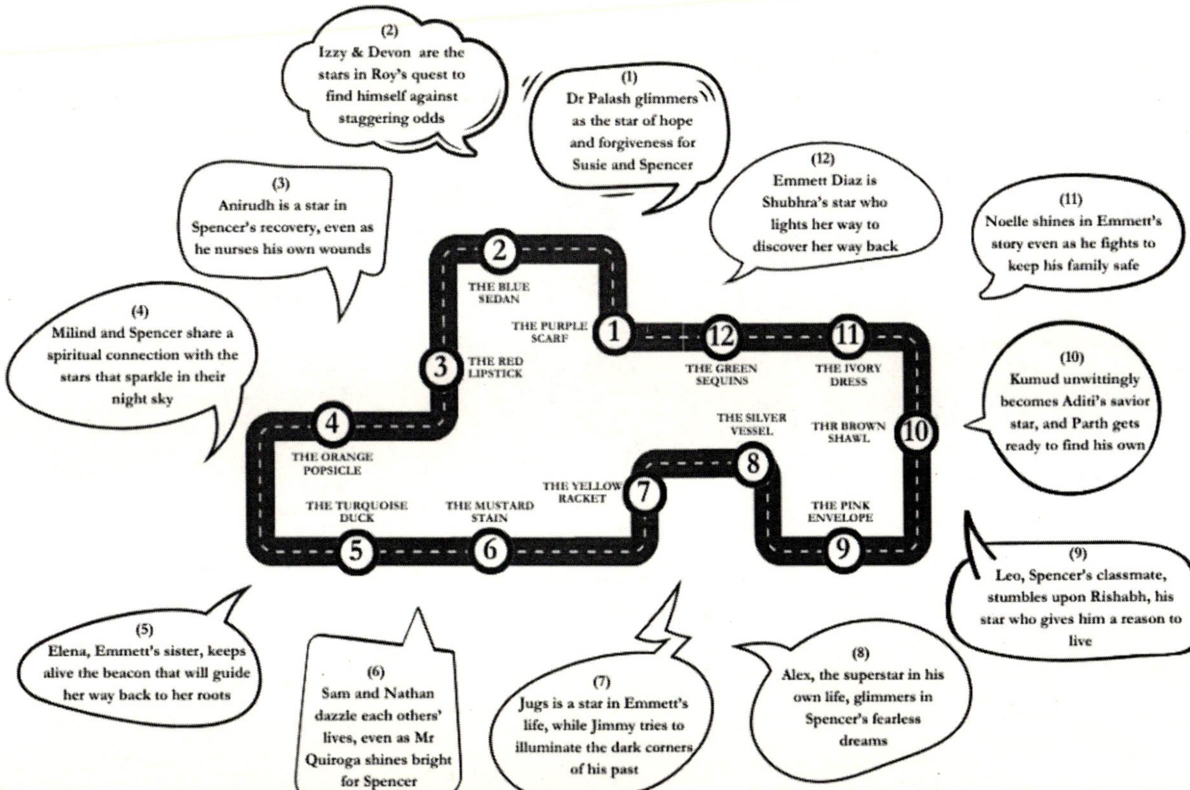

'Yesterday is gone. Tomorrow has not yet come. We have only today. Let us begin.'

— Mother Teresa.

Elementary Me

I don't like what they wear
I dislike all that they say
I don't follow the gait they bear
I disagree with the rigor they pray

Speaking the truth too easy
Fabricating lies a predicament
With wit and humor too cheesy
Striving to make hugs permanent

They say I just see positives
That I am too tolerant
So I feign being sensitive
Though I am so belligerent

Hostile, furious, in despair
Looking around for an anchor
Like the follicle on an uprooted hair
With no bearings, I wander

Laugh for him, giggle for them
And dance until you drop
Attend to every concern, every whim
Who am I? Just a prop?

The molds, the caps
The thick wick, the metal stand
What is my price? My tag?
Truly, what is my brand?

The myths I have spread
Over my yesteryears
Is that what I now dread
Defogged, the truth clear

Standing alone at the bay
Ringing ears and mind wary
Not daring what I want to say
My alter-ego gets scary

In the mirror, I behold, gape
The reflection, naked, pure
The color, the form, the shape
Cold, dead, blue almost azure

Laughing at me, mocking
Playing the devil's advocate
Pitiful, painful, shocking
Unyielding, at any rate

Jolts me awake, stark upright
As I submit, I finally see
The inescapable truth, the light
The essence of being me....

Author's Note

A book is not just words on a page. It is the telling of a story, not only of the characters on the pages but also of the people who tell it. Similar to any kid from the Delhi bourgeois of the Eighties, I grew up with a constant whisper in my ear about the importance of education. I was wise (or timid) enough to heed the advice. I studied. A lot. *I mean a whole freaking lot.* I did not know I had a choice. I read out of a necessity that exemplary grades were and a commitment to never let my parents down. Books were my best friends in that pursuit and we spent a lot of time hanging out. But I spent so much time with these friends that even they would have wanted to avoid me. However, I flew through the uber-important years of schooling as a model student and an obedient son.

Well, a hardcore introvert with few friends isn't cut out to be a rebel.

Fast forward a few years to me landing a seat at the IIT and shifting to a hostel (although still at the Delhi campus). I had to leave behind the safety net of my childhood home. The first few weeks were a miasmic shock brought on by exposure to unfamiliar languages and slang, cultures and demographics. Slowly, I started to appreciate why hostel life was touted to be a great teacher. It was the first time I had experienced such diversity, a colorful cornucopia I did not know India held within itself. Most importantly, it was here that I was introduced to a new realm—one of books and reading. I learned how you read to experience words and not to honor an obligation. I fell in love with fiction, the perfect segue from my routine textbooks, and within a few months, reading had become a passion.

I needed a passion. It was either reading or sitting alone in my hostel room, listening to sounds of ruckus and merriment in the hostel. Longing to be included but never fitting in.

I moved to the US to pursue higher studies after graduation, and it was then that I got into the business of reading. A library on the opposite side of my rented townhouse was the perfect invitation for a parched soul looking to reconnect with an old friend. Soon, I was reading on the metro; in breaks between lectures; on the university lawns; while having lunch, or sometimes even standing on the campus shuttle. Some would call it an addiction. In that alien nation, while reading diverse literature from authors all around the world, I found the biggest learning of my life—every voice counts and everyone matters.

Did I matter? Would someone listen if I talked? Did I not need to be an outlier anymore? If I could just talk.

Over the years, I have read hundreds of books, still mostly fiction, exploring myriad imaginative worlds crafted by authors across the globe. My house holds more books than there is room for. Sorry, Mummy. I cannot let go of the books I no longer 'need'. For books are like oxygen, and I do not know how to ration them rationally. I have lived books, dreamt words and relished the warmth of the fanciful yarns that writing geniuses of our times and before have woven for their readers.

My stars. My heroes. My inspirations. And the saviors of a boy who crash-landed into manhood without a friendly crutch to hold on to.

I don't know how or why, but five years ago, I started imagining my place amongst these literary stars. I started dreaming of becoming a storyteller or an author. Yes, that sounded insane to me as well, the first time I said it out aloud. But soon, I was writing blogs and poems, haikus, and stories. And every time I did, I started to find words.

My words. My voice.

They became my most intimate confidantes.

I felt I could reach others with my writing, the way the words of other authors had found me in my tenebrous hours. Books had given me peace when I grappled with the odds and brought me comfort when I stumbled.

And with that catharsis began a deeper journey into myself and the world around me. It has healed me in such countless ways that I cannot fathom the world before all of it began.

It's only words, but words are all I have (thank you, Boyzone!).

The first time I asked someone to read what I'd written was unimaginably nerve-wracking. Despite the encouragement (and a fair bit of flak), I felt a sense of pride and fulfilment. It felt like I had been seen and heard for the first time in my life. It made me feel that I mattered, that I wasn't here by accident. It gave me hope. And a purpose.

Right now, I am scared, even mortified, to present my first novel to the people of the world, knowing that those who have preceded me have set high benchmarks. But nothing else matters right now; I am only saying what I need to say and sharing what I need to share.

It was recently, during my research for this book, that I chanced upon the story of Ophiuchus, often considered the thirteenth sign of the zodiac. And I was intrigued by how it does not find a place in the modern zodiac, for it does not fit in with the precision afforded by the symmetry of the other twelve, each of them spanning a tidy thirty degrees of the celestial order.

Another misfit. Another outlier.

This thought got organically imbibed into the journey that writing this book has been all about—stories about those who do not fit well into the perfect order of the 'normal' world.

Those who exist only to disrupt the harmonic rhythm of perfection.

Each story in this book is woven around a sign of the zodiac and its classic associations with constellations, planets and luminary bodies, various colors & gemstones and personality traits. I am no expert on sun signs and I do not claim to understand the constellations either. So, don't mind the semantics. For more than that, my words are a celebration of those who do not fit the norms and chronicle their paths as they find their stars in their incongruous tales. This book is my homage to questioning retrograde patterns and forging an ethereal connection with versions of oneself that we do not even dare to accept because we are afraid of not fitting in, for lying on the wrong side of the trend line.

Most importantly, this book is about living without fear.

Or simply, living.

I hope you'll be able to find at least a smidgeon of yourself somewhere on these pages. I know I did while writing them.

"Imagine how we would be if we were less afraid."

Charlie Mackesy

The Boy, the Mole, the Fox, and the Horse

Some people don't find acceptance.

Many try to change themselves to make it happen.

A few others accept that it's okay to be excluded.

And some create a new normal.

This book is a tribute to all of them –
the ones who shine differently!

Illustrator's Note

Being a part of creating the illustrations for this book has been an incredible journey that I never thought I would have the opportunity to take. Although I have been dabbling in visual arts for many years, it was not until I started working on this book that I realized how exhilarating this process would be.

Art is my stress buster, a pastime, and a way of expressing my deepest feelings. I find all forms of art beautiful, whether acrylic, oil, or digital—providing a means for viewers to interpret my emotions and thoughts. Art is my passion, and with this book, my art has taken wings. I am deeply grateful to the author (and my cousin), Puneet Gupta, for trusting me with his words and believing that I could transform his vision into images.

Be it the image headers capturing the essence of the story; the depiction of the sun signs; the title page separators themed with the five elements or the serpentine abstraction for the thirteenth zodiac, I have thoroughly enjoyed this creative ride. While I know that the book might just be as fantastic to read without them, I hope that these visuals add a special something that the readers cherish and immerse themselves into.

This is my first time doing something like this and I am certain it won't be the last. Thanks to the encouragement from my parents; the love from my husband, Ashish, and the support of my siblings (*Hum Paanch*), I intend to stay the course and see where this first foray into book illustrations leads me.

Sweta Garg
Instagram: @pichhkari

Acknowledgments

When I started on my journey to get published, I was lost. Having spent two-and-a-half decades in the world of technology, this new ecosystem of agents, editors, arc readers, reviewers and publishers overwhelmed my senses. I express a million thanks to fellow authors from across the globe for educating me on how to go about it.

Thanks to my friend Satyam Srivastava for inspiring me with his journey from technology to administration and authorship and for helping me believe that I was not going crazy thinking I could become an author. I also want to express my gratitude to author Tanvi Srivastava and Dipti Nair for helping me understand the various processes and caveats involved in publishing and for pointing me to myriad resources related to finding agents and communicating with publishers. I'd also like to thank my mentor and author, Sattam Dasgupta, for making me see the freedom of self-publishing.

Many more thanks to…

…the guest authors from my podcast 'Authors of The World', hosted on my YouTube channel @alchemicstories and Instagram channel @scriptedsagas. You made me understand how we can all be united by the passion of telling stories yet follow our distinct journeys to accomplish being an author. You enriched me by sharing your eventful life journeys, unique creative processes and sincere advice. I cannot thank you enough for making me feel that I am not alone on this mission.

Thank you, Andrea Couture, Avanti Centrae, Collen Winter, Elizabeth M Kraus, Judith Adrian, Kenneth Humphrey, Laurie Buchanan, Luke Robert Eckley, Matilda Reyes, Nick Chiarkas, Pankaj Giri, Ranjith Radhakrishnan, Dr Ruby Gupta, Saralyn Richard, Satyam Srivastava, Sharon Michalove, Sherrill Joseph, Sudha Nair, Suzannah Grose and Tim Chapman—the best twenty guests one could ask for on a podcast about books and writing. I love you all.

A special thanks to Tracey Phillips and the Blackbird Writers group from Chicago for making my journey richer by introducing me to the many inspiring members of your writing family.

And most of all, thanks to…

…John DeDakis for being an acute reviewer of my manuscript and guiding me with painstaking notes and precise, pointed feedback, and Nick Chiarkas for introducing me to John.

…my first set of beta readers. Neelu Jethani, I still remember how you read the entire manuscript twice over and provided insightful feedback on the stories, plot loopholes, and an Indian reader's perspective. Thank you, Ananya Mittal, for bringing in a YA perspective to the feedback, which helped make the book more authentic.

…my fellow indie authors from the US, Luke R Eckley, Andrea Couture, Sudha GN and Laurie Buchanan, for being superb beta readers, critiquing my manuscript and providing honest reviews of my work. In particular, thank you, Andrea

Couture, for the phrase 'those who shine differently', which I have used in the book.

And finally, thanks to…

... my publishing team at IndiePress, a division of the prestigious Westland Books, for working with outstanding professionalism and a true collaborative spirit to bring my work to life. A special thanks to Sumit Bansal, Samyuktha, Jayantika, Sankhasubhro Nath (Jerry) and Krishna for deftly helping me navigate the nuances and intricacies of the entire publishing process. Also, thanks to the MAPS team for diligently formatting the manuscript into its final shape and form.

… my friend Dola Samanta for expertly guiding me on the book launch, social media strategy and marketing of this book.

... my illustrator, Sweta Garg, for the evocative illustrations she has created for the book, and for her endless support during the creative design process of this book. She's been an invaluable champion who has given me much-needed support.

... my editor, Priya Iyer, who has painstakingly labored by my side, iterating across versions and revisions, while always believing in the story behind the words, and helping me present my debut novel in its best avatar to my readers!

MORE BOOKS FROM THE SAME AUTHOR

Where Cookies Tell Fortunes is a twisted comedy. The play narrates a series of tangled events that unfold around diners at The Yin Yang Bistro —dating couples, friends, and family members. These people find themselves on a crazy journey of time, together yet separate. And amidst this chaos are unveiled stories of love, life and more. Where Cookies Tell Fortunes promises to tickle your funny bone, engage your senses, and keep you guessing at every turn!

Fortune cookies, rumored to be a Chinese tradition, were invented in the US. Yet, today, it is rare to finish a Chinese meal without a fortune cookie. Sometimes, nothing is as it seems, and everything is about something else. In a world where conventions are a norm and routines are lazily followed, fate can surprise you out of a slumber. The play is for me, for you, and for everyone around us. A homage to love and companionship….

This is a book of poetry with verses about life, love, loss and longing. The poems embody the following themes of self-love, emotional wellness and discovery of happiness amidst all odds.

It is okay to be lost. It is okay to not know how to be found.

It is okay to be different. It is okay not to meet expectations.

It is okay to fail. It is okay not to reach the finish line.

It is okay to just be. It is okay not to be the best version of yourself.

In a world obsessed with norms and stereotypes, have you found yourself a misfit?

Has your journey been made even tougher in your defiance to succumb to recurring demands for conformance? If yes, these poems will speak to your heart!

Once upon a time, there was a small family in a posh residential neighborhood, living in a swanky seventh-floor apartment. And they lived happily ever after until one of them killed themselves. Aditi, a young, college-going daughter of the household, is found dead.

Why did Aditi take her life? Did someone drive her to that end?

It's a story of the aftermath caused by Aditi's death and a simple note that states, 'I wish I could stay a little while longer.' While some try to answer these questions, some wonder if it was suicide. And some of them feel the weight of guilt weighing them down.

Guilty, yet not charged with any crime!

Does that make it worse?

This story takes you on a tumultuous ride exploring a jungle of relationships that the dead have with the living. It explores the life of the dead via the reactions of those left behind. The extreme incident pushes the characters into a mode of introspection, accusation and extrapolation.